NEVER ROMANCE A RAKE

NEVER ROMANCE A RAKE

LIZ CARLYLE

THORNDIKE
CHIVERS

This Large Print edition is published by Thorndike Press, Waterville, Maine, USA and by BBC Audiobooks Ltd, Bath, England.
Thorndike Press, a part of Gale, Cengage Learning.
Copyright © 2008 by Susan Woodhouse.
The moral right of the author has been asserted.
The Never Series #3.

The text of this Large Print edition is unabridged.
Other aspects of the book may vary from the original edition.
Set in 16 pt. Plantin.
Printed on permanent paper.

LIBRARY OF CONGRESS CATALOGING-IN-PUBLICATION DATA

Carlyle, Liz.
    Never romance a rake / by Liz Carlyle.
        p. cm. — (The never series ; #3.) (Thorndike Press large print core)
    ISBN-13: 978-1-4104-1105-1 (alk. paper)
    ISBN-10: 1-4104-1105-2 (alk. paper)
    1. Nobility—Fiction. 2. London (England)—Fiction. 3. Large type books. I. Title.
PS3553.A739N49 2008
813'.54—dc22   2008035098

BRITISH LIBRARY CATALOGUING-IN-PUBLICATION DATA AVAILABLE

Published in 2008 in the U.S. by arrangement with Pocket Books, a division of Simon & Schuster, Inc.
Published in 2009 in the U.K. by arrangement with Pocket Books, a division of Simon & Schuster, Inc.

U.K. Hardcover: 978 1 408 42155 0 (Chivers Large Print)
U.K. Softcover: 978 1 408 42156 7 (Camden Large Print)

Printed in the United States of America
1 2 3 4 5 6 7 12 11 10 09 08

*To Phil and Roscoe,
the Dynamic Duo*

Prologue

IN THE CANE FIELDS

The West Indian sun beat down on the still and verdant fields, searing all which lay beneath. Galleried white plantation houses shimmered in the heat, dotting the lush landscape like perfect, lucent pearls. Inside the fine homes, their broad corridors were steeped in shadow, and window louvers lay wide to catch the meager breeze, whilst slave children worked the fans which fluttered from lofty ceilings like massive raptors' wings.

This was a prosperous land; a near-magical place where money was wrung from the very earth itself, squeezed out drop by glistening drop in the gnashing teeth of the sugar mills, and rendered forth in every bead of sweat that poured off the men — and the women — who worked the cane. The land of sugar barons and shipping fortunes. A far-flung colonial outpost which was beyond the King's eyes — and often, beyond his laws.

But between the English ladies who languished in the heat on their divans, and the slaves who toiled in misery, there existed a third sort of people in the distant paradise. Sailors who longed only for home, most of whom would never see it again. Servants who had once been indentured, now enslaved by circumstance. Dock whores, street sweeps, and orphans — voiceless and unseen.

In this world of heat and indifference, two boys flew through the narrow rows of green, the razor-sharp cane leaves slicing at their arms and face, their breath coming in sawing heaves. They spared not a thought for the undulating ribbon of sapphire sea below, nor to the ramshackle house left on the hill behind. They had never seen a shaded divan, much less lain on one.

"That way." The bigger lad shoved the smaller hard on the left shoulder. "The swamp. He'll not catch us there."

They cut along the edge of the cane field; pale, skinny arms pumping furiously. The smaller boy dived beneath a low tree branch, skittered out, and pushed on. The stitch in his ribs cut like a knife. Blood pounded. Fear drove him. He could smell the brackish water just beyond. Another twenty yards.

8

Their bare feet threw up puffs of dust as they pelted along the field's edge. Almost. Almost. Almost there.

A drunken roar pierced the sweltering silence. Uncle leapt from the cane rows, crouching like some beast beneath the mangroves. Cutting off the swamp trail. The boys skidded in the dirt. Stepped back, and half turned. A skeletal Negro slipped out of the cane, blocking the path behind them, his face impassive but his eyes pitying.

The boys turned around, frail shoulders falling in surrender.

"Aye, cornered you little bastards, didn't I?" Uncle paced toward them, his steps remarkably sure for a man so intoxicated on rum and ruthlessness.

The younger boy whimpered, but the bigger did not.

Uncle stopped, his porcine eyes narrowed to glittering black slits, a riding crop swinging almost cheerfully from his wrist. "Fesh me the little one, Odysseus," he said, spittle dangling off one lip. "I'll teash the cheeky beggar to sass me."

The Negro approached, snatched the boy, then hesitated.

Like a flash of lightning, Uncle's crop cracked him through the face, drawing blood across his ebony cheekbone. "By

God, you'll strip the shirt off that little beggar and hol' him shtill, Odysseus, or it'll be forty lashes for you — and a week in the hole to repent."

Odysseus thrust the boy forward.

The bigger lad stepped nearer. "He didn't sass, sir," he piped. "H-He *didn't*. He didn't say a word. H-He's only eight, sir. Please."

Uncle grinned, and bent low. "Always the helpful one, aren't you, you little shite?" he said. "Aye, if you're so bloody bold, you can take his beating for 'im. Strip off his shirt, Odysseus."

The older boy was inching backward when the slave hitched him up short by the arm. "S-Sir," the lad stuttered, eyes wide, "I — I'm just trying to explain — n-no one sassed. W-We didn't say a word, sir. It was just the peacock. He squawked, sir, remember?"

But Odysseus began jerking the filthy linen shirt over the lad's head, impervious to his struggles. The smaller boy set both fists to his mouth, drew himself into a knot, and began silently to sob.

His brown eyes glistening with tears, Odysseus tossed the ragged shirt into the dirt of the cane field, and forced the boy's arms to the front, holding them there. The lad's thin shoulder blades stuck out like a heron's wings.

"You little bastards are going to rue the day." Uncle drew the crop through his fist as if savoring his task. "Aye, the day you got off that boat to bedevil me."

The older boy glanced back. "Please, sir," he begged. "Just send us back. We'll go. We *will.*"

Uncle laughed and drew back his whip. Odysseus turned his bleeding face away.

When the blows began, merciless and even, the little boy shut his eyes. He did not listen to his brother's cries. The sound of cracking leather. And whilst he shut it out, the sun kept beating down, the faint breeze picked up, and the rich people in their plantation houses savored their fans and sent their slaves skittering off for more lemonade. In the islands, God was in his heaven, and all was as it should be.

When the little boy opened his eyes again, Odysseus had gently hefted his brother over one shoulder and set out toward the house, the filth of the cane field caking his feet. The little boy cast one last look at Uncle.

His eyes glassy with drink and satisfaction, Uncle tugged his flask from his coat, tipped it toward the boy, and winked. "Aye, next time, you little snotnose," he promised. "Next time, Odysseus'll be carrying you from the fields."

The little boy turned and ran.

CHAPTER ONE

IN WHICH ROTHEWELL MEETS
THE GRIM REAPER

October was a vile month, Baron Rothewell thought as he peered through the spatter trickling down his carriage window. John Keats had been either a poetic liar or a romantic fool. In dreary Marylebone, autumn was no season of soft mist and mellow fruitfulness. It was the season of gloom and decay. Skeletal branches clattered in the squares, and leaves which should have been skirling colorfully about instead plastered the streets and hitched up against the wrought-iron fences in sodden brown heaps. London — what little of it had ever lived — was in the midst of dying.

As his carriage wheels swished relentlessly through the water and worse, Rothewell drew on the stub of a cheroot and stared almost unseeingly at the pavement beyond. At this time of day, it was empty save for the occasional clerk or servant hastening past with a black umbrella clutched grimly in hand. The baron saw no one whom he knew. But then, he knew almost no one.

At the corner of Cavendish Square and Harley Street, he hammered upon the roof of his traveling coach with the brass knob of his walking stick, and ordered his driver to halt. The brace of footmen posted to the rear of the carriage hastened round to drop the steps. Rothewell was notoriously impatient.

He descended, the folds of his dark cloak furling elegantly about him as he spun round to look up at his coachman. "Return to Berkeley Square." In the drizzle, his command sounded rather like the low rumble of thunder. "I shall walk home when my business here is done."

No one bothered to counsel him against walking in the damp. Nor did they dare ask what brought him all the way from the Docklands to the less familiar lanes of Marylebone. Rothewell was a private man, and not an especially well-tempered one.

He ground his cheroot hard beneath his bootheel, and waved the carriage away. Respectfully, his coachman touched his whip to his hat brim and rolled on.

The baron stood on the pavement in silent observation until his equipage turned the last corner of the square and disappeared down the shadowy depths of Holles Street. He wondered if this was a fool's errand. Perhaps this time his temper had simply got the best of him, he considered, setting a determined pace up Harley Street. Perhaps that was all it was. His temper. And another sleepless night.

He had come home from the Satyr's Club in the rose gray hours just before dawn. Then, after a bath and a stomach-churning glance at breakfast, he had headed straight to the Docklands, to the counting house of the company which his family owned, in order to satisfy himself that all went well in his sister's absence. But a trip to Neville Shipping always left Rothewell edgy and irritable — because, he openly acknowledged, he wanted nothing to do with the damned thing. He would be bloody glad when Xanthia returned from gallivanting about with her new husband, so that this burden might be thrown off his shoulders and back onto hers where it belonged.

But a surly mood could not remotely account for his troubles now, and in the hard black pit of his heart, he knew it. Slowing his pace, Rothewell began to search for the occasional brass plaque upon the doors of the fine homes which lined Harley Street. There were a few. *Hislop. Steinberg. Devaine.*

15

Manning. Hoffenberger. The names told him little about the men behind the doors — nothing of their character, their diligence — or what mattered even more, their brutal honesty.

He soon reached the corner of Devonshire Street and realized his journey was at an end. He glanced back over his shoulder at the street he'd just traversed. Damn it, he was going about this as if he were looking for a greengrocer. But in this case, one could hardly examine the wares through the window. Moreover, he wasn't about to ask anyone's advice — or endure the probing questions which would follow.

Instead he simply reassured himself that quacks and sawbones did not generally set up offices in Marylebone. And though the baron had been in London but a few months, he already knew that Harley Street was gradually becoming the domain of Hippocrates' elite.

At that thought, he turned and went up the wide marble steps of the last brass plaque he'd passed. If one was as good as another, it might as well be — at this point, Rothewell bent to squint at the lettering through the drizzle — ah, yes. *James G. Redding, M.D.* He would do.

A round-faced, gray-garbed housemaid

answered as soon as the knocker dropped. Her eyes swept up — far up — his length as she assessed his status. Almost at once, she threw the door wide, and curtsied deep. She hastened to take his sodden hat and coat.

Rothewell handed her his card. "I should like to see Dr. Redding," he said, as if he made such requests every day of the week.

Apparently, the girl could read. She glanced at the card and bobbed again, her eyes lowered. "Was the doctor expecting you, my lord?"

"He was not," he barked. "But it is a matter of some urgency."

"Y-You would not prefer him to call at your home?" she ventured.

Rothewell pinned the girl with his darkest glower. "Under *no* circumstance," he snapped. "Is that understood?"

"Yes, my lord." Paling, the girl drew a deep breath.

Good Lord, why had he growled at her? It was entirely expected that doctors would call upon their patients, not the other way round. But his damnable pride would never permit that.

The girl had resumed speaking. "I am afraid, my lord, that the doctor has not returned from his afternoon calls," she gently explained. "He might be some time yet."

This Rothewell had not expected. He was a man accustomed to getting his own way — and quickly. His frustration must have shown.

"If you should wish to wait, my lord, I could bring some tea?" the girl offered.

On impulse, Rothewell snatched his hat from the rack where she'd left it. He had no business here. "Thank you, no," he said tightly. "I must go."

"Might I give the doctor a message?" Her expression was reluctant as she handed him his coat. "Perhaps you could return tomorrow?"

Rothewell felt an almost overwhelming wish to leave this place, to flee his own foolish fears and notions. "No, thank you," he said, opening the door for himself. "Not tomorrow. Another day, perhaps."

He was leaving in such haste, he did not see the tall, thin man who was coming up the stairs, and very nearly mowed him down.

"Good afternoon," said the man, lifting his hat as he stepped neatly to one side. "I am Dr. Redding. May I be of some help?"

"A matter of some urgency, hmm?" said Dr.

18

Redding ten minutes later. "I wonder, my lord, you've let it go this long if you thought it so urgent."

The physician was a dark, lean man with a hook in his nose and a hollow look in his eyes. The Grim Reaper with his hood thrown back.

"If it had come and then gone away again, sir, it would not now *be* urgent, would it?" Rothewell protested. "And I thought it would. Go away again, I mean. These sorts of things always do, you know."

"Hmmm," said the doctor, who was pulling down the lower lids of Rothewell's eyes. "To what sorts of things do you refer, my lord?"

Rothewell grunted. "Dyspepsia," he finally muttered. "Malaise. You know what I mean."

The doctor's gaze grew oddly flat. "Well, you are a little more than dyspeptic, my lord," he said, looking again at Rothewell's left eye. "And your color is worrisome."

Again, Rothewell grunted. "I've but recently come from the West Indies," he grumbled. "Had too much sun, I daresay. Nothing more than that."

The doctor drew back and crossed his arms over his chest. "Nothing more than that?" he echoed, looking impatient. "I think not, sir. I am speaking of your eyes, not your skin. There appears to be just a hint of jaundice. These are serious symptoms, and you know it. Otherwise, a man of your ilk would never have come here."

"Of my *ilk* — ?"

The doctor ignored him, and instead swept his fingers beneath Rothewell's jawline, then down either side of his throat. "Tell me, my lord, have you suffered any malaria?"

Rothewell laughed. "That was one curse of the tropics which I escaped."

"You are a heavy drinker?"

Rothewell smiled grimly. "Some would say so."

"And you use tobacco," said the doctor. "I can smell it."

"That is a problem?"

"Overindulgences of any sort are a problem."

Rothewell grunted. A moralizing crepehanger. Just what he needed.

With quick, impatient motions, the doctor drew a curtain from the wall near the door, jangling the metal rings discordantly. "Step behind this, if you please, my lord. Divest yourself of your coat, waistcoat, and shirt, then lie down upon that leather-covered table."

Rothewell began to unbutton his silk waistcoat, inwardly cursing the doctor, the gnawing pain in his stomach, and himself. Life in London was ruining him. Idleness was like a poison seeping into his veins. He could feel it, yet could not summon enough disdain to shake it off.

Before today, he could count on one hand the times he had been sick enough to require a doctor. They did a chap far more ill than good, he believed. Besides, Rothewell had always been a great horse of a man. He had needed no one's advice, medical or otherwise.

Beyond the curtain, he heard the doctor open the door and leave the room. Resigned, he hung the last of his garments upon the brass hooks obviously intended for such a purpose, then glanced about the room. It was sumptuously furnished, with heavy velvet drapes and a creamy marble floor. A massive, well-polished desk occupied one end of the room, and in the center sat a tall table with a padded leather top. Dr. Redding's patients, it would seem, lived long enough to pay their bills. That was something, he supposed.

Beside the table was a pewter tray with a row of medical instruments laid across it. Rothewell stepped closer and felt an unpleasant sensation run down his spine. A scalpel and a set of steel lancets glittered wickedly up at him. There were scissors and forceps and needles — along with other tools he did not recognize. The chill deepened.

Good God, he should never have come here. Medicine was just one step removed from witchcraft. He should go home, and either get well of his own accord or die like a man.

But this morning . . . this morning had been the worst. He could still feel the burn of iron and acid in the back of his throat as the spasms wracked his ribs . . .

Oh, bloody hell! He might as well stay and hear what the grim-faced Dr. Redding had to say. To push away the thought of this morning, the baron picked up one of the more horrific-looking devices to examine it further. A medieval torture device, perhaps?

"A trephination brace," said a voice behind him.

Jumping, Rothewell let it clatter back onto the tray. He turned to see the doctor standing just inside the curtain.

"But if it is any consolation, my lord," the doctor continued, "I rather doubt we will find it necessary to drill a hole in your head."

■ ■ ■ ■

The day's drizzle had at last ended when the glossy black barouche made its third and final circle through Hyde Park. The Serpentine had risen up from its shroud of mist like something from an Arthurian legend, enticing the *beau monde*'s heartier souls to venture out to ride or to drive. And though the height of the season was many weeks past, the gentleman who so elegantly wielded the barouche's whip easily caught their eye, for he was both handsome and well-known — if not especially well liked. Alas, despite his beauty, society often saddled him with that coldest of English euphemisms, the vague stain of being thought *not quite nice.*

Though past his prime and ever on the verge of insolvency, the Comte de Valigny was nonetheless dressed with an unmistakable Continental flair, and his unimpeachable wardrobe was further accented by the sort of hauteur which only the French can carry off with aplomb. The stunning beauty who sat stiffly beside him was generally assumed by the passersby to be his latest mistress, since Valigny ran through beautiful women with rapacious efficiency.

The afternoon, however, had grown late, and it being both October and dampish, the crowd was thin. No one save a pair of dashing young bucks on horseback and a landau full of disapproving dowagers spared the woman much more than a passing glance. And that, to Valigny's way of thinking, was a bloody damned shame. He looked back over his shoulder almost longingly at the young gentlemen.

"*Mon dieu,* Camille!" he complained, returning a bitter gaze to her face. "Lift your chin! Cast your eyes more boldly! Who will look twice at a woman who will not look once, eh? You are not going to the guillotine!"

"Am I not?" purred his companion, looking haughtily down her nose at him. "I begin to wonder. How long have I been here? Six weeks, *n'est-ce pas?* Six weeks of this incessant damp and overweening snobbery. Perhaps I might soon welcome the executioner's blade?"

Valigny's expression tightened. *"Ça alors!"* he snapped, reining his grays to one side. "You are an asp clasped to my bosom! Perhaps, my fine lady, you should prefer to climb down and walk home?"

The woman turned and pressed her elegantly gloved fingers to her chest. *"Quoi?*

And taint my precious virtue by strolling unaccompanied through Mayfair like some common tart?" she asked mockingly. "But wait! I forget. They already think me a common tart."

"Be damned to you, Camille!" The comte snapped his whip, and the horses set off at a strong trot. "You are an ungrateful little shrew."

She set her shoulders stiffly back, refusing to cling to the side for balance. "I am, aren't I?" she said, as much to herself as to him. "Would to God it were spring! Perhaps then your foolish plan might — *might* — succeed."

The comte laughed loudly. "Oh, *mon chou!* I very much fear that spring will be too late for you."

She cut a disdainful glance at him. "*Oui,* this is true," she admitted. "And, *mon père,* too late for *you!*"

Pamela, Lady Sharpe, was standing at her sitting-room window, one hand braced on the back of a stout chair, watching the world of Mayfair go by when the tall man in the dark cloak came striding purposefully down the street. At first, she paid him scant heed. The rain had stopped, and something which might possibly have been a beam of sunlight was slanting over the roofs across Hanover Street. Lady Sharpe resisted the urge to clap her hands with glee.

Tomorrow, perhaps, there would be callers? Yes, almost certainly. And she was well enough to receive them. Indeed, she was dying to crow over her accomplishments. This had been a momentous week — but truth be told, it had been a banner year for Lady Sharpe. She had carried off the triple sweep of the social season, having launched her much-loved cousin Xanthia into society to shockingly good effect, and immediately thereafter marrying off her only daughter Louisa to an earl's heir.

And then, as her grand finale, after two decades of marriage to an amiable and understanding husband, Lady Sharpe had finally done what no one believed possible. She had borne Sharpe an heir. A lovely, blue-eyed boy who was his father's spit and image, bald pate in the bargain.

"My lady?" The countess's maid hovered at her elbow. "Perhaps you ought to lie back down?"

Just then, the dark man passed squarely by Lady Sharpe's window.

"Oh! Oh!" she cried, pointing. "Look! Anne, stop him! Go down! Fetch him up at once."

"Ma'am?" Anne's brow furrowed.

"Rothewell!" She gestured madly at the glass. "I sent a note round just yesterday. I really must see him! Oh, *do* go down this instant."

Anne lost a bit of her color, but she went downstairs — then ordered the second footman to hasten along Hanover Street after Lord Rothewell. The footman balked for an instant — the baron's reputation was not unknown to the staff — then finally did as he'd been bid. No appendages were lost in the process. Lord Rothewell had apparently bitten off his daily allotment of noses, and he followed the footman almost civilly upstairs.

The countess received him in her private sitting room, still attired in her cap and dressing gown, with her feet propped up on her husband's gout stool.

"Kieran, my dear!" she murmured, turning her cheek to be kissed. "You will forgive me for not rising."

"Yes, of course." Rothewell took the chair she motioned toward. "Though I cannot think, Pamela, that you've any business receiving anyone."

Lady Sharpe laughed lightly. "That is why you are my favorite cousin, dear boy!" she replied. "Your brutal honesty."

Brutal honesty. Rothewell wondered if the phrase was destined to haunt him today.

But Lady Sharpe's eyes were still twinkling. "Now, my dear! Why have you been ignoring me?"

"Ignoring you?"

"I sent an urgent note round yesterday," she chided. "One would think I'd been forgotten altogether after just a few weeks of confinement."

"Ah," he said quietly. "But I have scarce been home since yesterday, Pamela."

"Indeed, it's a shock to see you out in broad daylight." She wrinkled her nose. "I do dislike the sort of company you keep — and the hours. But never mind that just now. Am I to have your congratulations?"

Rothewell sat a little forward in his chair, his hands on his knees. "Yes, and my thanksgiving with them," he answered. "It was a dashed dangerous thing for you to suffer through, Pamela."

Lady Sharpe's finely etched eyebrows rose. "Why, what an odd thing to say. What do you mean?"

Rothewell forced himself to relax against the back of his chair. "Nothing, Pamela," he said simply. "I just hope you will not try to do it again."

"At my age?" Lady Sharpe gave a wry

smile. "I should think it highly unlikely."

"This has shaved a year off Sharpe's life, you know."

"I do know, and I'm very sorry for it." Lady Sharpe was toying with a ribbon on her handkerchief. "But Sharpe needs an heir, Kieran."

"He needs his *wife* — alive, preferably."

"Oh, you do not understand! Though you *should* do, of course — and better than most. You know what I mean."

He did know. But an heir? The notion had always seemed absurd. "What will eventually happen, Pamela, to my title?" he finally asked.

"What, when you are gone?" Lady Sharpe tossed her handkerchief dismissively. "One of those odious Neville cousins in Yorkshire will inherit everything. But little do you care."

"A very little, I daresay," he murmured.

Lady Sharpe was watching him quizzically. "You should get busy, Kieran." Her voice was uncharacteristically sharp. "You know what I mean."

Rothewell pretended not to understand. He set his hands upon his thighs as if to rise. "Well, old girl, I must get on. You need your rest."

"Pish!" said Lady Sharpe, waving him

29

down again. "If anyone needs rest, sir, it is you. It is rare I've seen you so haggard." She turned to her maid. "Anne, go and tell Thornton to present Viscount Longvale to his cousin."

The child? Dear God, not that. "Really, Pamela," said Rothewell. "This is not necessary."

"Oh, yes. It is." A mysterious smile curved her lips. "I insist."

Rothewell avoided meeting children at all costs. He always felt as if some sort of effusive response was expected of him. He was not effusive. He wasn't even especially pleasant. And children, more often than not, wished to be dandled upon one's knee, or to tug one's watch from one's pocket.

But Lord Longvale, as it happened, was apt to do neither. He was a doughy, pink-and-white lump with two impossibly tiny fists and a pursed rosebud of a mouth, and far too small to be of any trouble to anyone. Moreover, this child was Pamela's, a person for whom he possessed a rare fondness. So Rothewell steeled himself, forced a smile, and leaned rather tentatively over the bundle which the nurse held out for his inspection.

Strangely, his breath caught. The child was so perfect and so still he might have been sculpted of Madame Tussaud's magical wax. His skin was so delicate it appeared translucent, and his round cheeks glowed with an otherworldly color.

A remarkable stillness settled over the room, leaving Rothewell afraid to exhale. He could not recall ever having been in such proximity to a newborn babe.

Suddenly, two pale blue eyes flew open. The child squeezed his fists tight, screwed up his face, and commenced squalling with healthy gusto. The strange moment shattered, Rothewell drew back.

"I fear Lord Longvale has little interest in making my acquaintance," he said over the racket.

"Nonsense!" said her ladyship. "I am sure he is just showing off. Have you ever heard such a fine pair of lungs?"

Rothewell had not. Despite his swaddling, the child pumped his stubby legs and tiny fists back and forth relentlessly as he wailed. Rothewell was struck by the sheer force of will which emanated from the tiny creature. Yes, the child was very real indeed — and very much alive. And he was a scrapper, too, by the look of him. Rothewell found himself suppressing a sudden and improbable urge to smile.

Perhaps all of London was not dead or decaying after all. This little imp was precious and new, and quite obviously filled with promise. He would carry with him the hopes and the dreams of his parents into the future. Perhaps the cycle of life, death, and resurrection truly was eternal. Rothewell did not know if that thought brought him comfort or anger.

Lady Sharpe had opened her arms to take the child. "Let me soothe him a moment, Thornton," she said, tucking the bundle against her shoulder. "And then I suppose you'd best take him back up again. I believe we are making Lord Rothewell unaccountably nervous."

Rothewell did not return to his chair, but paced across the sitting room to one of the windows which overlooked Hanover Street. He felt strangely moved. He was but vaguely aware that the child's cries were slowly relenting. Eventually, the room fell silent.

One arm braced high against the shutter, Rothewell was still standing there, staring blindly at the falling dusk and wondering what it was about the child that struck him so when he heard Pamela speak again.

"Kieran?" Her voice was sharp. "My dear boy — are you perfectly all right?"

Caught in his musing, Rothewell spun round to look at her. His cousin sat alone in the middle of the room. The child and his nurse had vanished.

Lady Sharpe set her head to one side like a curious bird. "You've not heard a word I've said."

"My apologies, Pamela," he said. "My mind was elsewhere."

"I said I have a favor to ask of you," she reminded him. "May I depend upon you?"

Rothewell managed a smile. "I doubt it," he said honestly. "Women usually regret it when they do."

She leaned over and patted the chair beside her. "Come sit by me," she suggested. "And do be serious. This is important."

Reluctantly, he did so. He did not like the faint strain he could hear in his cousin's voice.

"Kieran," she said quietly, "are you still keeping company with Christine?"

Rothewell was taken aback by the question. Christine Ambrose was Pamela's sister-in-law, but the two were as different as chalk from cheese. And Pamela never, ever pried.

"I see Mrs. Ambrose whenever it suits us both," he said vaguely. "Why? Has Sharpe some newfound objection?"

"Heavens, no!" Lady Sharpe waved her hand dismissively. "Sharpe knows he cannot manage his half sister, and he does not try. But the two of you — well, you are not serious, Kieran, are you? Christine is not the sort of lady one would wish to . . . well, I don't quite know how to put it."

Rothewell felt his expression darken. He did not discuss his personal life — even Xanthia did not dare ask such things. Christine was thought rather fast, and he knew it. He also did not give a damn.

"I am afraid my relationship with Mrs. Ambrose is a private matter, Pamela," he said coldly. "But there will be nothing permanent between us, if that is your concern."

Nothing permanent. No, there was no future for him with Christine — not that he had ever contemplated such foolishness.

But Lady Sharpe's face had already brightened. "No, I thought not," she said, as if reassuring herself. "She is, of course, quite lovely, but Christine is —"

"Pamela," he said, cutting her off, "you tread on dangerous ground. Now, you wished to ask a favor? Pray do so."

"Yes, of course." Pamela was smoothing down the pleats of her dressing gown. "Thursday is the christening, Kieran. And I wish . . . yes, I have thought it out quite clearly, and I wish you to be one of

34

Longvale's godparents."

Rothewell could only stare at her.

"Oh, I mean to ask Xanthia, too," she swiftly added. "You are my nearest relations save for Mamma, you know. I was so happy when you came back from Barbados after all these long years away. Oh, *will* you do it, my dear? Please say you will."

Rothewell had jerked from his chair and returned to his spot by the window. He was silent for a long moment. "No," he finally said, his voice quiet. "No, Pamela. I am sorry. It is quite out of the question."

Behind him, he heard the rustle of fabric as his cousin rose. In an instant, she had laid a light hand upon his shoulder. "Oh, Kieran! I know what you are thinking."

"No." His voice was hoarse. "No, you do not, I assure you."

"You believe that you would not be a suitable godfather," Lady Sharpe pressed. "But I am quite convinced that is not the case. Indeed, I *know* it is not. You are a brilliant and determined man, Kieran. You are honest and plainspoken. You are —"

"No." He slammed the heel of his hand against the shutter, as if the pain might clear his mind. "God damn it, did you not hear me, Pamela? *No.* It is quite impossible."

Lady Sharpe had drawn back, her expression wounded.

He turned to fully face her, dragging one hand through his hair. "I beg your pardon," he rasped. "My language was —"

"Insignificant, really," she interjected. "There is goodness in you, Kieran. I know that there is."

"Pray do not bore us both with a recitation of my virtues, Pamela," he said, softening his tone. "It would be a very short list anyway. I thank you for the compliment you have paid me, but you must ask someone else."

"But . . . But we wish *you* to do it," she said quietly. "Sharpe and I discussed it at length. We are quite persuaded you are the right person for such a grave responsibility. You, more than anyone, know the importance of bringing a child up properly — or, I should say, the damage done to one who is *not* brought up properly."

"Don't speak nonsense, Pamela," he said gruffly.

"Moreover," she continued amiably, "Sharpe and I are not as young as we once were. What if we should die?"

He let his hand drop.

What if they should die? He would be of damned little use to them.

"Xanthia will see to the child should

36

something untoward happen," he managed. "She and Nash would raise the boy as their own if you wished it. You know that they would."

"But Kieran, the role of godfather is more than —"

"Pray do not ask me again, Pamela," he interjected. "I cannot. And God knows my character is too stained even if you do not."

"But I do not think you under —"

"No, my dear." With surprising gentleness, Rothewell laid her hand across his forearm and turned her toward her chair. "It is you who does not understand. Now you must sit down, Pamela, and put your feet up. You must. And I must go."

When they reached the chair, Lady Sharpe braced one hand on the chair arm and sank slowly into it. "When do Nash and Xanthia return?" she asked. "I daresay she will agree to do it."

"Tomorrow," he said, gently patting her shoulder. "Ask Nash to serve with her. He'll be honored. After all, he still isn't sure we like him."

"Do we?" Lady Sharpe looked up.

Rothewell considered it. "Well enough, I daresay," he finally answered. "We must trust Xanthia's judgment. And now I think on it, I'm dashed grateful to have him around."

"Are you?" The countess blinked. "Why?"

Rothewell managed a smile. "No particular reason, Pamela. Now, let me bid you good day."

His cousin gave a pitiful sniff. "Well, we did hope you might stay to dinner, at the very least," she said, beginning to pick at the pleats of her dressing gown again. "After all, you have no one at home now with whom to dine."

Rothewell bent to kiss her cheek. "I am a solitary beast," he assured her. "I will manage."

The countess craned her head to look up at him, her lips pressed thinly together. "But you and Xanthia lived and worked cheek by jowl for thirty years," she insisted. "It is only natural one might be lonely, Kieran."

"Lived, aye, but not worked," he answered, staring at the door, his escape route. "Xanthia was our brother Luke's protégé, never mine. They were the peas in the pod, Pamela. I was just . . . the leftover husk."

And then, before Pamela could dredge up her harangue yet again, Rothewell strode from the room.

CHAPTER TWO

IN WHICH LE COMTE HOSTS A CARD PARTY

The Comte de Valigny's thin fingers writhed like small white eels as he cleverly shuffled his cards. With eyes which were jaded and desultory, his guests observed the flicking of each card as he dealt it, and the shards of sparkling, bloodred color thrown off by his ruby ring in the lamplight.

They were five at the comte's parlor table on this particular night, each more dissolute than the next. Valigny's game was *vingt-et-un* with a fifty-pound minimum, and after long hours of play, the drawing room smelled of stale smoke and even staler perspiration. Unbidden, Lord Rothewell rose and shoved up one of the sashes.

"Merci, mon ami." Valigny shot a wicked smile in Rothewell's direction as he slid the last card across the giltwood table. "The game grows fierce, does it not?"

Two of the gentlemen at the table were indeed looking desperate. Valigny himself should have been, but in all the months Lord Rothewell had been playing with the comte, he had never once seen the man hesitate — not even when he should have done. Valigny played deep, lost often, and dealt out his notes of hand almost as blithely as he dealt out his cards. But his wins, when they came, were the stuff of legend. Thus was the addict born.

"Bonne chance, monsieurs." Initial cards dealt and bets placed, they each chose to draw. The comte was still smiling as he tapped one finger upon his exposed card — the queen of spades.

"Well, I'm damned." Sir Ralph Henries was slurring his words and squinting at the black queen. "That's twice in a row he's had it! Did you give that pack a proper shuffle, Calvert? *Did* you?"

"You just watched me do so," Calvert returned. "Good God, what have you to complain of? I'm halfway to the Fleet. Pour him another, Valigny. Perhaps that will keep him from whinging all night."

Sir Ralph looked up woozily. "I'm not whinging," he managed. "Wait — what's become of those girls? Dashers, weren't they? I liked the one with the . . . with the — what did you call it? The black leather thing and the — no, wait — am I mixed up, Vallie?"

"That was a few nights past, *mon ami.*" Valigny patted his hand solicitously. "Tonight we play at cards, hmm? Finish your hand, Ralph, or go home."

After a cursory glance at his cards, Rothewell half turned in his chair and let his gaze drift round the shadowy depths of the room. He was not perfectly sure why he had permitted Valigny to lure him here tonight. The comte's coterie of rogues was a low one, even by Rothewell's standards. But of late he had found himself slipping into lower and lower company, as if searching for the soul-sucking mud at the bottom of society's cesspool.

In keeping with this philosophy, he had stumbled across Valigny — he'd been too sotted to recall precisely where. But the comte was the sort of man whom one would ordinarily meet only in a Soho gaming hell, for Valigny did not belong to any of London's finer clubs. Or any of the lesser ones, come to that. If Rothewell was scarcely known within the *ton,* Valigny was beyond knowing. There had been some long-ago scandal — a ruined countess and a brace of pistols afterward, or so Christine Armstrong had once whispered. Rothewell could have cared less.

"Another, my lord?" The comte edged one

card off the pack with his thumb, his foppish lace cuff falling forward to cover half his hand. Rothewell inclined his head. Valigny sent the card sailing across the polished tabletop.

Somewhere in the depths of the house, a clock struck one. The game picked up, the play growing ever more reckless. Mr. Calvert, the most decent amongst them, was soon on the verge of insolvency — virtue rewarded, Rothewell thought cynically. Valigny drew a natural twenty-one twice in a row, once with his black queen, then proceeded to throw it all away again.

One of his footmen brought in more brandy and another box of the dark, bitter cheroots which the comte favored. Rothewell lit one. A second servant carried in a platter of sandwiches. Calvert got up to piss — or perhaps puke — into the chamber pot kept tucked in the door of the sideboard. Everything was conveniently to hand. God forbid anything should delay Valigny's play.

Lord Enders was a vicious player if ever one lived. He knew just how to taunt the comte, and pressed him hard. Rothewell was soon down six thousand pounds — a pittance compared to Valigny and Calvert. But he was still sober enough to find it bloody annoying. He motioned for one of the footmen to fetch the brandy.

The next hand soon dwindled to Rothewell and Valigny, who was betting as if his hand held perfection itself. Rothewell tipped up the corner of his card. The two of hearts and the king of diamonds down. The four of clubs up. Perhaps he had overstayed his luck.

"You are undecided, *mon ami?*" Valigny teased. "Come, be bold! It is only money."

"Spoken like a man who has never had to earn his own keep," said Rothewell grimly. He tossed off half his brandy, wondering if perhaps he should teach Valigny a lesson.

"Perhaps Rothewell's pockets are not as deep as rumor suggests?" said Enders in a tone which might — or might not — have been facetious.

The comte smiled at Rothewell. "Perhaps you should preserve your cash, my lord?" he remarked. "Indeed, if you are willing, we might play for something a little more interesting than money."

Rothewell's hackles went up. "I doubt it," he answered. "What did you have in mind?"

The comte lifted one shoulder, a study in nonchalance. "Perhaps just an evening of companionship?"

"You're not my type, Valigny," he said, pushing a pile of banknotes toward the center of the table.

"Oh, you misunderstand, *mon ami.*" Valigny's fingertips stilled Rothewell's hand, his elaborate white lace stark against Rothewell's still-bronzed skin. "Keep your money, and turn your card. If you lose, I ask only one simple thing."

Rothewell lifted the comte's hand away. "And what would that be?"

The comte cocked one eyebrow. "Just a very small favor, I assure you."

"Speak, Valigny. You delay the game."

"I wish for one evening — just one — with the delectable Mrs. Ambrose."

Rothewell was annoyed but not surprised. "You mistake my arrangement with the lady," he said darkly. "Mrs. Ambrose is not in my keeping."

"Non?" The comte looked genuinely confused.

"No." Rothewell left his money on the table. "She may bestow her favors upon whomever she chooses."

"And often does," remarked Enders flippantly.

"Ah, but one can only imagine what favors!" Valigny drew his fingertips to his lips for a kiss. "So by all means, let us play for money, my lord. I shall have need of it, I think. Mrs. Ambrose looks expensive."

"But worth it, one must suppose," said Enders, cutting Rothewell a sidelong glance, "if one does not mind her being a little long in the tooth."

The comte laughed, but nervously. Rothewell had lifted his gaze to Enders's face. "I hope, sir, that you did not mean your remarks as the insults they sounded," he said quietly. "I should hate to leave this game early merely to meet you again at dawn under far less hospitable circumstances."

Enders stiffened. "I beg your pardon, then," he said. "Your aim — and your temper — precede you, Rothewell. But unlike yourself, Mrs. Ambrose is not new to Town. We have all known her for years. Myself, I simply prefer the women I bed to be younger."

"*Mais oui,* much, much younger, if what one hears is true," Valigny chortled. "Still in the schoolroom with the hair in braids, eh? But what of it? Many men have such tastes."

Enders was a stout, middle-aged widower with thick lips and even thicker fingers. Rothewell had detested him on sight, and time was doing nothing to alter that opinion. He particularly did not care for the turn the conversation was taking.

Enders was still staring at the comte, his

gaze dark. "With enough money, a man can usually get what he wants, Valigny," he said. "You of all people should know that."

Valigny laughed again, but this time, there was an edge to it.

Rothewell finished the hand with a near-miraculous win; one which was to be followed by several more. But the conversation had left a sour taste in his mouth.

It was a little late in life, however, to be suddenly plagued by scruples. What business was it of his whom Enders fucked, or what Valigny thought of it? He was the last man on earth who should be pointing fingers. Still, it did bother him. And there was no denying Enders had a reputation for perversions of all manner.

The comte and Enders were still squabbling.

"Gentlemen, lesh not quarrel," said Sir Ralph, who was now dipping deep enough to be in charity with all mankind. "Youth in a chap's bed is all very well, aye? But at present, a rish woman should suit me even better. My purse has taken a proper thrashing."

"Well, good luck to you," said Enders sourly. "You may trust me when I say rich brides are a bit thin on the ground this time of year."

46

"*Oui,* there is nothing so comforting as a rich wife, eh?" The comte leaned intently forward. "This topic, you see, has been much on my mind of late. But you are already a married man, Sir Ralph, are you not? And you, too, Mr. Calvert?"

Both men agreed. *"Tant pis,"* said the comte, his expression a little gloomy. "But you, Enders, had no luck at your marriage mart this season?"

"There were poor girls and eyesores aplenty," Enders grumbled. "Always are. But the young girls with money are spiteful little bitches."

The comte flashed a wry smile. "*Oui,* life can be so very hard, can it not, my friend?" he said. "Ah, well! Play on, *messieurs!*"

But Rothewell was seized by the sudden impulse to simply leave his pile of money and walk out. Wealth had never mattered much to him — and of late it had mattered even less. He wanted, strangely, to go home.

And yet he knew once he got there and began to pace the floors of that vast, empty place, the disquiet would soon drive him into the streets again. To go anywhere. To do anything. Anything which might drown out those devils of the night.

He motioned for Valigny's footman to refill his glass and forced himself to relax.

For the next hour he drank more than he played, refusing to press his luck with another mediocre hand. Calvert wisely withdrew, but remained at the table nursing a glass of port. Sir Ralph was too deep in his cups to pose a threat.

Over the next dozen hands, the play rose to a fevered pitch. If the comte had played like a madman from the start, he apparently meant to end it like a lunatic, all but shoving his money at them. His desperation — and his purpose in hosting this debacle — were starting to show. The chap must be but steps from the sponging house.

Suddenly, Valigny made a grievous error, drawing an eight to the queen of spades and the five of hearts. Lord Enders swept up the winnings — two thousand on the one hand.

"Alas, my dark queen has failed me!" said the comte. "Women are fickle creatures, are they not, Lord Rothewell? Play on, *messieurs!*"

The next was dealt, everyone taking an extra card. But within moments, Sir Ralph, who had drawn first, was running a finger round his collar as if his cravat was about to choke him. It was the move of a rank amateur. Valigny caught the gesture and pounced like a cat, pushing up the wager again.

Sir Ralph belched and glanced at his down cards.

"Ralph?" the comte prodded. "Do you stand?"

"Bugger all!" said Ralph, flipping over his cards. "Overdrawn! Should have said so lasht round, eh?" He jerked awkwardly from his chair. "Think I'd besht say g'night, lads. Not feeling quite the thing."

Rothewell glanced over. Ralph did indeed hold twenty-three, and looked green enough to cast up his accounts. Valigny shrugged good-naturedly, then hastened his staggering guest in the general direction of the front door before Ralph could surrender to his collywobbles on the carpet.

Ralph aside, Rothewell did not miss the fine sheen of sweat on the comte's face as he passed. The air of desperation in the room had heightened. Yes, Valigny needed money, and rather urgently. But playing with Enders — or even with Rothewell himself — was a foolish way to go about it. They were amongst the most hardened gamesters in London. They would likely have the comte beggared within the hour — yet the knowledge brought Rothewell no satisfaction.

The entire evening had been unsatisfactory, really. He was wasting his time —

though, in a way, that was the very point of iniquity, wasn't it? To satiate oneself with revelry — liquor or sex or a hundred other wicked pursuits — which might numb a man to the truth of what his life had become.

But if he were honest, he would have to admit that the pursuit of wickedness no longer hid from him who or what he was to even the smallest degree — and drink, he was beginning to fear, no longer numbed him.

Had it begun with Xanthia's going away? No, not precisely. But after that, everything had simply gone to hell in a thousand little ways.

In any case, there was no point in lingering here. Since sin wasn't working, there was always gunpowder. If a man wished to hasten God's will, it might be less painful simply to go home and put a pistol to his head rather than remain here listening to Enders and Valigny pecking at one another.

The comte returned to the table, an expression of amused chagrin upon his face. "Alas, *messieurs, Madame* Fortune has forsaken me tonight, *n'est-ce pas?*"

"And Sir Ralph cannot bloody count." Rothewell began to push away from the table. "Gentlemen, let's retract our wagers and call it a night."

"*Non!*" Something which might have been fear sketched across Valigny's face. He urged Rothewell back into his chair, his smile returning. "I feel *Madame* Fortune returning to me, perhaps. May I not have a gentleman's chance to win back what I have lost?"

"With what stakes?" challenged Enders. "Look here, Valigny, I cannot take another note from you. Even if you win this bollixed-up hand, it is but a pittance to me."

The tension in the room was palpable now. The comte licked his lips. "But I have saved the best wager for last," he said rapidly. "Something which might be of interest to you — and a benefit, perhaps, to me."

Mr. Calvert lifted both hands. "I am but a spectator."

"Indeed," said the comte. "I speak to Enders — and to Rothewell, perhaps."

"Then speak," said Rothewell quietly. "The game grows cold."

Valigny braced both hands on the table and leaned into them. "I propose we replay this last hand now that Sir Ralph is gone," he said, glancing back and forth between them. "The winner shall take everything on the table tonight. Calvert will take the pack as a neutral dealer. We play only one another."

"Dashed odd way of doing things," Calvert muttered.

"What are you staking?" Enders demanded again.

The comte held up one finger, and cut a swift glance at the footmen. "Tufton," he barked, "is Mademoiselle Marchand still in her sitting room?"

The servant looked startled. "I'm sure I couldn't say, sir."

"*Mon Dieu,* just go find her!" Valigny ordered.

"Are . . . are you sure, my lord?"

"Yes, damn you," snapped the comte. "What business is it of yours? *Dépêchez-vous!*"

The footman yanked open the door and vanished.

"Insolent bastard," muttered the comte. He ordered the remaining servant to refresh everyone's drink, then began to pace the parlor's carpet. Calvert, too, was looking ill at ease. The hand still lay untouched.

"I don't know what sort of stunt this is meant to be, Valigny," Enders complained as his glass was filled. "Rothewell and I are winning, so we actually have something left to lose. Your next wager had best prove undeniably tempting."

The comte glanced back over his shoulder. "Oh, it will, my lord," he said silkily. "It will. Do I not understand your tastes and your — shall we say *appetites?*"

"Just who the devil is this Marchand person?" asked Rothewell impatiently.

"Ah, who is she indeed!" The comte returned to the table and lifted his glass as if to propose a toast. "Why, she is my lovely daughter, Lord Rothewell. My half-English bastard child. Surely the old gossip is not yet forgotten?"

"Your daughter!" Enders interjected. "Good God, man. At a card game?"

"Indeed, you go too far, Valigny," said Rothewell, studying the depths of his brandy. "A gently bred girl has no business in here."

Their host lifted one shoulder again. "Oh, not so gently, *mon ami*," he replied dispassionately. "The girl has spent the whole of her existence in France — with that stupid cow of a mother who bore her. She has seen enough of life to know what it is."

Enders's eyes flared wide. "Do you mean to say this is the child of Lady Halburne?" he demanded. "Are you quite mad?"

"No, but you may become so when you see her." Valigny's face broke into that all-too-familiar grin. "*Vraiment, mes amis,* this one is her mother's child. Her face, her teeth, her breasts — *oui,* everything is perfection, you will see. All she needs is a man to put her in her place — and keep her there."

"A beauty, eh?" Enders's expression had shifted, and when he spoke, his voice was thicker. "How old is she?"

"A bit older than you might prefer," admitted Valigny. "But she could prove amusing nonetheless."

"Then perhaps," said Enders softly, "you had best explain precisely what you are offering us here, Valigny."

Just then, the parlor door burst open. "*Oui,* an excellent suggestion," said the girl who stalked toward the comte. In the gloom beyond the table, she made a sweeping gesture toward the guests. "Just what are you up to this time, Valigny? Lining your pockets, I am sure."

The comte replied in rapid, staccato French. Rothewell could not make out the words, but Valigny's expression had suddenly soured. Her back half-turned to them, the girl let fly another torrent of French, shaking her finger in the comte's face. Her voice was deep and faintly dusky — a sultry bedchamber voice that made a man's skin heat.

The footman stood in the rear of the room, his face growing paler as the argument rose to a crescendo. He was worried about the girl, Rothewell realized.

"*Sacré bleu!*" the girl finally spit. "Do as you wish. What do I care?" Then she made an angry gesture with her hand, spun round on one heel, and swished toward the table. At once, Enders sucked a sharp breath between his teeth.

It was understandable. Once again, Valigny did not lie. A strange mix of lust and longing stabbed through Rothewell, an almost visceral desire. The girl — the *woman* — was exquisite beyond words. Her dark eyes flashed with fire, and her chin was up a notch. Her nose was thin, her eyes wide-set, and her lush hair formed a sharp widow's peak above a high forehead.

In the dim light her complexion appeared surprisingly rich, her hair almost black. She was tall, too. As tall as Valigny, whom she seemed in that moment to tower over. But it was an illusion. She was simply furious.

Rothewell pushed away his brandy. He did not like his reaction to the woman. "Kindly explain yourself, Valigny."

The comte gave a theatrical bow. "I meet your wagers, *mes amis,*" he announced,

"with one very beautiful, very rich bride. I
trust I need not sit her upon the table?"

"You must be mad," Rothewell snapped.
"Get her out of here. We are none of us fit
company for a lady, drunk and disreputable
as we are — even I know that much."

The comte opened his hands. "But my
dear Lord Rothewell, I have a plan."

"*Oui,* a plan of great brilliance!" the girl
interjected, lifting her skirts just a fraction
so that she might execute a deep, mocking
curtsy. "Allow me to begin anew. *Bonsoir,
messieurs.* Welcome to the home of my most
gracious and devoted papa. I comprehend
that I am now to go — how do you say it?
— upon the auction block, *oui?* Alas, I am
une mégère — a frightful shrew, you would
say — and my English is thick with the
French. But I am very rich" — she pronounced it *reesh* — "and passable to look
at, no? *Alors,* who will make my loving papa
the first bid? I am but a horse on the hoof,
messieurs, awaiting your pleasure."

"Come now, *mon chou!*" her father chided.
"That's doing it too brown, even for you!"

"*Je ne pense pas!*" snapped the girl.

Rothewell scrubbed his hand round the
black stubble of his beard, which was ample
given the lateness of the hour. He was not
accustomed to being the only sane person

in a room.

Valigny was still looking remarkably pleased with himself. The woman had gone to the sideboard and was pouring herself a dram of brandy as if it were nothing out of the ordinary, but her hand, Rothewell saw, was shaking when she replaced the stopper in the crystal decanter.

Rothewell turned to glance at Enders, but he was ogling the girl, his mouth still slack. A lecher without shame. But was he any better? No, for he'd scarce taken his eyes off the woman from the moment she'd entered the room. Her mouth could easily obsess him, and that raspy voice of hers sent heat into places it had no business.

Why, then, did Enders trouble him so? Why did he wish to reach over and shove that lolling tongue back in his thick-lipped mouth? Rothewell cut a swift glance down, and realized that beneath the table, Enders's hand was already easing up and down the fall of his trousers.

Good God.

"Look here, Valigny," said Rothewell, violently stabbing out his cheroot, "I came to get drunk and play cards, not to —"

"What's she worth?" Enders abruptly interjected. "And I'll brook none of her insolence, Valigny, so she can put that shrew business aside right now. Just tell me how much this leg-shackle will bring me if I win her."

Win her. The words sounded ugly, even to Rothewell's ear.

"As I say, the girl is well dowered," the comte reassured him. "Her worth will more than meet anything we've put upon that table tonight."

"Do you think us complete fools?" said Enders. "Halburne divorced his wife. She didn't have a pot to piss in by the time he was finished — and you had to put her up in some drafy old chateau in godforsaken Limousin — so we know her straits were desperate."

Valigny opened his hands expressively. "*Oui*, 'tis true," he acknowledged. "But one must ask, my dear Lord Enders — why did Halburne marry her in the first place, *hein?* It was because *she* was an heiress! Cotton mills! Coal mines! *Mon Dieu,* none knows this better than I."

"I'm not sure we care, Valigny," said Rothewell.

"You might soon come to care, *mon ami,*" the comte suggested lightly. "Because, you see, a bit of it has been left to the girl. She is the last blood of her mother's family. But first she must find a husband — an English husband, and a man of the — how do you say it? — *le sang bleu?*"

"A blueblood," muttered Rothewell. "Christ Jesus, Valigny. She is your child."

"*Oui,* and do not the English always barter their daughters to be bred like mares?" The comte laughed, drew out his chair, and sat. "I am just doing it openly."

"You are a pig, Valigny," said his daughter matter-of-factly from the sideboard. "Skinny, *oui,* but still the pig."

"And that would make you what, *mon chou?*" he snapped. "A piglet, *n'est-ce pas?*"

Calvert, who had until now remained silent, cleared his throat harshly. "Now see here, Valigny," he said. "If I am to be banker, I cannot proceed without Mademoiselle Marchand's agreement."

Again, the comte laughed. "Oh, she will agree — won't you, *mon chou?*"

At that, the girl hastened from the sideboard, and leaned across the table, eyes blazing. "*Mon Dieu,* I will agree!" she said, pounding her fist upon the table so hard the glasses jumped. "One of you haggard old roués marry me — *immédiatement!* — before I kill him. Neither of you could be worse."

Enders began to laugh, a nasal, braying sound, like an ass with a head cold. "A saucy piece, isn't she, Valigny? Yes, amusing indeed."

The girl moved as if to rise, but suddenly, she caught Rothewell's gaze, and their eyes locked. He waited for her to pull away, but she stared boldly. Her eyes were wide, limpid pools of black-brown rage, and some other inscrutable emotion. Just what was it that lurked hidden there? A challenge? Pure hatred? Whatever it was, it at least served one purpose. It kept Rothewell from looking directly down at the creamy swell of cleavage, which seemed destined to spill from her bodice.

"Come, *mon chou!*" cajoled the comte. "Stand up straight and mind your tone, eh? You may soon be a baroness if I play my cards poorly."

"Bah!" she spit, abruptly straightening up from the table. "Play your cards badly, then. I wish to have done with this business."

"Very well." Calvert still looked uneasy. "I suppose we may proceed."

Rothewell shoved his cards away. "No," he snapped. "This is lunacy."

"First hear what I offer, Rothewell," the comte suggested, all business now. "You have eight thousand pounds on the table."

"Yes? What of it?"

"And Enders has what? Another eight?"

60

"Give or take," agreed Enders.

"So I wager the right to marry my daughter against all that is on the table," said the comte. "If I win, *très bien.* You go home a little less well-off than you came in. But if I lose, then the winner can marry my daughter — but within the month, *s'il vous plaît.* Her grandfather's will settles upon her the sum of fifty thousand pounds on her wedding day, which you will halve with me. Let us call it a finder's fee."

"Fifty thousand pounds, halved?" Enders drew back. "But you cannot lose!"

"*Oui,* but if you win, you win far more than eight thousand pounds," countered the comte.

"True enough," said Enders. "But divided, that sum is nothing!"

"Come now, Enders, it is enough to make a man comfortable if not truly rich," the comte countered. "Certainly it is enough to meet your wagers."

"And her beauty aside, she's hardly young," Enders reminded him.

Rothewell looked back and forth between Mademoiselle Marchand and her father. Something was amiss here. Or being hidden. He sensed it with a gambler's instinct. The girl's spine was rigid, her chin still high. But she was casting surreptitious glances at

Lord Enders, and her bravado, he thought, was flagging.

She reminded him of someone, he suddenly realized. It was the French accent. That warm, honey-colored skin. Those dark eyes, alight with fury and passion. *Good God.*

He set his brandy glass away, afraid he might crush it in his fist. "I can think of nothing I want less than a wife," he gritted. "And plainly, Enders doesn't want one, either."

"Nonetheless, it is an intriguing offer." Enders leaned across the table, leering. "Her age aside, she's a pretty little piece. Bring her over here, Valigny. Into the good light."

The comte led the girl by the elbow into the pool of lamplight near the gaming table, a lamb to the slaughter. It was pure hell to watch — and despite his dislike of Enders, Rothewell was no better. He could not tear his gaze from her. It was like an accident happening before his eyes — and he was helpless to stop it. Valigny's fingers seemed to be almost digging into the flesh of her arm, as if he held her against her will. Without troubling himself to rise, Enders looked her up and down, his eyes openly lingering on her breasts.

Dear God, what manner of man would put his daughter through this? It was just as she had said — she was no more than horseflesh to Valigny. And now Enders was motioning with his finger for her to turn around.

"Very slowly, my sweet," he rasped. "Yes, very, very slowly."

When her back was toward him, he watched her hips lewdly as they moved beneath her dark silk gown, an unholy light in his eyes. Perhaps Enders ought simply to ask Valigny to hike up the girl's skirts so that he might fondle the wares firsthand? At that thought, a strange, disgusting wave of lust and nausea washed over him.

This was not right.

It was also none of his business. He could walk out. Go home this instant and tell Valigny and Enders to go bugger themselves. However desirable Mademoiselle Marchand might be, the woman could obviously fend for herself. He didn't give a two-penny damn about the money on the table and, he reminded himself, he had no morals to be troubled by.

And yet he was not leaving, was he?

Because she reminded him of someone. Because he had felt fleetingly drawn into the swirling black pools of her eyes. *Fool.*

Oh, what a bloody damned fool he was.

To shut out the wild notion edging nearer, Rothewell squeezed his own eyes shut.

But there was another reason for staying. A reason that cut deeper still. He knew what it was to be thrown to the dogs as if you were no more than a piece of rancid meat. Dear Lord, why must his long-dead scruples resurrect themselves at a time such as this?

Because Enders was going to take that beautiful girl. Take her to his bed and make her do God only knew what — or with whom — heaven help her. And she was but an innocent. Had Rothewell doubted it, the faint hint of fear he saw in her eyes at that instant when she glanced down at Enders would have convinced him.

An awful chill ran through him. Oh, Mademoiselle Marchand might be full of fire and spirit tonight, but men like Enders knew just how to beat that out of a woman, and more often than not, they enjoyed the doing of it.

Enders had finished leering at her arse. That much, at least, was over. Mademoiselle Marchand cut her gaze away from the men and closed her eyes as if steeling herself for something worse.

Enders touched her lightly on the wrist, his plump lips turning up in a lascivious smile as he leered up at her. "So you need a husband to tame you, my pet?" he whispered in his nasal voice. "I begin to find the notion perfectly delicious."

The girl did not open her eyes but drew a deep, steadying breath, her nostrils flaring wide. For an instant, Rothewell thought her knees might buckle. Enders had begun to stroke her wrist over and over with his wide, plump fingertips — a deceptively gentle gesture, given his predilections — and Valigny was doing nothing. And in that moment — that sad, sickening instant of understanding, when he was nothing like himself, but instead a stranger whom he had never met and could not possibly comprehend — Rothewell grasped what was about to happen. What had to happen.

Well, what the hell difference would it make to him?

The thought freed him. Almost. Good God, he was no hero. He must be as mad as all of them.

Enders and Valigny were still watching the girl. Calvert's face was turned away.

Across the table, Rothewell caught the footman's gaze. He set one finger to his lips, then eased his other hand over to fumble beneath the table and felt a moment of triumph. A stiff flap of paper was wedged deep into the crack between the table leaves.

"By God, I'll have her!" Lord Enders's booming voice fractured the strange silence.

Rothewell jerked back his fingers, and deftly slid Valigny's card beneath his waistcoat. Only the footman observed him.

"With an arse like that, she's worth the twenty-five thousand *and* the inconvenience," Enders went on. "Been thinking of taking a wife anyway. Perhaps, Valigny, we can make a deal without another hand?"

The comte beamed.

"No," said Rothewell gruffly, sweeping up the previous hand in one smooth motion round the table. "No, shuffle this, Calvert, and by God, we shall play."

Enders narrowed his eyes. "Will we now?"

"Yes, why not?" he said.

"But you've swept up the hand."

"I have money on the table, and I wish to replay it," Rothewell demanded. "That was Valigny's proposal."

"*Mais oui,*" said the comte. "A new hand and a neutral dealer. Come now, Enders. Calvert shall wield the pack."

Rothewell cast a glower at his host. "Sit down, then, Valigny, and play this god-forsaken game you've thought up." He turned in his seat, and jerked out the adjacent chair. "And for pity's sake, let us be quick about it."

It was indeed quick, mercifully so. Calvert dealt one card down to each of them, then hesitated.

"Go on," said Rothewell curtly. "We've already agreed to stake it all."

Calvert nodded, and went round again. The gentlemen tipped up the corners of their cards. In that fleeting moment, Rothewell made his move.

"Lord Enders, do you stand?" asked Calvert.

For a long moment, there was nothing but the sputter of the lamp. Finally, Enders spoke. "I am content, thank you."

"Valigny?" asked Calvert.

The comte tapped the table with his knuckle, and Calvert slid him one more card.

"My lord?" Calvert turned to Rothewell. "Will you draw?"

Rothewell shook his head. "I stand." Then, with one flick of his fingertip, he turned his cards faceup.

From the shadows, the girl gasped. Valigny made a strange, choking sound in the back of his throat. His lucky card — the Queen of Spades — stared up at them, her black eyes glowering with disapproval. Beside her lay the Ace of Hearts, impassive, but glorious.

"Gentlemen," said Rothewell quietly. "I think that's *vingt-et-un.*"

CHAPTER THREE

IN WHICH A PROFITABLE PROPOSAL IS MADE

Enders began cursing as soon as the cards fell. Valigny stared at the black queen for a long moment, then burst into peals of laughter. The comte's daughter closed her eyes, and set her empty glass down with an awkward *chink* as it struck the silver gallery tray. Her slender shoulders went limp, and her head fell forward as if in prayer.

She was relieved, Rothewell thought. *She was relieved.* At least he had accomplished something.

Or had he? The girl recovered herself quickly enough. When the comte finally stopped laughing, he rubbed his hands briskly. "Well done, my Lord Rothewell!" He turned to his daughter. "*Félicitations, mon chou.* May I be the first to wish you happy. Now take his lordship to your sitting room. A newly betrothed couple needs a moment alone, *n'est-ce pas?*"

She did not look at Rothewell but instead

swept from the room as if she were the black queen come to life. His emotions still ragged, Rothewell followed her past the stairs and down a long passageway. What in God's name had he just done?

Nothing, that was what. He owed Valigny twenty-five thousand pounds. He needed to keep that thought straight in his head.

Mademoiselle Marchand turned left. Her steps were certain and quick, as if she knew what lay ahead and meant to soldier through it. With her shoulders set stiffly back, she pushed through the sitting-room door with a quick, capable swish of her hips, turned up the lamp, and motioned Lord Rothewell toward a chair, all without pause.

He ignored the chair, since she did not deign to sit. Inside the small chamber, a low fire glowed in the hearth, and a second lamp burned by the worn but elegant chair which sat adjacent. Rothewell let his gaze sweep over the room, as if by taking it in, he might divine something of the woman's character.

Unlike the gilt and gaudy splendor of Valigny's parlor, this tidy sitting room was appointed with French furniture which looked tasteful but far from new. Leather-bound books lined the whole of one wall, and the air smelled vaguely of lilies instead of smoke, soured wine, and too much male perspiration. Clearly, this was not Valigny's territory, but his daughter's — and unless Rothewell missed his guess, the twain rarely met.

He turned to face her. "Have you a name, *mademoiselle?*" he enquired with a stiff bow. "I gather *mon chou* is not your preferred form of address?"

Her smile was bitter. "What's in a name?" she quoted pithily. "You may call me Mademoiselle Marchand."

"Your Christian name," he pressed. "Under the circumstances, *mademoiselle,* I think it necessary."

There was another flicker of annoyance in her eyes. "Camille," she finally answered in her low, simmering voice.

"And I am Kieran," he said quietly.

His name seemed of no consequence to the woman. She paced to the window and stared out into the gaslit street beyond. He felt oddly wounded. A carriage went spinning past in the gloom, the driver's shadowy form barely visible upon the box. Unasked, Rothewell started across the room to join her, but she cut an immediate and forbidding glance over her shoulder.

He hesitated. Why press forward with this travesty? Indeed, what had possessed him to pursue it at all? Pity? Lust? One last effort

71

to redeem his hopelessly blackened soul? Or was it simply a gnawing hunger for something which he had not already tasted to wretched excess?

And what had brought such a beautiful creature to such a desperate point — and she must indeed be desperate though she hid it like a master.

Rothewell dropped his gaze. A glass of what looked like strong claret sat on a dainty piecrust table by her chair, and a book lay open beside it. He glanced at the spine. It was not a novel, as one might expect, but *An Inquiry into the Nature and Causes of the Wealth of Nations* by the Scot, Adam Smith.

Good God, was the woman a bluestocking? Rothewell glanced again at her face, now in profile as she stared into the night.

No. With lips as lush as those, it simply was not possible. Moreover, she was too cool. Too Continental and sophisticated.

"Mademoiselle Marchand," he said quietly, "why are you cooperating with your father in this unholy scheme?"

At last she turned from the window, her hands held serenely at her waist, one laid neatly over the other. "I do it, *monsieur,* for the same reason as you," she replied, her French accent less pronounced now. "Because there is something in it for me."

"What, a title?" Rothewell sneered. "I assure you, my dear, mine is scarcely known. It will do you little good."

"I don't give a damn for your title, sir," she calmly returned, her chin up. "I need an English husband — one who can do his duty."

"I beg your pardon?"

"A husband who can get me with child — and quickly." She let her gaze run down him as if *he* were now the horseflesh on the block. "Surely you can accomplish that much, *monsieur,* despite your haggard appearance?"

Strangely, it was not the insult but her apathy which stirred his ire. "What the devil are you talking about?" he said darkly. "If you wish for a child, *mademoiselle,* there are many eligible bachelors in London who would doubtless oblige you."

"Alas, I am told they have all gone to the country for shooting season." She laughed with mocking lightness. "Oh, come, *monsieur!* With Valigny's reputation? And my mother's? I am thought scandalous, my lord. But you — ah, *you* do not look as if scandal much disturbs you."

"You have a tart tongue, madam," he returned. "Perhaps that is your problem?"

"*Oui,* but you'll not be long burdened with it," she answered evenly. "Just wed me, Rothewell, and do your duty. It will prove a lucrative wager indeed — less Valigny's cut of the settlement, *naturellement.* I will pay you a generous sum of money as soon as my child is born healthy. Then you may go on your merry, dissolute way."

"Good God," he said, his temper ratcheting up. "Just what is a man's seed selling for nowadays, Miss Marchand? Can you tell me? Have you put a price on it?"

She faltered but a moment. "It is worth a good deal to me," she returned. "A hundred thousand pounds, *monsieur.* How does that sound?"

"Good God," he said again. "I begin to believe you as coldhearted as Valigny."

A bitter smile curved her full, sensuous lips. "And I begin to believe it is your precious title which concerns you after all," she answered. "English arrogance is —"

"Titles and arrogance be damned!" he snapped, stalking toward her. "In any case, there will be no child. My God, there isn't even going to be a *marriage.* And what is this nonsense about a hundred thousand pounds? Valigny spoke only of a marriage portion."

"*Vraiment?*" Her brown eyes widened

74

disingenuously. "A pity I did not have my ear to the door, my lord. Valigny has told you but half the tale — the half he knows."

He moved closer — so close he could see the fringe of thick black lashes which rimmed her chocolate-colored eyes — and set one heavy hand on her shoulder. "Then suppose, Mademoiselle Marchand, that you tell me the other half? — and pray do so *now.*"

Her chocolate eyes seemed suddenly to shoot sparks. "Oh, you are just another spoilt, drunken rakehell, Rothewell, like all Valigny's friends." Her seductive voice was low and tremulous. "What would a fifty-thousand-pound marriage portion do for me? Why would I marry you? Out of the goodness of my heart? There is none! If ever there was, Valigny has trampled it out of me."

Rothewell was struck suddenly by three things. Her English was a good deal better than she'd been letting on. His cock was on the verge of stiffening, a strange circumstance indeed. And she was bloody well right about the money. Why *would* she marry him? What had she to gain? Her father would take half the marriage portion, and he, himself, would ostensibly take the other half.

"I'll have the truth out of you, madam," he gritted. "All of it. Now."

Something like hatred glinted in her eyes. "And so I shall tell you," she said. "Three months past, Valigny found out that I was left a marriage portion in the will of my grandfather, and it is eating him alive. *Oui,* he is addicted, *monsieur.* Addicted to the game, and always desperate. For the money to play his game, he will do anything."

Rothewell glowered down at her, strangely aware of her sharp, spicy scent, and of the tiny pulse point just below her ear. "Aye, go on."

For an instant, her dainty pink tongue toyed with one corner of her mouth, but Rothewell was almost too enraged to appreciate it. *Almost.* "There is more." She dropped her voice, her words swift and quiet. "Things Valigny does not know. But I wonder . . . I wonder if you can be trusted."

"No," he said flatly.

She let that thought sink in for a moment. *"Zut!"* she said beneath her breath. "You have me at sword point, *monsieur.* May I not rely on your honor as a gentleman?"

"That's a slender reed to grasp, my dear," he said. "But you may cling to it if you wish."

Her eyes shot daggers at him then. *"Mon*

Dieu, you are a devil!" she said. "A devil with the eyes of a wolf. But perhaps I must risk it."

"Why not?" he answered. "Could I possibly be more of a devil than your father?"

"*Oui,* that is most true." But her temper, he could see, was still hot and she was still hesitant. "There is more than a marriage portion for me," she finally said. "The solicitor of my grandfather advises me that his English — what do you say? His *propriété?*"

"His country estate, you mean?"

She nodded. "Yes, the land, the house, the title — all these have gone to a cousin. But all else — much else — is to be mine. There is money, *oui,* but also mills and mines for coal. Things which I do not understand — *not yet.* But it is worth many, many thousands of pounds."

Rothewell felt his eyes widen. It was true, then, what Valigny had said. But the man apparently did not comprehend the magnitude of what he'd just gambled away. "And Valigny knows nothing of this?"

"*Non.*" She lifted one elegant shoulder beneath the silk of her gown. "I was not fool enough to tell him everything."

Rothewell felt his suspicion growing. "If you are so wealthy," he said, "what need have you to marry at all?"

Here, Mademoiselle Marchand's lips thinned. "Alas, there is the — the what do you call it? — the fly in the honey?" she answered. "My grandfather was a vengeful man. I inherit nothing until I come here — to England — and marry a suitable man. A man of the English aristocracy."

"Ah, yes! There's that English gentleman again," said Rothewell.

She flashed a bitter smile, but to his frustration, it did nothing to lessen her allure. *"Mais oui,"* she agreed. "Then, however, to receive anything beyond my marriage portion, I must produce a child. My grandfather wished to ensure that the dreaded scourge — that frightful French blood of my father — was soon diluted out of existence in his descendants."

Rothewell took a step back. "I'm afraid you have netted the wrong sort of fish, my dear," he returned. "I have no interest in this misbegotten scheme."

She tossed him another disparaging glance, then edged away. "Of course you do," she snapped, crossing her arms over her chest. "You are a hardened gamester, are you not? Take a risk! You have a fifty-fifty chance the child will be female, and your precious title will be unsullied."

"Oh?" he growled. "Assuming I give a

damn for my title, what then?"

She gave a Gallic shrug. "Then, *monsieur,* you can divorce me," she replied. "I gladly will give you cause, if need be. I have had no offers of marriage, *c'est vrai,* but many offers of another kind. Offers made only with the eyes — so far. But it will be no problem for me simply to accept one."

Like the lash of a whip, his hand seized her arm, turning her to face him. "You would not dare, *mademoiselle,*" he gritted. "For if you tried that trick with me, it wouldn't be a divorce you'd get."

The woman had the audacity to laugh in his face. "Ah, suddenly principled, are you?"

He released her arm, but she did not back away. The hot, spicy scent of her filled his nostrils now. "I may not give a damn for my title, Mademoiselle Marchand," he snapped. "But I care a great deal about being made a cuckold."

"Oh, everyone has a price, Rothewell." Was there an unexpected note of melancholy in her voice? "You. Lord Enders. Valigny. *Oui, monsieur,* even I. Have I not just proven it?"

"A price?" he returned. "There may be little about me that is honorable, *mademoiselle,* but I have no need to marry a woman for her money. Indeed, I have no need — or desire — to marry at all."

"What nonsense!" She cut another of her cool glances at him. "That is precisely why you remained at the card table, *n'est-ce pas?*"

"No, damn you, it is not," he snarled.

Mademoiselle Marchand blinked her eyes, as if attempting to clear her vision. *"Non?"* she murmured, drifting back to the window. "Then why did you play Valigny's little game, Rothewell? What other reason could you possibly have?"

It was on the tip of his tongue to tell her it was because he could not bear the thought of Lord Enders's heaving himself atop so lovely and so innocent a young woman — but no. That would not do. It probably wasn't even true. Why should he give a damn what happened to Valigny's insolent by-blow? Oh, she was beautiful, yes. And infinitely beddable. But she had a tongue like a serpent, and eyes which seemed determined to pierce his darkest recesses.

How the devil had he got himself into this mess? There was nothing of the gentleman in him, and there never had been. He was no better than that scoundrel Valigny, or the sick, twisted Lord Enders.

Her piercing eyes were on him now, watchful. Insistent. "Why, Rothewell?" she said. "Now it is my turn to demand the truth."

"The truth!" he said bitterly. "Would either of us recognize it, I wonder?"

She stepped toward him, her eyes glinting. "Why did you gamble with Valigny?" she demanded. "Tell me. If not the money, why?"

His frustration finally exploded. He caught her by the elbow, and dragged her against him. "Because I want you, damn it," he snarled down at her. "Why else? I'm no better than Enders. I think I should like you under my thumb, *mademoiselle.* In my bed. Beneath me. I should dearly love to make you eat a few of your prideful words, and do my every bidding. Perhaps that is *why.*"

Satisfaction glinted in her eyes. *"Très bien,"* she murmured, stepping back as he released her. "At least I know what I am dealing with."

Rothewell forced down his anger. He was a liar — and he felt suddenly weary and ashamed. "Oh, you have no idea, Mademoiselle Marchand," he said, his voice dropping to a whisper. "For all your *avant-garde* upbringing, you cannot possibly know what you are *dealing with.* You have no business with a man like me. I release you, my dear, from this foolish, Faustian bargain of your father's. You are not his to barter — no matter what he might imagine when he is in his cups and desperate."

Mademoiselle Marchand had resumed her solitary vigil by the window and no longer faced him. Her delicate, thin shoulders had rolled inward with fatigue now, and much of the hauteur had left her frame. He had never seen another human being look so desperately alone.

Slowly, she turned and let her gaze take him in again, but this time it was his face which she studied. "No," she said quietly. "No, Lord Rothewell, I think shall stand by my father's bargain."

Rothewell gave a sharp laugh. "I don't think you understand, *mademoiselle*," he answered. "I have no need of a wife."

For a long, expectant moment, she hesitated, her mind toying with the knife's edge of something he could not fathom. She was weighing him. Judging him again with her all-seeing eyes. And it made him acutely uncomfortable.

She crossed the room to face him again and dropped her voice to a throaty whisper. "If you want me, Lord Rothewell," she said, "then have me."

"I beg your pardon?"

Mademoiselle Marchand leaned into him,

set her hands on his lapels, and dropped her sweeping black lashes. "Have me." He watched her lush lips form each word, mesmerized. "Give me your oath — your pledge as a gentleman that we shall marry and share equally in my inheritance — then have me. Tonight. Now."

"You must be mad," he managed. But he was drawing in the scent of her — that warm, spicy mélange that smelled of orchids and seductive feminine heat — and his traitorous body was eager.

Her breasts were pressed against him now. Her mouth — and that dark-as-midnight voice — were hot against his ear. *"Beneath you,"* she whispered. *"Under your thumb. Doing your every bidding.* That is your fantasy, *n'est-ce pas?"*

Rothewell dredged up what little restraint he possessed and set his hand to the back of her head. "Were I to have you, *mademoiselle,*" he whispered against her ear, "and act out even the most fainthearted of my fantasies, everyone from here to High Holborn Street would have to listen to the racket, because I'd have my hand laid to your bare backside."

She drew back, her eyes wide.

"No," he said, sneering. "I did not think that was what you had in mind. But if you insist on acting like a foolish child, then that is how I'll treat you, Mademoiselle Marchand. *Do not toy with me.* You will rue the day."

She dropped her gaze, and to his undying agony, backed away. "*Très bien,* my lord," she murmured, her voice amazingly cool. "You make your point. Is Lord Enders still in my father's parlor?"

Rothewell shrugged. "I daresay. What of it?"

She set off briskly toward the door. "Then I shall marry him after all," she replied over her shoulder. "It will be worth a vast deal of money to him — and to my father."

Rothewell beat her to the door, slamming his open palm against it. "Good God, woman, don't be a damned fool!" His voice was a low growl. "Enders is a lecher — and that term is a generous one."

"*Oui?* And what business is it of yours?"

He leaned into her. "*Listen to me,*" he rasped. "There is not a shred of honor in that man. You cannot bargain with him. Oh, he'll marry you — and then by law, every penny you possess will be his — and you will be his — to do with as he pleases."

She turned and set her back to the door, daring him. Looking him up and down as if she did not fear him — or Enders — in the least. The Black Queen. It was not what he was accustomed to.

Rothewell braced the other hand above her shoulder, effectively pinning her.

"It would appear you have me trapped, Lord Rothewell," she said coolly. "What do you mean to do about it?"

He meant, apparently, to kiss her. Almost savagely, in fact, driving her head back against the wood, and opening his mouth over hers without hesitation. As if on instinct, she raised her hands to shove him away, but it was too late.

Rothewell deepened the kiss on a rush of sensation, allowing his weight to pin her against the door. He slanted his mouth over hers, forcing his way into the sweet, spicy depths of her mouth.

She fought him but an instant, then opened willingly, entwining her tongue with his in a tantalizing dance of pleasure. Again and again, he kissed her, and felt himself slip into the depths of something dark and uncertain. It was as if the heat of her body seared his. The swell of her breasts and belly. The taut muscles of her thighs. All of it pressed down his length, urging him toward a rash, hot madness.

In the gloom, her breath came fast and urgent. He was vaguely aware that she was kissing him back, and rather boldly; rising onto her toes, the crisp silk of her bodice crushing against the wool of his lapels.

So lost was he in the moment, Rothewell was scarcely aware that his hands had left the door and gone instead to her face, trembling. In the street beyond, a clatter arose; a mail coach, perhaps, moving fast. The racket sliced through the heat, returning Rothewell to the present. Almost reluctantly, he drew his tongue across her sharp, white teeth one last time, then lifted his face from hers, his gaze locked to hers, their nostrils flared wide.

She, too, was trembling. Ah, there was a fear in her now. But not, he thought, of him.

Mademoiselle Marchand licked her lips uncertainly. "Tell me, my lord," she whispered, dropping her gaze to a point disconcertingly near his crotch. "Do you still wish me across your knee?"

There was bravado in her voice still, it was true. But like the hardened gambler he was, Rothewell began to scent panic. As the fog of lust slowly dissipated, he considered it, and let his arms drop. His gaze roamed over her beautiful, almost heart-shaped face, taking in her wide brown eyes and fine cheekbones.

"Tell me, my dear, how much longer do

you have?" he murmured. "I think I hear the fatal sound of a ticking clock — and I don't mean the one on your mantelpiece."

For a moment, she hesitated. "Six weeks," she finally whispered.

"Six weeks?" he echoed. "Why so little?"

Something like resignation sketched across her face. "I have had ten years," she answered. "Ten years in which to find the — what do you call it? The knight in shining armor?"

"Something like that," he agreed.

She flashed a bitter smile. "My grandfather decided this when I was very young. But I found the letters of the solicitor but recently — following my mother's death."

Rothewell looked at her, stunned. "Christ Jesus," he whispered. "She did not tell you?"

Mademoiselle Marchand shook her head. She would not hold his gaze. "I was a fool," she said softly. "A fool to think Valigny could help me. No decent family will receive him. He has wasted my precious time."

"Very well." Rothewell swallowed. "You have six weeks. And then what happens?"

She lifted her chin a fraction. "My twenty-eighth — how do you say it? — the anniversary of one's birth?"

"Your birthday?" said Rothewell, incredulous. "You must be *married* by your twenty-eighth birthday?"

"To obtain so much as the first sou, *oui,* I must first marry by twenty-eight, and bear a child of my husband within two years."

"And your father knows this?" Rothewell felt vaguely appalled. "He knows it, and he used you? To stake a card game?"

"Valigny, I fear, is without scruple," she said emotionlessly. Her eyes were still upon him, dark and knowing. "But be assured, my lord, that I *am* going to marry. Otherwise, there is nothing for me. Nothing but Valigny's generosity, which has never proven very reliable."

"I see," he murmured.

"So what is it to be, Rothewell?" she quietly continued. "Am I to marry you? Or must I take the licentious Lord Enders to my bed?"

Good Lord, she really meant to marry one of them? And the choice was to be his?

He looked again into her bottomless brown eyes. She was serious. Deadly serious.

Rothewell felt as if someone had just crushed the air from his lungs.

But Mademoiselle Marchand — Camille — was still looking at him, her expression oddly serene, her hands once more carefully folded. She was waiting. Waiting for his answer. He drew a deep breath, then let his gaze run over her once again. She was so beautiful she could almost have made the dead rise — *almost* — and there was no denying that despite all the emotion of this awful night, yes, he still desired her. The kiss had served only to fan the flame which had sprung to life the moment he'd laid eyes on her.

Well, he had begun this travesty, hadn't he? He might as well finish it. God knew it would make little difference to him.

"Have you a maid?" he asked abruptly.

"Oui, bien sûr," she said. "Why?"

Rothewell caught her almost roughly by the elbow. "Because we are going to find her," he said grimly. "And then we are going to your bedchamber to pack your things."

"In the middle of the night?" Her voice arched. "Why?"

"Yes. In the middle of the night." He had opened the door and propelled her through it. "Because I'll be damned if you will ever spend another under Valigny's roof."

Within the hour they were out of the house and Rothewell was helping Mademoiselle Marchand into his carriage. Her hand was warm and light in his own. He looked down to see her fingers, slender and neatly manicured. It was a capable-looking hand.

Since leaving her sitting room, he had moved as if in a dream, instructing Mademoiselle Marchand, barking orders at the servants, and holding Valigny deliberately at bay. And all the while, it felt as though he watched another man indelibly altering his life.

The maid turned out to be a thin, pale-faced girl who was terrified of Rothewell. As to Mademoiselle Marchand, her every gesture was calm, her expression unreadable. A very composed woman, he thought — unless she was being kissed senseless.

The footman called Tufton came down with the last bag and glanced at the carriage door with obvious concern. When he had lashed the bag to the back of the carriage, Rothewell stepped beneath the street-lamp, and thrust out his card.

"I am in Berkeley Square if you need me," he murmured. "I will keep her safe from him. You may depend upon that much."

The strain fell from Tufton's face. "Thank you, my lord." He tucked the card away and hastened back up the steps.

Rothewell looked up at his coachman. He was gravely reluctant to do what he knew he must, but his impetuous decision left him little choice. "To Hanover Street," he ordered.

"To Hanover Street?" echoed the coachman.

"Yes, to Sharpe's," he said. "And be quick about it."

The trip through London's darkened streets was a relatively short one. At Lord Sharpe's imposing town house, they were let in by the same cowering footman who had chased Rothewell down Hanover Street over a week earlier. They had obviously roused him from his cot, for his hair was badly askew and his shirttail half-out.

Rothewell made no explanation, but merely ordered the footman to put Mademoiselle Marchand and her maid in one of the guest rooms. He was not about to wake Pamela at such an hour. That done, he went into the front parlor, tossed his coat across the tea table, and glanced at the long-case clock by the door.

Half past three. Good Lord. He had lived an eternity in the last two hours. Accustomed to surviving on little sleep, Rothewell flung himself down in a nearby chair, threw his feet up onto his coat, and slipped into a state of numbness which was not quite sleep and not quite wakefulness. He did not rouse until the rattle of a servant cleaning a grate bestirred him sometime near dawn. He rose surprisingly free of the nausea and pain he had come to expect.

"Oh, dear!" said Pamela two hours later. She had come down wearing a loose-fitting morning dress striped with pink and cream, and was pacing before the hearth, her hem furling out with every turn. "Upstairs? The daughter of the Comte de Valigny, you say?"

"A rotter through and through, I know," said Rothewell.

Pamela stopped and frowned. "Lie down with dogs, Kieran, get up with fleas!" An overused proverb was as close to criticism as the countess ever came.

He lifted both hands. "I am not fooling myself, Pamela," he replied. "I know what is said of me. Valigny and I have been drinking and gambling and whor— well, other unmentionable things — together for months now. None of this looks good for her."

Pamela crossed the room, and sat down in the chair adjacent. "We mustn't judge the girl by her relations, for none of us, I think, would wish to suffer *that*," she said dryly, bending forward to refresh his coffee. "Nor perhaps should we judge you from your friends."

"Valigny has never been a friend," he said tightly. "As to being judged, we both know that it is done. That's why I brought her here."

"And not to Xanthia?" murmured Lady Sharpe. "I did wonder at it."

Rothewell flashed a wry smile. He did not like asking favors. "You are like the driven snow in this town, my dear," he said. "And Mademoiselle Marchand can ill afford to rub elbows with anything less. Of course her name will be irreparably blackened if I put her up in Berkeley Square."

"Quite so, quite so!" she agreed, springing from her chair again. "Well! What can be done? One must hope her mother has been forgotten."

Rothewell laughed harshly. "What, by the *ton*?" he asked. "They love gossip rather too well for that, my dear."

"Yes, I daresay you are right." She had set a finger to her cheek and was tapping it thoughtfully. "And this card game business, Kieran. Really, it is beyond the pale."

He set his jaw grimly. "Do you think I don't know that, Pamela?" he answered. "Seen in the light of day, yes, I regret it. If I had it to do over again, I would put a stop to the whole business."

Lady Sharpe's smile was muted. "Well, in

a way, you did," she remarked. "You have got the poor girl away from him, at the very least. But that lurid tale about the card game must never be heard of again, my dear. The girl will be utterly ruined."

Rothewell clenched and unclenched his fists. He was more than a little ashamed of his role in this debacle. "Look, Pamela," he said awkwardly. "This was a foolish notion. I shouldn't have barged in here."

Lady Sharpe waved her hand for him to hush. She began to pace again, her delicate blond eyebrows drawn together. Rothewell dropped his gaze and stared into the sobering black depths of his coffee.

What on earth had possessed him to load Mademoiselle Marchand into his carriage in the middle of the night? Why had he fallen in with her mad scheme? He had thought merely to do the woman a favor, with little inconvenience to himself. But life was never so simple as one thought it. That was a lesson he ought to have learned the first time he had asked a woman to entwine her fate with his.

He looked up to see Pamela pacing toward him. "Let me meet the girl," she finally said. "I shall think of something quite clever, Kieran, I assure you. Something to explain why she is staying here. But what, pray, do you mean to do with the chit in the long term?"

"Well, as to that —" Rothewell paused and eyed her over the rim of his coffee cup. "Well, as to that, I very much fear, Pamela, that I really do mean to marry her."

Lady Sharpe froze in her tracks. For once in her life, she was utterly and completely speechless.

Rothewell seized the moment. Amidst a good deal of stuttering and stammering on his cousin's part, he made the vaguest of explanations, thanked her again profusely, then bolted for the door.

It was time to go home, he thought as he dashed down the steps. Time to go home and write the Comte de Valigny a bank draft for his twenty-five thousand pounds. Then at least one part of this travesty would be over. The bastard would have his money — and whatever happened afterward would be none of his damned business.

Camille sat perfectly still in a chair by the window, looking down at the morning traffic in Mayfair. She had risen at dawn to wash her face and pin up her hair, for there had been no hope of sleep. Then she had sat down to await her fate — and here she remained; a stranger in a strange house, forgotten, perhaps. But what did a few more hours, or a few more months, matter? Had she not spent the whole of her life awaiting the pleasure of another?

Eventually, she assumed, Lord Rothewell would return. If he did not, Camille was fully prepared to take matters into her own hands. One could not wait on — or even depend upon — a man for very long. That much she had learned from her mother's mistakes. At least Rothewell had had the audacity to admit he was not to be trusted. That, she supposed, spoke well of him.

She was not perfectly sure just what she'd got herself into with Rothewell — but she knew very well what she'd got herself out of. Her fate at Lord Rothewell's hands could hardly be worse than the last three months she'd spent with Valigny. Certainly it would not be permanent. A quick marriage, and with a little luck, the blessing of a child to love. And then, at long last, she would be free. Free of her mother. Valigny. And, of course, Lord Rothewell. She would be glad indeed to see the back of him. His dark, glittering eyes, short temper, and hard questions would endear the man to no one.

She looked down and realized her hands were clenched again. With well-practiced will, she forced them to relax. Matters could be worse. There might even be a sliver of kindness in Rothewell. Of course she might well be mistaken. It was a risk she had weighed before leaping.

The other man — Lord Enders — oh, his type she knew well. He was nothing but a rutting pig — and a depraved one at that. She had not needed Lord Rothewell's counsel in that regard, for she had spent too much time in Paris, surrounded by her mother's coterie of desperate, over-painted friends, and the *débauchés* who courted them.

Just then, she heard Emily stirring on the bed behind her. She turned to see the maid lift her hand to block a shaft of early-morning sun as she sat up. "Beg pardon, miss," she managed. "I didn't mean to lie abed so late."

"It's quite all right, Emily." Camille returned to her vigil at the window. "You had no rest last night."

"Nor did you, miss," she answered.

Camille listened to the sounds of the maid dressing behind her. Emily doubtless wondered what was to become of them, and Camille had no good answers. At last, however, she turned round to watch the girl. "You mustn't worry, Emily," she said. "I am sure this will all work out."

"Yes, miss." Emily had begun to fold their nightclothes. "I'm sure you know best."

Camille suppressed a hysterical laugh. "We must hope so," she answered. "Of course, I would like to keep you on, Emily, whether I marry or not."

But she had to marry. She *must.*

Death had finally relieved her of the burden which had hung over her these last few years, and she had awakened from her mother's long illness as if from a dark dream, only to realize her life was empty. The awful truth was that she longed for far more than financial independence. She yearned for a *child* — a yearning which had only grown more acute with every passing year until it was like the pain of a knife's blade pricking at her heart.

And just when she had believed it would never be possible, that she must endure the pain with her arms empty — she had found her grandfather's letter. His eccentric bequest had laid open a path — but she now realized that that meant a marriage to Lord Rothewell, or to someone like him.

Oh, she could return to Limousin with her tail between her legs, sell what was left of her mother's jewelry, and perhaps survive for a time. But she was almost twenty-eight years old and no longer content with mere survival. And to return to her old life in France as a poor relation, clinging to the bedraggled hems of an ignominious family? No. No, it did not bear thinking about. She had seized this opportunity with her bare hands, and the only thing left to do was dig in her nails.

At that thought, she exhaled on a shuddering sigh. Her hands began to clench again, and the sense of hopelessness which had followed her from Paris began to edge nearer. Lord Rothewell really was her last hope. Despite her brash threat last night, Camille had been terrified of Lord Enders. So she had played upon that tiny sliver of decency she thought she'd glimpsed in Rothewell's eyes.

But perhaps the joke was on her. Perhaps Rothewell was worse. There was a darkness about the man of a sort she'd never seen before. Not evil. Not simple dissolution. No, it was a darkness of the soul, and it hung about him like a shroud.

At that, Camille did laugh. Emily looked at her strangely.

Yes, she really had lost her mind, Camille decided. She was becoming fanciful, and worse, melodramatic. Just a few steps further along that path, and she would turn into her mother.

Just then, there was a light knock at the door. Emily opened it. A footman stood rigidly at attention. The Countess of Sharpe desired Camille's company. Doubtless the lady was thrilled to hear that the illegitimate child of London's most disreputable scoundrel had been installed in one of her guest rooms whilst she slept.

Ten minutes later, Camille was ensconced in Lady Sharpe's private sitting room with a cup of coffee in hand. A proper cup, too. Not the cheap, watered-down brew which Valigny had insisted be served when there were no guests in the house.

Lady Sharpe was smiling at her with a brightness which was almost certainly forced. And yet throughout their brief conversation, she had thus far looked neither angry nor displeased. The countess was a round, sweet-faced woman well past her youth, but with an even temper and, Camille thought, a measure of good sense.

"And so you were brought up in the French countryside, my dear?" the countess enquired, leaning forward to freshen her cup. "It must have been lovely."

It had been anything but lovely, but Camille thought it impolitic to say so. "Valigny's uncle had a small chateau in Limousin," she answered. "He allowed mother the use of it, and of his house in Paris, too, when he had no need of it."

"He sounds very generous," said Lady Sharpe.

He had been generous — but like most men, he had expected something in return. *"Oui, madame,"* she agreed. "My mother was most grateful to him."

Lips slightly pursed, Lady Sharpe picked up her coffee, the cup chattering on the saucer. She was nervous, Camille realized, and there was a faint strain about her eyes.

"Well, my dear, now that we are a little bit acquainted," said the countess, "do tell me about this . . . this betrothal you have entered into with my cousin."

Camille lifted her chin a notch. "You disapprove, *madame,* I am sure."

Lady Sharpe's eyes widened. "I am not sure," she answered. "One might be almost grateful that you are willing to have him. But Rothewell has never shown even the slightest inclination toward domesticity."

Camille managed a weak smile. "You make him sound like a — a *petit chien* — a small dog, *non?* One which will not be trained to the house."

"Yes, like a puppy." The countess's eyes danced. "There is some similarity, I would agree — though Rothewell is anything but small or cute."

A long silence fell across the room then, and an air of seriousness returned. The countess wished to have an answer to her question. Camille held her gaze unflinchingly. "Lord Rothewell will have told you that this betrothal was agreed between himself and my father, *oui?*"

Lady Sharpe looked away. "He said something of it, yes," she admitted. "But you had never met him before last tonight?"

"I have met him now," said Camille.

"And you are willing to marry him?"

"Oui, madame," she answered. "I have given my pledge."

Lady Sharpe's lips thinned. "But . . . but *why?*"

"Why?" Camille echoed. "I am long past the age, *madame,* when a woman should be married. And here in England, my bloodlines are thought questionable at best. Rothewell has agreed to have me. Do you not think I should be grateful?"

Lady Sharpe's brows had drawn together. "But it all sounds so . . . so frightfully *practical.*"

Camille folded her hands neatly in her lap. "I am a practical woman, *madame,*" she said quietly. "I need a husband. I have no interest in romance or any other such *banalités.*"

"Oh!" said Lady Sharpe wistfully. Then her expression brightened. "On the other hand, you should suit Rothewell very well indeed, for a less romantic man I never knew. And if you expect so little of him — why, I daresay you will never be disappointed."

Camille managed a serene smile. "Yes, *madame,* a very practical solution, is it not?"

Lady Sharpe hesitated. "Nonetheless, my dear, I fear your path may not be smooth," she finally said. "Rothewell is someone for whom I care deeply — I see the good in him, you know — but he will not be an easy person to love."

Camille felt her eyes widen. "Indeed, *madame,* I do not expect to," she said. "This is but an arrangement."

The countess looked a little horrified. "Oh, my dear girl!" she said, her hand fluttering to her chest. "You must never enter into a marriage with someone you cannot grow to love."

"Pardon, madame?"

Lady Sharpe leaned intently forward. "People do it all the time, I know. But if a man is not worthy of your deepest affections, then on no account should you marry him. At best, you will be dooming the both of you to a life of quiet, empty misery."

Camille was taken aback. "But as I said, *madame,* I do not look for romance."

"Oh, heavens, child." Lady Sharpe all but rolled her eyes. "Romance and love have absolutely nothing to do with one another."

Camille was confused. "*Oui, madame.* If you say so."

The countess looked a little pained. "Have you no regard for him at all, then?"

"Regard?" Camille considered how best to put the woman at ease. "Lord Rothewell seems an honest man. That is admirable, *n'est-ce pas?* And I assure you, *madame,* that I shall be a dutiful wife so long as we live together."

Lady Sharpe looked a little mollified and began once more to refresh their coffee.

What more could Camille say of the man? She had met him but a few hours earlier, and Rothewell had not accounted himself especially well. She could still remember his sneer as he jerked her against him. His words were still burned into her consciousness — especially since she'd tried to use them herself.

I think I should like you under my thumb, mademoiselle. In my bed. Beneath me.

Camille closed her eyes, and swallowed hard. Dear God, was she making a dreadful mistake? Was she about to unleash something she could not control? She had not forgotten his warning, or the heat of his body as he had all but pinned her to the door. The strange sensation of her stomach bottoming out.

The countess was looking at her assessingly. "Rothewell needs an heir, Mademoiselle Marchand," she said, tilting the creamer over her cup. "You do wish for children, I hope?"

"Yes, *madame*," said Camille honestly. "As soon as possible."

Lady Sharpe set her hands on her lap. "Well, my dear, you seem a sensible woman. Now that I am relatively certain you know what you are getting yourself into, let us speak of the practicalities. I think some town bronze is in order, and then perhaps a wedding in the early spring would be —"

"Non," said Camille abruptly. "I mean — I do beg your pardon, *madame* — but I wish to be married at once. Lord Rothewell has agreed."

"Has he?" Lady Sharpe looked at her a little strangely. "Well, that must be worked out between the two of you, I daresay. Let me be blunt, then, if I may? My job, as I understand it, is to — oh, dear, how must I put this — to put a little distance between you and your father?"

"*Oui, madame,*" said Camille. "Valigny is not thought respectable, I comprehend."

"Oh, my dear, it isn't *quite* that," said the countess.

"*Mais oui,* it is precisely that," said Camille. "I take no insult, *madame,* from what is so. Until three months past, I had scarcely spent more than a fortnight at a time in Valigny's company, save for my infancy. But I wished to come to England. I thought it better to have his companionship than no one's."

"And you were quite right, to be sure." Lady Sharpe gave a comforting smile and leaned over to pat Camille's hand. She seemed so very kind.

Camille drew a deep breath. "*Madame,* if . . . if I might ask?"

"By all means, my dear." The countess looked at her enquiringly. "What is it?"

Camille weighed her words. "Lord Rothewell has told you of my mother? Who she was?"

Lady Sharpe's face fell with sympathy. "Yes, of course. I never met her, but I'm told she was a remarkable beauty."

"And her . . . her husband? Lord Halburne? Do you know him?"

Lady Sharpe slowly shook her head. "Sharpe once met him, I believe," she mused. "But Halburne lives the life of a recluse and is almost never seen in town."

Camille exhaled audibly. "*Oui,* that is what Valigny said," she whispered. "But I was not sure . . ." Her words trailed weakly away.

"Whether to believe him?" Lady Sharpe waited for Camille's nod, then patted her hand. "In this case, I daresay you can."

"*Bon,*" murmured Camille. "I will not see Halburne, then? I will not — what is the phrase? Bump against him?"

"Bump into him," Lady Sharpe corrected. "No, my dear. I rather doubt it."

"*Merci, madame,*" Camille rasped. "*Merci.*"

But Lady Sharpe was looking pensive, and her mind was clearly drifting elsewhere. "I had a French governess as a girl," she finally said. "A very well bred lady by the name of Vigneau. Her family was from St. Leonard. Was your village near there, by chance?"

"*Oui, madame,*" said Camille. "Not so very far. And there are many Vigneaus thereabouts."

"Mademoiselle Vigneau was with me but briefly," said the countess. "I was very fond of her, but alas, her family called her home, for they had arranged a brilliant marriage to a local nobleman."

"How fortunate for her," said Camille.

"How fortunate for us, perhaps." Lady

Sharpe was tapping her cheek again. "It should not be so great a stretch as to manufacture some vague acquaintanceship between all of us, I think. Something which would explain why you've come to stay with me."

Just then, there was a sound at the door. Camille looked past Lady Sharpe's shoulder to see a very tall, very willowy woman in a dark blue carriage dress standing in the passageway. Lady Sharpe turned around in her chair.

The lady was flushing. "Oh dear," she said. "You have a caller. I thought to find you alone at such an hour. Forgive me."

Lady Sharpe rose and went to the door, both hands outstretched. "My dear, you must come in," she said. "And you are right. It is too early for a caller. But Mademoiselle Marchand, you see, is my houseguest. Do come and meet her."

The woman did so, impatiently unfurling the ribbons of her bonnet as she came. Unless Camille missed her guess, the lady was a few months gone with child.

"I really must apologize," she said again, lifting off the hat to reveal a somewhat severe arrangement of dark, glossy hair. "I slipped right past poor old Strothers rather than be announced. I was hoping, you see, that you might have the little one down already."

"In a little while, perhaps," said Lady Sharpe, urging the caller toward Camille. "Xanthia, may I introduce Mademoiselle Marchand? This is my cousin, Lady Nash."

The lady already had her hand out, her smile widening. "You are French, are you not?" she said almost excitedly. "Of course one can see that from the cut of your gown and pelisse. You make me feel perfectly gauche — and perfectly fat."

"You are too kind, *madame*," murmured Camille.

"Now do sit down, my dear," said Lady Sharpe, going to the sideboard for another cup.

"Well, I can stay but a moment," said the lady, settling gingerly into the chair. "My carriage is waiting, for I'm just on my way down to Wapping."

"Yes, I see." Camille realized Lady Sharpe was uneasy. "And did your brother mention nothing . . . er, nothing of my houseguest to you?"

"Kieran?" said Lady Nash, her expression mystified. "Lord, no."

Camille felt her heart sink. *Kieran?*

Dear God. This was Rothewell's sister. Camille wished a hole might suddenly open beneath her chair and swallow her up.

But Lady Nash was still speaking, and dropping lump after lump of sugar into the coffee the countess had thrust upon her. "In any case, I've not seen him since Wednesday. Why? Has he made Mademoiselle Marchand's acquaintance?"

"Well, yes," the countess said. "And left me in an awkward position, it would seem. Kindly chastise him for it, if you please."

"Why, I never overlook the opportunity to do so." Lady Nash glanced back and forth between them. "Now really, ladies. The cat's clearly got into the cream pot. Will one of you kindly drag him out again?"

"Indeed I shall," said the countess a little lamely. "Though your brother may not thank me for spoiling his surprise. Mademoiselle Marchand, you see, has just accepted Rothewell's proposal of marriage."

The lady froze, one hand set protectively on her belly. "I . . . I beg your pardon?" she said. "What did you just . . . ?"

"Kieran and Mademoiselle Marchand — *Camille* — are to be married," she said again. "You must give her your congratulations."

The lady looked horrified. "Is this a joke?"

Camille felt her face flame. Dear God, how had she imagined this might work?

Everyone could see what she was. Everyone was going to hate her. She should never have poked the first toe into the English Channel, let alone sailed across it with her scoundrel of a father.

"Xanthia!" Lady Sharpe chided. "You should be happy for them."

Lady Nash had lost her lively color. "You are perfectly serious, then?" she said. "Well. Well, of course, Mademoiselle Marchand, I do wish you very happy. It is just that I am . . . shocked. Yes, that would be the word which leaps most readily to mind."

"Merci, madame," said Camille. She rose stiffly from her chair. "It is an arranged marriage, if that matters. We but recently met. I shall leave you now. I am sure you have things which are better discussed in private."

Lady Nash caught her hand as she passed. "I do beg your pardon," she said swiftly. "I am stunned, Mademoiselle Marchand, that is all. And my manners have slipped. It has nothing to do with you."

"Do sit back down, my dear," Lady Sharpe urged. "We have merely surprised Xanthia, that is all. I shall rake Kieran over the coals for this, you may be sure. He has left us both in a devilish awkward position."

Camille turned and made a faint curtsy to Lady Sharpe. "Thank you, *madame,* for

111

your kindness and your hospitality," she said coolly. "I should like to return to my room now."

She felt the heat of their gazes on her back as she hastened across the room. Once she'd reached the corridor, she closed the door behind her and fleetingly fell against it, her knees shaking too much at that moment to manage the steps. But it did not matter. One could have heard Lady Nash's ensuing shriek of horror halfway up the staircase.

Lady Nash hated her. And everyone else would, too.

But somehow, Camille came away from the door, blinked back her tears, and straightened her spine. There was no point in panicking, or feeling sorry for herself, was there? This was the price she must pay for her parents' iniquities. Even the Bible said so.

She could not change who she was, nor make people like Lady Nash approve of her. In any case, she had lived through worse. She must soldier through it, and hope Lord Rothewell kept his word. He did not look like a reliable sort of man — but then, did such a creature exist? Rothewell, she supposed, was as good a bet as any.

Trammel was in the foyer having the chandelier winched down for dusting when Xanthia burst into the house in Berkeley Square. She had not bothered to knock. Though she was married now, this was still her home so far as she was concerned.

"Good morning, Miss Zee," said Trammel over one shoulder. "Stop! Stop! That's far enough."

"I beg your pardon?" asked Xanthia shrilly. Was *everyone* topsy-turvy today? "Might I remind you, Trammel, my name is still on the deed to this house?"

The butler lifted his gaze from the mass of sparkling crystal, then his visage cleared. "Oh, no, not you, Miss Zee. It's the chande—" Here, the crystal prisms gave an ominous shudder — *"I said stop, blast you!"* Trammel was clearly shouting up the stairs now. "Stop, and tie it down *now!"*

The tinkling of glass halted at once. He came away from the staircase and looked at her consolingly. "I beg your pardon, ma'am," he said, throwing his coffee-colored hands in the air. "Everything is just all helter-skelter today."

"You don't say," muttered Xanthia, surveying the array of crystal that dangled before her eyes. "Lud, that's a dusty fright, isn't it? But why are you bringing the chandelier down? We never light it. We never

113

even look up at it."

At that, the butler threw up his hands again. "One of the master's notions, ma'am."

"In his cups again, is he?" Xanthia set one hand against the small of her back, which was aching from her enraged march across Mayfair. "And making unreasonable demands? Never mind, Trammel. I've come to have a word with him."

"Actually, my lady, I think he might have been more or less sober," said Trammel, leaning nearer. "Or was when he gave the orders about the house."

"What orders, exactly?" asked Xanthia suspiciously.

Trammel cast his doleful gaze heavenward. "We're to clean it 'from top to bottom, inside and out,' " he replied. "Carpets up, draperies down, every piece of plate polished, and even the attics to be aired out — by the end of the week, no less! And if we miss so much as a dusty corner, he's going to send us all to the devil."

"And you believed him?" asked Xanthia.

"Oh, no, Miss Zee," the butler assured her. "I have known the master for too long. But some of the new housemaids *did* believe him. He threw a book at Mrs. Gardener last week when she went in to dust the library.

Passed out on the red chaise, he was. And how, pray, was she to see him back there?"

"How indeed." Xanthia's hands balled into fists. If she had to hire her brother yet another housekeeper, *he* would be going to the devil. "Where is he?"

Trammel exhaled with relief. "In his study, ma'am," he said. "But do have a care, please. Obelienne says his mood is very strange today."

"Oh, I'll just bet it is," she said, already halfway down the passageway.

Miss Obelienne was their cook, and had been for nearly ten years. She and Kieran were fortunate that Trammel and Miss Obelienne had agreed to come from Barbados to London with them. They seemed to be the only servants who were willing to put up with her brother. The others had been leaving like lemmings since Xanthia's marriage a few months earlier.

Despite her frustration, Xanthia did not fail to notice the familiar scents which assailed her nostrils as she moved through the shadowy depths of the house — the scent of well-polished cedarwood and warm spices and something uniquely Bajan which she could not name. These were the scents of their childhood, hers and Kieran's. They had carried them from the West Indies to

England with them, and even now, they brought back memories.

She found Kieran standing at one of the windows which overlooked the garden, his massive frame blocking much of the light. He held a brandy glass in hand and did not turn round until she spoke.

"My God, it is barely eleven," she said, trying to untie her bonnet. "Rather early for spirits, isn't it?"

He turned slowly, but looked entirely sober. "Eleven, is it?" He took a deliberate sip, eyeing her over the glass. "That would make it rather late, not early. I have not yet been to bed, you see."

To her annoyance, the bonnet strings had snarled again. "Honestly, Kieran, have you lost your mind?" she cried, dropping her hands, with her bonnet half-askew on her head. "I have just come from Pamela's! Do you know what I found there? *Do* you?"

Some strange emotion sketched across his face. "Ah, that," he said softly. He set his glass on his massive mahogany desk and circled around toward her. "Hold still," he ordered. "You are making the tangle worse."

"Honestly, Kieran!" she said again, as he bent over the knot. "What were you thinking? A woman you just met? Besides, you cannot possibly wish to be married."

He crooked one dark eyebrow. "Can I not?" he murmured, glancing up from his work. "Have you some hidden power of omniscience you've been keeping from me, Zee?" At last he pulled the ribbons apart and gingerly lifted the bonnet from her head.

Xanthia was still glowering at him as he set the hat aside. "You have never shown the slightest interest in marriage," she complained. "You have never even been seen in the company of a respectable woman — and no, I do not count Christine! And now this poor, poor girl."

"What is so bloody poor about her?" he asked, going to his desk and pulling out a cheroot.

Xanthia began to wave her hand. "Oh, for God's sake don't light that thing!" she said. "I shall retch, I tell you."

"I see." Kieran pulled open a drawer and dropped the cheroot into it.

"No, you don't see!" Xanthia knew her voice was rising as she marched toward the desk, but she seemed unable to stop it. "My mouth hung open so long, she now thinks I disapprove of her. She was horrified. *I* was horrified."

"*Do* you disapprove of her?" There was a hint of warning in his tone.

"Why, I hardly know," said Xanthia. "I certainly do not want you to marry her!"

"Because — ?" He arched his eyebrow again, as if to intimidate her.

"Because you will ruin her life, Kieran," she said, "unless you mean to mend your wicked ways. And you don't, do you?"

"I am afraid it is rather too late for that, old thing," he said. "I am a wretched old reprobate and habituated in sin."

Xanthia circled round the desk and settled gingerly into a side chair. This was not going well. Since the babe had begun to grow, she had felt irritable and restless. Thoughts, sounds, smells, frustrations; everything was magnified tenfold. And that included her temper. Still, she mustn't take it out on her brother — even if he did deserve it.

"How on earth, Kieran, did you manage to meet Valigny's daughter?" she asked quietly. "Surely he did not formally introduce you?"

"No, I won her," he said, picking up his brandy, "in a card game."

"Oh, God!" Xanthia squeezed her eyes shut and set a hand on her belly. She was beginning to feel clammy, and a little weak in the knees. "Oh, I am going into labor! I just know it. And it shall be all your fault."

To her surprise, Kieran lost a bit of his

color, and came round the desk with a magazine in his hand. "You are just over-wrought," he said, gently fanning her. "Breathe, Zee, for pity's sake. You cannot have the child yet — *can* you?"

Xanthia did not open her eyes. "I think not," she murmured. "But what does either of us know? I do feel as though I might faint. Please tell me, Kieran, that you did not just claim to have won Mademoiselle Marchand in a card game?"

"Well, I won the right to marry her," he qualified. "It isn't quite the same thing, I daresay."

Xanthia opened her eyes, and somehow pulled herself erect in the chair. "You are perfectly, serious," she said.

"Quite so," he said. "I was at Valigny's last night."

"Yes, I know," said Xanthia dryly. "I pried that much out of Pamela. Who else witnessed this debacle?"

"Enders and Calvert," said her brother.

"Lord Enders! Horrors!" said Xanthia. "That vile man! — Oh, lud! Will either of them talk? If they do, you know, the girl will be quite ruined."

"I have been musing on that." Kieran sounded perfectly detached. "Calvert is marginally a gentleman. Enders I shall have to threaten. Valigny, too, before it's over, I daresay."

How could anyone contemplate marriage with such an utter lack of emotion, Xanthia wondered? Mademoiselle Marchand might be improving her situation — but only a tad. "Her own father!" she whispered. "And with Lord Enders! How could he?"

Kieran lifted one shoulder, and tossed off the last of his brandy. "Valigny has no scruples — *and* he keeps low company. Myself, for example."

"Well, you are a rank amateur compared to Lord Enders."

"Thank you," he said, "for your unshakable faith in me."

Xanthia scowled at him. "So you really mean to go through with this?"

Kieran opened the drawer again, extracted a piece of heavy foolscap, and tossed it onto the desk. Xanthia took it. A special license. It was written out in crisp, blue-black ink, properly signed and sealed.

"How?" Xanthia demanded, rattling the paper. "How did you get this so fast?"

"Your old friend Lord de Vendenheim down in Whitehall," said her brother. "He knows people who know people. And, as it happens, he owes me for a rather large favor, so this morning I went round to

Whitehall and called in my debt."

"He also owes me a thing or two, you will remember," she said in an injured tone. "I very nearly got myself killed in that smuggling business of his."

"Oh, no, my girl!" said Kieran, propping one hip against his desk. "What you got was *married* and *pregnant* — probably not in that order — neither of which was Vendenheim's doing."

Xanthia lifted both hands as if she might tear her hair out. "This is not about me!"

Her brother looked at her unblinkingly. "But I should far rather talk about you than myself, my dear. It feels so much less . . . what is the word? Intrusive, I think, will do nicely."

"Why, Kieran?" she cried. "Just tell me why you are doing this! I have my suspicions, you see. I want — no, I *need* — for you to tell me I am wrong."

"Careful, my dear," he said. "You are sounding just a little histrionic."

He was right, but she hated to admit it. "Just answer the question," she snapped. "Expectant mothers are not quite sane at the best of times, and just now I am favoring that silver paper knife on your desk."

Rothewell cast a glance down at it, then shrugged. "You shall have to stab me in the back, then," he said, going to the sideboard. "Because I need another brandy desperately enough to risk death. As to your question, I don't suppose you would believe I felt sorry for the girl?"

"Sorry enough to marry her?" Xanthia scoffed. "Not in a million years."

She listened to the crystal stopper being pulled from the decanter. Her brother's hand was perfectly steady as he poured. It always was. Only his temper seemed to suffer from his bad habits. Kieran did not sleep when he should, eat when he ought, or stop drinking when any reasonable man would have done. *Moderation* was not in his dictionary. Nor was *marriage*, Xanthia could have sworn.

Suddenly, he set the bottle down. "You are having a child," he said, bracing his hands wide on the sideboard. He looked not at her, but at the gilt mirror above it. "Nash's heir, quite likely. And Pamela has done the same for Sharpe. Sometimes, Zee, a man — even one so steeped in depravity as I — begins to wonder at his legacy. One wonders if . . . if there will be anything left when one is gone."

At last he turned around. She watched him warily for a long moment. Legacy, her arse, thought Xanthia. She had suspected

122

from the first, really, what this was about. Now she was almost sure. *Sorry enough to marry her?* Telling words, those.

"No," she finally said. "No, you won't cozen me with that one, either. You've never give a thought to your legacy and you aren't now. Don't forget, Kieran. *I have seen her.* Pamela has not."

Kieran looked at her strangely. "Don't be ridiculous," he said. "You just said you saw her *with* Pamela."

Slowly, Xanthia shook her head. "No, I am not speaking of Mademoiselle Marchand," she said. "I am talking about Annemarie."

Her brother's visage stiffened. "What the devil do you mean by that?"

But he knew what she meant; Xanthia could see it in the taut lines of his mouth, and in the faint twitch of his cheek where he had clamped his jaw together.

"I mean our dearly departed sister-in-law," she repeated, gentling her tone. "Yes, Mademoiselle Marchand bears more than a passing similarity to Luke's dead wife. The dark hair and eyes. That lovely dark skin. The rich French accent. Perhaps she doesn't look like Annemarie — not the way Annemarie's daughter does, no — but there are some striking similarities."

Her brother stared at her, his gray eyes suddenly glittering like silver. "I will thank you to cease this line of conversation, Xanthia," he gritted. "Get out. Go home now. I am tired, and I've no wish to listen to such nonsense."

Xanthia braced her hands to rise. "You cannot even admit it, can you?" she answered. "But you must, Kieran. That poor girl deserves to marry for love. Not because you pity her. Not because she reminds you of someone you once loved, but because —"

"Just get out, damn you!" he exploded. Then, to her horror, he hurled his glass into the fireplace. Crystal crashed and splintered. "Just get out, Xanthia! The dead are simply dead, and they aren't coming back. Do you think I don't know that? *Do you?*"

His face was twisted with rage. The brandy had caught on the banked coals and was licking up the back of the hearth in delicate blue flames. Unsteadily, Xanthia rose. Dear God. She really had pushed him too hard this time. "Kieran, I never meant —"

"Just get out!" he bellowed. "You did mean it, Xanthia. You always do. You just keep dredging it up." He set the heel of one hand to his temple as if it hurt. "I swear to God, sometimes I think you'd needle at a bleeding wound. But Luke is still dead. His wife is still dead — and I have done all I could bring myself to do for her daughter. I have done my duty, damn you."

"And Martinique knows that you have always looked after her," said Xanthia. "But you couldn't look *at* her, Kieran. Good God, you sent her two thousand miles away from Barbados just because she reminded you of her dead mother. Of Annemarie. And now this poor girl — Camille — she deserves to marry someone who will love her for who she is. Not because she is another dark-eyed beauty who needs to be rescued."

Kieran stalked toward her. "But I did not rescue Annemarie, did I?" he snarled. "Luke had the pleasure — and the pain — of that task."

Xanthia laid a trembling hand on his arm. "Just wait a while, Kieran," she whispered. "That is all I ask. Just wait until you and Mademoiselle Marchand come to know one another."

"Why?" he gritted. "So she can refuse me? So that she can find a way out? That is what you mean, isn't it?"

Xanthia lifted her hand uncertainly. "I am so sorry," she murmured, dropping her gaze to the rug beneath them. "You are quite right. This really isn't my business, is it? I will go, Kieran. Just promise me . . . promise me you will get some rest?"

When he did not snap back one of his angry retorts, Xanthia looked up. Her brother's face had gone white. His silvery eyes were shut, his visage twisted — not with rage, but with pain.

"Kieran?" She returned her hand to his arm. "Kieran, what is it?"

She felt a deep shudder run through him. "Aaahh, God!" he cried. Then he seemed to collapse beneath her like a house of cards, going down onto one knee, his fingers clawing desperately at the edge of the desk, the other hand clutching his lower ribs.

She had run to the door and flung it open before she knew what she meant to do. "Trammel!" she cried. "Trammel! For God's sake, come here!"

The butler was there in an instant. Panic sketched across his face when he saw Kieran. He knelt beside him on the floor, and hooked one arm under her brother's. "Can you get up, sir?" he asked. "I shall help you up to bed."

Xanthia stared down at their bent heads, Trammel's tight gray curls contrasting sharply with Kieran's dark mane. When Trammel lifted, her brother grunted, and tried to stand. Somehow, the butler got him up, then turned to look at her.

"It's all right, Miss Zee," he said. "He gets like this sometimes."

"As of when?" Xanthia demanded.

"A while now," he said vaguely. "Your brother needs a warm meal and a rest, Miss Zee, that's all. He's not been to bed" — here, the butler flashed a faint smile — "not in this house, at any rate — for three days."

Xanthia surveyed him anxiously. Kieran must have had more to drink than she realized. But now he did indeed look steadier on his feet. The twisted agony had left his face to be replaced by a mere grimace. "Oh, go home, Zee, for God's sake," he managed. "Haven't you a husband now to meddle with?"

Xanthia watched them go, Trammel's steps slow and dependable, Kieran's heavier but steady now. She was worried. Very worried. This business with Mademoiselle Marchand made less sense the more she learned of it. Kieran's was a logical and incisive mind, one which did not rationalize or cloud the truth, even when it brought him pain. He was a sinner, yes, but one who carried the burden of his own sin like a penance on his back. And his love for Annemarie — well, that he had worn like a heavy chain about his heart.

So what had changed since Xanthia's leaving this house? Kieran. He had changed. And she realized now, more than ever, how little she understood him — and what was worse — how little Kieran understood himself.

CHAPTER FOUR
A STROLL IN THE GARDEN

In the end, Lord Rothewell did not return to his cousin's house the following morning with a parson in tow. Lady Sharpe persuaded him that perhaps a fortnight's delay in marrying would do little harm and, quite possibly, a vast deal of good. Camille could not find it in her heart to explain that she no longer cared what society thought of her; not when the countess herself so clearly *did* care. And so Camille embarked on a whirlwind tour of fashionable London — or what little there was of it, given the lateness of the year.

On Tuesday there was an afternoon of shopping in Oxford Street with Lady Sharpe and her daughter Lady Louisa, who lived nearby. Friday brought a visit to the Royal Academy with Lord Sharpe, a large, affable man who knew nothing of art, but happily squired her around and introduced her to everyone they met. In between were a small soiree in Belgravia, a literary reading in Bloomsbury, and a visit to Kew Gardens.

At each outing, Lady Sharpe would introduce her to an endless stream of new faces — some of whom inevitably strolled away whispering. The countess's glib anecdote about her late governess went over well enough, but the subject of Camille's parentage was unavoidable.

"Never mind, my dear," the countess would console her. "By next season — when it really matters — your name won't raise so much as an eyebrow."

Indeed, despite the whispers, Lady Sharpe seemed to know everyone who was anyone, and to be able to almost extract invitations from thin air. Lord Rothewell might have been *persona non grata* within the *ton,* but his family certainly had connections.

As to Rothewell, he surprised Camille by paying a very brief call each day, usually in the afternoon. He said little but merely watched her across the room with his silvery, glittering gaze as Lady Sharpe served tea and prattled on about their plans.

For the most part, Rothewell looked as dissolute and brooding as ever, putting Camille in mind of an angry, caged beast, and to her undying annoyance, his occasional sidelong glance could still make her stomach bottom out most alarmingly. She wished desperately to forget that hot, mad kiss they had shared in her sitting room, and to stop thinking of how his body had felt as he had pressed her so relentlessly against the door.

But she could forget neither, and oftentimes, could not even take her eyes from the infernal man. Oh, it would not do to fall in love with Lord Rothewell. He would give her his name. He would give her, she prayed, a child to love. But never, ever would he give her his heart, and she must not become so weak and so naive as to hope for it.

On Saturday, Camille was invited to drive in the park with Rothewell's brother-in-law, Lord Nash, a man so elegant he could have cast the most debonair of Parisian dandies into the shade. He drove a team of twitchy black geldings hitched to a phaeton so delicate and so high Camille feared they'd strike a pothole and splinter to kindling. But Lord Nash proved to be both an admirable whip and a kindred spirit, being but half-English himself.

He put her at ease talking about his childhood spent on the Continent, outrunning Napoleon's mayhem, and about the death of his uncle, which had required his family to come to England.

"And was it terribly hard, *monsieur?*" she found herself asking. "Did you feel like a fish out of the pond?"

He laughed. "Yes, the *ton* was a challenge," he confessed, cutting his horses neatly through the Cumberland Gate. "Until I grasped the fact that one must simply look down one's nose at them."

"Look down one's nose?" Camille echoed.

"Indeed, for that is the only thing they respect," he replied. "You see, Mademoiselle Marchand, one must think of the *beau monde* as something like a horse's arse."

"A horse's arse?" Camille suppressed a laugh.

"Quite so," said Lord Nash with specious solemnity, "for it is a well-muscled and potentially dangerous thing which is nonetheless capable of respecting something far smaller than itself" — here, he gave his whip a demonstrative little snap — "but only if you can make it fear your sting just a little. And to do that, one must simply behave with more condescension."

"Oh, dear!" said Camille through her laughter. "Do I dare?"

"My God, woman, you are half-French," said Lord Nash. "I can think of no creature better suited to such a task."

"Très bien," she said. "I shall try it."

Lord Nash looked down at her and smiled — a smile that reached all the way to his eyes. He did not dislike her. Indeed, even his wife had come to tea the day before. As a husband, Rothewell would doubtless be a cheat and a scoundrel, but at least his family was kind.

Eventually, Lord Nash drew his phaeton up alongside the pavement in front of Hanover Street and leapt down to lift her out.

"Your wife tells me that you are anticipating a blessed event," she said when her feet touched the earth again. *"Félicitations, monsieur."*

He smiled again, but this time it was the smile of a worried husband. "And my congratulations to you," he said quietly. "I understand you will be making an announcement in a few days' time."

"Merci, monsieur." Camille, too, flashed a weak smile. "It is a fearsome prospect, marriage, *n'est-ce pas?* I would welcome any advice which you should care to give."

Lord Nash seemed to hesitate. "I am sorry," he said. "I do not know Lord Rothewell very well. I married his sister just a few months past. I know my wife both adores him and despairs of him. I speak for both of us, Mademoiselle Marchand, in wishing you good luck."

Good luck.

As she went up the stairs and into the house, Camille considered Lord Nash's choice of words. Not *congratulations.* Not *may you have many happy years together.* Just *good luck* — as if she were wagering on a lame horse, or investing in a lead mine. But Lord Rothewell was just a little more complicated than a horse's arse. To manage him, she might need a very large whip indeed.

By her second day in Hanover Street, Camille had had the great good fortune to find the nursery — with little Lord Longvale tucked happily in it. She had been initially taken aback to learn that Lady Sharpe had just borne a child, but not surprised to see that the countess doted upon the babe. No blanket could be soft enough, no bathwater temperate enough, no draft more dangerous than those which entered Lord Longvale's sphere. The entire house revolved around the child's needs, and within a few days, so did Camille.

The countess was pleased when Camille asked to spend time with the boy. The nurse, Lady Sharpe suggested, would be glad to have an hour to herself, for she was a family retainer who had left retirement to attend the child. Lord Longvale was too young to do much more than sleep, but Camille was happy enough to sit by his cradle with a piece of needlework.

When the nurse had errands, Camille would happily report to the nursery. From time to time, the child would stir, and sometimes even cling to the end of Camille's finger when it was offered. Then, whilst his pale blue eyes gazed up at her, he would blow a spit bubble, or thrash his legs happily until he had kicked the covers from his feet. For Camille, it was utterly captivating — and utterly heartbreaking.

On this particular day, Camille had taken a book to read, then laid it aside. A shaft of midmorning sun was slicing through the nursery's draperies and illuminating the child's face like some holy icon. Lord Longvale was a truly precious gift. Such a child would have been priceless to her. She was prickly and bitter, yes — perhaps life had made her so, or perhaps it was simply her nature — but she was still a woman. She still felt a woman's yearnings.

Camille closed her eyes and felt the babe's tiny fingers clutching at her thumb. She prayed to God she had not waited too long. Surely, had she tried harder, she could have found a husband before now? Surely it needn't have come to this? A marriage to a man she did not know. A man who would marry her for money, without even the pretense of affection.

Ah, well. Maudlin sentiments brought one nothing. Camille extracted her thumb, pulled the child's blanket back down to cover his woolen booties. A *marriage*. A *child*. Perhaps she was soon to have both.

Camille remembered her mother's histrionics when she had announced, at the age of seventeen, her intent to elope with the gardener's son. Hartshorne in hand, Lady Halburne had taken to her bed for a se'night.

It was not that her mother had believed Camille too young — and probably not that she'd thought the gardener's son beneath them. Indeed, she rarely thought of Camille at all until Camille announced her intention of leaving. And then the illnesses and the petulance would come on. The swoons. The chills. The lingering diseases which she swore were certain to ravage her beauty and leave her with nothing but her precious daughter's love and companionship.

It was easy to be taking in by such balderdash when one was young, and craved a parent's affection — or anyone's affection, come to that. In those times, Camille at last became her mother's foremost concern. Her most treasured possession. Until the next handsome gentleman came along, or her mother scratched up enough money to go to Paris for a few months' amusement.

And so her dreams of the gardener's son had gone the way of all flesh — along with a local squire of comfortable means, a hollow-faced widower with four children, and a novice priest who suffered a sudden crisis of faith upon glimpsing Camille's ankles as she hopped across a puddle. None of those men had been meant for her — but any of them would have done better than the debauchee she had landed. Any of them could have given the babe she longed for. And yet she had let the clock tick on.

Lord Rothewell no doubt thought she wanted a child for financial reasons — if, there again, he thought of her at all. If he was as much like Valigny as one would assume, he thought only of the money she would bring him and the pleasures on which he would squander it.

Her somber musings were interrupted by the squeak of door hinges. She looked up to see Lady Sharpe enter the room. "Rothewell has come to call," she said, her voice grave. "He wishes to stroll in the garden with you."

Camille felt a sudden panic. "But the babe —"

The countess was offering her hand. "No, up with you, my dear," she said. "Take your shawl. I shall stay until Thornton returns."

Camille rose. Lady Sharpe gave her hand an encouraging squeeze. "You do not have to marry him, Camille," she said quietly. "No one would blame you if you did not. But you do have to speak to him privately."

She set her shoulders stiffly back. "I am not afraid of him, *madame,*" she said. "His bark is loud, perhaps? But I, too, can bite."

The countess smiled. "Dear, dear," she murmured, sliding into Camille's chair. "Has my wicked cousin met his match, I wonder?"

Camille snatched her shawl and her book, then made her way downstairs to find her betrothed husband. She prayed to God the man was a little more sober and a lot less disheveled than the last time she had been alone with him. He had seemed irascible, too. But then again, staying up all night drinking and gaming doubtless took a toll on one's temperament and wardrobe. Camille hoped, too, that he did not cast one of those silvery, sidelong looks in her direction and set her knees to melting. Surely she was not such a fool as that?

Lord Rothewell awaited her in a sunny parlor toward the back of the house. Camille found him staring out into the gardens, his legs slightly spread, one hand grasping a thin black crop, which he was slapping impatiently against his riding boot, the other set at the small of his back. And in looking at him thus, she was struck once again by the sheer size of the man.

She had thought perhaps his height and breadth had been some sort of emotional misimpression brought on by her anger the first night they had met. But she was increasingly aware that it was not. Rothewell was simply a large man and a commanding presence. His dark coat seemed stretched over dauntingly wide shoulders, and the black leather boots which encased his calves rose far higher than any mortal man's ought.

Yes, from this angle, at least, there was a good deal to admire — and yet no one would have thought him elegant, despite his obviously expensive clothes. When she broke this spell by speaking his name, would he turn round and disappoint? His complexion, she knew, was too dark; his hair nearly black, and from this vantage point, far too long. Indeed, Lord Rothewell looked like a man who belonged in the countryside, for he was simply too large and too austere for the elegant environs of Mayfair. And for some reason, looking at him today made her breath catch.

She lingered on the threshold an instant too long.

"Good morning, *mademoiselle*," he said without turning. "I trust I find you well?"

Camille froze. Then she realized he was watching her reflection in the window. "*Oui,* I thank you," she said coolly. "And you, *monsieur?*"

He let his empty hand drop, and turned around. "Well enough, I daresay." His voice was a low, emotionless rumble. He came away from the window and offered his arm. "Might I have the pleasure of your company in the garden?"

"Mais oui." Camille laid her book on a table by the door, and tossed her woolen shawl about her shoulders.

Rothewell glanced down at the book and raised his eyebrows as his eyes trailed across the title, *An Epitome of Book Keeping by Double Entry.* "You have remarkable taste in reading, *Mademoiselle* Marchand," he commented, drawing one finger lightly down the spine.

She regarded him levelly. "You would prefer, perhaps, a stack of novels, *monsieur?*" she remarked. "*Après tout,* money makes the world go round — and perhaps those who have little of it should at least understand how it works?"

For the first time, his sardonic smile almost reached his eyes. "Ah, but you shall eventually have plenty of it," he remarked, "if all goes according to plan."

"*Oui,* but what good is a fortune in the hands of a fool?" she asked. "If I am so fortunate, *monsieur,* then I mean to manage well what *le bon Dieu* has given me."

To her surprise, he nodded solemnly. "Then you are very wise, *mademoiselle,*" he answered. "Never trust anyone else to steward your wealth or steer your future."

She looked at him in some surprise. Camille had expected that he might argue. If she understood English law, her income would be his once they were wed. It was a risk she would have to take.

They went down the steps in silence, Rothewell deftly hooking his crop on the rear gatepost as they passed. In the garden, the breeze held a chill. Already the bitter tang of coal smoke spiked the autumn air. Winter was coming, thought Camille, cutting a sidelong glance up at Lord Rothewell. Coming, perhaps, into her life.

Her every instinct warned her to back away; that this, perhaps, was a man who was as much dangerous as dissolute. A man well beyond her range of experience. But she did not turn around. She did not even hesitate.

Halfway down, the lawn was terraced, but the steps were of uneven stone, and a little steep. Rothewell leapt down before her, graceful as a cat, then turned to slide his hands beneath her shawl, grasping her round the waist.

"*Merci, monsieur,* but I —"

Too late. He lifted her easily. Her hands grabbed instinctively at his shoulders, and when they spun round together, the moment felt suspended in time. As if he held her perfectly still in the air, their bodies entirely too close, her fingers curling into the soft wool of his coat. They were face-to-face, his mesmerizing gray eyes just inches from hers, her heart hammering oddly in her chest.

Watching her, Rothewell lowered her down his length. But the earth felt suddenly unsteady beneath her feet, and Camille did not remove her hands. Rothewell still grasped her waist, his large, heavy palms warming her skin through her dress. She remained there, looking up at him until a clatter in the alley beyond rent the silence.

He released her waist.

"*Merci,*" she murmured, lowering her

hands. But her heart would not still, and the warm masculine scent of his cologne lingered in a dizzying, sensual cloud. Camille felt almost frighteningly aware of him as a man — but that was her only clear thought amidst the sudden, maddening whirl in her brain.

They strolled toward the center of the garden as Camille tried to still her heart and gather her thoughts. Farther on, a high arrangement of boxwoods concealed a sheltered circle of fading rosebushes, and here Rothewell stopped and laid his hand over hers where it rested upon his arm.

When he spoke again, his voice was surprisingly gentle. "I came to tell you, Mademoiselle Marchand, that I have sent your father a bank draft for his twenty-five thousand pounds," he said in his impossibly deep voice. "You are now free of any obligation to him."

She stopped abruptly on the path and looked up at him. *"Mon Dieu!"* she whispered. "Where did you get twenty-five thousand pounds?"

Rothewell hesitated for a moment. "Ah, that," he said dryly. "I waylaid a Blackheath mail coach at gunpoint."

She was almost relieved to see the glint of irritation in his silvery eyes. *"Vraiment, mon-*

sieur?" she replied. "Then you robbed a coward. I should have waited to see how good a shot you were before stopping."

"I don't doubt it," said Rothewell. "The French are notoriously foolhardy in battle. But I am quite a good shot, Mademoiselle Marchand. You would have waited at your peril."

Camille decided it prudent to alter the subject. "And you still wish to marry me, *monsieur?"* she said. "Otherwise, you see, I have no way to repay you."

He looked down at her steadily. "I am here, am I not?" he answered.

"You must know by now that that your sister disapproves of our marrying," said Camille. "Is she quite a good shot, too, I wonder?"

"Yes, as it happens." His expression had tightened. "But in this, her opinion is of no consequence. Moreover, it is not you of whom she disapproves. It is I — and I shall deal with it."

Ah, a family quarrel. Camille decided it might be more prudent to hold her tongue. As Lord Rothewell resumed his sedate pace, he cut a glance down at her, his expression inscrutable.

Why on earth was he marrying her, Camille wondered, if he could come up with

144

twenty-five thousand pounds on a drunken whim and a few days' notice? But he had, and at last her foolish bargain with Valigny was over. She was surprised by the flood of relief that knowledge brought her. This made twice that Lord Rothewell had come to her rescue.

No. Camille jerked herself up sharp. She must not look at it like that. This man was no hero, and she must on no account romanticize the situation. Rothewell was, if not her father's friend, certainly his cohort. They were cut from the same piece of cloth, with the same vices. The same victims. And Rothewell had a good reason to marry her, for she had told him, foolishly perhaps, the one thing she had kept from Valigny — the true magnitude of her inheritance.

The path narrowed as they approached the end of the garden. Lord Rothewell stood quite close now; so close she could again catch the scent of his cologne on the air; something that smelled distinctively of sandalwood and citrus. It was an infinitely male scent, one which she remembered well from that fateful night at Valigny's.

Just then, his arm brushed hers as they walked, and her heart gave another of those odd little flip-flops. Suddenly, Camille was seized with the notion to bolt.

But to what? She had little money. No formal education to speak of. And no family that would own her, unless one counted Valigny's shallow-minded kin, who, whilst not precisely throwing her into the street, had nonetheless ignored her existence.

Rothewell must have read her thoughts. He stopped on the path and turned her to face him. When he spoke, the mood surrounding them suddenly altered in a way which made her unaccountably nervous.

"Mademoiselle Marchand, Pamela's delay has given me time to think," he said, his warm, heavy hands settling on her shoulders. "You do not have to marry me. This bargain was Valigny's, not yours. You can walk away if you choose."

"*Oui,* but to what, *monsieur?*" she asked simply. "And with what?"

"You have a cousin, have you not?" he suggested. "The man who inherited your grandfather's title? Perhaps he has the connections to arrange a marriage?"

She laughed bitterly. "I don't even know his name, and I am sure he does not wish to know mine," she replied. "Consider, *monsieur.* I am the bastard daughter of the woman who shamed his family, *n'est-ce pas?* And if I never marry, never bear a child, then he will probably inherit all, instead of just a long title and a big house. No, he will not thank me for turning up on his doorstep."

Rothewell winced. "I fear you are a good judge of human nature," he muttered. "Perhaps a situation could be found for you?"

"Employment, *oui?*" she answered. "Such as a companion or a — a *gouvernante?*"

"A governess, yes. But that dooms you to a life of poverty, I daresay."

"I am not afraid of hard work, *monsieur*," she said honestly. "I should thrive on it. To use my brain — *oui,* it would be like a dream. But the things I could best do, no woman would be allowed. And the things society permits women to do — *non,* for the daughter of the disreputable Comte de Valigny, it will never happen."

His silvery gaze drifted over her face for a moment as if searching for something. "Pamela tells me you adore children. Do you, Camille?"

"Oui," she said casually. "Who does not? But no one is going to hire Valigny's by-blow to care for their children."

"No, not likely." He smiled faintly. "But do you wish for children of your own? Your grandfather's will notwithstanding?"

"I should like it very well," she replied

equivocally. But she was lying, and she wondered if he knew it. A child to love — oh, it was her deepest wish. Her only hope, it often seemed.

For an instant, their eyes locked, and again she had the sense that he was searching for something. Grappling with some notion she could not comprehend. She was beginning to think she better understood him as a drunken roué. This strong, stern man seemed far more controlled, and much less predictable.

"You once spoke, Camille, of your wish to live alone," he continued, his voice a low, soft rumble. "I dislike the notion, but we live in a world of uncertainty. Are you strong enough to rear a child alone?"

"I am strong enough," she answered firmly. "Never doubt me, my lord. I am strong enough. To persevere. To survive. To do whatever must be done."

When she said no more, Rothewell led her toward one of a pair of benches which sat in the center of the rose garden and drew her down beside him. She noticed he had begun, unbidden, to use her Christian name.

"I want to understand something," he finally said. "I want to know how you came to be here in England. What led up to this point in your life."

It was not an unreasonable demand, given the circumstances. Lord Rothewell wished to know more about her. He was going to marry her. In all likelihood, she would bear him a child. So why did his curiosity feel intrusive? Had she somehow imagined the man would simply turn up one day with a parson in tow, no questions asked?

And then it struck her that his questions, his explanations — all of this — was a sort of intimacy. The giving and sharing of one's life. But she had no wish to share her life with anyone; to be emotionally bound by even such a simple act as this — getting to know one another. She was afraid of Lord Rothewell. She did not wish him to rescue her. She could not bear to have her heart broken as her mother's had been. She just wanted a child. Someone of her own to love. And then she wanted to be left alone by Rothewell and by the rest of the world — because in the end, that was how life worked anyway.

But Rothewell was holding her gaze, his eyes unwavering, and to her shock, Camille felt that odd sensation in the pit of her stomach again. She knew it for what it was, too, though she had rarely felt it. Lord Rothewell was not a beautiful man, no. But he was striking, with his hooded gray eyes and his hard facial bones. And the set of his jaw said he wanted an answer to his question.

Camille dropped her gaze to her lap. *"Très bien,"* she finally said. "What do you wish to know, *monsieur?*"

"I am not perfectly sure," he admitted.

Fleetingly, Camille wondered if perhaps this was as awkward for him as it was for her.

"I suppose I wish to know what happened between your mother and Valigny," he said. "She was the Countess of Halburne, was she not?"

Camille nodded. "*Oui,* or so she called herself," she answered. "But Halburne divorced her when I was two or three. Perhaps the name was no longer hers to use?"

Rothewell shrugged. "I cannot say," he admitted. "There were no divorces where I came from."

"Where you came from?" She looked at him in some surprise. "Do you not come from here, *monsieur?*"

He shook his head. "No, I spent the whole of my life — or pretty near it — in the West Indies," he said. "I have lived in London less than a year. The place still strikes me as strange."

Camille considered it. Perhaps she and Rothewell had more in common than she had imagined. "My mother died in the spring," she said. "I daresay it little matters what one calls her now."

"I am sorry you lost her," said Lord Rothewell. "From what did she die, if I may ask?"

"Hard living, *monsieur*," said Camille. "Hard living, declining beauty, and — perhaps — a broken heart."

Again, he flashed the faint half smile, and Camille found herself wondering what he would look like if he smiled with the whole of his mouth. Younger, she thought.

"A broken heart?" he said. "Broken by whom? Surely not Valigny?"

"*Bien sûr*, she adored him," said Camille honestly. "Always, he was the one thing she could never have — not for very long."

"Ah," said Lord Rothewell. "You did not live as a family?"

Camille felt suddenly wistful. "Briefly, *oui*," she said. "After that, *Maman* was just Valigny's occasional mistress. He never remained long in one place, and had many women. Of course, it was France, and *Maman* took lovers, too. But I think always, *monsieur*, all that she wished was to make

151

him jealous."

"Did it work?"

Camille nodded. "*Oui,* sometimes," she said. "He would return to her, and there would be money for clothes and for jewels. Sometimes a gift for me. He would pamper her until she began to bore him, then he would go away again."

"And they never married?" Rothewell asked. "Did Valigny have a wife?"

Camille shook her head. "He wed a girl in his village, *Maman* said, when he was young, but they, too, divorced," she said. "For a time, it was common in France. *Maman* truly believed Valigny would marry her someday."

"They could have done, after Halburne freed your mother," he remarked.

Camille gave a sour smile. "Oh, but Valigny concocted a new story when the time came," she answered. "He claimed the church would not allow him to marry again — a convenient discovery indeed."

Rothewell looked at her incredulously. "*Valigny* is a devout Catholic?"

Camille's laugh was bitter. "*Non,* a devout liar," she said. "Years later, *Maman* discovered his wife had died shortly after her second marriage, so Valigny had long been released from any religious obligation.

Instead, for Valigny, Lord Halburne's divorce was — how do you say it? — the last straw on the camel?"

Rothewell smiled. "The straw that broke the camel's back."

"*Oui,* the camel's back," Camille continued. "After Halburne divorced her, *Maman's* father wrote to her and cut her off utterly. Valigny finally realized that there would never be an inheritance. His gamble had not paid off. After that, Valigny slipped in and out of *Maman's* life. We were fortunate his family accepted us — at least nominally — and left the roof over our heads and gave us a meager allowance."

"And now your grandfather has left a part of his estate to you," Lord Rothewell murmured. "But with harsh stipulations."

"*Oui,* it was a decision made long ago," she answered. "At the time he cut *Maman* off. As to the stipulations, something, I daresay, is better than nothing."

Rothewell was no longer looking at her, but into the shadows of the boxwoods beyond the rose garden. "Tell me about her," he said. "Your mother, I mean. About how she came to be involved with Valigny and exiled to France."

Camille gave a bitter laugh. "*Maman* met him during her come-out," she answered.

"Valigny told her that for him, it was love at first sight."

Rothewell crooked one eyebrow. "And she believed that, did she?"

Camille shrugged. "Some days, *certainement,* she believed. Especially at the first. And she loved him back. Desperately. She did not see — or would not allow herself to see — what he was."

"How did they come to be living in France?" he asked.

"*Maman* was betrothed to Halburne," she answered. "Against her wishes, of course, for she claimed to love Valigny. But her father disliked Valigny excessively, and after the marriage was arranged, he refused to let her see him. She finally agreed to the wedding — to escape her father, I think — then shortly afterward, *Maman* slipped out to meet Valigny. In response, Halburne slapped a glove to Valigny's head."

"To his face, yes," said Rothewell. "And so there was a duel for the lady's honor?"

Camille nodded. "*Oui,* Lord Halburne was shot," she said. "Valigny stood unscathed. When *Maman* heard this, she thought it *très romantique.*"

"And you do not?"

"*Non.*" Camille felt her temper spike. "I think it was *très stupide.* And irresponsible.

154

And cowardly in the bargain."

"I see." Rothewell watched her levelly for a moment. "And then what happened?"

"They fled to France. This was in the early years of the war."

"Good God," muttered Rothewell. "Halburne was expected to die?"

"It was said that he would, *oui,* and that because of it, Valigny could never return to England," Camille answered. "But somehow, Halburne did not die. Instead, he divorced *Maman.*"

Rothewell gave a low whistle. "What a row that must have been."

"*Oui,* and a terrible embarrassment for Lord Halburne," she whispered. "And now my coming here will surely stir up old gossip — and old hatred."

Rothewell shook his head. "You will not likely meet him," he said. "Moreover, he cannot fairly blame you. Valigny, however, is a different kettle of fish."

Camille shrugged. "After the war ended, *monsieur,* Valigny resumed his visits here. If there has been trouble, it has not reached my ears."

"Then Halburne is a damned sight more forgiving than I would be." Lord Rothewell fell silent for a long moment, then he set his hands on his thighs as if to rise. "Well. We have a decision to make, I suppose. Do you wish, Camille, to go through with this business of marriage?"

"*Mais oui,* I thought this was decided," she said.

He regarded her through hooded eyes. "You would willingly marry a haggard old roué?" he said, echoing the insult she had once flung at him.

She cut her gaze away, and did not answer. "I am some years older than you, Camille," he went on. "And I have lived a very different life."

She jerked her head around. "You know nothing of the life I have lived, *monsieur,*" she said. "I am not some naive innocent with whom you must concern yourself. I have no wish to be swaddled."

"That's good to know," he remarked, "given all your barbs and nettles."

Camille felt her face warm. "Your pardon," she said hastily. "I am too brusque. How old are you, *monsieur?*"

He looked taken aback. She could see him mentally calculating in his head. "Five-and-thirty, more or less," he finally answered.

"*Ça alors!*" Her eyes widened. "No more than this?"

"My dear, you are just full of compliments this morning," he murmured. "I can scarce wait for our wedding day."

"Pardon, monsieur," she said. "It is just that you look . . . or you seem —"

"Yes, I know," he interjected. "Old and haggard."

Her blush deepened. "*Non,* that is not perfectly true," she murmured. "You are very handsome, as I am sure you know, but you have the look of a man who knows much of life."

"Aye, more than I might wish, perhaps," he said musingly. "When do you wish to marry?"

"Tomorrow," she answered. "I have no time to waste."

"I understand the feeling," said Rothewell dryly. "But perhaps it would be best, Camille, if we were seen courting for a time."

"Better for whom, *monsieur?*" she asked.

His mouth drew tight for a moment. "Better for your reputation, perhaps, in the long run," he said.

"Why do you care?"

"*Madame,* you will be my wife."

"And you do not wish to be tainted by gossip?"

Irritation glittered in his eyes. "If you knew anything at all of my reputation, Camille, you would not even contemplate marriage to me," he snapped. "But for my wife

— possibly for my child — yes, I should mind the taint of gossip a great deal."

He moved as if to rise. She surprised herself by touching him lightly on the arm. "My lord, I ask you again. Why do you do this?"

Rothewell's expression went blank. "I am told that at my age, one needs a wife and an heir," he said, jerking to his feet.

"*Pardon, monsieur,* but you do not strike me as the sort of man who listens to what he is told," she said, following him into the shadows of the garden. "Let us at least be honest with one another."

When he did not respond, she caught him lightly by the elbow and felt the tautness of a hard, well-muscled arm beneath the wool of his coat. He spun around, and their gazes caught.

For a long moment, Lord Rothewell said nothing. "My sister recently married, and I have no one to manage my home," he finally answered. "It is a simple enough matter, is it not?"

Camille watched him warily for a moment. He was lying. She knew it. "*Alors,* this is to be a true marriage of convenience?" she asked. "I will see to the running of your house, and you will give me a child?"

He nodded curtly.

"Très bien," she said. "I accept this. But do not attempt to persuade me to trust you, Rothewell. All men are faithless. I will not depend upon you."

He fell silent for a time, and she awaited the lies. Perhaps, even, some halfhearted pledge of fidelity. But that was not what she got.

"Indeed, you would be well advised not to depend upon me," he answered. "You must build a life for yourself, Camille. I will not be available to you."

There. She was fairly warned.

Perhaps she would not have to leave him in order to be left alone. Or perhaps, despite his pride, he would be glad enough to let her go — so long as her inheritance came as promised. It was a bit of a gamble, yes. But once again, what choice did she have?

She felt the heat of Lord Rothewell's gaze and looked up. His eyes were hard, his jaw harder still. To her surprise, he lifted his hand, and brushed the back of it along her cheek, a surprisingly intimate gesture. "For all your barbs and nettles, you are a beauty, Camille," he murmured. "That first night — yes, I knew you were — and yet, a man sometimes doubts himself."

"Mon Dieu, did you imagine I might have

grown a beard and a tail overnight, *monsieur?*" Camille felt surprisingly wounded. "Or were you too drunk to remember what I looked like?" She held his gaze, and refused to look away. She was no shy, innocent miss, and she'd be damned if she would act like one no matter how dashing and handsome he appeared.

"I had been drinking, yes, and I was tired," he acknowledged. "And I shan't deny that I have on occasion misjudged a woman's beauty during a long, hard night."

Camille laughed. "That must come as a shock when one awakes to a gorgon in one's bed the next morning."

He smiled faintly, but it was somehow turned inward. His gaze drifted over her, and for an instant, some nameless emotion sketched across his face. Not lust, she thought, but something harder to comprehend. Longing? Or regret, perhaps? But how foolish she was. Men like Rothewell did not feel regret — and if they longed for something, they found it, and took it.

"Oh, well," he finally said. "A man usually gets what he deserves, Camille. But you — ah, your beauty would disappoint no man — at any time of day."

"Merci bien," she replied.

But she had become acutely aware that

the mood was oddly shifting. They stood near the far wall of the garden now, and he was holding her gaze, his silvery eyes almost mesmerizing.

The world seemed suddenly more distant, as if the here and now existed only in this place — this small circle of dying roses and dead leaves — with only the two of them in it. And Lord Rothewell was . . . different somehow. *Dangerous.* Oh, this man was dangerous. To her sanity. Even, perhaps, to her heart.

When he lifted his hand to gently cup her cheek, Camille felt suddenly as if the earth had tilted. "It will be no disappointment, Camille, to have you in my bed," he murmured, threading his fingers through the hair at her temple. "Have you any experience? Or am I to be your first?"

But Camille was now trembling inside with an emotion she did not comprehend. She did not like this disconcerting reaction to his touch. *"Ça alors!"* she snapped. "What sort of question is that?"

"A logical one, I should think," he murmured, tucking a wayward strand of hair behind her ear. The scent of his cologne — the scent of *him* — was enveloping her. Cowardice got the best of Camille, and she shut her eyes.

"Do not mistake me, *monsieur,* for the fool that my mother was," she managed. "I saw enough of her world to last me a lifetime. I know the value of *virginité* far too well to sell it cheap."

"That sounded like a *yes,*" he murmured. "But I would find you desirable, Camille, regardless."

Camille felt herself shiver, and yet an unseasonable warmth seemed to swirl about them. "You do not have to flirt with me, *monsieur,*" she murmured. "I know what my duty is to my husband, and I will do it."

"I do not flirt." His voice had gone husky. "Kiss me, Camille."

"Mais pourquoi?" she whispered.

"Because," he said quietly, "for the second time in my life, I should like to taste innocence."

His grip on her arm seemed to tighten. She said neither yes, nor no. And despite the fact that her eyes were still shut, she was acutely aware of his mouth hovering over hers. Of his strong arm banding round her, and their bodies coming inexorably together as her thoughts spun out of control again.

It was inevitable. And strangely, in that moment of heat and scent and soft words, Camille did not care. She wanted him. Her arms slid round his waist unbidden. His mouth skimmed along her jaw, brushing at her ear. "Teach me, Camille," he murmured. "Teach me to be gentle."

Her body went willingly, fully against his. Unlike the first time, Rothewell settled his lips over hers in a kiss which was slow in its seduction. His mouth slanted back and forth, molding softly and perfectly to hers, drawing her into him. Coaxing her. His hands were big, his body sheltering, and the kiss exquisitely tender, ratcheting up her pulse. Melting her to him. Yes, *seduction* was the word for this.

Fleetingly, she wondered if she'd lost her mind. But this was her fate, and she had agreed to it. Why resist? Her body was already answering his, and he knew it. Rothewell drew his tongue enticingly across her lips, tempting her to surrender. In response, Camille tipped back her head. He made a sound — something between a sigh and a groan — and crushed her against him as he plunged his tongue into the warmth of her mouth. And then she was truly lost, caught up in the heady spiral of passion.

Her hands slid beneath his coat and went skating up the warmth of his back, making him shiver. It was empowering. Compelling. He drew back and brushed his lips across the apple of her cheek. "Camille," he whispered.

He returned his mouth to hers, surging inside with a kiss more urgent than delicate. Her stomach bottomed out again. A little desperately, she drew his tongue into her mouth, and something hot and urgent went spiraling through her, all the way down, drawing at her very center, making her gasp. He sensed it, and deepened the kiss, one big hand cradling the back of her head.

Dimly, Camille realized her breath had sped up, and that Rothewell had one warm, heavy hand on her hip, circling through the fabric. His other hand came up to caress her breast beneath the veil of her shawl, gently at first. His mouth skimmed down her throat, then his heated lips brushed the plump swell of her breast as his hand weighed it, almost lifting it from her bodice. Camille ached for his mouth — to feel it *there.* The jutting weight of his erection was unmistakable against her belly now. Her breath was coming too fast. Blood seemed to be rushing to her head, and desire pooled in her belly.

Camille was not naive. She knew how men and women made love. When his thumb slipped beneath the ruching of her bodice, and tugged it down, she did not protest.

Her right breast sprang free. On a soft, hungry sound, Rothewell captured the nipple with his lips and drew it into the melting warmth of his mouth. *Yes.* As he suckled her, Camille began to feel boneless, without the will to refuse him anything. She wanted this. Ached for *him.*

The wind chose that moment to act up, gusting through the rose garden, sending a swirl of dry leaves rattling across the paths and about their feet. Somehow, it jerked her back into the present. To the reality of where they were. In the garden. In broad daylight.

Abruptly, he set her away. The breeze on her bare nipple was an exquisite pain. She opened her eyes and stepped back, frightened by the intensity of her response to him. She could not get her breath. Panic began to flood through her limbs.

At once, Rothewell caught her elbow, and drew her back to him, restoring her dress to order. "Forgive me." His voice was hoarse, his breathing rough as he pulled her fully against him, and spread a broad, solid hand across her back. "Forgive me, Camille," he murmured into her hair. "I am too forward."

Camille's cheek was against his chest, the soft wool of his lapel tickling her face. He felt wonderfully warm and solid. And yet the panic was shifting to a cold fear which was snaking through her, even as his hand began to make a slow, sweet circle between her shoulder blades. His soft words and gentle touch made him no less dangerous. Was this not precisely how a man lured a weak-willed woman onto the shores of emotional ruin?

Dear heaven, he was a rake just like her father — and yet in an instant, he'd had her all but pleading for more.

Oh, this was not wise. Did she want the sort of life her mother had lived? She drew a deep, shuddering breath. The marriage bed was one thing — and it was unavoidable. But this — oh, God, this sense of tumbling into something heady and wild . . . it simply would not do.

She lifted her head from his shoulder, and pushed abruptly away. "A most interesting exchange," she managed. "But strictly speaking, *monsieur,* this is not necessary, is it? For the having of children?"

"What do you mean?" he rasped.

She glanced up at him. "This . . . this dalliance? All the kissing?"

He was silent for a moment. "No," he finally said. "No, strictly speaking, it is not necessary. I think you know that."

"*Oui,*" she admitted. She did know. And she knew, too, she had to preserve her heart.

Her sanity. She had to keep herself safe from this man.

The intermittent gusts of wind were becoming a strong and steady breeze. The coldness inside her was moving into her limbs now. The fear was wrapping round her heart.

Camille dipped her head, pulled her shawl back around her. *"J'ai froid,"* she murmured.

Lord Rothewell offered his arm. "Then we must get you inside."

She looked up at him. "You speak French?"

His face was an emotionless mask. "Well enough," he answered. "Come, Mademoiselle Marchand. Allow me to see you safely inside."

She took his arm, still unsettled. She was again *Mademoiselle Marchand.* She had not meant to insult him. But under no circumstance could she allow herself to become besotted by this man. What had she been thinking, to ache for his mouth so hungrily? Was she as much a fool as her mother had been? She glanced away and felt suddenly ashamed. Not of her desire — but of her utter lack of caution.

They reached the back door, and Rothewell picked up the riding crop which he had hung upon the gatepost. She watched him warily for a moment. "May we be married at once, *monsieur?*" she asked. "I do not wish to wait any longer."

For a long moment, he simply stood there, rhythmically slapping the crop against his boot. "Another week, perhaps, for propriety's sake," he finally said. "I shall tell Pamela."

"Très bien," she murmured, lowering her gaze. "I thank you, *monsieur.* Will you come inside?"

He shook his head. "No. I think not."

Camille gave a perfunctory curtsy. "Then I shall say *bonjour, monsieur,*" she answered. "And thank you again."

"For what?" he asked tersely.

"For the money you have paid to Valigny, of course," she answered, holding the door.

"Ah. The money. Yes, let us never forget about *that.*"

His jaw even harder than usual, Lord Rothewell made a tight bow, then went back down the steps, and out by the garden gate.

Lady Sharpe had lingered with her son no more than five minutes when Thornton returned, bringing with her the baby's bathwater. The child's routine was important, the countess consoled herself before surrendering her precious bundle to his nurse.

"I shall be in Sharpe's study, should you need me," she said after kissing the child's forehead.

Downstairs, a small stack of correspondence and invitations awaited her, as they always did this time of day. Lady Sharpe prided herself on being a creature of habit. She went dutifully through all the letters regarding matters at home in Lincolnshire, dictating replies to those she could, and instructing Mr. Bigham, her husband's secretary, to give the remainder to Sharpe himself.

She was just turning her attention to the invitations when a familiar voice in the hall beyond caught her ear. Lady Sharpe nearly leapt from her skin. "Bloody hell!" she muttered.

"I beg your pardon, ma'am?" Bigham turned, gaping, from the papers he had been sorting.

Lady Sharpe's face heated. "Nothing, Bigham," she said. "We've a guest. That's all." *Yes, and a most unwanted guest, too.* The countess was frantically wondering what was best done about it when the footman appeared.

"Mrs. Ambrose, ma'am," he gravely announced.

Too late. Lady Sharpe's sister-in-law

swept round him, her color high, a bright green hat set at a jaunty angle atop her pale blond locks. "Pam, my dear!" she exclaimed, circling the desk to kiss the countess's cheek. "I've just got back from a week in Brighton, and it was — oh, dear — are you doing Sharpe's work for him again? I shouldn't, if I were you."

"One does what one can," she murmured, motioning Christine to a chair opposite the desk. "It is very hard for him to be away from the estate at this time of year."

Christine shrugged one thin, angular shoulder. "Well, you could hardly travel, bloated, fat, and miserable as you have been," she said, dropping languidly into the chair. "Honestly, Pamela, you will likely *never* get your figure back. It really is too horrid to contemplate at such an age."

Lady Sharpe gave a muted smile. There was no point in explaining to Sharpe's widowed and cheerfully childless sister how little her lost figure mattered — not when one had the recompense of a son and heir. Moreover, she needed to get Christine out of the house.

"I am afraid, Christine, that I was just on my way out," she lied. "Why do you not accompany me down to the Strand? I need a new . . . andiron. Or two. Yes, a new set of andirons."

Christine stuck out her lip. "How frightfully dull," she said. "Now, if you could be persuaded to go down to Burlington Arcade, perhaps? I need a reticule to match this hat. Oh, wait — ! Where is Sharpe? I must borrow a hundred pounds first."

Anything to get Christine out of the house. "I shall get the cash box," said the countess, starting to rise. Just then, Mr. Bigham laid another piece of paper on the stack. "What is that?" she asked, distracted.

"An invitation which was hand-delivered from Lady Nash, ma'am," he said solemnly. "A dinner party tomorrow in honor of her brother's eng—"

"Yes, yes, Bigham, that will do!" said the countess sharply.

"A dinner party in honor of Rothewell?" crowed Christine, reaching for the ivory card. "How shocking! He will not approve, I daresay. I shall go, of course — merely to tease him about it."

Lady Sharpe snatched the card and fell back into her chair. Rothewell had done it to her again, blast him!

Christine was staring at the invitation suspiciously. "Why may I not see it, Pam?"

Lady Sharpe sighed. "You may, I suppose," she said. "But I am afraid, Christine, that you won't be invited to this one."

Christine's perfectly shaped eyebrows rose. "I beg your pardon? Has Xanthia become so high in the instep she no longer knows me? That haughty husband of hers is but an earl, for God's sake — and barely even English."

Lady Sharpe pursed her lips. "Xanthia likes you very well, Christine." A second lie on the heels of her first! "But I am afraid there has been some shocking news. You shan't like it — and it is not really my job to tell it."

Christine had gone perfectly still. "Oh, Lord, I knew I shouldn't have gone to Brighton!" she said. "He is ill, is he not?"

Lady Sharpe felt her eyes widen. "Ill?"

Christine leapt up, and began to roam the room. "Rothewell — he's been behaving very oddly," she said, sounding more aggrieved than grief-stricken. "At times, he refuses to see me. He won't eat. He seems so distant. He cancels plans. Once he looked to be in pain. Oh, dear, what a bother this will be!"

"A bother?"

Christine whipped around, her lips in a pout. "We have been invited to a house party in Hampshire," she said. "He'll use this, I daresay, as another excuse not to go."

"No, he will not be going to any house party," Lady Sharpe agreed. "Christine, my dear. I am very much afraid to say — well — that Rothewell is getting married."

Camille watched the garden gate slam behind Lord Rothewell. His shoulders were stiff, his pace determined as he circled around in the direction of Hanover Street. Her hand still holding the door, Camille realized she had been unkind, and she was ashamed.

She had been angry with herself, not him. But that kiss — it had been too much. By the time it had ended, she had been boneless and disoriented. As if her weak knees had allowed her to melt into a warm puddle of desire, something Lord Rothewell could easily tread through on his way to the next woman he might bed.

She closed the door without fully appreciating just how prescient the notion was — until she heard the bloodcurdling scream from Lord Sharpe's study.

"Madame?" Camille cried. Her shawl slithering halfway off as she ran, she made a mad dash down the passageway.

She almost collided with the thin blonde who burst from the study and into the corridor, with Lady Sharpe on her heels.

Camille brought herself up short, sending her shawl falling to the floor. But the blond woman had espied her and jerked to a halt, quivering with what looked like indignation. One finger thrust at Camille, the lady looked back over her shoulder.

"Is *this* what he has thrown me over for?" she cried. "This — this insipid little brown mouse running madly about?"

The countess had her fingertips to her temple. "Christine, for God's sake," she said. "Preserve just a scrap of your dignity!"

"What has happened?" Camille demanded, looking past the woman to Lady Sharpe. "*Madame,* you are unhurt?"

Eyes flashing with irritation, Lady Sharpe dropped her hand and nodded. "I am fine, my dear."

And then the woman's words struck her. *Is this what he has thrown me over for?*

Camille stiffened her spine and stood with all the elegance she could muster. *"Pardon, madame,"* she said, turning to the lady. "I think we have not met?"

The woman's eyes narrowed. "And she's *French!*" she exploded. "The little baggage is French! How dare he?"

"Christine, for God's sake, calm yourself!" hissed Lady Sharpe. She cut a sympathetic glance at Camille, but she also looked deeply vexed and more than a little embarrassed.

Regrettably, there was but one way to handle such a misfortune. Camille stepped deeper into the fray and smiled at the woman. "*Alors,* you are the mistress?" she asked, forcing her chin up. "And you have just learnt of me? *Quel dommage!* It is most unfair, is it not?"

"Why — What — *Who* are you?" the woman demanded.

Camille managed a bemused look. "Why, just the — the — what did you call it? The brown mouse, *oui?* I am afraid I do not know the word *baggage.*"

A horrific shade of red was crawling up the woman's face now. She was trembling with outrage.

"Oh, I should not worry, were I you, *madame.*" Camille was angry, yes, but a malicious little part of her was enjoying herself. "It is a very big world, *n'est-ce pas?* You are his mistress, and perhaps that will not change — but rest assured, I am not leaving."

"Why how *dare* you!"

Camille shrugged, and picked up her shawl. "But I do dare, *madame,*" she said quietly. "And I think you must come to grips with it. In another week, you may still be Rothewell's mistress — but this mouse shall be his *wife*."

Lady Sharpe looked as if she couldn't decide whether to laugh or to cry. Suddenly, she glanced over her shoulder and brightened. "Oh, look!" she said, waving a hand toward the window. "There is Rothewell now. He must be awaiting his horse. If you have a bone to pick, Christine, you should pick it with —"

The woman was halfway down the steps before Lady Sharpe could finish.

Camille caught the flying door before it swung round to smack Lady Sharpe in the face. *"Au revoir, madame!"* she sang before closing it. *"Et bonne chance!"*

Rothewell turned, the color draining from his face. Camille waved at him and slammed the door. Lady Sharpe gave a snort of laughter, then clapped a hand over her mouth.

Camille twisted her mouth wryly. "Well, *madame,* this mouse could use a glass of sherry if you would be so kind?" she said, resolved to hide her hurt. "Perhaps something even stronger. And then, if you please, *madame,* you must tell me just who that lady was."

Lady Sharpe looked at her and laughed

again. "You really must do something, my dear, about that frightful Franglish of yours," she said. "It really does tend to come and go, does it not?"

"*Oui, madame.*" Camille lifted her skirt and curtsied. "As it is needed — or as the nerves dictate."

"Come along, then." The countess went back into the study. "I think I shall join you in that sherry, Camille, whilst I savor thoughts of the punishment Rothewell is reaping right about now."

"It was badly done, *assurément*," said Camille. "A man should hide his mistress away before making a proposal of marriage, do you not think, *madame?*"

Lady Sharpe took two glasses from a door in the sideboard and set them on a tray. "Yes," she cheerfully agreed. "If he means to keep one at all."

"*Oui*, but what man does not?" asked Camille rhetorically.

The countess's face fell as she poured. "Dear child!" she murmured. "Many men do not — and you must see to it that Rothewell does not."

Camille blinked her eyes for a moment. "*Mon Dieu, madame,* but how can such a thing be done?"

"Oh, you will think of something,

clever girl."

"Shall I, *madame?*" asked Camille doubtfully.

Lady Sharpe handed her the sherry, then eyed her across the second glass. "Oh, yes," she said musingly. "I am quite persuaded, you see."

"Persuaded of what, *madame?*"

"Persuaded," she said, lifting her glass high, "that Lord Rothewell has met his match."

Camille wished she was equally confident. Over the next two days, she thought often of Rothewell's mistress. Indeed, she was almost grateful to the poor woman. Their awkward meeting had driven a stake neatly through the heart of whatever nascent passion Camille might have been tempted to nurture for her future husband.

The lady's name, the countess later explained, was Mrs. Ambrose, and she was Lord Sharpe's half sister. Camille's heart had sunk at that pronouncement. It would have been far easier to think of her husband's mistress as a member of the demimonde. Instead, her blood was far bluer — and more English — than Camille's, a fact which begged but one question — why wasn't Lord Rothewell marrying his beautiful blond mistress? There could be but one answer. *Money.*

CHAPTER FIVE

IN WHICH LORD NASH HOSTS
A BETROTHAL PARTY

"Marriage, someone once said, is a desperate business," quoted Lord Rothewell, lifting his chin so that Trammel might better knot his cravat. "And by God, I am beginning to agree with him."

"Marriage is a desperate *thing*," the butler corrected, standing back to admire his handiwork. "And it was Selden, the great English jurist, I believe, who said it."

"Indeed?" Rothewell surveyed his reflection in the gilt cheval glass. "It is very lowering, Trammel, for a chap to know his butler is better educated than he could ever hope to be."

Trammel's eyes had lit on a loose string at the baron's right cuff. "I should hope that it is more lowering to be dressed by one's butler," he said, going to the baron's dressing case for a pair of scissors. "You might give some thought to hiring a proper valet, sir, now that you are marrying."

"No need," said Rothewell gruffly. "Just get me through this dinner party tonight, Trammel, and the wedding. Then you may go back to thrashing the staff at your leisure."

Trammel neatly snipped off the string, then reached for Rothewell's brocade waistcoat. As he slid it up the baron's arms, he gave a *tsk* of disapproval.

"What now?" Rothewell grumbled. "My petticoat showing?"

The butler stepped round, then flicked a glance up at Rothewell's face. "You have lost more weight, my lord," he said. "You need to eat more regularly."

"Just give me my coat, damn it," said Rothewell. "Miss Obelienne's been complaining again, I collect."

Trammel shrugged, and fetched the coat. "When the plates go back but half-eaten, my lord, a cook takes it personally."

"Get a damned dog to sit under the bloody table, then," Rothewell complained, "if it will stop her nagging."

The butler started toward the dressing room, shooting him a reproving glance as he went. "You are soon to be a married man, my lord," he said. "You must learn to endure a female's nagging with a little more grace."

Rothewell closed his eyes and pinched hard at the bridge of his nose. There was no point in snapping at Trammel — not when he likely spoke the truth. What had he been thinking, to enter into this mad scheme? And if he meant to do such a foolhardy thing, why had he not done it at once, as Mademoiselle Marchand had wished? By now he could have wed her, bedded her, and got this bloody damned itch out of his system.

It was as if Trammel read his thoughts. "There was a message from Lady Sharpe this morning," he called from the dressing room. "Did Slocum give it to you?"

"Oh, yes." Rothewell suppressed a groan. He was in Pam's black books, and deservedly so.

The butler brought out a freshly folded handkerchief.

"That will be all, Trammel," said Rothewell, tucking it away. "Take the evening off — no, even better — take all the lads down to the King's Arms for a pint. Someone may as well enjoy this evening. God knows I won't."

"Yes, sir." Trammel bowed, and left.

Rothewell went to the sideboard, and yanked the crystal stopper from a decanter of cognac. Then, on second thought, he shoved it back in again. In his present mood, he would likely not stop drinking once he started, and the notion of being less than completely sober in Mademoiselle Marchand's presence was a daunting one.

He needed his wits about him when dealing with her. She had already persuaded him to marry her. To impregnate her. To kiss and fondle her in broad daylight like some bought-and-paid-for tart. Even now, if he closed his eyes, his head swam with her exotic, spicy scent. God only knew what might come next. Well, perhaps nothing. Perhaps they would not even be on speaking terms. It was likely, given their last exchange.

God damn it, he hated this. Hated having to care what another human being thought of him — even if he had asked for it. Even if it was *her.* And he probably wouldn't care in the end. Mademoiselle Marchand would understand soon enough just what she had married and be glad to leave him to himself.

In any case, the brandy was best left alone for now. Rothewell paced across the room and looked at the mantel clock. He was not due at Nash's for another half hour, and it was less than a ten-minute stroll to Park Lane.

He went to the window and stared out almost blindly. A lone carriage was circling the empty square — a shabby hackney coach with a tired brown horse. It went round twice, and then a third time, as if the driver were lost amongst the opulent lanes of Mayfair. Rothewell felt a sudden stab of pity for the poor devil. He knew the feeling — that sense of being disoriented. Of being an insignificant thing in a greater and grander place.

Was that what he was? *Lost?*

He did not know. Rothewell left the window and looked about the vast, empty room in his vast, empty house with a strange sense of dread, a feeling so old and so familiar, he could no longer shake it off with ease. After almost a year, this place still was not his home. Nor had Barbados ever been home. He had been sent there — shipped off like a load of coal slag — after the death of his parents, along with Luke and Zee, then but a babe. And on that hellish plantation, they had lived through horrors unimaginable to anyone — anyone, that is, who was not a slave.

They had worked, he and Luke, until their fingers bled. They had borne drunken beatings and emotional torment so horrific and so often he could no longer remember it, so deep had he shoved it in the recesses of his mind.

Food and clothing had been luxuries, shoes nonexistent — not because their uncle couldn't afford them but because he took pleasure in his wards' deprivation. There had been no education save that which could be had by lamplight after Uncle passed out drunk, using what books they could take from the dusty library shelves. No joy. No hope. The three of them had clung together unflinchingly and loved one another fiercely — and in this way, they had somehow survived.

Even now, Rothewell wasn't sure how it had all happened. His parents had loved them; that much he *did* remember.

The Nevilles had been poor, in a shabby-genteel sort of way; their father a simple country squire, their mother the sixth daughter of an obscure baronet. They had died as simply as they had lived, of a bilious fever, which tore through the village, striking down high and low alike.

In the tragic aftermath, none of their relations in England had been willing to take their children, not even Pamela's mother, Lady Bledsoe, their aunt Olivia, a singularly coldhearted woman. So they had been sent out to the West Indies, where their father's elder brother, a devil and a drunk and a violent son of a bitch, had been exiled.

As a young man, the sixth Baron Rothewell had throttled a footman in a drunken rage — his sister's lover, to be precise — a fool who'd had the grave misjudgment to blackmail Aunt Olivia just weeks before her wedding. The future Lady Bledsoe, who was as sharp as her brother was stupid, had not taken it well. Knowing her brother's propensity for drink and violence, she had suggested that the footman, rather than his own ineptitude at the card tables, was the root of his nagging insolvency.

The footman, of course, had stolen nothing save Olivia's virtue, and probably not even that. After he lay dead, Olivia cried and swore the footman had tried to attack her. Her father swept it all under a rug as best he could, and bought his dolt of an heir a one-way passage to Barbados.

Uncle figured much of it out, of course, once he'd sobered up — somewhere off the coast of Portugal. The realization had served only to make him more vicious. Once or twice he'd got drunk enough — and angry enough — to complain of his sister's duplicity, and in this way, the tale had fallen on Luke's ears. Rothewell kept Aunt Olivia's secret, which was more than she'd ever done for him.

So, after living through that sort of childhood with those sorts of relatives, here he was. Thirty years later, he still had no home. No place where he felt — well, whatever it was one was supposed to feel. Was he fool enough to hope that some last-ditch effort at marriage would fill these rooms and take away that awful blackness?

At that, he laughed aloud, and briefly reconsidered the cognac bottle. Surely it had not come to this? If his life was empty, it was because he had made it so — willingly, and with his eyes wide open. And the ache he sometimes felt in the pit of his stomach was just that; his ruthless innards repaying him for a lifetime of abuse.

And so it would be. His mouth curled in a bitter, inward smile. He was not a man much given to repentance. God knew the truth of what a man was, and no last-minute conversion or contrition could cover it up. His bargain with Valigny had been no act of Christian charity; no long shot at redemption. He had felt sorry for the girl, yes. But beyond that, it had been an act of raw lust, plain and simple, and he could not let himself think otherwise.

Restless and on edge, Rothewell threw himself into a chair and snatched up Pamela's letter again. The words *dashed awkward position* and *utter lack of thought* fairly leapt off the page to smack him in the face again. Then there was *grievous insult* topped by *unimaginable humiliation* — the former in regard to Christine Ambrose, the latter to Mademoiselle Marchand. But Pamela's obloquies were interchangeable, were they not? He had managed to antagonize everyone equally.

Rothewell threw the letter down, and scrubbed a hand round his freshly shaved chin. He did not tolerate criticism especially well — not even when it was deserved. But this was *Pamela.* And Christine was her sister-in-law. He should have thought of that before hauling Mademoiselle Marchand across town and dumping her on Pamela's doorstep.

And yet the notion had never occurred to him. He and Christine were not a couple. They both regularly took other lovers, but even that limited arrangement had gone stale of late, and their relationship had assumed the qualities of an old shoe, comfortable, but a little worn.

Regrettably, it now appeared Christine had ascribed an entirely different meaning to that lull. She had marched down Sharpe's front steps, her eyes blazing, her whisper laced with icy certitude. *"Oh, you are going to pay for this, Rothewell,"* she had said. *"On* that *you may depend."*

Christine had had the great good fortune to catch him with his defenses down, his mind obsessed by what had just transpired in Sharpe's garden. With the taste of Mademoiselle Marchand's lush, exquisite mouth still in his, and the sting of her cold barb still burning in his flesh. *She did not want to be kissed. Or embraced. Or dallied with.* Fine, then. He would just fuck her. That was all he wanted to do anyway.

Again, Rothewell pinched his nose. Dear God, what was wrong with him? Yes, he very much feared he was going to pay — but not in the way Christine had envisioned. Camille Marchand — if he were placing money on a fight — would make a far more chilling opponent. With her, there was no explosion of temper, no idle posturing. She was hard. Hard in an unflinching, almost ruthless way. Funny how a man could recognize his own traits in others.

In any case, he was not risking money, he was risking his peace of mind, or what little of it was left to him. And now he might well have to live out his last with a haughty shrew. A haughty shrew who did not wish to be kissed, but merely impregnated. Good

God, what had he done?

Tonight they were to be toasted and congratulated by his extended family — or whatever of it Pamela and Lord Nash had managed to dredge up. They would be expected to smile at one another, perhaps even to dance with one another. To look happy and proud. But he was none of those things, and he seriously doubted Mademoiselle Marchand was either. Instead, she would be looking daggers at him the whole evening, and expecting him to curry her favor and forgiveness. Well, to hell with that. The sooner she knew what she was marrying, the easier her life would be. Perhaps she would cry off and put a bullet through the head of this ill-considered farce.

Perhaps he needed that drink after all? Rothewell looked up. The mantel clock was about to strike the hour. He was now late. Damn. Late for his betrothal dinner.

No one, of course, would be surprised.

In Park Lane that night, the row of fine carriages stretched from Lord Nash's door all the way to Upper Brook Street. Camille sat opposite Lord and Lady Sharpe in their elegantly appointed barouche, though the drive to Park Lane had been short.

"We shall have our hems to worry about,"

Lady Sharpe had fussed over breakfast. "There will be rain before the evening is out, mark me."

Camille craned her neck to look up at what little of the sky she could see. Lady Sharpe, she feared, had been right. So she had taken the precaution of wearing one of her darker gowns, a forest green satin which had been her mother's. With no money for a new wardrobe, Camille had kept those things of her mother's which were still fashionable and at least marginally modest. The gowns she had taken up an inch, and that was that. The green was daring, Lady Sharpe had agreed, but still this side of propriety, given Camille's age.

Camille smoothed her hands anxiously down her skirts and awaited their chance to alight. She was almost disconcertingly eager to see Lord Rothewell again. She owed him, perhaps, an apology — but *he* owed *her* an explanation.

Oh, she could not stop him from keeping a mistress. But she would not have that cat hissing and spitting in her face again, and the sooner Rothewell knew it, the smoother life would go for both of them.

As she watched the scenery inch forward, Camille told herself she was not jealous of Mrs. Ambrose. The woman's ivory skin and pale blond locks meant less than nothing to her. But then she remembered Rothewell's lips on hers in the garden, and the strange ache began anew. She tried to force it away by returning her gaze to Lady Sharpe.

"It is most kind of Lord Nash to host this dinner party, *madame*," Camille said. "But I feel . . . oh, I don't know the right word."

"Nervous, I daresay," Lady Sharpe murmured. "Poor dear. In a few days' time, you will be married to a man you scarcely know. And tonight you must meet a great many more relatives."

"*Oui, madame,*" said Camille quietly. "It is daunting."

"Daunting but necessary." The feathers in her small hat bounced as she nodded. "Nash's stepmother, the Dowager Lady Nash, and her sister Lady Henslow shall be there — the most frightful gossips in town."

"Gossips?" said Camille. "*Ça alors,* this will make matters more difficult."

The countess wagged a finger. "No, no, no, dear child," she said. "Gossip is unavoidable. One can only hope to steer it. Tomorrow the talk will be of Rothewell's engagement, and yes, of your mother's unfortunate situation. That will be but a five-minute conversation. Then the gossips will have to acknowledge that the family has embraced

192

you, and has trotted you out just as we would any blue-blooded bride."

Camille had to acknowledge it made a certain amount of sense.

The carriage rocked to a halt, and Camille felt a flush of heat from her breasts up her throat. Soon. Soon, she would see him again.

Oh, but what a goose she was! Lady Sharpe's optimism aside, Rothewell was not apt to be a faithful husband. He had no reason to be. For her part, Camille understood how the world worked. She must remember she wanted but one thing of Lord Rothewell — and it was not, she reminded herself, the man's heart.

They were greeted at the door by Rothewell's sister, who smiled, and clasped both of Camille's hands in her own. Lady Nash had reconciled herself, it seemed, to her brother's unfortunate marriage. Camille forced a smile and kissed her hostess's cheek.

A whirlwind of introductions followed, along with the oft-repeated tale of Lady Sharpe's French governess. The first to hear it were Nash's stepmother, a lovely but rather silly woman, and her sister, a stout, good-humored matron of perhaps sixty years. The matron's husband, Lord Hens-

193

low, attended, as did two pretty girls, Lord Nash's half sisters. There was a handsome golden-haired gentleman — a business associate of Lady Nash's — and his wife, a quiet, strikingly beautiful woman. The pair was introduced as the Duke and Duchess of Warneham. And Lord Nash had a younger brother, Anthony Hayden-Worth, a politician who flirted charmingly with the ladies.

It was all a bit much to take in. Camille had been prepared to be faintly snubbed — that, she could have borne. But these people were entirely civil. Even warm. She went in to dinner on Lord Nash's arm and passed what should have been a pleasant two hours. Except that it was not. She kept looking down the table at Rothewell. She knew what he was, yes. So why did she keep remembering their kiss in the garden? Remembering how his mouth had molded to hers? How he had touched her, arousing in her a hundred complicated emotions?

Fleetingly, she closed her eyes. Oh, he was not for her, that dark-haired devil with his lean, hard face and somnolent eyes. She might well marry him, but she could ill afford to be besotted by him. She knew his type too well and had seen the ruin heartbreak brought firsthand.

But even now, she could not quite take her eyes from him — not even when Mr. Hayden-Worth had asked her a perfectly earnest question about the resignation of the Villèle cabinet. Camille had been required to turn round and ask him to repeat himself. The gentleman had cheerfully done so, then tore off on a rattle about France's position on covert slave-trading, a subject of obvious interest to him. Camille was compelled to nod and answer his questions until his mother appeared to kick him beneath the table, ordering him to keep his politics from the dining room.

And so Camille's gaze had returned to Rothewell, almost against her will. He was picking at his food, she noticed. That seemed odd, for he looked to be a man of great appetites, in every sense of the word.

He had been late tonight, arriving well after all the other guests, and Camille's pique had been replaced by a sudden sense of foreboding. Rothewell's sister's smile, too, had begun to look a little brittle as her eyes kept darting toward the door. Whilst a withdrawing room full of guests had laughed, sipped champagne, and offered their congratulations, Camille had quietly convinced herself that Rothewell was not coming at all.

She was trying to decide if she felt relieved or jilted when he swept into the entrance hall wearing a long black opera cloak and carrying a gold-knobbed walking stick. Camille watched through the double doors of the withdrawing room as a footman lifted the cloak from his shoulders. Beneath it Rothewell wore his usual black, accented by a pewter brocade waistcoat and an expression just as forbidding as Camille remembered.

Upon seeing her, however, he had crossed the room at once, then shocked her by pressing a kiss to her hand; a surprisingly fervent kiss, too, not some faint gesture made upon the air. Camille had found herself blushing, much to the delight of Lord Nash's stepmother and aunt.

Now the dinner was over and the ladies were awaiting the gentlemen in the long blue-and-gold withdrawing room. Camille watched from a distance as Rothewell's sister poured more coffee for those who wished it, then turned her attention to the lady next to her. Camille drifted toward the grand piano which she had noticed upon her arrival. It was a gorgeous beast of an instrument in warm, burled wood with gilt trim and carved legs so delicate one wondered how it held its weight. A little awed, she sat down upon the bench, and stroked her hand across the wood.

"Beautiful, is it not?"

Camille looked up, startled to see Rothewell standing near. She had not seen the gentlemen return from their port. A sudden vehemence roiled up inside her. *"Mais oui,"* she answered coolly. "It is *incroyable.*"

For a moment, he said no more. She hardened her gaze, and a look passed between them, dark and turbulent. He knew, of course, that she was angry. *Good.*

She was chilled by her wish to lash out at him. To tell him, in no uncertain terms, that his days with Mrs. Ambrose were numbered. But that would not do, when so many eyes were upon them. It would have been a hollow warning anyway.

Rothewell rested one forearm on the piano and leaned nearer, as if tempting her to slap him. "I know very little about music, of course," he went on, as if the dark moment had never occurred. "But I do know good craftsmanship when I see it."

"The gilt and carving alone must have cost a fortune," she managed to reply.

Rothewell surveyed her in silence for a moment. "You look lovely tonight, Camille," he murmured. "Are you well? Has everyone been kind to you here?"

Was that a note of genuine concern in his voice? "*Merci,* my lord," she answered, some of the fight going out of her. "Everyone has been most gracious. And the kiss — the kiss on my hand — it was unnecessary. But thoughtful."

"Thoughtful?" he echoed flatly.

Just then, Lord Nash saw them from across the room and approached with a cup of coffee in hand. Camille suppressed a vague sense of disappointment. "Do you play, Mademoiselle Marchand?" he asked.

"*Mais oui,*" she said. "The fortepiano, mostly."

"This is a six-octave Böhm," said Nash, drawing up beside her. "It was bespoke from Vienna. The veneer and giltwork were my stepmother's doing."

"*Mon Dieu,* to possess such a thing." Camille's voice was laced with awe.

"By all means, try it," Lord Nash encouraged. "You will fall in love, I think."

His choice of words sent a strange frisson up Camille's spine. She tried to focus on the piano. Oddly aware of Rothewell's gaze, she carefully laid back the fallboard, then set both hands down on the keys. The chord which rang out was both light and rich. Extraordinary.

"And now you behold the true beauty of

the Böhm." Lord Nash surveyed her over his cup. "The giltwork and carvings are meaningless by comparison."

Camille played a few notes. "*Oui*, the sound — the *résonance* — all is perfection, *monsieur*."

"I know it is bad form to ask a guest of honor to perform, Mademoiselle Marchand," Nash continued. "Still, I hope you will?"

Camille looked up at Rothewell, who said nothing but inclined his head almost imperceptibly. Camille drew a deep breath and smiled. Then she lifted her hands, and set them dramatically down upon the keyboard. As was usual with her, she did not choose the piece, so much as the piece chose her. The sound washed over the room in luxurious, rippling waves as if from another's hands.

As she played, Camille was aware of nothing but Rothewell's strong, steady gaze upon her hands as they moved upon the keyboard. Soon, she was lost to the music, unsure even of how long she played. Music was her solace. Her means of survival. It always had been — and during the last three years, as her mother's illness had worn on, confining Camille and stripping from her all other joys, she had become more than competent at the piano.

Long moments later, when at last the final chords rang out, Camille lifted her hands from the ivory, and looked up to see Rothewell's sister standing beside him. From the other side of the sofa, someone was slowly clapping.

"Well done! Well done!" said Lord Nash's stepbrother, standing. "My hat — if I wore one — would surely be off to you, Mademoiselle Marchand."

Murmurs of appreciation ran through the small crowd, then one by one, most returned to their coffee and their conversation. Though he watched her still, Rothewell's expression was strange, almost bleak. Then he, too, turned and walked away. He went to the window, and stood there rigid and alone, staring out into the night.

"That was extraordinary, *mademoiselle*," said Nash, setting his coffee aside. "A Haydn sonata, was it not?"

"*Mais oui*, Number 54 in G-major." But Camille's attention was fixed on Rothewell's back.

"*Allegretto innocente*," murmured Nash. "What a remarkable piece to choose."

Camille forced her attention to her host. "*Oui*, his sonatas are not as popular as his symphonies, I think?"

"Nonetheless, you played it to perfection, Mademoiselle Marchand." Nash smiled. "You did not give in to the temptation to rush it or to drive it too harshly, as so many do with Haydn."

"My lord, you are too kind. *Merci.*"

"No, it was extraordinary," Rothewell's sister chimed in. "Thank you, Mademoiselle Marchand." She glanced at her husband. "My dear, Gareth wishes to speak with you. Something about a filly coming up at Tattersall's?"

"Ah, that," said Nash. "We are going to have a look on Thursday. Unless he has changed his mind?"

His wife lifted one shoulder. "You must ask him, I daresay."

Lord Nash excused himself, and crossed the room to join the golden-haired duke. Lady Nash smiled down at Camille. "Will you play again, Mademoiselle Marchand?"

She jerked her head up. "Camille, please."

Lady Nash's smile warmed. "Camille, then."

"No, I shan't be greedy," she went on, rising. "I must let one of the other ladies take a turn."

Lady Nash laughed lightly. "I rather doubt, my dear, that any of us will wish to humiliate ourselves by following *that* performance," she said. "And I see that Tony is getting up a hand of whist with the others. Would you care to come upstairs and see our nursery?"

It was another olive branch, perhaps. Camille seized it. *"Merci,"* she answered. "I would like to."

Rothewell was not perfectly sure how long he stood there by the windows, looking out into a night so dark, there was nothing to be seen. He watched instead the watery reflection of the room. Of *her.* The Black Queen. As proud and as beautiful as she had been on the night he'd first laid eyes on her.

The music did not resume. He was glad. Relieved, really. He realized that he had broken into a cold sweat and extracted his handkerchief to blot his forehead. He felt vaguely ill, like a boy on the verge of his first round of fisticuffs, knowing he would likely be pummeled.

Good God, it was just music. Just a beautiful woman playing the piano. But playing it with an almost sensuous grace, her mind lost to the music as if it were a lover's caress. Her finely boned hands had moved across the keyboard with an elegance he had no right to know, and yet he could not help but imagine those hands caressing him with that same passion. Would she ever long to touch him as she had longed to touch that piano?

No. No, why should she? What a mistake this marriage was going to be. Camille was everything that he was not. Delicate. Polished. Graceful. And underneath all of it, she was passion personified. Never had he known a woman so clearly full of heat and light. Her husky bedroom voice still made him shiver, and her scent still filled his nostrils, though he had walked away from the piano minutes ago.

Tonight her black hair was swept high on the back of her head again, revealing that delicate place just below her ear where Rothewell imagined he could see her heartbeat. He had watched her, almost mesmerized, and felt something inside himself tear away.

Yes, a fight was indeed coming — and at the most inopportune point in a man's life. And just now, it felt like a fight he was destined to lose.

"Rothewell?" The voice was impatient. "Wake up, old chap."

"What?" He turned just as his friend Gareth took him by the arm.

"I think you've gone deaf." Gareth, the

Duke of Warneham, grinned at him. "We've been calling you from across the room. Zee has absconded with your bride."

Rothewell looked round the room. "Yes, I see," he muttered. "Probably warning her off, eh?"

"Probably." Gareth's grin did not fade. "You don't deserve her, you know."

It was meant lightheartedly, he knew, but the words hit so close to home, Rothewell nearly flinched.

But Gareth was still talking. "Listen, Rothewell, I've a mind to go to Tattersall's Thursday morning with Nash. He's looking to buy a filly — a famous one, I gather, but I've forgotten whose. Want to come along?"

"No, I'm sorry," Rothewell managed. "I have some things I must get done."

"Yes, it's too early in the day for you, I know," said Gareth. "Moreover, the end of your bachelorhood draws nigh, doesn't it? You must have much on your mind." Gareth set a hand on Rothewell's shoulder, and his smile faded. "Antonia and I are so pleased for you," he said, dropping his voice. "We wish you many years of happiness, Kieran."

Many years of happiness. Well, that was not apt to happen.

He thought again of how brittle and angry

she was. Ironic how one could recognize it in another and not see it in one's self. What was it Xanthia had said? "You will ruin her life, Kieran."

Those words had stung even as he had acknowledged there might be a hint of truth behind them. Was his sister right? Was he destined to drag Camille down into his own misery rather than lift her from her own?

Shaking off the mood, Rothewell returned his attention to Gareth, thanked him, then resumed his solitary vigil by the window.

Camille followed Rothewell's sister up a wide, twisting staircase to the second floor. As they went, Lady Nash talked about what they might name the child. They were favoring Mihalo if a boy, and Katerina if female, her hostess explained, for they were the names of Nash's maternal grandparents.

Halfway along the passageway, she stopped, and pushed open a door. Camille followed her into a large, airy chamber with high ceilings and three wide windows. It smelled of beeswax and well-scrubbed floors. A sturdy rocking chair and a tufted armchair sat by the bank of windows. In the center of the room was an old wooden cradle stripped bare. The fireplace was surrounded by a tall brass fender, liberally padded with leather. But beyond that, the room was empty.

Lady Nash turned round and opened her arms expansively. "Well, Camille, this is it," she said. "My blank slate. My canvas, as it were. I only wish I knew where to begin."

Camille turned around in the room. "You have invited the wrong guest, *madame*, if you seek advice," she said ruefully. "Perhaps your female relations might advise?"

Lady Nash's expression shifted. "I have no one, really, save Pamela," she said quietly. "And Nash's stepmother, of course. She is well-intentioned, but a bit scatty. No, I really just wished a moment of privacy with you, Camille. I wished to . . . well, to apologize, I suppose."

"Pardon, madame?" Camille murmured. "To apologize for what?"

Her smile muted, Lady Nash set a hand on her faintly rounded belly, and eased down into the rocking chair. "I know I have seemed less than enthusiastic about this marriage," she said quietly. "But it has nothing — *nothing* — to do with you. I swear it."

Camille joined her in the other chair. *"Merci, madame,"* she replied. "I am much relieved."

"As am I," said Lady Nash, her gaze distant. "At first, I feared . . . well, never mind that. The truth is, Camille, you seem a thoroughly sensible woman. You may, in fact, be just what my brother needs. But is *he* what *you* need?"

"I need a husband," said Camille quietly.

Her hands braced on the arms of the rocker, Lady Nash shook her head. "Every woman wants more than that," she replied. "To fall in love with a handsome prince. To be swept off one's feet. You ought not settle for less than your dream."

"I have no dream, *madame,*" she lied. "The decision is made."

Lady Nash pursed her lips. "Then you must make Kieran toe the mark," she said warningly. "You must give him and his bad habits no quarter. You must love him, and defend him fiercely — sometimes, perhaps, against himself. For if this is the marriage you mean to make, then you must make the marriage into something worth having. Only then will there be hope."

Camille looked at her quizzically. "Hope for what, *madame?*"

Her head relaxed against the arching back of the rocking chair. "Call me Xanthia," she said. "Or Zee."

"Merci," she returned. "Xanthia."

Lady Nash's gaze seemed far away. "I love my brother, Camille," she said fervently. "I love him with all my heart. Never doubt it. He is an extraordinarily strong man, with a capacity for love which I suspect you cannot yet imagine."

"I . . . I must trust your judgment in this, *madame*."

Lady Nash turned to face her. "He was not always like this, you know," she said quietly. "He was not always so cold and grim. He did not always drive himself hell-for-leather. Or drown himself in drink and . . . well, dissolution. Inside, Camille, that is not who he is."

"You had a good and loving family, *madame*?" Camille suggested. "Sometimes even that is not enough for a wayward soul."

Lady Nash gave a bark of bitter laughter. "Oh, God no!" she said. "I never even knew my parents. Perhaps your father left something to be desired, Camille, but at least you knew him. You knew he loved you."

Camille was quite sure Valigny had never loved anyone save himself, but it did not bear being said just now. "If you had no parents, how did you . . . come up? Is that the word?"

The distant look deepened. "We were sent out to Barbados to my father's older brother," she answered. "He was the sixth Baron Rothewell, and the worst ever to bear the title, I am sure."

"In Barbados?" murmured Camille. "*Alors,* he was a . . . a governor? A diplomat?"

Lady Nash shook her head, heedless of her hair scrubbing on the back of the chair. "No, nothing like that," she said. "There was a scandal, I collect, when he was a young man, and he was sent away by his father. He was given a plantation — a run-down, ramshackle thing which threw off just enough money to keep him in brandy and bad company."

"*Oui, je vois,*" Camille murmured. "It was a difficult childhood?"

She focused on a point somewhere far in the distance. "It was horrific," she quietly admitted. "And it could have been even worse for me, I daresay. But my brothers saved me from the worst — and took the brunt of it instead. Kieran, especially. He never could keep his mouth shut. And Uncle was . . . not kind, to say the least."

Something like grief or guilt needled at Camille. "But why did they send you to such a horrible man?"

"It was decided by my aunt — Pamela's mother — that we should go there because Luke was our uncle's heir, and Uncle had no wife or children," she said.

"And Luke — he was your brother, too?" said Camille. "*Pardon,* but I do not follow."

Lady Nash's eyes looked weary. "Yes, our elder brother, but he died some years past," she explained. "There was an accident. Kieran inherited most everything; the plantations — we had three by then — and a large part of Neville Shipping. And, of course, the baronial seat in Cheshire, which is vast."

Camille felt her eyes widen. *"Vraiment?"* she murmured. "Rothewell possesses an estate? And plantations?"

Lady Nash looked at her strangely, then laughed. "My God, Camille!" she said. "No one will accuse you of marrying him for his money."

Camille's mind was suddenly racing. *Marry him for his money?* Was Rothewell not the impecunious rake she had believed him?

"And this Neville Shipping," she murmured. "That is a . . . a very great thing? A prosperous thing?"

Again, she gave a trill of laughter. "It had better be," said Lady Nash. "I have slaved away at it for nearly the whole of my life. Luke taught me to read and write using the manifests. Kieran and I own a quarter each, our niece owns a quarter, and Gareth —

the Duke of Warneham — owns the balance."

"A niece?" Camille searched her brain. "The child of your dead brother?"

Lady Nash smiled. "His adopted child, yes," she said. "Martinique. She is married and living in Lincolnshire now. Luke wed her mother when Martinique was a child. But there, I am throwing out too many names. You needn't worry about any of this."

Camille's head was spinning. Rothewell had an estate and plantations. A sad childhood. A brother who died too young. A sister who worried for him. This marriage was beginning to feel terribly real to her. These were real people. A family — with all the tragedy and drama and history a family brought with it. This was not just *Rothewell.* And never mind the fact that he had deceived her about his wealth.

At the outset, she had told herself she did not wish to know him. Did not need to know him. She needed his name and his seed, and nothing more. So why did she now hang upon his sister's every word? Why was she so angry about Mrs. Ambrose? Was not one scoundrel very like another?

Suddenly, Lady Nash sat erect in the rocker, her hands braced on the arms as if she might spring to her feet. "Just promise me this, Camille," she said quietly. "Promise me that you will be a good wife to him — or as good a wife as he will permit you to be. I love him, you see. And . . . And I want you to love him. Promise me — *promise* me — that you will be kind to him. That you will love him."

Camille tore her gaze away, unable to look Lady Nash in the face. What was she to say? How could she promise anything to anyone? "We cannot know what the future holds," she finally answered. "I . . . I will be a good wife, Xanthia. I will do my best to be kind."

Her omission, she thought, did not go unnoticed. Sadness sketched across Lady Nash's face, then she rose from her chair. As if on impulse, she hugged Camille, then just as swiftly set her away again.

"Well, I have neglected my guests too long, I daresay," she said quietly. "Come, Camille. Shall we go back down?"

Once inside the drawing room, Lady Nash excused herself to confer with one of the footmen regarding the coffee service. Most of the guests were playing cards now at one of two tables which had been pulled to the center of the room. Rather than hover over them, Camille drifted around the perimeter, admiring a fine collection of French landscapes. She was particularly absorbed by one when she felt a light touch at her elbow.

She turned to see one of Nash's younger sisters at her side. "Cards are so frightfully dull, are they not, Mademoiselle Marchand?" she said, smiling.

Camille smiled back. "They can be, *oui.*"

The young woman stuck out a hand. "Lady Phaedra Northampton," she said. "You cannot possibly have got all these names the first time round."

"*Merci,* I did not," Camille confessed.

Lady Phaedra was perhaps a bit past twenty, and vivacious despite her drab gown and gold spectacles. She gestured at the wall. "You are an admirer of French classicism, *mademoiselle?*"

Camille turned back to the painting. "I like Poussin," she admitted, pointing at her favorite elements in the painting. "I like his subtle use of color here. And here. It allows his extraordinary skill with line and light to emerge."

"You are quite sure this is a Poussin?" asked Lady Phaedra lightly. "He did not ordinarily sign his work."

Camille turned to look at her, wondering if this were some sort of challenge. "I could be mistaken, perhaps. But I think not. I have had the good fortune to see many of his works."

Just then, Rothewell approached. "Do not let this one goad you," he murmured, leaning toward Camille. "She imagines herself more intelligent than us mere mortals."

Lady Phaedra drew herself up an inch. "Well, at least I know my *Rosa centifolias* from my *Rosa rugosas,* which is more than I can say for some people," she answered, her eyes following Rothewell. Then she softened her tone, and returned her gaze to Camille. "As to the painting, Mademoiselle Marchand, I haven't any notion. The last pair of experts my father trotted in were equally divided. And Nash simply likes the painting, so he doesn't care who painted it."

Lady Phaedra's mother drifted toward them. "I have always thought that one especially pretty," she remarked, motioning at the painting. "The hills, the trees, and those tiny little horses. Very clever indeed. But I prefer the kind Nash has upstairs. The ones with all the bowls full of fruit and such."

"Still lifes, Mamma," said Lady Phaedra indulgently. "They are called still lifes."

"But they are all *still,*" the dowager complained. "They are paintings. They cannot very well go anywhere, can they?"

Lady Phaedra chose not to argue with this

logic. "Nash's late mother was part Russian," she explained. "She had quite good taste in art. As Mother says, there is a collection of fine Flemish still lifes in the library upstairs, if you would care to see them."

"A capital notion," said Rothewell out of nowhere.

Camille spun around to see he was studying the alleged Poussin as if it held the secrets of the universe. Her breath caught at the intensity of his gaze.

"Lovely, then," said Lady Phaedra cheerfully. "Up we go."

The dowager whacked her daughter lightly on the arm with her fan. "Don't be obtuse, Phaedra," she said. "The happy couple might wish to go alone."

"An excellent notion, ma'am," said Rothewell. "I believe I am developing a fondness for art."

"And roses," interjected Lady Phaedra, grinning. "Did you know that, Mademoiselle Marchand? Lord Rothewell has a vast knowledge of rose gardening. You must ask him to expound upon it sometime."

"Thank you, Phae." Rothewell bowed stiffly. "But at present, I find myself equally fascinated by painting."

The dowager had taken Camille by the

hand. "The paintings are in the far end of the library. If the room is locked, you'll find a key under the vase by the door." Then she smiled and leaned nearer. "We will not send out a search party if you linger."

Lord Rothewell watched Camille from the corner of one eye to see if she would hesitate. The notion of privacy was as appealing as it was disquieting. He turned, and offered his arm to her.

"The talk about roses," she asked as they went up the stairs, "what did it mean?"

"What, Phae?" Rothewell looked down, feeling faintly embarrassed. "Nothing. She is simply teasing me."

"*Oui*? About what?"

"About a foolish white lie I once told her — an excuse to escape a tea I did not wish to attend."

"I see." Camille seemed to hesitate. "And tell me, *monsieur,* are you lying now?"

Rothewell stopped on the steps. "About what?"

Her dark eyes flashed with some inscrutable emotion. "About your fondness for paintings, of course."

He let his eyes roam over her face. "Yes," he said honestly. "I don't give a damn for art or roses, if you must know."

"Ah," she said softly. "Do you know

anything at all of art?"

Rothewell hesitated. He doubtless looked the worst sort of rustic in her eyes. But he'd be damned if he'd pretend to be something he was not — even for her. "I know blue from red," he finally answered. "And oils from . . . the other kind. That is the extent of it."

"And yet you wish to see more paintings?"

"What I wish is to speak with you in private," he finally snapped. "And I can see no other way of doing so. Forgive my presumption. Would you rather not be alone?"

"Alone should suit me very well indeed," she said, starting up the stairs again. "For I have something to say to you, *monsieur.* And I am not afraid of you. I think you know that much by now."

She should have been afraid. If she had sensed for one moment the thoughts which ran through his head as he watched her silk skirts slither over her hips as she climbed the stairs, yes, she would have been very afraid indeed.

The library was easy to find. A pair of vases on pedestals flanked the entrance. Rothewell found the key and locked the door behind them. Inside, the room was faintly musty, like any library which was little used. A pair of sconces burned just beyond the doors, but the rest of the room lay in shadow. He found a candle and lit it, then strolled a little deeper into the room. An entire wall had been given over to paintings, with sconces placed every few feet between them.

"Shall I light the others?" he asked.

"*Merci,* but the candle will do," she said. "We are not here, I think, to look at paintings?"

"No, we are not." He set the candle on one of the reading tables, and turned to face her. "We are here because I owe you an apology."

Her finely etched eyebrows rose. Finally, he had shocked her. "*Mon Dieu,* does everyone mean to apologize to me this night?"

"I can speak for no one save myself," he replied.

She smiled almost sourly and half turned away. "You refer to Mrs. Ambrose, *n'est-ce pas?*"

Rothewell followed her as she strolled past toward the wall of paintings. "I do," he answered. "That scene yesterday at Pamela's — I take full responsibility for it. It was unfair to you."

"*Oui,* it was." She looked back over her shoulder. "And unfair to *Madame* Ambrose,

I think?"

"That, too," he said grimly.

Camille turned around, and he thought he saw a flicker of pain in her wide, bottomless eyes. For an instant, she hesitated. "I cannot stop you, my lord, from keeping a mistress," she said after a long, uncertain moment had passed. "But so long as we live together, I shan't have this *affaire d'amour* of yours flung in my face. Do you understand me, Rothewell? I will not be humiliated as my mother was. I will *not*."

Her voice was raw, but despite it, Camille stood before him, cool and exquisite, like an ornament of spun glass placed just beyond his reach. Something inside his chest seemed to twist. He suddenly wished to kiss her again. To hold her and kiss her until her beauty was in dishabille. Until her inky hair was tumbling down and tangled in his fingers. Until her mouth was softly parted and her eyes were somnolent with desire. His weakness angered him. Ruthlessly, he shoved the thoughts away.

"Our discussion of Mrs. Ambrose is finished, Camille," he said, setting his hands on her slender shoulders. "I have apologized."

Camille's eyes hardened. "It is far from finished, *monsieur,*" she gritted. "I demand

219

your word as a gentleman."

"What, jealous?"

Her eyes sparked with fire. "Oh, you would like that, wouldn't you?" she retorted, her voice a hot whisper. "You would like to have that power over me. To hold my heart in your hands. But I am not such a fool, Rothewell. I will not give you my heart. I can ill afford it."

His hands tightened on her arms. "I have asked you to be my wife," he gritted. "And I am asking you to be honorable and faithful. Not one thing more do I require of you, *mademoiselle.* Do not put words in my mouth."

"Très bien," she snapped. "Then keep your *affaires* private, *monsieur.*"

He gave her a little shake. "At least say my name, damn it," he growled. "Stop calling me *monsieur,* as if you just met me."

"Fine," she said, "Lord Rothewell."

"Not that name," he growled. "Kieran. If you cannot dredge up a little indignation at the thought of my keeping a mistress, do you think you could at the very least use my Christian name?"

"So, you mean to be a faithful husband?" she challenged, her eyes wide and mocking. "Oh, do not lie to me, my lord. You are a rake and a rogue to your very core, and we both of us know it."

Something inside him snapped. He jerked her hard against him, and set his mouth to hers in a kiss which was more brutish than tender. His mouth took hers hungrily, lust shooting through him like a hot, living thing. He wanted her angry. Wanted her, he supposed, to slap him senseless. To shut out the truth of her words. He thrust his tongue into her mouth, claiming her, forcing her head back. Forcing her to submit. It was a fierce, fleeting thing, and when they came apart, her eyes blazed, and her breath came sharp and short.

"There," he said, his own breath coming roughly. "Now do not claim, Camille, that you are so indifferent to me. Use my Christian name. Stop this foolish pretense of yours. Stop acting as if you mean to go to the marriage bed like some lamb to the slaughter."

A rosy flush ran up her throat. "You are very full of yourself, *Kieran*," she said in her quiet, husky voice. "And trust me, I am no lamb."

"No, you are not, are you?" His voice, too, had dropped an octave. "This is going to be a marriage, Camille. If we can do no more, we should at least try to be . . . I don't know. Amiable, I suppose."

Amiable? Rothewell wished to jerk the word back as soon as it left his lips. He was not amiable — to anyone.

But Camille was watching him, and for an instant, the hard mask fell. She was lonely, and alone, he thought, but afraid, perhaps, to be otherwise. She had his sympathy. And in another time and place, he wondered if things could have been different for them.

"Camille," he whispered, "may we not try to get along?" Such simple words — and, so far as he could recall, the only thing he had ever asked of any woman. The thought shamed him a little.

"I . . . I do not know." She clasped her hands before her, and in the slight curve of her shoulders, he could see an infinite weariness. "But I know this: I cannot afford to grow attached to you. I cannot come to depend on you. You have said as much yourself and, *mon Dieu,* I admired you for your honesty when you said it —"

"No, what I said was —"

Camille threw up her hand. "Let me finish, *s'il vous plaît,*" she said. "Do not give in to this — this bourgeois guilt you seem suddenly to be toying with. You desire me, but do not pretend you feel anything for me beyond lust. I will think the better of you for it."

"Christ." He dragged a hand through his hair. "It's just that I wish . . ."

"*Quoi?*" She whispered, lowering her eyelids as if hiding some emotion. "What do you wish, Rothewell? That life were fair? I think you know that it is not."

He shook his head. "I wish that we had met under different circumstances. Before I became . . . what I am. Before you became so cold."

"Is that what I am?" she asked softly. "Cold?"

"Yes, and hard," he added. "Your heart has been hardened by life, Camille. You expect . . . well, the worst, I suppose."

And perhaps she was about to get it, he inwardly acknowledged. He was a poor choice of a husband, for any number of reasons. He probably wouldn't be faithful. Perhaps not even honorable. Hell, he had cheated at cards just to get the chance to bed her. But his mind kept turning back to the scene of her pounding her fist on Valigny's card table and challenging one of them to marry her. She had been ready for martyrdom — and he carried the sword.

Tonight she was even more beautiful, the creamy swell of her breasts just visible above the fabric of a dark green gown, which flattered her every turn. His gaze drifted over the warm olive skin of her swanlike neck. Over the emerald earbobs which swayed from the plump earlobes he wanted suddenly to suckle. He returned his hands to her shoulders, and pulled her nearer.

"Camille, you are marrying me because you have no other choice," he said quietly. "Do you think I don't know that? But before you stand up with me before God, you should know what I expect."

"Bien sûr." Her dark eyes narrowed. "What do you expect?"

"Kissing," he said quietly. "Perhaps a great deal of it."

"Ah, as you just kissed me a moment ago?" she asked.

"Yes, I daresay." She meant to make this difficult, he realized. "Camille, this cannot be about having a child and nothing more," he found himself saying. "You deserve something better than a man who will simply take his pleasure from you."

"I see," she said quietly. "You wish to seduce me."

"Yes. Yes, I suppose I do," he admitted.

She cut her gaze away, a rare show of surrender. "I need a husband, my lord," she answered, blinking rapidly. "And I have already shown that I am weak. Yes, I desire you. Your touch . . . it maddens me. Your seduction of me will not present much of a challenge, I fear."

Rothewell shook his head. He was deeply dissatisfied, and he was not perfectly sure why. It was the same sort of frustration he had felt on the night he'd first met her, when Camille had so dispassionately offered her body to him then and there, in exchange for his promise of marriage. He had been damned tempted, too.

He remembered another such beauty who had needed rescuing, but on that occasion, it had been he who had made the offer. The many pleasures of Annemarie's body in exchange for his undying love and financial support. He was hardly the first man to propose that to her. And she had been glad enough to seal the bargain — in a way he would never forget. After long years in the darkness, his life had suddenly seemed filled with light. Until his brother had chosen to interfere.

But Camille was not Annemarie, no matter what Xanthia believed. Oh, the resemblance was there. Dark hair and flashing eyes. Honeyed skin. That sensuous French accent. And yes, it had been the first thing about Camille that had struck him. Tempted him. But any resurrected fantasies of Annemarie would likely not survive one interlude in Camille Marchand's bed. This woman had a passion and a backbone Annemarie had never possessed.

A woman so rare deserved to be surrounded by joy. To be made love to on a bed of rose petals. To have poetry written in her honor. And none of these things would he ever do for Camille Marchand. It wasn't in his nature. She would have to settle, at least for a while, for a good deal less.

Though he had not spoken in some minutes, Camille had made no effort to step away. Caught in the moment, he lifted his hand and stroked the back of his knuckles along her cheek.

Her sweep of black lashes lowered, fanning across her warm skin.

"You were right about one thing," he finally said. "I desire you. Far more than I would wish."

She looked up at him, unblinking. "You wish to kiss me again, *n'est-ce pas?*"

He lifted his hands to cradle her face, then stroked his thumb round the corner of her mouth, and then across her sensuous bottom lip. He felt the plump swell of it quiver beneath the pad of his thumb. He drew it down just a fraction, to reveal her small white teeth, and the pink tip of her tongue. He leaned forward, and skimmed his mouth along the shell of her ear. "Yes," he murmured. "And it is very necessary, Camille. *Absolutely* necessary."

"Necessary?" Her voice was thready.

"This kissing." He drew back and smoothed his thumb across the apple of her cheek. "You once asked me . . . was it necessary? And it is. Like air to my lungs. Kiss me again. Kiss me, Camille."

She tilted her head and rose onto her toes without opening her eyes. Slowly, ever so slowly, Rothewell lowered his mouth to hers. He wanted to savor each second, tucking it away in the recesses of his memory. Storing it away for a time when, perhaps, he would not have this pleasure.

Their lips touched, hers trembling at first. His were certain. And with a gentleness that amazed even himself, Rothewell molded his mouth softly to hers. After a moment's hesitation, Camille was kissing him back in earnest. Unbidden, she opened beneath him, and drew his tongue deep into the warmth of her mouth. It was sweet. So achingly sweet. Something in the pit of his belly seemed to melt.

Her hands came up to hold his face, mirroring his earlier gesture. As if she might control his motions, she held him there, their tongues sinuously entwining, her breath coming more urgently with every moment. He wanted her. Good God, how he wanted her. It was not unbridled lust. It was not Annemarie. He just wanted this woman — Camille — and with an intensity that would have worried him were he not so desperately lost in her kiss.

Somehow, he turned and set her back to the wall below one of the sconces. He wished suddenly that he had lit them all; that he could see the flickering light play over the fine bones of her face, and the silken sweep of her eyelashes. Without taking his mouth from hers, his hands went up to cradle the mounds of her breasts.

Camille gasped faintly at the touch of his hands. When he hooked his thumbs in the laced edge of her bodice, she said nothing, and let her head go back against the wall. She felt enervated, as if she were entirely at his command — and in that moment, she did not care. With a deft tug, he drew the fabric down, taking her chemise with it, until the dusky pink nipples were exposed.

He hesitated as if waiting. For her protest. For the back of her hand. But the dark silence of the library was rent only by the sound of their breathing. She was so tired of fighting her desire for him. Whatever he was, no matter why he wanted her, she ached for him. And when he bent his head to draw her left nipple between his lips, she gasped at the hot ribbon of pleasure it engendered.

He took that as a sound of approval. He drew her breast more fully into the warmth of his mouth, suckling until she began to make small, breathy sounds of pleasure. Then he moved to the other breast, first circling the nipple with his tongue, then sucking at the very tip as he gently nipped with his teeth.

"Ooh, *oui!*" she murmured. Her hands went to his shoulders, restless and urgent.

Gently, he slipped one hand between her shoulder blades. "No, let me, Camille," he breathed against her ear as the hooks of her gown slipped free. "Let me unfasten this."

She did not feign innocence, or further protest. Instead, she gave herself up to the skill of his well-tutored touch. And when he returned his attention to her small, perfect breasts, cupping their weight in his hands, she opened her eyes. *"Mon Dieu,"* she murmured dreamily.

He kissed her long and deep. Her head moved restlessly against the wall. "Kieran, I want —" she whispered. "I want — oh, I don't know."

"Perhaps I can guess."

But as Kieran cradled one breast and kissed her deeply, and his other hand fisted in her skirts, he realized he should be horsewhipped. He was not so wrapped up in her he could not appreciate the precariousness of their situation. Or the fact that she was a virgin. Instead, he inched her skirts up into his fist, then eased one hand between them, touching her lightly in her most intimate place.

"Camille," he whispered. "You are going to marry me. In a few days' time. We will be married, yes?"

"Oh, *oui, je suis* . . ." She stopped and swallowed hard. "I am so . . . yes. *Yes.*"

With a lifetime of experience in having sex in places he had no business, with women he scarcely knew, Rothewell inched down her drawers until they slithered into a puddle of silk at her feet. Oh, Lord. *Her feet.* He wished desperately they were hooked behind his neck. They looked slender. Like her legs. Exquisite. And then he touched her again, and heard her gasp. All else, even her small, perfect breasts, was forgotten.

He eased two fingers into the tangle of curls, and felt the answering slickness. "Oh, *mon Dieu,*" she murmured.

"Ah, Camille, Camille," he moaned against her mouth. But this was madness.

This was no place to make love to an untutored virgin. But none of this — none of it — reached past his brain to his nether regions. In one smooth motion, he pushed her skirts higher, went down on one knee, and stroked his tongue through the soft curls which guarded her pleasure. This time her gasp verged on something more.

He parted her gently, pressing her thighs wide until his fingers found the soft, warm folds of her flesh. Gingerly he drew a finger through the silken wetness. She gave a little moan of surrender when he eased one finger inside. He wanted to give her pleasure. Exquisite, extraordinary pleasure. The kind of mind-clouding pleasure that might make her go unquestioningly to the altar, and not look back at the truth.

With one hand fisted in her skirts, he plunged his tongue deep. She cried out again, but softly. A withering little sound of surrender. Her breathing slowly grew more raspy. Over and over he drew his tongue through the folds which guarded her pleasure until he could feel the little nub of her arousal, unmistakably firm and trembling.

"Kieran, Kieran," she whispered, her hands coming down to seize his shoulders.

He felt her climax inching near. She was murmuring something over and over in

French, he didn't know what. Her head was back, her breath jerking roughly now. She was passion personified. Beautiful. With one finger and his thumb, he opened her wider, teasing her with quick, delicate strokes until he heard her cry out in the darkness. There was a moan. And then she was shaking, her limbs stiffening as she shuddered with the pleasure. He kissed her lightly across the soft, pale flesh of her lower belly as she trembled, then nuzzled her curls one last time. Beautiful. She was so beautiful.

When she had returned to herself, still gasping for breath, he jerked to his feet, his hands going to the fall of his trousers. Quickly he released the buttons, shoving down his drawers and trousers in one motion. "Let me lift you, love," he rasped. "Put — Put your legs round my waist. Yes. Like that."

"Oui," she whispered. "Yes. Inside me."

She felt weightless. Heavenly. He lifted her another inch, and the hot length of his cock slid into the wetness. Carefully, he positioned himself, and pushed gently. He felt her stiffen at the invasion, and then relax again in his embrace.

"Camille, I might hurt you." He let his eyes roam over her face. "Christ. I don't know."

She buried her face against his neck. *"N'importe,"* she whispered. "I want this. I want you, Kieran, inside me."

He knew, vaguely, that he would regret it. That it was tasteless — and probably the worst possible position for a woman of no experience. But he could not wait. His desire for her now blinded him. The scent of her, of him; all of it swirled about them in a sensual heat.

"Ah, Camille," he said, unable to resist the silken, welcoming warmth. He pushed again, and felt a faint resistance. She sucked in her breath on a gasp of pain.

"Oh, hell," he said through gritted teeth.

"Don't," she whispered. "Please. Don't stop."

He eased himself deeper, and felt Camille relax to take him. To draw him in. Literally. Figuratively. He began to move slowly inside her, savoring the sweetness. She wrapped her arms about him and kissed him deeply. He reveled in her every motion. Cherished her every sound. He was lost to the passion, and yet fully, completely aware. His thrusts came faster.

"Camille," he groaned, pushing deeper. Her head was back, her eyes closed, her exposed breasts rising tantalizingly with every breath. "Camille, say my name again."

"Kieran." The word was a soft sigh.

His climax came upon him with merciful swiftness, and he did not try to hold it back. He thrust. And thrust again, trembling as the warmth of his seed finally spilled inside her. It felt like the end of a perfect dream. A dream which had felt nonetheless inevitable. The release sent relief shuddering through him. And then Camille's slender arms were twined around him, her face buried against his neck as he returned to himself.

It was done. The paper in his pocket had just become a mere formality. They were joined now; joined in a way he would let no man put asunder.

No one looked at Rothewell and Camille — suspiciously or otherwise — upon their awkward return from the library. Indeed, the other guests were so obviously *not* watching them, the omission left Camille a little embarrassed. She joined Lady Phaedra on one of the sofas, and hid her shaking hands. After a few moments of their idle chitchat, Rothewell once again withdrew from the crowd and took up his solitary vigil by the window. He looked strangely distant. Almost pained. Camille's heart sank. Had his seduction been a disappointment to him after all?

The Dowager Lady Nash joined them, and the conversation turned to Parisian fashions. Camille responded to the lady's questions almost mechanically. She watched from one corner of her eye as Xanthia joined her brother by the window and rested her hand upon his arm, her expression concerned. Rothewell appeared strangely pale, and had set one hand almost protectively over his lower ribs.

"Excusez-moi." Camille rose abruptly in the middle of a discussion about ladies' hats. "I . . . I should speak with Rothewell."

She went at once to the window. "My lord, you are unwell?" she murmured, drawing up beside them.

Xanthia cast her an uncertain glance. "Kieran?" she asked pointedly. "Are you?"

His lips thinned as if with irritation — or pain — and his forehead, Camille noted, was beaded with perspiration. "Thank you, it is nothing," he managed.

Then, without another word, he left them by the window, and crossed the room to pour himself a brandy at the sideboard.

Xanthia cursed beneath her breath. *"That,"* she muttered, "is the very last thing he needs."

Camille suspected Xanthia was right. But Rothewell was a stubborn man. She rather doubted his sister's chiding — or hers — would change that.

She did not have long to fret about Rothewell's mood, however, for the first of the guests began leaving shortly thereafter. Lady Nash looked exhausted by the time she escorted the last of them to the door. She hugged everyone in turn, Camille included, and sent them down the steps to their waiting carriages.

Camille climbed into the shadows of Lord Sharpe's barouche, greatly relieved to be making her escape. She wanted very much to be alone. To lie in bed and consider the gravity of what she had just done — and, if she were honest, to relive it in her mind. She looked down and realized that her hands were still trembling a little at the memory of Rothewell's touch. Hastily she pressed them to her thighs and forced herself to smile.

Just then, Rothewell himself came down the steps, his walking stick in hand, and his sister on his arm, urgently whispering.

Lady Sharpe leaned out the still-open door. "Kieran, may we take you up in our carriage?"

Rothewell's head jerked round. "It is out of your way," he answered. For a man so dark, his face looked deathly pale. What had

Lady Nash said to him?

"Oh, do come along, Kieran," said Lady Sharpe again. "A gentleman should see his betrothed safely to her door, do you not think?"

"You should go," said his sister quietly, setting one hand between his shoulder blades.

Lord Sharpe, still standing on the pavement, held his hand toward the door. "The womenfolk have decided, old fellow," he said. "You may as well climb in gracefully."

Rothewell's troubled expression did not abate, but he thanked Sharpe and climbed inside to sit opposite the ladies. Lady Sharpe kept up a constant stream of pleasant chatter as the carriage made its way the length of what Camille now recognized as Mayfair. She was curious to see Lord Rothewell's home.

The house, as it happened, was in Berkeley Square, and it was very elegant indeed. Camille marveled that she had ever thought Rothewell penniless. Perhaps he had been fleetingly strapped for cash, or perhaps he was simply unable to resist the lure of the game. But impoverished he certainly was not.

The grand front door swung open, and a servant appeared, a slender Negro gentleman wearing a starkly elegant black coat. The butler, she thought, studying him.

Rothewell, however, did not stir. He was looking across the carriage at Lady Sharpe.

"I think," he said very quietly, "that we have waited long enough for this wedding."

Lady Sharpe stiffened. "I beg your pardon?"

Rothewell turned his gaze to Camille. "I wish us to be married," he said. "In the morning."

"In the morning?" said Lady Sharpe incredulously. "Kieran, no one is ready."

"We are as ready as we shall ever be, Pamela," said Rothewell firmly. "I wish us to be married at once. Sharpe, will you make the arrangements?"

Lord Sharpe seemed to agree with this course of action. "Indeed, old chap, if that is your wish," said the earl, his bald head nodding. "Have you a special license?"

"Yes, for some days now." Rothewell looked at Camille. He was doing this, she supposed, because he had taken her virginity tonight. She had not thought him as old-fashioned as that.

"My dear, I think we ought not wait." His voice was surprisingly gentle. "Will you trust me?"

Will you trust me?

Camille swallowed hard at the words.

Rothewell's mesmerizing, silvery gaze held hers across the gloom, and for an instant, it was as if they were alone in the carriage. This was it. Her last chance to refuse him. To cling to her sanity, perhaps, and to the safe but empty life she had lived for so long.

Lord and Lady Sharpe, too, were looking at her, awaiting her answer.

Camille closed her eyes. No, it was too late, she realized, to refuse. Not because of what they had done tonight. She wished it could be so simple as that. But no, it was too late because of how he made her feel. Because he was what she wanted. God help her, *he was what she wanted.*

Fool. Fool. Oh, what a fool she was.

Camille opened her eyes, and drew a deep breath. *"Oui, monsieur,"* she said, her voice amazingly steady. "I should be honored to marry you tomorrow."

CHAPTER SIX
IN WHICH ROTHEWELL TASTES
WEDDED BLISS

In the end, Rothewell and his bride stood up to speak their vows in the late afternoon before a blazing fire in Lord and Lady Sharpe's withdrawing room, with only Xanthia and her husband in attendance. It was an unusual time of day for a wedding, but it was a wedding under unusual circumstances.

Lady Sharpe, however, did her best to maintain a celebratory air. With only a few hours' preparation, and despite a miserable cold snap which brought gray skies and a whipping wind, the good lady had decorated the room with springlike bouquets of white lilies and sprays of fresh greenery, and laid out a cold supper which would have done a sultan proud.

Camille, however, barely saw the flowers. Despite her outward calm in the carriage, she had passed a sleepless night, her mind going over and over everything which had passed between Rothewell and her in the library. This marriage was not to be the mere formality she had wished to believe it. This was a holy sacrament. Already she had given this man her body, and even as she stood before the priest and the blazing fire, surrounded by the dizzying scent of the lilies, she was frightened by the depth of her reaction to him.

She felt as if she were stepping off the edge of a precipice, and into a black, unknowable void. Involuntarily — and perhaps absurdly — Camille's nails dug into the wool of Rothewell's coat sleeve.

The priest opened the prayer book, and began to read. *"Dearly beloved, we are gathered here . . ."*

The words quickly faded from Camille's consciousness in a buzz of sound and a blur of light. She had to remind herself to breathe.

Rothewell, perhaps sensing her discomfort, laid his hand over hers and drew her nearer. The gesture oddly strengthened her and stopped her knees from shaking. She managed to murmur her vows, and when Rothewell whispered, "Give me your hand," she responded mechanically, then watched in mute amazement as he slid a band of bloodred rubies onto her finger.

"Send thy blessing upon these thy servants, this man and this woman, whom we bless in thy Name," intoned the priest, *"that, as Isaac and Rebecca lived faithfully together, so these persons may surely perform and keep the vow and covenant betwixt them made, and may ever remain in perfect love and peace together, and live according to thy laws; through Jesus Christ our Lord. Amen."*

In perfect love and peace together. Camille closed her eyes and let the gravity of the words sink in.

But was there to be either love or peace for her? She had given herself to this man; this dark, seemingly dangerous man whom she still did not know. And would likely never know.

When the blessing was finished, Rothewell's hand fell away. Camille watched as the stones twinkled and blurred before her, and realized in some embarrassment that she was on the verge of tears.

The final prayer followed, then Camille was caught in the crush of one embrace after another.

Two hours later, after having been kissed and toasted and set to blushing more times than she could count, Camille sat shivering in Rothewell's carriage, waving good-bye to her new sister and to her kind and generous hostess. Despite the unseasonable cold, Lady Sharpe stood upon the top step, fluttering a lace handkerchief as the horses clopped away. Camille's time of sanctuary was at an end.

"Well, Camille," said her husband in his low, rumbling voice, "we have done it."

Camille drew a steadying breath. "*Oui*, we have done it," she echoed. She prayed to God that neither of them regretted it.

He spoke not another syllable during their short journey through Mayfair. It was to be, she suspected, the first of many silences their marriage would endure. Rothewell was a man of few words.

By the time they reached the house in Berkeley Square, dusk had settled over London. The air was sharp, and once again thick with the metallic tang of coal, which burned in the hearth of nearly every drawing room and coffeehouse in London. They entered the shadowy portals to be greeted by the same butler whom Camille had seen standing on the top step the previous evening.

Rothewell introduced the servant as Trammel. Inside the broad, unadorned entry hall, the air was laced with some exotic, spicy scent. The only ornament, a fine Persian carpet in shades of red and gold, rolled down the passageway and up the stairs. The butler bowed and welcomed her warmly, then threw open the doors to a large if somewhat austere drawing room.

"Given the dreadful chill," he said, "I thought my lady might wish tea?"

"Or something stronger, perhaps?" Rothewell suggested. "My new wife has something of a backbone, Trammel, when it comes to wine and spirits. And if I recall, she prefers claret."

"Merci," said Camille, surprised that he had remembered — or even noticed. "Any sort of strong red wine would be most welcome."

Trammel made a gesture to a waiting footman, then motioned them into the room. Inside, a low fire burned in the grate, but as Camille's eyes adjusted to the light, something small came hurtling off the sofa. The creature skidded to a halt at Trammel's feet, its tongue lolling cheerfully out.

"What the hell is that?" said Rothewell, frozen.

"Oh, yes," said Trammel as the tiny creature danced about their feet. "This is Chin-Chin, my lord."

"The devil!" said Rothewell.

"Bonté divine!" declared Camille, her anxieties instantly forgotten. "Is he a cat?"

244

"Yip! Yip!" said the creature, as if insulted.

"He is a dog, ma'am," said the butler. "Some sort of Asian spaniel, I'm told."

"A *dog* — ?" Rothewell looked down dubiously. "We've got rats in the alley twice his size. What is he doing here anyway?"

Trammel drew himself up an inch. "You said, sir, to get a dog," he replied as Camille and Rothewell settled by the fire. "Yesterday afternoon, in fact."

"The devil!" said Rothewell again. He sat down, wincing a little as if in pain. Camille said nothing — it would have done little good — but made a mental note to keep a watchful eye on him.

The little creature, however, held no such reservation. He leapt onto the settee beside Rothewell and set his chin upon his fore-paws. His hindquarters, however, remained in the air, his backward, fanlike tail waving madly.

Camille leaned over to stroke him. "*Bonjour,* Chin-Chin," she cooed. *"T'es trop mignon!"*

"Where, pray, did he come from?" asked Rothewell. "Wherever it was, by God, he's going back tomorrow."

"Alas, my lord, Chin-Chin is homeless," Trammel intoned. "He has nowhere *to* go."

"Homeless, my arse," said Rothewell, glaring down at the tiny black-and-white fluff ball. "He's fat as a Christmas goose, and freshly brushed. Now where the devil did you get him?"

Trammel sighed as if put upon. "Across the square at Mrs. Rutner's — excuse me, *Lady Tweedale's* — house," he said. "The late Mr. Rutner brought him back from a trading venture in Malaya. But Lord Tweedale took a dislike to the poor mite after their marriage and threw him out. Said he'd rather have a bulldog."

Rothewell made a sound of disgust. "Well, with a name like Tweedale, he can't afford to take any chances, can he?" he said. "If I were Mrs. Rutner, I'd send him packing and keep the dog."

"Mon Dieu," murmured Camille, picking up the little spaniel and tucking him beneath her chin. "What sort of person gives up a pet to appease a tyrant?"

Rothewell snorted. "A spineless one," he said.

"But you are trying to give yours away, sir," said the butler, drawing the tea table nearer to Camille.

"Damn it, Trammel, *it isn't my dog.*"

Further argument was forestalled by the reappearance of the footman carrying a galleried silver tray with a decanter of ruby-colored wine and two glasses. Just then, the spaniel leapt from Camille's lap back onto Rothewell's settee. The little dog circled twice, then flopped down against Rothewell's well-muscled thigh with a satisfied grunt. Clearly, he had chosen his new master — and did not appear to be mourning the inconstant and cowardly Lady Tweedale.

Camille smiled and poured the wine.

An hour later, Trammel returned to inform Camille that her trunks had arrived. Camille refused the butler's offer of a late meal, and Rothewell surprised her by following suit. It struck her as odd that such a man would have no appetite.

After a brief stroll through the lower floors of the house, they retired a little awkwardly upstairs. Rothewell's bedchamber, Camille noted, was a study in asceticism. No carpets or bed hangings adorned the room, which was neither large nor grand. The bed, however, was a massive mahogany affair with tropical carvings on the towering bedposts, and it had not, she was sure, originated in England. The counterpane was woven of heavy, cream-colored cotton, and the windows were hung with similarly colored draperies. On the whole, the room was colorless, but Camille found it oddly soothing. Perhaps that was the intent.

Trammel helped Rothewell remove his coat, then rang the bellpull. "I fear the chambermaids are not quite ready for you," he said to Camille. "We turned out the adjoining room this morning when we learnt of the wedding."

So she had been expected. She had half feared that Rothewell might treat his staff with the same detachment he apparently treated marriage; something to be thought about — or mentioned — on a whim.

At that thought, shame flooded over her. Was she any better than Rothewell? Had she not set out to marry someone — anyone, really? Indeed, she had offered herself to him the very first night they'd met in exchange for marriage. She had wanted a husband, to escape Valigny and her cold, hollow existence. Whatever came of it now was as much her fault as anyone's. And if she gave her heart to this man, that, too, would be her fault.

The room which was to be her bedchamber was directly connected to Rothewell's, with neither a dressing room nor a sitting room as a buffer. At the entrance, she hesitated and sniffed suspiciously.

"Fresh paint, ma'am," said Trammel. "I

apologize. The door was just put in last week."

Camille stepped back and looked at it, curious. "Was it?"

"There were no connecting bedchambers in the house," the butler went on as they entered a lighter, much larger room. "His lordship wished you to have the main bedchamber. He has taken the smaller."

Yes, expected indeed. So much for her theory about Rothewell's detachment. He had given her his bedchamber? Oh, how she wished that he had not.

Inside, the furnishings were similar to those she had already seen, but the bed was smaller and more delicately made, and the room contained a writing desk and a brocade settee. All the lamps were lit, and two maids were in the process of rolling out the carpets and rehanging the draperies. They were inordinately curious, and kept cutting sidelong glances in her direction when they thought she was not looking.

As to the room, she could not fault Rothewell's servants. It smelled clean and well aired, and she saw not a trace of dust anywhere. Her trunks sat by the dressing-room door, one of them open to reveal her carefully folded nightclothes.

"I have sent for hot water, my lady," said

Trammel, returning to Rothewell's door. "Your maid is in the kitchen having a late supper. Shall I send her to assist you?"

"*Non,* not tonight, *merci.*" Camille looked about the vast room, feeling vaguely lost. "Tell Emily to retire for the evening. We can see to all this unpacking tomorrow."

When the water arrived, and the last of the maids departed, Camille locked the door so that she might bathe and brush out her hair. As she removed the evening's finery, she was surprised by the weariness which overtook her. Her bones seemed to ache with the weight of it.

The water was blessedly hot, the soap a good French-milled cake scented mildly of almonds. She splashed her face, then methodically washed. But when she noted the slight tenderness between her legs, it sent her hurtling back to that one instant of pain when Rothewell had claimed her. The scent of him. The heat. His strength as he had lifted her against the wall, impaling her. Camille shivered. It seemed a lifetime ago, instead of mere hours.

She closed her eyes, and set her hands on the edge of the washstand to steady herself. The evening — all of it — seemed like a dream to her now.

But it was not a dream. Camille shook off

the feeling and turned to stand before the cheval glass. Slowly, she let her gaze run down her length. So this was the woman Lord Rothewell had wed. The woman he had made love to last night. Passionate, impetuous love — and in the wickedest of ways, too.

Pictured thus, she did not look like the sort of woman who would stir a man to such lust. Indeed, she looked small and thin. One would have imagined him with someone more voluptuous. More exciting and experienced.

But he had chosen to marry her. And not for her money, it now seemed. And not for love. That left only kindness, so far as she could see, and Rothewell was not a kind man. If ever he had been, something had wrung it from his heart, or so he wished people to believe.

She sighed, then drew on her nightclothes and began to put out the lamps. Would Rothewell come to her bed tonight, she wondered? Or invite her to his? She would agree, of course. In part, because it was her duty. And because she wanted a child so desperately. But there was another, deeper, more frightening reason.

She did not have to wonder at it long. As she passed by the connecting door, there was a soft knock. The door swung open to reveal her husband silhouetted in the lamp-light, his broad shoulders and height filling the doorway. He wore a dark silk dressing gown and, it appeared, little else.

When he held out his hand, it seemed the most natural thing in the world to take it. It was a warm hand, callused in places, and still hard with masculine strength. Wordlessly, he drew her into the room.

Trammel was gone, and the lamp by his bed was turned down to a mere flicker. A half-empty glass of brandy sat upon his night table, and the glow from the hearth cast a warm sheen over the room.

"Ah," she murmured, glancing at the foot of the bed. "I see you have a happy bed-mate."

"Not for long." Rothewell tossed a disparaging glance down at the dog.

Chin-Chin gave a huge yawn, then snapped his mouth shut and wriggled deeper into the bedcovers.

Rothewell scowled. "Look at the little beggar," he said. "He acts as if he owns the bloody place."

"What do you mean to do with him?"

"Tomorrow, I'll take him back across the square, I daresay, and put the fear of God in Tweedale."

As if he understood English, Chin-Chin slunk off the bed with a resentful glance and went to the hearth rug, stretching himself out before the fire.

Camille laughed and squeezed his hand. "Will you indeed?" she said. "I am not at all sure he means to go."

Suddenly, Rothewell closed his eyes, and dropped his voice. "I hope, Camille, that you will not regret this," he rasped. "I hope that I have done the right thing."

He was not talking about the dog, and his uncertainty strangely touched her. Camille stared into the fire, once again wishing he would revert to the arrogant, drunken rake she had first met in her father's parlor.

"You have done only that which I asked you to do from the very first," she admitted.

Some nameless emotion flared in his eyes when he opened them. "I may have occasion to remind you of that, my dear."

Camille lifted one shoulder. "If there are regrets, whom can I blame save myself?"

For the first time that she could recall, he looked away. Several minutes passed before he spoke again. "In the library last night," he finally said, his voice hoarse, "had I exercised a little restraint, this sudden marriage would not have been necessary."

"I believe, *monsieur,* that there were two

of us in that library," she said a little tartly. "Do not suggest to me that I had no choice. I know what my choices are, and I make them as it suits me."

Rothewell glanced down at their clasped hands. "Until last night, Camille, I . . . I was toying with the ungentlemanly notion of backing out of this betrothal. Would you have let me?"

"*Oui, bien sûr,*" she said. "But not gladly."

"Pamela would have helped you," he said. "Had either of us asked, she would have thought of something. She has grown fond of you. In her heart, she does not wish to see you tied to me."

"But she is your cousin, *monsieur,*" Camille answered. "How could she not wish it?"

"Because Pamela knows the kind of husband I'll be," said Rothewell. "A bad one. But you already know that, do you not? You don't expect much out of me, so you won't be disappointed, I daresay."

"I have few expectations, my lord," she said quietly. "And you know what they are."

He looked at her with something like sorrow in his eyes, and to her surprise, his hands came up to gently cradle her face. "You will not . . . develop any foolish, feminine attachments to me, will you, Camille?" he murmured. "You are too wise for that, I think."

"*Oui,*" she said softly, dropping her gaze. "I am too wise."

Camille shifted to move away, but he surprised her by drawing her into his arms. "All our regrets and bad luck aside, we *are* married," he said. "And it has been a long day for us both, I think. For a few hours, let us pretend that life, perhaps, holds a little more hope than we think. That happiness can be a real and tangible thing — even for the likes of such jaded folks as us."

When Camille made no answer, he kissed her lightly, then threaded one hand through her hair. "Such glory," he murmured, pulling back to look at her.

"*Pardon?*" she whispered.

He smiled, a rare thing. "Your hair," he murmured. "Since the moment I laid eyes on you, I have wanted to see it down." Again, he slid his fingers through it. "Like black silk, hanging to your waist. Will you promise me something, Camille?"

She swallowed hard. "I . . . *oui,* perhaps. What do you wish?"

He brushed his mouth over the apple of her cheek. "I wish, Camille, that so long as I live, you will never cut it," he said. "Will you promise me that? Is it too great a thing for a husband to ask?"

She found his choice of words a little odd. "It — It is not such a great thing," she admitted. "*Oui,* if it matters to you."

As if pleased by her agreement, Rothewell pulled her into his arms and kissed her gently with only his lips, but thoroughly, as if they had all the time in the world. Yet Camille could think only of how she had felt with her body joined to his last night. Of the passion and almost uncontrollable yearning which had burnt inside her. She came against him stiffly, hesitantly, wondering how on earth she was to give this man her body whilst holding on to her heart.

"Open your mouth, Camille," he whispered against her lips.

He pressed her body closer, and a shudder of suppressed lust ran through her. She opened her lips beneath his, reveling in the feel of his tongue slowly thrusting into her mouth. He slid deep, tasting her, plumbing the depths of her mouth and her soul until finally, Camille felt herself surrender. She rose onto her toes, melting to him, her breasts pressed high against the silk of his dressing gown.

With her eyes drowsy slits, the lamp and the firelight seemed to twinkle in an otherworldly blur, much as her wedding ring had done. Rothewell's hand was on her buttock, slowly circling, urging her hips to his. In mere moments, she felt lost — lost to all good sense, filled only with warmth and need and sensation.

He broke off the kiss on a groan, his nostrils wide. His hands went to the tie of her wrapper, drew it impatiently free, and pushed the garment from her shoulders. Her remaining clothes soon followed, and then she stood before him, her body as bare as her soul. The chill of the room drifted over her, making her nipples harden and her cheeks flood with color.

Rothewell's eyes slid down her length, hot and hungry. "You are so lovely," he rasped. "I want you, Camille. I want you in my bed tonight."

She turned, drew back the covers, and lay down.

His gaze raked over her again, his eyes flaring appreciatively. He loosened the tie of his dressing gown and let it slither to the floor. Camille almost gasped aloud when she saw him fully naked. Rothewell was quite shockingly male, even to one who had often seen the masculine nude in painting and sculpture. Despite the width of his shoulders, he was sleek and muscled like a cat, his waist almost impossibly lean. His chest was solid, and his arms were not those of some idle nobleman, but those of a man who had known hard work.

Rothewell's thighs were thick, and lightly dusted with hair, and between them his manhood hung firm and almost disconcertingly large. As if to shield it from her view, he set one knee to the bed, and crawled over her, again clasping her face almost tenderly between his hands as he kissed her deep.

"Do you want me, Camille?" he whispered when he broke the kiss. "Do you want . . . this?"

She looked away. "You can make me want it," she whispered.

He slid a finger beneath her chin and gently turned her face back to his. "You are a passionate woman, yes," he said. "There is no shame in that, Camille. No weakness. Is that what you think?"

Camille did not wish to think at all. And so she did the one thing sure to distract him. She closed her eyes and pulled his face to hers, kissing him deeply.

For long moments there was nothing but the sound of their growing passion in the gloom. Rothewell made love to her with his mouth, and with his hands, gently and unerringly. She sighed beneath him. With his careful skill, he drove her sighs and her hunger to a fevered pitch.

His ravening mouth sought her breast, his eyes closing in a sweep of thick black lashes across his cheeks. As if he meant to madden her, Rothewell suckled at her nipple until it drew into a hard, aching peak. Until the dark desire began to twist through her body again, tugging at her womb in that sweet, familiar way. His lips slid softly to her breastbone, his tongue coming out to draw a sweet, simmering trail of heat all the way down to her navel. There, he kissed her, licking it lightly then delving inside until she shuddered.

At that, he made a sound of pleasure deep in his throat and let his hands slide round to her buttocks. With one knee, he gently urged her legs wider. When she obeyed his command, he let the weight of his erection ease through her warm, slick folds, just grazing the sweet spot he had tormented last night.

"Oui, oui," she whispered, her head thrashing a little on the pillow.

He entered her a little roughly. Camille sucked in her breath through her teeth, but the feeling was one of both pleasure and pain.

"Good God," he rasped. "Forgive me."

"I want this," she whispered. "Oh. Do not

stop." Her hands had gone to the hard muscles of his hips, her fingers digging deep. Her wetness was audible now, almost embarrassingly so.

Rothewell lifted his weight from her body, his heavy black hair falling forward, casting his face in deep shadow as he drew back and entered her again. "Ah, Camille!" he cried. "Oh, sweet."

He captured her hands in his, pushing them high above her head, then thrust again, the muscles of his throat and his belly going taut. It was a perfect rhythm of pleasure. Her need circled higher and higher, his every stroke pushing her toward that delicious, frightening edge.

He made love to her, it felt, with every element of his being; loved her until her breath came sharp in the night, and she was crying out for him. Vowing her need — and perhaps even more than that. The intensity spiraled inside her. She wanted to feel, not think. Not to doubt herself or to doubt this.

His driving thrusts pushed her closer and closer. The heat and scent of his body enveloped her. His breathing grew rough. His strokes deepened. She let her head arch back against the pillow again, let herself go to him without reservation. When she came, it was not the flash of brilliance and heat of the previous evening, but a tender, languid slide into the abyss. Her soul, it seemed, flew to him, and he went with her over the edge, crying her name.

When Camille returned to the present, Rothewell still lay atop her, the breath heaving in and out of his chest. She whimpered when his lips moved down her throat, the stubble of his dark beard lightly scrubbing her tingling skin. She felt alive, as if for the first time. As if the whole of her life — the waiting and oftentimes, yes, the loneliness, had been but a preamble to this. To this . . . sheer and utter joy.

When Rothewell lifted his head and looked at her, some inscrutable emotion still burned in his eyes. His hand, when he lifted it, shook. It was not her imagination. He cradled her cheek, kissed her again, then rolled to one side, drawing her protectively to him, burying his face in the tangle of her hair.

A part of her knew, even then, that this was a time out of place. A moment of fantasy and otherworldly joy. But her heart was raw, her mind not yet ready to return to the grim certitudes of her existence. Not yet ready to consider the folly of what she was allowing to happen. So Camille let herself imagine that happiness was a real and tangible thing. That her husband loved her. And that she had married him for a reason which went beyond her own selfishness.

CHAPTER SEVEN
A SLIPPERY SLOPE

Rothewell awoke sometime near dawn to the sound of his house bumping and clanging to life. Today, for once, he found it vaguely comforting instead of annoying. He rolled up onto his elbow and listened. Grates were being cleaned, coal hauled in, drapes drawn, and the upper servants were hastening along the corridors, stepping lightly as they passed his door. Rothewell was not known for his good humor when his sleep was disturbed after a hard night.

A hard night. He dropped his gaze to the woman who lay beside him, and a harsher reality returned. Camille Marchand — *Lady Rothewell* — lay on her side, one hand curled into his bedsheet, her dark hair spread out like a fan of black silk across his pillow. Even as his desire for her began to build again, he considered his folly. He had vowed to be strong — for her sake and for his. And then, inexplicably, something had happened last night. He had *allowed* something to happen. To change.

On that thought, Rothewell collapsed back into bed and dragged an arm across his eyes to shut out the muted daylight. It was the beast, perhaps, weakening him. But good Lord, he was not some besotted fool — and he did neither himself nor Camille any favors by behaving as if he were. It was just sex with a beautiful woman, he reminded himself. It could be no more than that. And yet, the depth of his feelings last night, seen in the bright light of day, were just a little chilling.

Camille. *Camille.* He had no wish to break her heart — but there was no denying he had lost a little of himself last night, and no one was more shaken by that than he was.

It was strange to awaken to find her in his bed. And the dog, if one could even call it that, was now asleep by her feet. Good God, how had this all happened? His home had heretofore been an impermeable fortress. He did not entertain, or invite anyone to so much as pay a morning call. And now someone was inside his walls to stay. That was all very well; after all, he had agreed to marry her. But *sleeping* with her — sharing a bed for something other than sex — today that felt like a dangerous and sentimental business. It would not happen again. And the dog — Jim-Jim, or whatever the hell it was called — was going back to Tweedale's before breakfast.

The frustration did not stop him from rolling over, however, and allowing himself the pleasure of looking at Camille. Her face held the soft blush of sleep. Her lips were slightly parted, and she looked far younger than her twenty-seven years.

Rothewell was beginning to fear his wife mightn't be as hard-hearted as she let on. That might prove unfortunate. He did not want anyone's sympathy, or to be mollycoddled. He did not want the girl growing attached to him. He hoped he could give her a child, yes. But he still rued the day he had laid eyes on that lively little bundle of Pamela's. Perhaps it had been his grim mood at the time, but in that moment, something inside him had caught — or torn? — no, *altered.* That was the word he wanted.

The babe had been so beautiful. So full of life. A real person, wholly fleshed out, with his own will and determination. He had been the embodiment of hope and light and innocence; things heretofore unknown to Rothewell. And now this woman . . . this beautiful woman . . . Good Lord, he was going soft.

He listened to the sound of someone sweeping in the passageway beyond his door, and wondered if he could make love to her again this morning — but without losing his head.

He did not have long to wonder. When he glanced at her again, Camille was looking up at him, wide-awake, her eyes roaming over his face. Searching, he thought, for something.

"Good morning," he murmured. And then, after a few long and lingering kisses, he turned her onto her back and mounted her. He was not ungentle — no, he would never be that, he vowed. But he held himself a little apart from her as he coaxed her and entered her, and yes, even as she spasmed, and cried out beneath him, though it cost him dearly to do so.

Long moments later, when his business was finished and she lay limp and sated, Rothewell rolled away, feeling suddenly irritated with the world. Why? His body was spent. His hunger well slaked.

Camille must have sensed something was wrong. "Rothewell?" She reached out and laid a warm, soft hand upon his chest.

Gingerly, he pulled back the covers and sat up on the edge of the bed, his elbows on his knees.

He realized at once he should have drawn on his dressing gown. He could feel the heat of her gaze trailing over his back, could hear her faint gasp. Hell, he could hear the unasked question upon her lips. And when she reached out to touch him, her fingers tracing lightly over the web of scars, he did not even flinch.

"Rothewell?" she said again, her voice wavering.

Good Lord. Not now, on top of all else. He turned and forced a grim smile. "What?"

She pushed up a little awkwardly, her dark eyes solemn as they regarded him. "You are well?"

"Well enough, I daresay," he answered.

Her gaze trailed over him, her mind forming the words. "Your . . . Your back," she finally said. "The scars — they are . . . *mon Dieu,* I don't know what they are."

He felt his faint smile turn to a sneer. "I was a recalcitrant youth," he answered. "Spare the rod and spoil the child."

She looked at him unflinchingly, and yet he could see the pity in her eyes. "I do not think this was a rod," she said, setting one hand to the small of his back.

"No, it was whatever my uncle had closest to hand," he said. "A sapling branch, a horsewhip, his cane. He had a wide appreciation of all things flagellatory."

"How can you speak so lightly of it?"

Impatiently, he rose and snatched his drawers from the chair over which he'd tossed them the preceding night. The dog leapt down from the chair he'd retreated to and came to join him.

"It wasn't meant to be light, my dear," he said, hitching up his drawers. "It was my uncle's philosophy — a philosophy that extended to anyone or anything in his path. If you think this looks bad, you should have seen his slaves. Or my brother."

Camille watched him — her husband — jerking on his clothes, and wondered what she had said to frustrate him. When his trousers were hitched up over his lean hips, Rothewell turned to face her. He seemed different this morning. Distant once again.

"I'm going to Tattersall's this morning with Warneham and Nash," he said, scrubbing his hand round a day's worth of dark beard stubble. "Tell Trammel to introduce you to the staff."

Camille tried not to feel disappointment. Rothewell had not misled her into thinking this was anything other than a marriage of convenience. And the passion last night had been . . . well, just a physical release for him, no doubt. The realization was a little lower-ing. This morning . . . ah, that had been more what she'd expected of him.

"*Très bien,*" she murmured.

He bent down and scooped up the dog, then dropped him on the bed beside her. "Have someone see to him, will you?" The words were not curt, but merely emotion-less. "He'll want . . . walking and feeding and such, I suppose."

"*Oui, bien sûr.*" Shutting away the hurt, Ca-mille folded back the bedcovers and rose. She pulled on her nightdress and wrapper, then went to the windows and began to draw the draperies. "When may we expect you back?"

"I don't know." His voice was emotion-less. "I keep late hours. If you will excuse me, I shall ring for my bathwater now."

She shrugged and started toward her bed-chamber door. It was his loss if he wished to be an ass this morning. But as she crossed the room, something by his wash-basin caught her eye. She glanced over her shoulder. Trammel had come in at once and stood listening to Rothewell. Camille went to the washstand, picked up the small towel which lay there, and turned it to the morn-ing light. For an instant, she could not get her breath.

Blood. There was no mistaking it. Spatters of pinkish, watery blood, not a bright red streak from a shaving cut. Moreover, one look at Rothewell would confirm that he had not recently shaved.

Camille was not perfectly sure how long she stared at the bloodstains, but when she looked up, Rothewell was staring at her. He looked . . . not angry, but a little querulous, perhaps. As if he were challenging her to make something of it. Camille lifted her chin, and considered it.

No, she would not give him the satisfaction of an argument. It was probably nothing, and in his present mood, he might well tell her to mind her own business. She laid the towel back down, then opened the connecting door. Just then, she heard Rothewell utter a vile curse. She turned around to see that Chin-Chin had cocked his leg over one of his new master's evening slippers.

With an inward smile, Camille left. She was almost relieved to see her maid standing by the dressing-room door, a pile of stockings in her hands. "*Bonjour,* Emily."

"Oh!" said the maid, a little taken aback. "It's just you, miss. I thought . . . dear me, I don't know what I thought."

Camille managed to smile as she slipped off her wrapper. She tried not to think of the blood; tried not to think of the many things it might mean. "It's all right, Emily," she said. "We will get used to living here, I daresay."

Emily cut a strange look in her direction. "Yes, miss — I mean, my lady," she answered.

"Everyone has treated you well so far?" Camille enquired.

Emily nodded. "Of course, I've met but a few — the kitchen maids, the footmen who carried up our trunks, and the butler — but he doesn't look like any butler I've ever seen."

Camille went to her windows, and stared down into the square. "Mr. Trammel is from Barbados," she said. "The cook is his wife, according to Lady Nash. I am sure they are excellent at their jobs." Otherwise, Camille silently added, they would not have long survived in Rothewell's employ.

"Well." Emily brightened. "Will you be wanting your bathwater, miss?"

"I suppose," said Camille. She had begun to chew absently on her thumbnail. "Yes, bathwater. And then the blue muslin day dress? I think it's time I dressed, and went down to meet the staff myself."

In a fit of stubbornness, Rothewell decided

to walk down to Hyde Park Corner, eschewing Trammel's advice that he not only stay in, but that he *put his feet up!* Rothewell would be damned before he'd do the latter, and with Camille in the house, he was not sure he could bear to do the former. He had already seen one too many questions in her beautiful brown eyes, and he'd no intention of answering any of them. Thank God she had slept through the brief, bad turn he'd taken in the wee hours of the night.

Contrary to Trammel's grim prognostication, the walk did not kill Rothewell, nor did London's morning air — contrary to his own long-held suspicion. Instead, it did a vast deal to clear his head. Going to bed before dawn perhaps had its benefits, though he did not plan to make a habit of it. Indeed, he rather doubted he'd see dinnertime sober, or his bed much before cockcrow, provided the beast did not come crawling back out to gnaw at him tonight.

Yes, in marriage, he had decided, it was best to begin as one meant to go on. There was no point in giving Camille the idea that theirs would be a normal union of husband and wife — not that she necessarily would care — and no point in allowing himself to feel regret. A man got whatever time God allotted him, and developing hindsight or hope too late in one's life would only make matters worse. To Rothewell's way of thinking, you made your bed — or your grave — and you lay in it without complaint.

Rothewell turned down the narrow lane to Tattersall's and found his friends in the Jockey Club's subscription room poring over the descriptions of the horses to be auctioned that day. Tattersall's was London's premier auction venue for bloodstock, and all of London's most raffish turfites passed regularly through their doors. Lord Nash had been practically enshrined there.

Today, Nash's booted legs were languidly crossed, his dark head bent to Gareth's lighter one, both men wholly absorbed in their task. For a moment, Rothewell considered not interrupting. He was glad the two had come to be friends. There had been a time he feared it mightn't be possible, for both men had once been in love with his sister Xanthia. But the dark and dashing Lord Nash had won out.

For his part, Gareth was now the Duke of Warneham, and but a few weeks' married himself. And only in seeing Gareth as he was now — in love and happy — did Rothewell realize how desperately *unhappy* the poor devil had been for all those years which had come before.

For many years, they had lived almost like a family; he, Xanthia, and Gareth, united by their miserable childhoods and a general mistrust of nearly everyone else. And yet Gareth had always kept a part of himself *to* himself. The change in him was truly revealing.

Just then, Gareth looked up and smiled as a shaft of morning sun caught his golden locks. He was considered by the ladies to be a remarkably handsome man, Rothewell knew, and today he looked almost like Gabriel come down to earth. But he still swore like the wharf rat he was. "Damn me if it isn't the devil himself!" he said. "And up before noon, at that."

"Good morning, gentlemen."

"Rothewell!" said Nash jovially. "Do join us. I was just about to bankrupt myself."

Rothewell crossed the room, propped his walking stick against a nearby table, and sat down. "Don't let me stop you, old fellow," he said. "My sister can afford to keep you up in a pretty grand style, I daresay."

"Yes, I know." Nash grinned, showing his very white teeth. "Isn't marriage a fine institution?"

"He has no idea," said Gareth, laughing. "Not *yet.*"

"Actually, I am now qualified to render an

274

opinion on that lofty subject," said Rothewell, looking about for a servant. "Have you
any coffee round here, Nash?" he asked. "I
could do with a pot."

Nash motioned to no one in particular,
and three of the lackeys dashed off to do his
bidding. Then he centered his gaze on
Rothewell. "Now," he said quietly, "about
that first part, old boy. I think you must tell
Warneham your news, for I have not."

Gareth leaned forward in his chair. "Kieran, what have you done?"

"I was married," he said. "Late yesterday."

The golden-haired duke fell silent. "Ah,"
he finally said. "There was some issue with
— er, the lady's honor?"

Rothewell shook his head. "No, not precisely."

"Well, either there *was* or there *wasn't*,
Kieran," said Gareth. "There's nothing
imprecise about it. But keep your counsel,
please. Just tell us what we're to tell people."

"That we decided life was short," he
answered. "And that there was no point in
waiting to do that which we'd planned to
do anyway." It was a surprisingly honest
answer, if not a complete one.

Gareth fell back into his chair. Neither he
nor Nash had believed he meant to do it at
all. He could see that now.

"Yes, well," said Gareth. "Well, we wish you very happy, I'm sure. And Lady Rothewell?"

"What about her?" asked Rothewell.

"We wish her happy as well," he hedged. "Do you think . . . Kieran, do you think she *will* be? I don't mean to give advice, but —"

"Then don't," Rothewell interjected. "Camille has what she asked for. We will rub along well enough, I daresay."

A servant appeared with a tray carrying the coffee and set it down between them. Nash poured, his gaze focused on the spouting coffee as he spoke. "Sometimes, Rothewell, women deserve just a little more than they ask for," he said pensively. "Those are the rare ones, I'll grant you. Still, one might give it some thought?"

Rothewell took the proffered cup. "Like fidelity and love?" he suggested. "Or jewels and gowns? The latter she may have as it pleases her."

"And the former?" Nash asked.

Rothewell sipped at his coffee. "It is not in my nature," he answered. "If it ever was, it long ago deserted me."

Gareth made a dismissive sound. "Balderdash!" he said. "This is a second chance for you, Kieran. She is a lovely and gracious girl. You could make her fall in love with you, you know — and love her in return if you would just let sleeping dogs lie."

His coffee cup half-raised, Rothewell turned to face him. "Now why is it, Gareth, that I suspect you are just about to roust up those sleeping dogs?" His voice was cold. "I do not presume to give you advice, and I will thank you to do the same for me."

But Gareth's expression had stiffened in a way which Rothewell knew meant trouble. "Sometimes, Kieran, you are a bloody damned idiot," he said, his voice low and a little angry. "You are still grieving over a woman who was never worthy of your grief. You were just a boy, and Annemarie played you for a grass green fool. Face it, Kieran. She got precisely what she wanted in the end — *and it wasn't you.*"

Rothewell set down his coffee with an awkward clatter. "No, Gareth, what she got in the end was a fiery grave," he said. "She and my brother both. Somehow, I am not sure that was what she had in mind when she married him."

Nash held up both hands, palms out. "All right, I am well out of this," he said. "I just came to buy a racehorse, then slink quietly home with my pockets empty and my mouth shut."

But Rothewell was still staring darkly at

his old friend. Abruptly, he shoved back his chair. "Nash, I wish you every success," he said, his voice gruff. "As for me, I am off."

Gareth jerked to his feet. "Where the devil are you going?"

Rothewell picked up his walking stick. "Far away," he snapped. "I've a sudden fancy for a hand of cards, a bottle of brandy, and a plump, promiscuous woman who'll fuck me blind."

Even Nash's eyebrows went up. "A little too soon for that, isn't it, old chap?"

Rothewell made no answer, and headed for the door.

Behind him, a second chair scraped. "That man is a damned fool," he heard Gareth say. "I had best go with him."

Rothewell whipped round to tell Gareth to go bugger himself, but in such haste that he did not see the gentleman who had just pushed through the door. They collided squarely, Rothewell nearly tripping over his feet.

"*Bonjour,* my Lord Rothewell!" The Comte de Valigny backed up and made a pretense of dusting himself off. "By the way, I hear I missed the wedding!"

Rothewell was fleetingly speechless. "You!" he finally managed.

Valigny set his head to one side. "*Mais non,*

not buyer's remorse already!" he said. "She is a handful, my *petit chou, n'est-ce pas?* Worry not. You will be broken to the plow soon enough, *mon ami.*"

Rothewell shoved his way through the door, followed by the sound of the comte's pealing laughter.

Camille went belowstairs with a mix of curiosity and trepidation. In France, the chateau staff had consisted of a handful of aged retainers who had been there forever, and who were officially in the employ of Valigny's uncle. They had regarded Camille and her mother almost as guests who had overstayed their welcome. The keeping of a budget, however, Camille well understood, for the managing of such things had fallen to her at a young age, and there had been very little money. Economy and careful accounting had been necessary.

She found Mrs. Trammel in the kitchen tongue-lashing the scullery maid and holding a lethal-looking carving knife in her hand. The cook was a tall, lithe woman of indeterminate age, with sharp, high cheekbones and ebony skin which was far darker than her husband's. She spoke with a musical lilt unfamiliar to Camille, and wore a white scarf over her braided hair and small gold hoops, which swung from her earlobes. Her every move spoke of confidence, and the kitchen staff stood well back when she passed.

Camille stiffened her spine, marched in, and introduced herself.

"You may call me Miss Obelienne, *madame*," she said when they were ensconced in her private sitting room. "Would you like a cup of tea?"

"*Merci*," said Camille. "That would be lovely."

Miss Obelienne bowed and went out again, only to return with a kettle which was already hot. The tea, which was kept in an earthenware jar upon her worktable, smelled of herbs and flowers. Whilst it steeped, Obelienne cut slices of what looked like a cake without frosting, dusted with coconut.

Camille picked at the cake, and sipped tentatively at the exotic brew whilst they discussed the running of the house. Two upstairs maids, she was told, handled the routine housework. The kitchen staff numbered four, the footmen three, and the stable staff another four.

"*Alors*, there is no housekeeper?"

Miss Obelienne shook her head. "She gave notice a fortnight past. The master, he is

hard to live with when one is not accustomed to his ways. It is as well. She was not
needed."

Camille was surprised when the cook
explained that she and her husband now
managed those duties between them. As to
the shopping, two regular costermongers
came round each morning, eggs and milk
were brought in every other day from a farm
in Fulham, and the preferred butcher was
in nearby Shepherd's Market.

Miss Obelienne's gaze fell to Camille's
cake plate. "You do not like it?"

"It is unusual," Camille hedged. "And
very spicy. What kind of cake is it?"

"Not a cake, *madame,* but a pone," said
the cook in her rhythmic lilt. "Cassava pone
from the islands. Once it was the master's
favorite." Her mouth turned down into a
frown.

"Was it indeed?" Camille murmured. "It
certainly is unique."

The cook took this as a compliment.
"Miss Xanthia's ships bring me spices and
roots to make many exotic things."

"*Oui,* I can taste ginger and nutmeg," said
Camille, wiping a crumb from her lip.
"What is cassava?"

Miss Obelienne motioned for her to follow and crossed the room to a locked

281

cabinet. After sorting through the keys in her apron pocket, she opened two mahogany doors to reveal an arrangement of apothecary drawers. She drew open a large one at the bottom and extracted something which looked familiar.

Camille studied it, searching for the English words. *"Une patate douce?"* she finally asked.

"*Non,* not a sweet potato." The cook snapped the tuber in half to expose its creamy flesh. "A root, *oui.* But in the islands, we make a sort of flour of it."

Camille reached for it. "May I taste?"

The cook drew it back. *"Non, madame,"* she said. "If not properly prepared, cassava is deadly."

Camille jerked her hand away. "Deadly?"

Miss Obelienne smiled faintly and dropped the root back into the drawer. "I show you the spices." She was distant, Camille noted, but not unfriendly. She began drawing open the smaller, upper compartments, obviously proud. The air grew redolent with sharp fragrance. "Nutmeg. Cinnamon. Ginger. Allspice," she recited. Then the names became even more exotic. "Aniseed, cumin, mace, tamarind, saffron . . ." There were thirty or more before she was done.

Camille was amazed. "All these come from the West Indies?"

The cook shook her head. "All over the world," she said. "Miss Xanthia has many hand-chosen for me. A few I get in the markets." She pulled open another drawer containing a small cloth bag with some harsh black markings which appeared to be an oriental language.

"What is that?"

Miss Obelienne upended the bag and two small gnarled roots spilt into her hand. *"Rén-shēn,"* she said, her smile oddly mischievous. "Man root. From China."

Camille tried not to blush. *"Rénshēn,"* she echoed. "What is it for? Sweets? Or savories?"

"It is not quite a spice," said the cook, holding it up for further inspection. "It makes a man . . . vigorous. Potent."

Her cheeks flaming, Camille sniffed it. It had no noticeable odor save for that of earth and gardening. She wondered what Miss Obelienne was suggesting. "Xanthia's ships bring this?"

"No, *madame.*" Miss Obelienne stuffed the roots back into the raw silk sack. "Covent Garden Market."

They returned to their cake and tea, now tepid. "In the past," the cook continued in

283

her lilting voice, "Miss Xanthia approved the menus each week. You will wish to resume this, *madame?*"

Camille considered it. "What have you been doing in her absence?"

Obelienne's eyes narrowed. "The master, he does not eat," she said bitterly. "You must see that this is remedied."

Camille's smile was muted. "I shall try," she said. "But I fear he will prove hard to manage."

"*Oui, madame,* but you must do it." Her gold hoops swung as she reached for one of the baize ledgers on her worktable — a worn book labeled *Menus.* "I will show you a typical week in Miss Xanthia's time."

She opened the ledger and passed it to Camille. Camille scanned the tidy columns. Many of the dishes were decidedly French, others Camille suspected were of West Indian origin. "You have experience with Continental cuisine, I see," she remarked.

Obelienne inclined her head almost regally. "I come from Martinique," she explained. "My mother was cook to an important French family."

Camille regarded her with new interest. "You speak French, *oui?*"

The cook's smile was faint. *"Bien sûr, madame,"* she answered. "But mostly *Kwéyòl,* which you might not understand."

This, then, explained the unusual rhythm of her voice. But Camille was still confused. "You worked for the Neville family in Barbados, *n'est-ce pas?*"

Again, the slow nod. "*Oui, madame,* but my mistress was from Martinique. She was sent to Barbados, and I was sent with her. I was a young girl in those days — a maid of all work, you would say. After a time, my mistress, she married. Into the Neville family."

"Into the Neville family?" Camille echoed.

"Oh, *oui.* To Luke Neville, *madame.* The master's elder brother. He is gone now."

Camille remembered what little Xanthia had said regarding her brother. "I don't know much about him," she confessed. "Lord Rothewell has never really spoken of his brother."

"*Oui,* he drinks brandy instead," said Obelienne flatly. "To make the spirits go away. But in their place, devils come."

Camille did not know what to make of that remark. Obelienne was looking at her impassively from across the worktable.

"Well," said Camille as cheerfully as she could, "it would appear you have the kitchen in good hands, Miss Obelienne. I should look over the household accounts next, I suppose?"

Again, Obelienne regally inclined her head. She pulled another ledger from the stack, opened it, and passed it to Camille. "You have the look of her," she said quietly.

"Pardon?"

"My mistress." Obelienne let her dispassionate gaze drift over Camille. "*Non,* not the face. Not like the daughter. But the similarity — *oui,* it is there all the same."

"The daughter?" Camille was confused. "You are speaking of my husband's niece?"

Obelienne slowly nodded. "You, too, are very dark and very beautiful," she said quietly. "Like Annemarie. And so I will pray, *madame,* for you."

"Pray?" Camille looked at her sharply. *"Pourquoi?"*

"I will pray that your beauty does not become a burden to you."

The remark would have seemed insolent, had not Obelienne appeared entirely sincere. But Camille's head was beginning to swim with names and grim warnings. *"Merci,"* she said awkwardly, reaching out for something more tangible; something she understood — an accounting ledger. "Now, what have we here? Are these the greengrocer's receipts?"

As if the strange moment had never occurred, Obelienne bent her head to the account book.

Camille spent the remainder of the morning meeting with Trammel, who was a good deal less enigmatic than his wife. Chin-Chin followed at their heels, venturing off only to sniff at a chair leg or poke his head behind a drapery as Trammel introduced the footmen and the maids, and asked Camille a great many questions about how she wished things done. Throughout it all, Camille simply kept her nose up a notch and pretended she knew what she was about. The manufactured confidence seemed to work. The servants bowed and scraped as if her marriage actually meant something.

At the same time, no one seemed especially shocked by the sudden appearance of a wife. Their impetuous ceremony aside, it seemed generally assumed that Lord Rothewell's marriage was one of convenience. His sister had married and gone. Someone was needed to keep house. At least no one expected starry-eyed bliss from Camille.

"Have you been with the family very long, Trammel?" she asked, as they looked over the china and plate.

Trammel pulled out the next drawer. "Yes, ma'am. Since I was a young man."

Camille put the teacup she'd been toying with back on the shelf. "So you came from Barbados," she said musingly. "Were you ever a — that is to say, legally, were you . . ." Her words faded.

"A slave?" Trammel suggested. He cut her a sidelong glance as he moved deeper into the pantry. "No, my lady, I was hired by Mr. Neville — Mr. Luke Neville — but he had a title by then, of course. He needed a servant to oversee the house properly. We were acquaintances."

"As in friends?"

"Yes, after a fashion," he agreed. "Mr. Neville was some years older than his brother and sister, and ran Neville Shipping out of Bridgetown. My father was in the business of refitting the ships which came into port, and he owned a large inn, which I managed for him."

"Oh, my." Absently, Camille bent down to scoop up the dog. "All that will be a tremendous responsibility for you someday."

Trammel flashed a dry smile and set his hand down upon the pale marble top of the dish cupboard. "No, he has other children," he said, looking at his bronze skin. "White children. Legitimate children."

"You . . . you were not acknowledged?"

He shrugged and reached up to lift down

288

a huge silver bowl. "Inasmuch as the children of a man's mistress can be," he said. "You must understand, ma'am, that Barbados is not like England. There are many shades of skin — and kin — in the islands."

"Yes, I see," said Camille quietly. It seemed as if there was at least one thing she and Trammel shared. "The uncle," she said, "the old baron, I mean. Did you know him?"

Trammel shook his head. "Only by reputation." The words — and his tone — held a wealth of meaning.

"Someone once suggested he was cruel," said Camille vaguely. "Perhaps it was Lady Nash."

Trammel studied the silver bowl. "The man was possessed by devils, or so his slaves said," the butler murmured. "But then, what else would one expect them to say?"

Possessed by devils. It was hauntingly similar to what Obelienne had said of Rothewell.

The remainder of the morning passed without incident, and Camille's starry-eyed bliss looked even more improbable when Rothewell did not return home for luncheon. She ignored the stab of irrational disappointment, asked the attending footmen to take Chin-Chin for a walk, then ate a meal of cold roasted chicken in the dining room alone.

As she did so, her gaze drifted about the space which, like the rest of the house, was a little bare. Or perhaps bleak was the better term? Oh, each room was furnished with life's essentials, and they were of fine quality, too. But there was no character. No soul. No paintings or portraits. No needlework or flowers or even empty vases. It was the house of a family with no memories.

Or perhaps the house of a family with memories they wished to forget? Suddenly, a vision of Rothewell's scarred back flashed before her eyes. Camille dropped her fork onto the china plate with an awkward clatter.

It had been horrible. Deep, disfiguring welts cut into the flesh across the whole of his back. But the scars were white with age, and if the memories of them left Rothewell with any emotion stronger than aggravation, one could not have discerned it by his response.

"If you think this looks bad, you should have seen his slaves," he had said. *"Or my brother."*

Camille shoved back her chair and rose. She could not think about the inhumanity of it. She could not concern herself with the hurts he might have suffered or the cold emptiness of his home. She could not begin to worry whether he ate, or if he was ill. If she did, it was but another step nearer that slippery slope of emotional attachment. She could not grow fond of him. She could *not.*

But it was almost too late, and she knew it. Her fingertips going to her mouth, Camille pondered it. Surely — *surely* — she was not falling in love with the infernal man? Surely it was just simple lust? She was, after all, her mother's daughter.

But had not her mother also fallen for a scoundrel? And once done, no amount of Valigny's maltreatment had been unable to undo it.

Surely she was stronger than that. Wiser than that. She had to be. It was one thing to feel sorry for Rothewell and quite another to be a fool for him. She had to live with him, yes — at least for a time. And she desperately wanted his child. She wanted to make love with him, but not love him, and the line between those two things was beginning to seem so agonizingly fine, she could only pray for the ability to walk it. For if she slipped, she feared she would be tumbling into an emotional abyss.

So deep was she in these contemplations that she leapt when the dining-room door suddenly swung open.

"Camille!" Rothewell's sister swept in, her

arms open. "I just had to drop by. Yesterday seemed so . . . unfinished."

"Unfinished?" Camille smiled and accepted Xanthia's embrace.

"Kieran is such a wretch!" his sister declared, her eyes dancing good-humoredly. "Have you any idea how much he frustrates me? I was hoping for a big wedding."

"*Mais non!* Even I did not wish that. I am sure your brother did not."

Xanthia drew back and caught Camille by the elbows. "Well?" she demanded. "Where is he?"

Camille felt her eyes widen. "Why, he said he was going out to meet Nash. Do you need him?"

Xanthia's gaze darkened. "Do you mean to say he is out?" she asked. "Out on the first day of his marriage?"

Camille let her hands fall, and Xanthia did likewise. "You need not chastise him, Xanthia," she said. "This is a marriage of convenience. It would be best if we all accepted that."

Xanthia tossed her shawl across a chair as if she meant to stay. "Perhaps the two of you might make a little more of it if he were to actually remain at home," she complained, drifting deeper into the room. "Besides, his appearance worries me. I wish he would rest. The night of our dinner party, I feared he was having another sick spell."

"Another?" Camille pounced upon the word. "How often does he have them?"

Halfway down the length of the dining table, Xanthia spun around. "Why, I don't know," she said. "Kieran will tell me nothing, the stubborn man. He claims his stomach is merely dyspeptic — which one cannot doubt, given how he abuses it."

Camille motioned toward the two wide doors which opened onto the withdrawing room. "Will you stay a moment?" she asked. "We might ring for tea. The day is growing chilly."

Xanthia gave a sideways grin. "Congratulations, my dear. You deflect the topic almost as cleverly as he does."

Camille's smile was quiet. "The tea, Xanthia?"

Xanthia stuck out her lower lip. "Very well," she said. "Your point is taken."

"*Pardon,*" said Camille. "But my position here is a difficult one. Your brother is not in love with me. Certainly he is not obedient. I have no leverage — yet."

"*Yet.*" Xanthia's face broke out into a smile. "That sounds promising. Listen, why do we not go for a brisk walk in the park, Camille? I've been shut up in Wapping all day. The doctor says I need exercise." She set her hand over her belly in that sweetly protective gesture now familiar to Camille. It left her just a little envious.

"I shall just fetch my cloak."

Camille found herself inexplicably eager to escape her new home, a place which should have felt like a refuge from all the uncertainty in her life. A bastion against the loneliness. Instead, she found herself feeling more alone than ever. She was suddenly very glad for her new sister-in-law's company.

In minutes, she and Xanthia were making their way down Berkeley Street. The few pedestrians whom they met all wore heavy cloaks or greatcoats, their collars turned up as they pushed through the wind which came rushing up from the river.

In the busy expanse of Piccadilly, carriages clogged the street. A tumbrel laden with hay had broken an axle, sending a golden brown cascade across the thoroughfare. One of the coachmen had begun to shake his fist and swear, whilst a beer cart was attempting to turn round near the top of St. James's Street, making matters even worse. And amongst it all, two newsboys competed to see who could shout out the most lurid headlines. London, Camille decided, was as madding as Paris.

Xanthia took Camille by the hand, and together they wound their way through the snarl of horses and carriages. Deep in Green Park, both the noise and the breeze finally subsided. They walked in silence for a time, but companionably close together. Camille was beginning to rather like Rothewell's sister.

"How much longer until the child comes?" Camille asked.

"Oh, several months," said Xanthia vaguely. "But I feel as big as a cow."

"Mais non," said Camille. "You are slender still. With your cloak, one must look very closely to notice it at all."

"My back hurts sometimes," Xanthia admitted. "But oh, I *long* to feel the child move. When will that be, do you think?"

Camille narrowed her eyes against the sun, which was peeping through the clouds now. "I do not know," she answered. "But I know you are very fortunate."

Xanthia cut a strange glance in her direction. "You wish for children, then," she remarked. "How many would you like?"

Camille drew her cloak a little tighter, and felt her cheeks color. "Oh, one," she confessed. "I should be so happy with just one."

"Knowing my brother, my dear girl, I

295

daresay you'll have more than that," said Xanthia dryly.

"Rothewell likes children?"

"No, he likes —" Xanthia's eyes twinkled. "Oh, never mind that! I just think that Kieran will adore children once they begin to appear. I think they will . . . oh, I don't know. Give him hope for the future?"

"Why does he not have hope now?" asked Camille. "*Pardon,* Xanthia, but your brother seems . . . *zut,* what is the right word for it?"

"Dare I say jaded?" Again, Xanthia's tone was dry

"Non." Camille's brow furrowed. "In French, we say *désolé.*"

"Sad?"

She shook her head. "More than that," she answered. "A sadness that comes from regret. An emptiness in the heart."

"Ah, that." Xanthia cut a strange look at Camille.

Their pace had slowed, but for a time, neither spoke. The breeze picked up slightly, lifting the soft tendrils of hair which peeked from beneath Xanthia's bonnet. Her cheeks had grown pink in the sharp autumn air. Camille sensed that something was weighing on her.

Finally, Xanthia exhaled on a long sigh

and turned to look at her. "Camille, are you in love with my brother?"

Camille shook her head. *"Non,"* she said, praying she spoke the truth. "I hardly know him."

"He is thought a very handsome man," Xanthia conceded. "Assuming one likes the rugged type. Many women do, you know."

"Like Mrs. Ambrose?" Camille quietly suggested. "I fear your brother is in love with her."

Xanthia halted on the path and laughed. "Lud, no! That spiteful cat? He would not dare."

"You do not care for Mrs. Ambrose?"

Xanthia kicked a stone from their path with the toe of her shoe and slowly resumed her pace. "She once played a cruel trick on someone whom I love very much," she said musingly. "My niece, Martinique. I cannot prove it, mind you. Still, I know she did it, and I shall never forgive her. And she will wish you to the devil as soon as she lays eyes on you."

"Oui, I am already wished there," said Camille. Hesitantly, she explained to Xanthia what had transpired at Lady Sharpe's.

At the end, Xanthia was laughing. "Oh, I *do* wish I'd seen it!" she said. "What a minx you are, Camille! No wonder Pamela is so sure you are right for Kieran."

Camille wished she had Lady Sharpe's confidence. "I was just so angry," she returned. "And angry at him for having put Lady Sharpe in such an awkward position when she had been so very kind to me."

There was a bench just ahead near the top of Constitution Hill. Impulsively, Xanthia took Camille's hand and drew her to it. "Sit down," she said. "I wish to tell you something."

"Oui?" said Camille, wondering at her urgency.

Xanthia sat and snagged her lip between her teeth. "It is something I ought not tell," she said. "But it is something you ought to know."

"Which means it is something else which your brother should explain," said Camille. "But again, you know he likely will not."

Xanthia flashed a relieved smile. "You understand," she said. "I am not by nature a gossip."

"Never could I think such a thing."

Xanthia paused as if gathering her thoughts, her eyes distant. "My brother was in love once," she said. "At least I think he was in love. Actually, it was something worse — obsession, perhaps. But he was very young, and he handled it badly."

"The very young often do," said Camille pensively. "It is so very hard to be in love when one is young, *n'est-ce pas?* All the world seems a tragedy."

"A tragedy, yes." Xanthia clasped her hands in her lap, an almost girlish gesture. "You see, Kieran fell head over heels for Martinique's mother," she confessed. "But then, every man who saw her did."

Camille's brow furrowed. "*Oui,* but was she not the — the *sœur du conjoint?* — the wife of your brother?"

"No." Xanthia shook her head vehemently. "No, not then. At first, Luke merely felt sorry for her. Her name was Annemarie, and she was breathtakingly lovely."

"And she was French?"

Xanthia looked at her strangely. "No, not French," she answered. "Not entirely, at any rate. But she had been the . . . well, there is no pretty way to put it. When Annemarie was very young, she had been kept by a wealthy shipping magnate in the French West Indies. Martinique's father."

"*Mon Dieu!*" said Camille, feeling at once in sympathy with the girl. "This is not known, for your niece's sake, I hope?"

"Not here in England," said Xanthia. "But on the island there were always rumors. When the Frenchman cast Annemarie off, you see, he sent her away — she and the child, along with a couple of underservants. He sent them to Barbados and gave her two of his oldest ships, which he told her she could sell when she got there. But Annemarie did not sell them. She decided to try to run rum and sugar herself — as an owner, of course, hiring her own captains. And that's how she met Luke, you see. He was often round the docks, and he had a head for business. He tried to help her learn to make a living."

"Beautiful women rarely have such a burden," said Camille a little dryly. "Could she find no one to keep her?"

"Kieran offered," said Xanthia swiftly. "Many times, apparently. He was foolishly young and besotted, too — along with every other man in Bridgetown. But Annemarie knew lovers did not last. She tried to keep the business afloat, quite literally, but soon she was drowning in debt. Dishonest captains and merchants took advantage of her. She could be overcharged for refitting, for victualing, and never know the difference."

Camille didn't quite grasp it, but she nodded. *"Oui."*

Xanthia's shoulders fell. "Luke tried to help," she said. "But finally, her creditors swooped down to pick over what little carrion was left. Annemarie really was quite desperate. I daresay Kieran thought it was his chance. I will never forget that afternoon. He came in from the fields early, which he never did, then dressed in his best and rode into town."

"Oh," said Camille softly. "This story does not end well, does it?"

Xanthia's eyes were sorrowful. "No," she answered. "Of course, Kieran didn't tell me why he was going, but like any younger sister, I always had my ear to the door. He meant, he said, to make her one last offer — a house in town, a carriage, servants, and a governess to tend the child — things he could barely afford, for we were still undoing the damage Uncle had wrought. But in the end, she accepted him."

Camille could not suppress a gasp. *"Mais non!"*

Xanthia nodded. "Oh, yes," she answered sadly. "She did. Kieran spent the whole afternoon with her, and when he returned late that evening, he was the happiest man on earth."

"Mon Dieu!" Camille was horrified. "And then?"

Xanthia's face fell even further, if such a thing were possible. "And then Luke came home," she said. "He had been up at Speightstown on some sort of business. That night at dinner, Kieran was cock of the walk. Finally, Luke asked why. And when Kieran told him — well, I can honestly say I had never seen Luke so angry. Not even when Uncle was at his worst. Luke was simply enraged that Kieran would make such a proposal to her. He accused Kieran of taking advantage of Annemarie when she was desperate."

"And what did Kieran say?"

Xanthia closed her eyes. "He said, *'But she is a sangmêlé, Luke. A sangmêlé who sleeps with men for her living. What did you expect me to propose? Marriage?'* "

"*Ça alors,*" Camille whispered.

Xanthia's lips were a thin line. "You know the term, then?"

"*Oui,*" said Camille. "Of mixed blood. Like *Monsieur* Trammel?"

"Similar, yes," said Xanthia. "But he didn't mean it, Camille. He didn't mean that she was a whore. He was only repeating things he'd heard round the docks. He was so young. Younger, even, than Annemarie. And she — why she could have refused him. She could have kissed him on the cheek or swatted him on the rear, and sent him politely home again. But she didn't. She said *yes*."

"And your brother Luke?" asked Camille quietly. "What did he do?"

Xanthia shook her head again. "He threw down his linen napkin and called for his horse," she said. "And when he came home the next day, it was done. He had married her. I suppose he had been in love with her all along. I really don't know. Luke . . . he had been both brother and father to us, I suppose, and he believed in always doing the right thing. Kieran used to call him our white knight — and there was a time when he meant that as a compliment."

Camille felt heartsick. "What a sad story," she whispered.

"I think it is worse than that," Xanthia replied.

Camille turned to look at her. "What do you mean?"

Xanthia would not hold her gaze. "God help me, but I think . . . I think Annemarie knew what she was doing," she whispered. "I think she knew — or suspected — that Luke was in love with her. And she simply used Kieran as leverage."

"*Mon Dieu!* That is despicable."

Xanthia just shook her head. "You cannot fully grasp these things, I think, until you've grown up," she said. "But now I believe that if Annemarie had really wanted a protector, she would have chosen one of her more wealthy suitors. Most sugar barons had money to burn, but Kieran — well, he was still working daybreak to dusk just to get our plantation out of debt. He was handsome, yes. Perhaps the handsomest man on the island. But what courtesan would choose looks over money?"

"C'est vrai," Camille murmured. It had been the one difference between her mother — who had been born to assume a man would provide her life's every luxury, and was bewildered when it did not happen — and a more practical woman who had been born into poverty. "Always, it is the money. The security."

"And what is more secure than marriage?" Xanthia lifted both shoulders a little wearily. "Kieran, of course, moved out of the house."

"Where did he go?"

"To a vacant overseer's cottage," said Xanthia quietly. "It was the first time the three of us had been apart — ever. I missed him terribly, of course, even though the cottage was nearby. After a while he began to come to dinner on occasion, and soon Gareth — he's the Duke of Warneham now — turned up on the island, and Luke took him into the business. But things were never the same again."

"Yet your brothers continued to work together?"

"Oh, yes." Xanthia appeared to be blinking back tears, but whether it was from the cold air or grief remembered, Camille could not say. "But Luke put most of his effort into the shipping business, and I followed him there. Kieran continued to build up the family fortunes and expand our plantations. Kieran did very well for us. Together, he and Luke made us rich."

"And the new wife? She was happy?"

"Yes, but society accepted her most grudgingly," Xanthia confessed.

"Because of her blood?"

Xanthia shook her head. "She never talked about it, though some did know," she said. "Annemarie's complexion was . . . like the creamiest of coffee. So lovely. But her years with the Frenchman — and poor Martinique's birth — those things she did not entirely outrun. And I remember on that first day — the very moment she swept into our home — there was this . . . this faint look of *triumph*. Like she had got what she was after."

"She sounds unpleasant."

"That's part of the sadness," Xanthia said. "She wasn't. Annemarie was a loving mother, and she was very kind to me when she really did not have to be. But her life had been so hard. She had risen from toiling barefoot in the cane fields to being a rich man's mistress — and she did not intend to go back to the fields ever again. Unfortunately, on her way up the social ladder, she stepped on Kieran. And he has never — *never* — got over it."

"*Oui,* that explains much," said Camille quietly. "He must have loved her desperately."

Xanthia shook her head. "As I said, it was more of an obsession," she answered. "And he has allowed guilt and hatred to fester like a boil in his heart — a boil he won't lance, and will scarcely even acknowledge. All of us have had to pay the price for that; myself, Martinique, sometimes even Gareth."

"But . . . But whom does he hate?"

Xanthia looked at her, her eyes bleak. "Himself," she whispered. "Camille, he hates himself."

"And now your brother Luke is dead, and the hurt between them cannot be mended," said Camille hollowly. "What a sad end. *Alors,* she is dead now?"

"Yes, a long time ago." Xanthia sighed deeply. "The rest of it you must get from

Kieran. Perhaps I have already spoken too freely."

"*Mais non!*" Camille protested. "Is it not best that I should know? And who else was to tell me? Your brother? He will never share such things with me."

"Then it is his loss." Xanthia rose and stared unseeingly down the hill. Just then, a clock somewhere below in Whitehall tolled the hour, the sound heavy and melancholy beneath the leaden sky. "It has grown cold, has it not?" she murmured. "And late. Perhaps we should go back?"

Camille realized her hands were freezing despite her kid gloves. "*Très bien,*" she murmured. "Let us go."

Xanthia smiled with specious gaiety. "Well," she said, as they set off again, "what color, Camille, shall I paint the nursery in Park Lane? And I shall have a second one, you know, at our counting house in Wapping."

"Something bright, I suppose?" Camille suggested. "Yellow is *très jolie.*"

But even a discussion about nurseries could not quite lift the pall which had been cast over Camille. This was the first day of her marriage, and she had not seen her husband since the early morning — something which bothered her far more than she wished to admit. And now his sister had opened another painful window on his past.

Once again the impenitent rake she had believed she was marrying was becoming a real and complex person before her eyes. Camille was beginning to *feel* a myriad of emotions for him — frustration, anger, lust, and now a strange sort of tenderness — when what she really wished to feel was nothing at all.

Xanthia went up the steps with her when they reached the house.

"Will you come in?" Camille asked.

Xanthia smiled brightly. "Just long enough to see Kieran," she said. "I am sure they finished at Tattersall's eons ago."

But Camille's husband had not returned. And as the hours dragged on into evening, it occurred to Camille that perhaps he did not mean to do so. He was making, she supposed, some sort of point. Despite his flashes of tenderness, Rothewell had made it plain this was a marriage of convenience.

Well. His point was most assuredly taken.

CHAPTER EIGHT
IN WHICH ROTHEWELL RECEIVES A GREAT DEAL OF UNWANTED ADVICE

The news of Baron Rothewell's marriage was received with very little fanfare by those whom it reached that day. He was not well enough known in decent circles to create much of a stir, and within the indecent circles, he was to be mourned as a man who had likely surrendered to a scoundrel's last refuge — marrying for money — and would doubtless return to his senses, and his old haunts, sooner rather than later. No one, however, could have predicted that "sooner" would mean the day after his wedding.

At the Satyr's Club, Rothewell spent the early afternoon being entertained in one of the lounges by a nearly bare-bottomed lass named Periwinkle whose primary skill appeared to be — as the Duke of Warneham would later describe it to his wife — giggling and sipping the club's cheap champagne whilst squirming about on Rothewell's lap.

The duke looked around the tawdry room and felt his skin crawl. On the opposite end of the lounge, a pair of nightingales at the pianoforte were feigning refinement by singing a duet from a comic opera currently popular in the West End. A third was attempting to step through the dance which went with it, but having little success despite the crowd of men who cheered her on.

The establishment was a far cry from St. James's bastions of upper-class masculinity, such as White's Club. Here, the musty velvet draperies and poor lighting aside, one could plainly see the furniture was worn. The walls were hung with faded silk, and the carpets possessed several suspicious stains. The place reeked of sex and of sin — and of several less savory things. It was quite obviously designed for the sort of man who did not give a damn about ambience or class. The sort of man who preferred to sate his passions and drown his soul with life's darker pleasures. A man like Rothewell.

"Thank you, no," said Gareth when Periwinkle attempted to spread her assets around. "My wife would likely have my fingernails ripped out."

This sentiment served merely to make Periwinkle laugh so hard some of the champagne went up her nose and she had to excuse herself.

"This really is perfectly disgusting," Gareth complained to Rothewell, who had one arm slung carelessly along the back of the settee. "Half-naked girls dancing and singing — and the fully naked ones just a staircase away. Not to mention the whiff of opium I caught round by that back parlor."

"Opium?" Languidly, Rothewell extracted a cheroot from its silver case.

"Oh, don't come the innocent with me, Kieran!" Gareth snapped. "You cannot be at sea for as long as I was and not know the stench of that vile scourge. I did not know London had been so tainted by it."

"Indeed?" Rothewell looked supremely bored.

"And in Limehouse, for God's sake," Gareth continued. "What kind of gentlemen come out here, anyway? I think, Kieran, that you should go home to your wife."

Rothewell surveyed him from beneath heavily hooded eyes and drew on his cheroot. "You may be henpecked, old chap, but I don't intend to be," he finally replied. "Besides, who invited you to follow me here? I was trying to escape you and your damned moralizing."

"So you are merely making a point? You

311

wish to show your new wife who's in charge? Is that it?"

Rothewell was quiet for a moment. "I'm beginning as I mean to go on," he finally said. "I don't wish my wife to harbor any fantasies. My marriage is not like yours, Gareth. It is not a love match."

"No, and it never will be if you 'mean to go on' like this." Gareth waved an arm about the room. "Why would you want this, Kieran, when you haven't even attempted to make something better with her? Perhaps it isn't to be — God knows I'm not naïve about such things — but you'll never know if you don't try. Instead, you are already trying to escape her."

"Better? What will be better for her is never to be disappointed." Rothewell had begun to tap one finger upon the back of the sofa. "Besides, women ask too many questions."

The duke looked at him pointedly. "What kinds of questions? And what harm would it do you to simply answer them?"

Rothewell remained impassive. "I don't have to answer your questions, either."

The duke glowered at him. "You do not need to, Kieran," he snapped. "I know the answers. You come here because this is what you think you deserve. And because you wish to be numbed by the wretched excess of it."

Abruptly, Rothewell jerked to his feet. "Bugger off, Gareth," he said, heading toward the door.

The duke sighed, and rose. "Always so eloquent! Where are you going now?"

"To Soho," the baron snapped. "To play cards. And don't follow me, damn you. I don't want a bloody nursemaid."

But Rothewell was to find no peace in Soho, either. There was an especially pernicious gaming hell he favored beneath a tobacconist's shop just off Carlisle Street. The dark little hole of a place was run by a retired blackleg with no ears by the name of Straight — which he wasn't — whilst the shop upstairs fronted for a notorious fence from Seven Dials who dealt stolen watches and snuffboxes out the back.

Rothewell still wasn't sure what had happened to Eddie Straight's ears — and didn't really want to know — but he knew the hell drew just the right sort of crowd if a man wished to avoid the petty yammerings of the *beau monde*. Save for the occasional young buck on a lark, the *ton* never darkened doors like Straight's. And since it was a good way to get a shiv in the back, no one at Straight's ever asked a man questions, either.

Rothewell found himself a trio of disreputable cohorts — East End sharpers whose tricks he already knew — who were in want of a fourth for their table. Then, whilst tossing off the better part of a decanter of brandy, he proceeded to throw away some two or three hundred pounds over the course of a few hours. He did not care enough to actually keep count. And that, he knew, was fatal.

The mantel clock struck midnight. Rothewell tossed down his hand and stabbed out his cheroot. "Gentlemen," he said, using the term liberally, "fortune has forsaken me tonight."

"That may be," said Pettinger, the chap holding the bank. "But there were some remarkable rumors going round Lufton's earlier this evening."

"What sort of rumors?" demanded one of the other men.

"Rumors which suggested that Rothewell had had some very *good* fortune yesterday," he chortled. "If Valigny is to be believed."

Rothewell felt his jaw twitch. "Valigny is almost never to be believed, Pettinger," he snapped. "You've played cards with him often enough to know that."

Pettinger laughed. "Very true! But tell us,

Rothewell, was he lying this time?"

Rothewell rose abruptly. He did not like the suggestion in Pettinger's tone. "You may congratulate me, gentlemen," he replied. "I have had the honor of making Valigny's daughter my wife. Now if you will excuse me, I believe I shall try my hand at the dice."

Rothewell bowed to the sharpers and retreated to the hazard table.

"Gawd save 'im," he heard one say as he departed. "The chit must be a reg'lar gorgon."

It was a fair assumption, Rothewell admitted to himself. And it was like vinegar to his stinging wounds — the ones Gareth had already inflicted. People were already speculating about his wife, he grudgingly admitted, when the fault lay not with her, but with him. A reasonable man — a man wed under convivial and happy circumstances — would have been at home with his bride.

At the hazard table, Rothewell found himself leaning into the action as if he cared, but placing minimal bets unthinkingly. Inside, he was seething — at himself, and at Valigny. That goddamned jumped up Frog had spies everywhere.

Who else, he wondered, was busy leaping to unfair assumptions about Camille? It was the one thing, illogically, which he had not considered when stalking out of the house this morning. He had not wished to bring that down upon her. She would have trouble enough as it was, he expected, before their marriage was over. And then, if the story of Valigny's card game ever got out . . . good Lord. Camille would be utterly humiliated. And all of it — *all* of it — would be partly his fault.

He was jolted from his contemplations by a nudging elbow. "Stamp 'em, Rothewell," said the young man impatiently, shoving the dice box into his hand. "You're casting."

Pettinger, who had followed him to the table, promptly laid a hundred pounds against him. Someone across the table gave a low whistle.

"Gentlemen?" Rothewell lifted his eyebrows. "Anyone else have so little faith in me?"

The remaining bets were laid and finished. Rothewell promptly tossed out double fours.

"Eight!" said the man at the head of the table. "That's the main."

Rothewell hesitated. He had the sense luck wasn't with him tonight. But now it was too late to pass. With a flick of his wrist, he sent the dice smacking against the opposite rail.

"Bloody hell!" someone uttered. "Eleven!"

Rothewell groaned, and many of the

spectators with him. The throw meant an automatic loss for him. At least his punishment had not been drawn-out, and his death had been swift. What more could a man hope for in the end?

Rothewell passed the dice box, and wished the next fellow luck. After that, he watched and bet haphazardly for a time, but his heart was not in it. He began to drink more earnestly. Oh, he'd *been* drinking all evening. But now it felt more like a plan than a pastime.

He soon gave up hazard altogether and took his brandy to a dark and empty corner where he could sulk and smoke alone. But restlessness and dissatisfaction still pricked at him like a sharp needle. Gareth had been wrong, he realized. It wasn't Camille he was trying to escape. It was himself.

When the brandy was half-gone and the crowd twice as thick, Rothewell gave up all pretense of contentment. Tonight, for whatever reason, he simply did not belong here. Even half-sotted, he found nothing in this place to tempt him. He shoved his glass away with the back of his hand and prepared to rise.

"Rothewell!"

He looked up to see a lean, elegant figure waving as he slipped through the crowd toward his table. Rothewell cursed beneath his breath. *Good God.* He really was not in the mood for this.

George Kemble was looking extraordinarily well — but then he always did. "*You,* here at Eddie's?" Kemble flapped his hand at the thick cloud of smoke. "A little too refined for your tastes, I should have said."

Rothewell scowled at the insult but didn't bother to throttle him as he might have with a lesser man. Kemble was a friend of his sister's — and, he supposed, of his. Though the last time they'd seen one another, Kemble had stolen his phaeton and his two best horses on a whim.

"I ought to choke the breath of life from you, Kem," he said. "But today, old chap, is your lucky day. I haven't enough ambition in me to kill anyone."

Kemble lifted both eyebrows and pulled out a chair. "Well, they do say marriage tames a man," he said, sitting down uninvited. "But a great, strapping stallion such as yourself? Rothewell, you disappoint. And you look at death's door, by the way."

"Queue up, damn you, if you mean to complain about it." Rothewell shoved his glass away. "It'll be a dashed long wait."

Kemble feigned a chiding expression. "I do hope you've not taken up the Chinese

318

vice, dear boy," he said. "The Satyr's Club is rife with it."

"I'm ill-humored, not witless." Rothewell pushed the brandy bottle toward him. "Here. Have the rest of this swill. It will occupy your tongue."

Kemble wrinkled his nose. "Surely you jest? I wouldn't even drink Eddie's water if I saw it running out the pipe with my own two eyes. But everyone knows you haven't any standards." He scowled at the label. "My God. You really are sick. This is tolerable Frog water."

"Then drink it, and be quiet," he said. "What are you doing in here anyway?"

Kemble's smile was muted. "Never ask such things, old boy," he answered, wagging a finger. "That way you'll never be an accessory after the fact."

Rothewell snorted. "A friend of Straight's, are you?"

"Since we were young hooligans running loose in Whitechapel." Kemble pulled the cork and filled the empty glass. "Want to know how Eddie lost his ears?"

Rothewell blanched. "God, no."

Kemble's face fell. "It's a delightfully gruesome story," he said, sighing. "Oh, well. I can always rag you about your marriage to Valigny's daughter. Poor, poor girl. Really,

Rothewell. He's nothing but Continental trash."

"Just keep it up," said Rothewell, rising, "and I'll drag you out back to that thieves' den they call an alley and beat the living hell out of you — and remember, Kem, I know your little tricks. Your shivs and your brass knuckle covers and the like. And I outweigh you by about five stone. Yes, by God, the mere notion of pummeling something has my blood stirring again after all."

"So glad to have been of service!" Kem chortled, downing the glass. "Well, must run! I've a thousand things to do."

"Or a thousand things to fence," said Rothewell.

"Tut, tut!" said Kemble. "One mustn't fling about unsubstantiated rumors. I have my good name to think about."

"Yes," said Rothewell dryly, "and I'm the new churchwarden."

With one last flashing grin, Kemble melted into the teeming crowd. Rothewell left his dark corner as he'd entered it — alone and deeply frustrated. He waded into the morass of human foolishness in hope of finding a servant who might go and fetch his greatcoat, his steps so steady few would have guessed how much he'd had to drink.

Just then he felt a warmth pressing close

beside him. He turned to see a blonde in a worn satin gown sidling up — one of Straight's regulars, he assumed. Women who were paid to entertain the patrons and keep them at the tables. She was small with a coquettish face, but he couldn't put a name to it.

"Lord Rothewell!" Eyes sparkling, she set her head to one side like a curious bird. "Do you remember me?"

He hesitated but a moment, uncertain. "Of course, my dear," he lied. "How could a man forget?"

"I've a sudden wish to watch the faro table," she said, slipping her hand round his elbow. "Perhaps such a handsome man needs a lady on his arm to bring him luck?"

Rothewell hadn't the heart to tell her she was neither a lady nor apt to bring him anything but the clap. "Thank you, my dear, but no," he said quietly. "I believe it is too late to salvage my evening."

The blonde pressed herself against him. "We could go into the back, then?" she suggested. "Just a little something to make you forget your ill luck?"

It was the last straw for Rothewell. He lifted her arm from his waist and stepped away. Fleetingly, something like panic lit her face.

"I'm sorry," he said firmly. "Not tonight."

The expression — if it had existed — vanished. Without another word, she backed away, then melted into the crowded room.

Rothewell settled his business with Straight, found his greatcoat, then went up the steps to set briskly off in the direction of home. The walk back to Berkeley Square was scarcely a mile, but he wished sorely that he had had the sense to come out in his carriage.

The truth was, he abruptly realized, that he wanted to see Camille — even though seeing her was like playing with fire. He just needed to reassure himself that . . . well, he did not know what. He had simply been struck by a sudden distaste for who and what he was, and with it came a strange, fierce longing to go home.

Home. Well. Perhaps he had one after all.

But at this hour, he was not apt to see Camille. She had likely been abed for hours. And he could not very well just barge into her bedchamber. What was he to say? *I'm drunk and feeling sorry for myself?* No. That was a weak and intolerable sentiment. Not even to himself would he admit such a thing.

Impatient, he stopped beneath a street-lamp to check the time. But his vest pocket held no watch. Nor did his coat pockets, he realized as he patted through them. How very odd. He never left home without his watch.

And then it struck him. The woman in the faded gown! Rothewell cursed violently. Hang upon his arm, indeed! The little strumpet had pawed him over as neatly as if he'd been some rustic farm boy newly come to town. At this very minute, his watch was likely going out the back door and down the alley. Bloody hell. With luck like his, it really was time for him to go home. A pilfered watch was the least of his worries.

The night was chilly, but fortified by his temper and his brandy, Rothewell pressed on through the gaslit gloom of Soho, keeping to the less dodgy streets lined with their orderly, middle-class homes. To take his mind off Camille, he actually began to look at them. Neatly swept steps. Glossy black shutters. Flowers, sometimes in pots upon the stairs, or in boxes beneath the windows. A man began to notice odd things, he supposed, when time became a precious commodity.

Or perhaps he was simply drunker than he realized? No matter. As he looked at the houses, his mood began slowly to shift. Even in the dark, their narrow faces appeared oddly snug and inviting. Not like his house.

Funny how he'd never seen it before.

Near the end of Portland Street, a front window was still lit in one of the houses. Despite the gloom, one could see that the tidy window boxes cascaded with yellow and purple pansies. Inexplicably, Rothewell hesitated, and stared up at the soft, welcoming light which spilled through the window. He could hear laughter, muffled yet cheerful. Through the sheer veil of drapery, one could see the silhouette of a seated woman, her hair up in what looked like a soft arrangement. She turned, and reached up with both arms. A man bent down to embrace her. For an instant, they clung to one another, the very picture of domesticity.

And then the man straightened up, and stepped back. Rothewell began to imagine what they might have been laughing about. Something delightfully mundane, he supposed. And now she was reminding him, perhaps, to take his tonic before going to bed. Or he might be offering to carry up her hot water. They likely had few servants, and worked from daylight to God only knew when. And yet he envied them. He *envied* them. They sounded happy. They had a long life together to look forward to.

There was a sudden knot in his throat. His chest ached and his eyes stung — the coal smoke, no doubt. Dear Lord, he was becoming that most annoying of creatures, a sentimental drunk. He had been mad — *mad* — to give in to his desire for this woman. And now his only hope was to keep a carefully cultivated distance, lest her already difficult life was to have the added poignancy of grief and loss piled onto it.

He left the little house at a brisk clip, his walking stick clicking lightly against the pavement as he went. He did not expect any warm, welcoming light to spill through his windows in Berkeley Square. He did not expect pansies, though for all he knew, there were some. Why did he not know this? Why did he not remember?

But the feeling of happiness which the house behind him had exuded had nothing to do with geography. It had nothing to do with class or wealth or soft embraces. It had to do with the people who lived and breathed and loved there. In his heart, he knew that. And he knew that it was not meant for him.

CHAPTER NINE
A STUBBORN SILENCE

Lord Rothewell had forgotten all about the watch by the time he reached his front door. He had also forgotten that he'd surrendered his bedchamber to his wife. Rather than disturb a servant, he let himself in with his key, tossed his greatcoat over the newel post, and headed up the staircase.

For almost a year now, he had been treading up the steps of this house in the gloomy hours near dawn, some nights more sober than others. And like a horse headed to the stable, each time he turned right, then left, and entered the second door on his left. Tonight was no exception. Despite the fact that he was drinking, Rothewell prided himself on his catlike grace. Bumbling, tripping, and staggering were for lesser men.

Once inside, he found no lamp lit for his arrival, and no sound of Jim-Jim's *clickity-click* paws, either — he'd forgotten about taking the little imp back to Tweedale.

Shrugging it off, Rothewell shucked his coat and tossed it over his usual chair. But there was no chair. The coat sailed to the carpet with a soft *whuff.* Undeterred from his folly, Rothewell stripped naked and pitched his clothes on top of it.

Suddenly there was the rustling of bed linen. *"Qui est là?"* someone whispered.

Bloody hell. Camille.

"It's just me," he answered, feeling his way along the foot of the bed. "My apologies."

There was a moment of silence, then, "Apologies?" Her voice was cool in the pitch-black room. "For what do you apologize, Rothewell? Barging into my *chambre* uninvited? Or staying out all day and night?"

His hand on the bedpost, he stiffened. "You are my wife now, Camille," he replied. "I do not believe I am required to ask permission to enter your bedchamber — or to go out."

Camille heard the gruffness in his voice, and the almost imperceptible slurring of his words. What gall the man possessed — especially after a night of carousing. It took her a moment to sit up and light the candle by her bed. He must have heard her rattling around.

"You might not wish to do that," he said

327

warningly.

"*Non?*" she said as the wick caught. "*Pour-quoi?*"

"Because I'm naked."

Camille turned around slowly, willing herself to appear nonchalant. "Indeed you are," she murmured, letting her gaze trail down him as she rose from the bed. "*Quel dommage,* Rothewell. You have taken off your clothes for nothing."

He stood there for a moment, his expression as daunting as his naked body. "I see," he finally replied. "And you think I came in to . . . to do what, precisely?"

Camille lifted one shoulder and pretended not to notice his sculpted arms. The dark dusting of hair on his chest. And then there was — *good Lord!* She jerked her gaze up. "I daresay you came in to do whatever a man normally does when he is naked in a woman's bedchamber," she returned, coming to her feet. "But if you think I will succumb to *that* —"

"Now wait," he ordered, holding up his hand. "Wait just a damned minute."

"*Non,*" she said sharply, pacing away from him. "*You* wait. Do not ever come to my bed after you have been out drinking and whoring all day and half the night."

He followed her, glowering. "Look, Camille, I haven't —"

"Do not dare lie to me," she interjected, spinning around to face him. "I can *smell* her on you."

"No, you can't," he said firmly.

"And you're drunk," she returned, unwilling to concede even an inch of moral high ground.

"Somewhat, aye," he admitted.

"There is no *somewhat* to it," she snapped. "Either one is or one isn't — and you reek of it."

This time, he sneered. "New standards, Camille?" he asked. "I was drunk when I agreed to marry you. You made no objection then. Had I known that eternal sobriety and a shrew in my bed were part of the bargain, perhaps I would have declined the honor."

Camille's spine went rigid. She was scarcely aware she'd raised her palm to slap him. In a flash, his hand came up, catching hers.

Rothewell looked at her in stupefaction. Then he grabbed her wrist and jerked, hitching her up against him. "By God, don't you *ever*." His voice was an awful rasp in the gloom. "Don't you ever — *ever* — try to hit me again, Camille."

They were so close, she could smell the

anger and the heat of his skin. She should have been terrified. But all she felt was hurt and outrage. "I am not afraid of you, Rothewell." Her voice was low and angry. "You are nothing but a rake and a bully and I am not afraid of you."

He stared down at her, his eyes narrow, his nostrils wide with anger. "God damn it, Camille," he roared. "I am *not* your father. I am nothing like Valigny."

"Are you not? Tonight, you seem very like him to me."

Rothewell stared down into his wife's eyes. She was angry, yes. He had left her alone in a house where she knew no one so that he might slink off to brood on his own troubles. Gareth was right. It had been a callous thing to do. And what was the difference, really, between him and Valigny? Damned little, he supposed. The truth shamed him.

As her gaze held his, his mind searching for the right words to say, the fight inside her seemed to collapse. She looked lonely, and suddenly very alone.

"Come, Camille, don't," he whispered, embracing her gently. "I'm sorry. Let's not allow the servants to hear us quarreling."

"*Et alors?*" Her face twisted as if she might cry. "Let them hear. I do not care."

He drew her nearer, and set his mouth to

her ear. "Yes, my dear, you do," he gently countered. "Rail at me till hell freezes over — but quietly, all right? I don't wish you to be the subject of gossip."

She pulled back a few inches. "Do not do that," she whispered. "Do not be kind to me. I . . . I don't know who you are when you do that."

He stared down at her, at the wide, limpid brown eyes and sweetly heart-shaped face, and he knew suddenly why he had come home. Dear God. Rothewell swallowed hard. "So you'd rather I be the cheating rakehell you were expecting? Is that it?"

She shook her head and cut her gaze away. "I do not know," she whispered, almost to herself. "It might be easier if you were."

"At least it's something I'm good at," he muttered. Then, with one finger, he turned her face back to his. "Look, Camille, you've married a cad. I don't deny it. But I'm sorry if I hurt you."

"*Vraiment?*" she retorted. "Now I am to be grateful for your honesty?"

Her gaze was heating again — with temper, not lust — but he was drowning in it. Yearning for something he could not explain. Slowly, purposefully, he bent his head and kissed her, half-expecting the little hellcat to try to backhand him again. He kissed her like he meant it, opening his mouth over hers, and stroking his tongue along the seam of her lush lips.

Camille hesitated at first, pushing half-heartedly at his shoulders with the heels of her hands. But her mouth, her lithe, trembling body — ah, they did not hesitate. She opened so sweetly beneath him, allowing him to delve into her mouth, her tongue entwining sinuously with his. In response, something inside his chest lifted as if suddenly unburdened.

And yet, even as he deepened the kiss and thrilled to her soft moan of surrender, he could sense her conflicted emotions. Her hands were still on his shoulders, but no longer shoving him away. When at last she twisted her mouth from his, it was sudden. Her breathing was rough, her eyes a little teary.

Rothewell speared his fingers into her hair at the nape of her neck, and banded the other arm even tighter about her slender waist. She wanted him — wanted him, perhaps, as desperately as he wanted her — but she was none too happy about it.

Cradling her head as she turned her face away, he stroked his lips over her ear, along her jaw, and all the way down the long, perfect length of her throat. "Camille," he murmured. "Please, Camille, you are my wife."

She muttered something in French; cursing herself, he thought.

He dropped his hand to the turn of her derrière, cupping one sweet swell of it in his palm. It filled his hand perfectly, just as he'd known it would. He didn't care that she'd just tried to slap him, or that she'd insulted him. It was a sign, he feared, of how far he had fallen. "God, how you tempt me, Camille," he rasped. "I have burned for you from the first moment I laid eyes on you."

Was he mistaken, or was she trembling ever so slightly? *"Oh, mon Dieu!"* she whispered, lowering her lashes in an inky sweep. "You madden me. I — I cannot think straight."

Rothewell took it as surrender and kissed her again, a little too roughly. Nonetheless, Camille rose onto her toes to kiss him back with newfound urgency. He surged into her mouth triumphantly, slanting his mouth over hers again and again as he lost his head to the taste of her.

Camille's hands roamed down his shoulders, stroking his bare biceps, then sliding round his waist, down the small of his back. Lower and lower until she caressed the muscles of his buttocks. Until he groaned, and a faint shiver ran down him, too.

Rothewell had begun this game in total control, but that control was fast slipping away. He had forgotten this morning's vow to keep his distance. Camille was like fire and ice in his arms. Their bodies were entwined now; heart to heart, her belly pressed to the hard, eager weight of his erection. *He wanted her. He wanted her.* His blood throbbed to the sound of it. He was going to pick her up and carry her to the bed. He was not going to let her say no. He would convince her. Would woo her if he had to.

Suddenly, she pushed him away — and she meant it. *"Très bien,"* she said, her breath gasping. "Just . . . just do it, then."

"Do it?"

"Just . . . have me, Rothewell. That's what you want, *n'est-ce pas?"* She left him and went to the bed. "I am weak. And I — I want a child. So just . . . do it."

But it was as if his feet were nailed to the floor. "Camille, what is wrong?"

She sat down on the bed slowly, her small feet peeking from beneath the lace hem of her nightgown. "Nothing. I just want you to . . ." Her words trickled away, and she shook her head.

He stood there feeling foolish. And naked.

"Just say it," he demanded.

Her heavy black hair swung over one shoulder as she leaned forward, almost as if in pain, wrapping her arms almost protectively round her stomach. "I just . . . I just cannot be like this with you," she whispered. "I cannot afford to lose my —"

"Lose *what?*" he demanded. "Camille, what are you afraid of?"

At that, she looked up at him with anguish in her eyes. *"Myself,"* she whispered.

Confused, he went to the bed, his cock still erect, damn it all. He set one knee to the mattress and tipped up her chin. Good Lord. He had not pursued a woman in almost two decades. Not since his mad, impassioned *affaire* with Annemarie.

Desperately, he looked down into Camille's eyes, searching for the right thing to say. The thing that would impassion her again, and get him what he wanted — her. *All* of her. But he was no good at it. He was too rough and too blunt to know how to court a woman.

"Bloody hell, Camille, just kiss me again," he said. "Everything was fine two minutes ago."

She shook her head and drew a deep breath. "I just want to do it without . . . without all the emotion," she said. "I thought this was to be just a transaction, Rothewell. My grandfather's money. Your seed."

His cock twitched impatiently. "My dear, I am not a stud service."

"*Oui, oui.* You are." Her voice was gentle as she pushed past him and rose. "Rothewell, don't you see? That's all you can be to me."

"By God, I never agreed to that!" he answered tightly — though in truth, it would have been better for them both. "And don't you dare try to convince either of us that I did. I made it plain what I wanted that night at Valigny's."

At that, her mouth twisted bitterly. "*Oui,* let us see if I can recall it," she said. "Ah, yes! You wished me to 'eat my prideful words, and do your every bidding.' That is right, *n'est ce-pas?* Is that what you mean?"

"What if it is?" he growled. "Are you willing? After all, Camille, you married me."

"*Coûte que coûte,*" she whispered, cutting her gaze away from his jutting erection.

Whatever the cost. Her words served only to further frustrate him. "You are just angry," he snapped. "Angry I stayed out so late. Admit it."

"I would not lower myself," she said quietly. "I don't give a damn where you go

336

or what you do — or with whom you do it."

"Yes, you do, my dear," he replied. "That's precisely why you're so damned cross with me. And frankly, now that I think on it, I'd rather a nagging bitch for a wife than a frigid one."

She flicked a derisive glance up at him and half turned, as if to walk away. "Just keep your end of the bargain, Rothewell," she said. "I want a child."

He set his hands on her shoulders and jerked her back to face him. "You want a child?" he rasped. "By God, I'll give you a child, Camille. I'll lock you in this bedchamber and ride you till kingdom come. You'll have to beg me to stop."

"Will you indeed?" she said sweetly. "How charming. But if you dare —"

He cut off her words with his mouth. He wasn't even sure when he made the decision to do it. He knew only that he couldn't bear the accusation in her eyes. Couldn't bear knowing that he wasn't really good enough. That she was settling because of who her father was. That he would never make her happy — and a thousand other regrets. Fleetingly, she twisted beneath him, pushed at him, and then, just as before, she surrendered. More than surrendered.

Rothewell crawled onto the bed — crawled

over her — taking her back with the force and strength of his body, his mouth never leaving hers. She exhaled on a shudder, allowing his hands to roam her body at will. He thrust and thrust into her mouth, a sensual promise of what he meant to do.

In response, her eyes softened and closed, her velvety black lashes fanning across her olive skin. His hand caressed her breast, weighing it, lightly thumbing her nipple through the fine lawn of her gown. The sweet nub hardened to his touch, and she gasped into his mouth.

He lifted his lips from hers. "Camille," he whispered. "I'm sorry. I'm sorry."

She lay on the bed, passive and silent, her arms outstretched like an avenging angel. And she was. God had sent her, he feared, to teach him an awful lesson. The torture of wanting what he could never fully have. How to survive on dry crust when he yearned to feast.

The muscles of her throat moved up and down, but she did not speak. And he realized that, foolishly, he wanted her to want him. To feel at least a little tenderness in her heart for him.

How vain and hopeless that was. The crust was all she meant him to have, and by God, he would take it.

He reached down and pushed up the hem of her nightgown. Shoved it up and dragged it off, ripping a stitch in the process. He straddled her, kneeling, as his hungry gaze took her in. *Good God in heaven.* The woman was perfect. Small, high breasts. Long legs, beautifully turned. And between them — ah, *that* might as well have been the Holy Grail, for he could not have desired any vessel more.

He dragged her farther up the mattress, then pushed her legs wide with his knee. He let his palms slide up the silken flesh of her inner thighs, and higher still, brushing his thumbs along the plump folds of feminine flesh which guarded her center. Gently, he parted her. She gasped at the intrusion.

"My God, Camille," he whispered. Rothewell burned with impatience to take her. To claim her once more with his body. She was his wife, and he ached for her.

Somehow, he checked his impatience. He shifted his weight and rolled to his side. He let his hand skim down the flat of her belly, until his fingers threaded through her soft thatch of curls. He lay half atop her now, his face buried against her neck as his fingers returned to stroke her. Deeper. Again and again. Already her breath was roughening. Moisture began to slick his fingers. But he wanted her hungry. Aching. It was inexplicably erotic to touch her that way, to open her, to stroke her until her own juices flooded his fingers whilst she lay open and languid. Waiting. Waiting to be taken.

He lifted his head, and brushed his lips along her collarbone, then lower. When he captured her breast in his mouth, she cried out in French, a weak, thready sound. The sound of a woman who had given up her body to his pleasure — and, he hoped, to hers.

Rothewell suckled her greedily, drawing the whole of her nipple into his mouth, teasing the hard nub with the very tip of his tongue, then biting ever so gently. She arched up, crying out. And then to his shock, she began to tremble in earnest. Her hands raked into the bedcovers, her nails digging deep. It was a moment suspended in time. Crystalline. Perfect. He watched, awestruck, as the pleasure took her, her hips arching to his touch.

When she lay still on the bed, her breath hitching and her eyes still closed, he kissed her deeply, then mounted her. With one hand, he guided himself gently into the warmth. The heat of her surrounded him. He drew back, waited for her to relax, then deepened the thrust.

He had thought he would feel impatient; that he would spill himself like some virgin schoolboy up to the hilt in his first woman. But it was worse than that. He could not rush. He felt . . . right. Perfect. And perfectly unhurried — as if he were slowly drowning in her beauty. Camille's somnolent eyes watched him as he thrust, luring him onto the shoals like a silent siren. He prayed for the strength to survive it — this, her, all of it. Already she was driving him mad. Breaking his heart — and he'd scarcely known he had one.

Camille's eyes were lazy with spent passion. Her face was smooth now, her mouth relaxed. Her body called to him — drew him like the pull of the ocean — as if she meant to coax the essence of life from his loins. His arms set wide above her shoulders, he bent his head to kiss her. Her cheeks, her eyebrows; he let his lips move over her face. Suddenly, he sensed a shift in her. Camille's breath came faster. Her knees drew up, one foot sliding sinuously along his inner calf. Her hips arched to his, and her hands left his back to roam restlessly over his buttocks.

"Mon Dieu," she whispered. "Ahh —"

Just as they had done with the bedcovers, her fingers dug into the muscle of his hips as he rode her. She cried out again beneath him, a soft, sweet sound of triumph. They drove one another over the edge, tumbling and falling into the brilliant abyss as one. And fleetingly, he felt at peace.

When he came back to his conscious self, his arms were shaking. "There," he said, touching his forehead to hers. "There, Camille. I have done it."

Her serious brown eyes searched his face. "What, *chéri?*" she whispered. "What have you done?"

"I have given you what you needed," he rasped. "And I hope I have given you our child. If not, well, we must simply try again. And again. Until I get it right."

A faint, drowsy smile played at her lips, but she said no more. He rolled onto his side and drew her to him, her back against his chest. He felt joyous, yet oddly shaken, as if something he had known with a certainty seemed suddenly unfathomable. His own mind, perhaps. Or his heart.

Rothewell curled his body protectively about hers and closed his eyes. When Camille shivered in his embrace, he reached down and drew the counterpane up to cover them. They lay together, perhaps even dozed, for a time. Each moment with her in his arms felt precious, but the candle she'd lit was much shorter now, and daylight was not far away. The house would be stirring.

Rothewell allowed himself to roll up onto his elbow, just for the pleasure of looking down at her. Her beauty was breathtaking. And it would be eternal, he thought. It had been a long time since he had looked at a woman so. Perhaps he never had? A strand of her hair had slipped from behind her ear, dark as ink against the perfection of her cheek. Gently, he tucked it back again.

She turned her head slightly on the pillow, like a flower turning to the sun, and gave a lethargic *umm* of pleasure.

She was happy, he realized, at least in this moment. It was an amazing if simple thing to muse upon. He doubted if he had ever made any woman happy. Merely satisfied, which was not the same thing, he now realized. Oh, the emotion would not last; happiness was ever fleeting. But at least for now — yes, in this moment — he did not feel as if he had ruined her life. Perhaps he could avoid doing so. He did not want her to love him, or grow attached to him. Did he? Surely he was not so selfish. Perhaps, if he could avoid acting the cad, she would someday have fond memories of their time together.

On that thought, Rothewell set his lips to

the turn of her shoulder, tucked the bed-covers up higher, then rolled onto his back. He stared up at the frieze of acanthus leaves which ran around his ceiling. He had been wrong to leave her yesterday, and he was not fool enough to think himself forgiven. He had distracted her with pleasure, no more.

The truth was, Camille had a right to ask questions. He could refuse most of them, yes — with a modicum of diplomacy. Instead, he had snapped at her. Diplomacy was not his strong suit. In Barbados, he needed only to please Xanthia, who always overlooked his harshness and never punished him with the past. Well, save for once. The time he had quarreled so openly with Martinique over marrying her husband. Then — in private — Xanthia had thrown his cruel words in his face like a vial of boiling acid.

Rothewell thanked God his niece was gone and out of his hands — for her sake. He had done the girl no good whatsoever, and a great deal of harm. And oftentimes, he had known it even as he had done it. He had been a bastard, unable to stop himself — much as he had been with Camille yesterday.

If he could not look past his own wounds

in order to care for a child — a child Luke had loved and entrusted to his care — what manner of ill did that bode for his new wife?

He stirred, a little restless, and propped one arm behind his head. It was odd, but in the past few months, thinking of Martinique no longer meant thinking of her mother in the same breath. It did not mean an instant resurrection of that memory of Annemarie wrapped in his brother's bedsheets the morning after her wedding, looking past him with regret in her eyes. Or the vision of Annemarie wrapped in the shroud in which they had carried her, dead, from the cane fields.

He shifted restlessly on the bed. Annemarie was his past. This woman — this vibrant, beautiful woman who perhaps resembled Annemarie but was in reality nothing like her — was his future, so far as he had one. They were going to make a child together. A child who would, he hoped, be a better, happier person on this earth than he had ever been. Perhaps that's what all this was about. Perhaps he was trying to expiate his sins.

Just then, there was a faint scratching at the connecting door. Rothewell slipped from the covers and opened it a crack. A shadowy form streaked past his ankles and bounded onto the bed. A faint sense of relief struck him, but he crushed it.

"Aye, you'd best enjoy it," he whispered to the dog. "It's back to Tweedale at cock-crow, old boy."

The dog just snorted, and flopped down across Camille's ankles. Rothewell slid back into bed and tucked himself close to her. But just as he settled into the perfect position, his stomach growled loudly. Camille, whom he had believed asleep, turned to look at him solemnly.

"Sounds like I swallowed a bad-tempered alley cat, doesn't it?" he said, rolling toward her. He nibbled lightly at her neck.

"*Oui,* and you are talking to the dog, too," she said. "Chin-Chin is not leaving, you know."

"You think not, eh?" he answered. "Don't get attached to him."

When Camille spoke again, her tone was grave. "When did you last have a proper meal, *s'il vous plaît?*"

He stroked one hand down the length of her arm, considered it. "I cannot perfectly recall," he admitted.

For a long, expectant moment, she said nothing. Then she sighed, and said, "I wish to ask you something."

Rothewell bit back his instinctive refusal.

Perhaps he was getting old. "Very well."

"I shall ask just this once." She was still lying on her side, staring into the banked coals of the hearth. She did not crane her head back to look at him again — deliberately, he sensed. "If you cannot — or will not — answer, I shan't nag," she went on. "Indeed, I shan't even ask again."

"I find brevity an admirable quality in a wife," he said.

He watched over her shoulder as she toyed with a bit of fringe on the counterpane, wrapping it round and round her finger, then releasing it. For a moment, he thought she had changed her mind. When she did speak, it was abrupt. "You are sick, *n'est-ce pas?*"

When he did not respond, Camille turned her head on the pillow to look at him, her eyes wide and searching.

For an instant, he held her gaze. Then, unable to bear it, he looked away.

She exhaled slowly. "How bad?"

Rothewell looked at the ceiling and struggled for an answer. "I've lived a hard life, Camille," he finally said. "And it hasn't killed me yet."

His words hung in the air for a long moment. "You are sick," she said again. This time it was not a question.

Rothewell threw back the covers and rose from the bed, the dog following him. There was nothing more to be said. "It will be daylight soon, Camille," he answered. "I will leave you to your rest."

He gathered his clothes from the floor in silence and made his way through the gloom to the door. But she was hurt, he knew. Already, damn it, he was doing what he had vowed not to do. And for the first time since that fateful day in Harley Street, he suddenly wanted to cry. To mourn the missed opportunities and rage at the cruelties of fate. He wanted to weep for the young man he had once been, and for the lovely young woman who deserved something so much better.

She sat up, and spoke again as his hand touched the knob. "Rothewell," she said quietly, "you will remember what I said?"

He turned and studied her through the candlelight. "About what, Camille?"

"About asking again." Her voice dropped to a tremulous whisper. "I shan't, I tell you. I *shan't.* I will not beg you — not for anything. Ever. Not even for this — what we do in bed together — no matter how much pleasure you give me. Do you understand?"

And as he stood there naked, his hand on

348

the door, his heart half-breaking, he understood. She was forcing him to make a choice — the choice, perhaps, between true intimacy and raw pleasure. But he wasn't sure he had ever known true intimacy — not even with Luke or with Xanthia — and his decision was already made. He would not burden her. He would not cast a shadow over her hope, when her hope was to conceive their child.

Camille was still staring at him, her eyes wide in the gloom. Stiffly, he nodded and drew open the door.

CHAPTER TEN

IN WHICH CHIN-CHIN
GOES TO THE CITY

The following days in Berkeley Square took on a strange, almost otherworldly rhythm. Camille lived them mechanically, torn and a little heartsick.

To the bewilderment of his staff, Rothewell began to spend a greater part of each day at home, where he would shut himself up in his study with his brandy, his books, and the little spaniel, a creature he nonetheless disavowed at every turn. Occasionally, however, Camille would pass the closed door and hear Rothewell talking, and she knew, strangely, that it was the dog to whom he spoke. She began to feel a little twinge of envy.

At times Rothewell also looked decidedly unwell, but if he suffered violent spells of illness — which Camille suspected he did — then he hid it from her. Neither of them mentioned her parting words on the night of their argument; it was as if a silent truce had been drawn between them.

In hindsight, Camille realized she had been foolish to interfere. From the very first, Rothewell had asked nothing of her, save that she be faithful, and if possible, amiable. He had made it plain that his life would never really include her.

"You would be well advised not to depend upon me," he had said. *"You must build a life for yourself."* And she had agreed to that. Indeed, it was what she had wanted. So why did his words cut her so deeply now?

As was his habit, Rothewell scarcely slept, but he came to Camille's bed most nights, often in the hours just before dawn, when he returned home from an evening spent doing God only knew what. She no longer questioned him about it, and otherwise saw little of him. Camille tried to tell herself it scarcely mattered. Despite the lovemaking and the occasional shared meal, there was a carefully cultivated distance between them. And though it hurt, Camille did not attempt to eliminate that distance. Her husband had put it there quite deliberately — and, after all, she tried to convince herself, intimacy was not what she required. In fact, it was what she had sworn to avoid.

But her efforts to save her heart, she feared, were in vain, and slowly, Camille was beginning to face a second bleak truth. His broad shoulders and overt masculinity aside, her husband was ill. Even in the short weeks she had known him, his face had thinned.

And then there were the other signs, the signs Camille knew too well from her mother's long illness. The restlessness. The hollow eyes. The inappetence and bad temper. Rothewell was drinking — and perhaps grieving — himself to death.

She told herself she would not do it. She would not dance attendance on another person who was bent on slowly killing themselves. And yet, she could not leave him — because, she told herself — she wanted a child. But the reality was becoming far more complicated than that.

Camille tried not to think about it. Tried not to think of *him.* Of his whispered words and heated touch. Of how she lay restless and eager in her bed each night, awaiting the moment when he would come to her. And so the days passed quietly and all too slowly in Rothewell's bland, empty house. It was a lonely existence, but Camille was accustomed to solitude.

The solitude was briefly severed one afternoon when Rothewell escorted Camille into the City to meet her grandfather's solicitors, so that she might give them the evidence of her marriage. It was a meeting she had dreaded since discovering her grandfather's letter hidden amongst her mother's things. But the visit had been easier with Rothewell's stern, forbidding presence at her side.

To his credit, Rothewell took pains to give every impression theirs was a marriage of respect, if nothing more. He allowed her to speak for herself, whilst he remained standing in the background, leaning on his gold-knobbed walking stick and staring out the window.

When at last the senior solicitor finished his business, his brow was furrowed. "Well, thank you for coming in, Lady Rothewell," he said. "Our felicitations on your marriage. My lord, we will arrange a draw of fifty thousand on the late earl's estate when the banks open tomorrow."

Rothewell turned from the window. "For the dowry, do you mean?" He lifted a forestalling hand. "I have no need of it. You may hold it in trust for my wife, or if she prefers, for any children of the marriage."

Camille managed not to gape. "We shall discuss it," she said swiftly, "and let you know."

The solicitor's look of confusion deep-

ened. "Then we shall await your decision."
He rose as if to show them out, then hesitated. "You understand, do you not, that
the balance of your grandfather's estate
remains in trust pending — we hope — the
birth of your first child?"

"We understand," said Camille, rising to
her feet.

Still the man hesitated. "I must confess,
my lady, to a deep curiosity," he said. "Why
did your mother not answer this letter
twenty years ago, when it was still possible
you might have been reconciled with your
grandfather?"

The question stung. Remembering Lord
Nash's advice, Camille stood and looked
down her nose at him. "What need had I of
a reconciliation, *monsieur?*" she asked. "One
cannot reconcile with a man one has never
met."

The solicitor was immediately flustered.
"I beg your pardon," he answered. "What I
meant to say was . . . well, why did . . ." He
was clearly searching for a tactful phrase.

"Why did my mother hide his letter from
me?" Camille supplied. "Because, I daresay,
there was one thing she feared more than
poverty. She feared dying alone. A human
frailty, *n'est-ce pas?*"

"I see," said the solicitor somberly. "Perhaps you are right."

Camille managed a distant smile. "My grandfather would never have taken her back," she said. "*Maman* knew that. Why would she give her only child a reason — and the means — to abandon her?"

The solicitor did not argue but instead merely thanked her again for coming.

Rothewell came away from the window, offered his arm, and saw her safely back down the stairs. Together, they left the solicitors bowing obsequiously in their wake, and for the first time, Camille felt the full import of being an earl's granddaughter and a baron's wife.

Rothewell, however, looked preoccupied as he helped her into his coach. He followed her in, and Chin-Chin immediately leapt into his lap. The dog had insisted upon following them from the house, whining until Rothewell simply picked him up and took him along.

"You did not need to do that, Rothewell," said Camille as the carriage rocked into motion.

"What, the money?" he said, scratching the dog's ear. He fished in his coat pocket, and extracted something, which he fed the dog.

"*Oui,* because already you paid Valigny

half, so by rights, half of it should be —"

Rothewell cut her off. "I did as I pleased, Camille," he interjected. "I usually do, you'll recall."

Camille hesitated, and he pinned her with a pointed stare. "As you wish," she answered. "And stop feeding the dog, *s'il vous plaît.* You are making him fat."

After a few moments had passed, he spoke again. "What, precisely, did that old letter say, Camille?" he asked, his long fingers absently stroking the dog's silky fur.

Camille looked at him, surprised he cared. "It was just the ramblings of a bitter man."

"This is the letter you never showed Valigny?"

"I dared not," she said quietly. "I learnt young that one must never fully trust Valigny. Why? Do you wish to see it?"

Rothewell looked out the window. "I rather think I should like to," he murmured.

"*Bien sûr,* I shall find it."

She watched the shadows move and shift across his stern profile as they turned into Cheapside. A quiet fell over the carriage, broken only by the rhythmic *clop-clop-clop* of the horses' hooves and the rumble of the carriage wheels as they lumbered back toward St. Paul's. His hand never stilled, rhythmically stroking the dog. It was as if he sought solace from the creature, solace, perhaps, which he should have received from his wife. Fleetingly, she closed her eyes and wondered if she was an utter failure.

After a time, he spoke again, still without looking at her. "I am sorry, Camille, that Valigny is your father," he said softly.

"As am I," she answered. "*Maman* — she loved me, in her way. That I never doubted. But Valigny? *Non.* Never. I was but an annoyance to him."

Some inscrutable emotion sketched across his face. "You deserve something better, Camille. Something better than" — here, he lifted his hand in a vague, dismissive gesture — "any of this."

It was her turn to stare blindly through the window. "Perhaps I do not," she said quietly. "I am just the bastard child of a selfish man. The world does not look kindly upon such as I."

"Hush, Camille," he said sharply. "Let the world think what it will, but never belittle yourself. You are nothing like your father."

Camille did not answer him. What more was there to say? She had long ago stopped feeling sorry for herself. And long ago stopped trying to win Valigny's love. For all the paternal affection the man had shown her, she could have been the child of some stranger — or worse, of an enemy.

But was her coldness so deep and so permanent — were her emotions so tightly shut off — that she was failing as a wife? Was she no longer able to open her heart? That was not what she wanted. It was *not* the person she wished to be. Perhaps it was no longer the sort of marriage she wanted.

She looked again at her husband's profile, so grim and yet so handsome in the sun. Was there any hope for the two of them? Was there any chance of real intimacy? Intimacy which went beyond the bedchamber? And yet, even if she were willing to risk being hurt, she scarcely knew how to take that first step. How to reach out and shatter the glass wall they had erected between them.

"When I was five years old," she said suddenly, "I decided that my name was Genevieve."

Rothewell turned from the window, one eyebrow politely arched. "Did you indeed?"

"*Oui,* and that I was a princess who had been kidnapped by the evil Comte de Valigny," she went on, feeling supremely foolish, but somehow driven. "I told my nurse that my real papa — a great and powerful king, of course — was coming to find me and take me away."

Rothewell flashed a rueful smile. "Yes, and then they would all be sorry, wouldn't they?" he murmured. "Was that the idea?"

Her face fell. *"Oui,"* she said quietly. "You know how this fairy tale ends."

"I fear so," he said. "I liked to pretend that a powerful Ottoman corsair was my father, and that he had sent me to Barbados to keep me safe from his enemies. When he returned, I imagined, and saw what my uncle had done to me, he would cut off Uncle's head with his scimitar. I believe I even shared that sentiment with him — or something very like it."

Camille gave a cluck of sympathy. "I daresay he laughed in your face."

"No." Rothewell's expression was suddenly emotionless. "No, he locked me in the slave hole for three days with no food or water. Then he passed out drunk, and Luke stole the key from his pocket. When he sobered up, Uncle was too preoccupied by stripping the hide off Luke's back with his bullwhip to spare me a moment's notice."

"Mon Dieu!" Camille's gloved hand had flown to her mouth. "You . . . you were but children!"

"Oh, not for long," said her husband quietly. "Not for long."

The horror of it chilled her. "Rothewell,"

she managed to whisper, "what is this thing, this hole? Something very bad, *n'est-ce pas?*"

"Just a pit Uncle had dug in a swampy spot near one of the sugar mills." Rothewell's gaze had returned to the window, but his mind had returned to the West Indies, Camille sensed. Even his hand had stilled, and now lay frozen upon Chin-Chin's back.

"It was a deep hole," he finally continued, "like a sort of cistern or a well. There was always brackish water in the bottom, and if there was rain — and God, there was always rain — the hole would begin to fill."

"Mon dieu!" she whispered. "How did you get out?"

"You could not," he said. "One simply prayed the water didn't rise too high. There was a heavy grate atop it, and my uncle had the only key. He built it to punish the slaves, but after our arrival, he grew increasingly fond of it."

Camille felt herself begin to shake. "But this is monstrous!" she cried. "Why . . . Why did someone not stop him?"

Rothewell's head at last swiveled around, his gaze locking with hers. "Someone?" he said quietly. "Who is someone, Camille? There was no one who gave a damn."

360

She shook her head rapidly. *"Non, non,"* she whispered. "This I cannot believe. There were people . . . the parish, the priest. A magistrate. Someone who should have looked out for such things."

After a moment had passed, Rothewell sighed. "It was a colonial backwater, Camille," he said. "There was a woman who came from the church once — concerns had been raised, I collect, about Xanthia living under my uncle's roof, given all that went on beneath it — and there was talk of taking her away to live with a family in Bridgetown. But nothing came of it."

Then his gaze shuttered, and he turned once again to his window.

They said no more for the duration of the drive through the City. But when the carriage rumbled beneath Temple Bar, Rothewell seemed to bestir himself as if from a dream. "Are you happy, Camille?" he asked. "In Berkeley Square, I mean? You are satisfied there?"

For an instant, she hesitated. "I have never had a home of my own," she said quietly. *"Oui,* I like it well enough."

"I am glad," he said quietly. "I would never wish you unhappy."

"But if I might —" She paused, and snagged her lip between her teeth.

"Yes?" He looked at her pointedly. "Go on."

"I have some things still at Limousin," she said. "Sentimental things which I should like to send for."

"But of course. What sort of things?"

"*Bagatelles,* really," she said. "Things to . . . to warm the house. A pair of landscapes which I like, and some *objets d'art.* A set of needlepoint pillows and a portrait of my mother. A few of my favorite books."

"More of your dry financial tomes, eh?"

It took her a moment to realize he was teasing. "A few, *oui.*" She found herself blushing. "But also some geography and history — even a novel or two. The house, you see . . . well, it feels a little bit empty. I know you have not been there long. And I just thought that . . ." She searched her mind for the right word.

"You find it uncomfortable?" he suggested, once again stroking the dog pensively.

"*Certainement pas,*" she said hastily. "It is a lovely home and very comfortable indeed. I should have said it merely lacks ambience."

He seemed to consider it. "I daresay you are right," he said, his gaze fixed upon the shops along the Strand. "Xanthia and I wouldn't know ambience if we tripped over it. You should furnish it however it pleases you."

Their conversation fell away, and after a few minutes had passed, in which his eyes remained fixed beyond the window, he surprised her by calling to his coachman to halt.

"Why are we stopping?" she asked.

"It is a surprise," he said in his grim, raspy voice.

When the steps were down, he climbed out to help her descend. Inordinately curious, Camille laid her hands on his shoulders. Rothewell lifted her out as if she weighed nothing, then turned and set her lightly onto the pavement. Behind them, Chin-Chin danced about on the banquette, whining.

"Oh, bother!" said Rothewell under his breath. "Come along then." With that, he plucked up the dog and tucked him into his waistcoat.

They doubtless made an interesting sight strolling along the shop-lined Strand, with Rothewell's dark, rather ominous form towering over Camille's slender, far shorter one, and the little dog's head sticking incongruously from Rothewell's waistcoat.

Her hand on his arm, they strolled languidly past drapers and haberdashers and china shops until, a few yards along, Rothewell turned into an elegant, bow-fronted shop with a polished hook harp in the window. The small sign which swung from a brass bracket read JOS. HASTINGS FINE STRINGED INSTRUMENTS.

Inside, the place smelled of beeswax and of freshly sanded wood. Harps, harpsichords, and even a small spinet sat about the shop, the latter in a state of disrepair. Camille looked about in wonderment as a thin, pale gentleman came from behind the counter.

"Good afternoon," he said. "The harp catches one's eye, does it not?"

"*Oui,* it is most lovely," said Camille a little breathlessly.

The man steepled his fingertips lightly together. "You have excellent taste, ma'am," he said. "It is a McEwen single-action, and they just don't make them like that anymore." He bowed slightly to Rothewell. "Shall I price it for you, sir?"

"No, thank you," he said, extracting his card with one hand as he supported Chin-Chin with the other. "What we want is a piano. A grand piano."

A look of greed flashed across the man's countenance but was quickly veiled beneath a mask of obsequiousness. "You have certainly come to the right place, my lord!" he said, glancing at Rothewell's name. "The grand piano is the finest instrument money can buy. I have a lovely Babcock due in from Boston in a few weeks' time."

"No, not an American piano," said Rothewell a little irritably.

"Sir, the Americans really are not to be sneezed at." The man looked wounded. "The Babcock has a modern one-piece, cast-iron frame; one which will far outlast your lifetime."

Rothewell's mouth twisted wryly. "That I do not doubt," he said. "But what we want is the sort of piano you sold last year to the Marquess of Nash."

"Mon Dieu," Camille whispered, clutching at Rothewell's arm.

The pale man grew paler still. "Oh, dear," he murmured. "The six-octave Böhm. A truly exceptional instrument, of course."

"Of course," said Rothewell, ignoring Camille's grip. "How long shall it take?"

The man winced. "Sir, those are Viennese-made, and very hard to obtain."

"How long?" he said firmly.

"Why, it could be months, my lord," he said. "The Babcock can be had on a six-month order, and a good English piano in half that. But the Böhm — why, the one we just received was bespoke almost a year ago."

"You have one?" said Rothewell, his voice suddenly sharp.

"Well, yes," the pale man admitted. "But it is *bespoke*."

"Indeed? By whom?" Rothewell had extracted his purse.

"Well, by the French ambassador's wife," he answered.

Rothewell laid a banknote in his hand. "Then unbespeak it," he said quietly.

The pale man looked down at the banknote and swallowed hard.

Camille gasped.

"Well," said the man unsteadily. "Well, I daresay . . . I daresay there could have been a delay in shipment." He paused to lick his lips. "And after all, ambassadors come and ambassadors go, do they not?"

"Yes," said Rothewell grimly. "And I will not *go*. Away, I mean. *Ever*."

The pale man cast him a nervous glance, and tucked the banknote into his coat pocket. "It seems we have struck a bargain," he said brightly. "Congratulations, my lord."

"We are in Berkeley Square," said Rothewell. "When can you deliver it?"

The man cast a nervous glance toward the

366

back of the shop. "Early next week?" he answered. "But through the alley, I think, my lord. *Not* the front door."

"*Mon Dieu,* why did you do such a thing!" Camille protested, as he helped her back into the carriage ten minutes later. "Really, Rothewell, it was not necessary."

Indeed, she considered, she and her mother could have lived an entire year in reasonable comfort on the cost of the new piano alone — and never mind Rothewell's bribe.

Rothewell settled himself into his seat and extracted Chin-Chin from his brocade cocoon. "Walk on!" he cried to the coachman. Then, returning his somber, silvery gaze to hers, he said, "We are married now, Camille, and I wish my wife to have only the best. But the piano — ah, *that* is for me."

"For you, my lord?" She set her head to one side and studied him.

His eyes drifted slowly over her. "So that I might have the exquisite pleasure of hearing you play," he explained, his voice dropping an octave. "It is customary, is it not, for a wife to — er, to *entertain* her husband with her many talents?"

Camille felt a frisson of desire mixed with embarrassment, but she refused to look away. "And do I, my lord?" she whispered.

"Do I entertain you satisfactorily thus far?"

For a long moment, he said nothing. "Oh, I think you know the answer to that question, my dear," he finally answered. "I think you know very well indeed."

Oddly pleased, Camille relaxed against the seat and said no more.

Upon their arrival at Berkeley Square, Rothewell escorted her into the house with the dog trotting at his heels, then vanished. Camille went upstairs to find her grandfather's old letter, and rushed into Rothewell's bedchamber. Her shoulders fell with disappointment when she found the room empty.

She had hoped that he might be there; that she might reach out for him and feel again that sense of emotional intimacy they had shared so briefly in the shadowy confines of his carriage. It was a heady, almost dangerously seductive feeling, that wish to unburden oneself to someone who cared, and to yearn to be the vessel for the outpouring of another's grief — restrained, perhaps, though Rothewell's was. Still, they had shared something of themselves with one another.

Lingering, she drew in his tantalizing scent, cool and diffuse in the shadowy stillness of the room. She looked about the austere, ordinary walls. So many of her first impressions in this house were beginning to make sense. The lack of anything intimate, such as a portrait or a trinket. The emotional bareness of the décor. If she poked through her husband's drawers or riffled his desk, Camille sensed, she would find nothing. Nothing but folded clothes and unused letter paper. They had been three children who had possessed nothing of sentimental worth. Nothing which they wished to remember.

And into this cold, austere place, he had brought her — a cold and austere wife; one whom he seemed at times to wish to make even more so. Why? Why had he married her? Did he not wish for warmth and love? Perhaps they were kindred spirits, she and her husband, both afraid to want for anyone or anything. Afraid to hope. Afraid to love. But his voice in the carriage — that had been neither cold nor austere. And for the first time outside the bedchamber, he had looked at her with both tenderness and raw desire, his suggestive words running over her skin like molten honey.

Camille set her forehead to the smooth, cool wood of his bedpost, and fleetingly closed her eyes. She was falling. Falling fast and hard. And suddenly it dawned on her that she did not want to fail as a wife. She wanted to shake off the coldness, perhaps even at the cost of her own pain.

But could her wounded, withdrawn husband ever be convinced? Or was this the marriage — and the emotional distance — he would always insist upon? Her hand trembling a little, Camille laid the letter at the foot of his bed and left.

If Rothewell read the letter, he did not mention it. Camille found it on her writing desk the following day and tucked it back into her prayer book in which she had brought it from Limousin.

The following week, Rothewell surprised Camille by proposing a visit to Neville Shipping. The drive to the Docklands was fascinating, taking Camille deep into a part of the city she had never seen. The sounds and smells were gloriously uncultured — fetid mud, rotting fish, steaming meat pies, and the scent of the sea carried in by the massive merchant vessels which floated almost cheek by jowl across the Thames.

As they made their way along Wapping Wall, the alleys they passed were choked with stacks of barrels, crates of squawking poultry, and craggy-faced men with red noses and rough surtouts. Men of the sea, and of the slums. Rothewell pointed out the front door of Neville's offices, a grimy, nondescript building of four stories which was wedged between a cooperage and a shop selling rope and sailcloth.

At the front door, Rothewell lifted her down, spun her neatly over the pavement, and set her high on the doorstep. Camille looked down to see the pavement below splattered with what looked like fish offal and sodden straw.

"A vile place," he muttered, kicking a fish head from his path. "I daresay I'd no business bringing you down here."

"Not at all," Camille protested. "I think it fascinating."

Inside they were greeted by Xanthia, who was clearly stunned to see her brother. She tossed down the pencil and ledger she'd been poring over and came at once to the door. "This frightful account!" she said, obviously exasperated. "Thank God someone has come to save me from it."

After a brief introduction to Mr. Bakely, the head clerk, Xanthia gave them a quick tour of the counting house. The ground floor was one large room, surprisingly well-appointed, and generously lit from the wide rear windows which overlooked the Thames. The half dozen clerks, she noticed, gave Rothewell a wide berth but bowed to her as she passed between their desks.

"Do come upstairs," Xanthia suggested when they were through. "Mr. Bakely, give me back the ledger and I shall sort it out upstairs. Will you have one of the lads bring tea?"

With the offending book tucked under her arm, Xanthia started up the steps. They followed her up to a surprisingly grand, high-ceilinged office with a window which looked down on the teeming Pool of London. Glass bookcases lined one wall, whilst two wide mahogany desks, one of which was covered with neat stacks of baize account books and a pile of correspondence, dominated the room. The second was neat as a pin.

Xanthia paused to lay her ledger facedown atop the pile of correspondence. Amazed, Camille went directly to the window. "*Alors,* are any of those vessels yours?" she asked, staring down at the water.

"One, yes, and she's a fast, Boston-built beauty, too." Xanthia set her hand on Camille's shoulder and leaned past her, pointing. "The *Princess Pocahontas,* just there by Hanover Stairs."

"Only the one?" Camille had expected a vast flotilla.

Xanthia laughed. "We have another down at the West India Docks and one just upriver at St. Catherine's. Remember, my dear, that a ship in the Pool is a ship which is costing us money." She paused to set her hand over her heart. "That is my sacred duty. To keep our assets under sail."

Camille could feel Rothewell's comforting warmth just behind her. "Zee handles the planning and scheduling now," he explained, setting one hand at Camille's waist. "Gareth keeps up with the inventory and the money — or did do, at any rate."

Camille turned from the window. "The Duke of Warneham?" she said, bemused.

Xanthia's smile was a little twisted. "Gareth has been the duke but a short while. But now they believe Antonia — the duchess — is with child, so that's that, I daresay."

"Do they?" remarked Rothewell. "Perhaps that accounts for his moods."

Xanthia looked at him oddly, then went on. "I am happy for her, of course," she said. "But Gareth will be keeping himself at Selsdon now, I am sure. We have hired Mr. Windley, who is very good indeed."

"You are pleased with him, then?" asked her brother solicitously.

The smile twisted further. "Have I any choice?" Xanthia asked. "He'll do well enough. But no ordinary employee can ever be as dependable or as diligent as an owner." Here, she paused to look directly at her brother. "Moreover, I am not perfectly sure Mr. Windley is pleased with the Docklands. There was an unfortunate incident yesterday with a cutpurse in Mill Yard."

Rothewell winced. "I pray he stays on."

"Indeed," said Xanthia tightly.

Rothewell smiled a little grimly. "You wished my signature on something, Zee?"

She inclined her head toward her desk. "Several things from the bank," she said. "And I wish you to actually *read* them this time, if you please."

Xanthia began to lay out a long row of papers.

Rothewell groaned, and sat. "Give your recalcitrant account book to Camille," he suggested, lifting it from the desk. "She just finished some dusty tome about bookkeeping."

Xanthia raised her brows in mild surprise. "Well, idle hands do the devil's work," she remarked lightly. "If you can get those columns to balance, Camille, I shall be forever in your debt. Use Windley's desk."

"I should be pleased to try," she answered.

A little surprised at Rothewell's suggestion, Camille took the book and sat, plucking a pencil from a box on the desk. With

Xanthia standing over him, pointing out various bits of language in the papers they were reviewing, Rothewell read dutifully for a time, then began to dash his signature here and there as his sister instructed.

Camille rose uncertainly when they were done. "Here," she said, carrying the book, open, to Xanthia. "The clerk failed to carry over this charge for sailcloth. And the digits got reversed in that last line item for victualing."

Eyes widening, Xanthia looked down at the book. "Indeed?" she said. "Why, look! I do think you must be right. Does it balance?"

"*Oui*, it should do," said Camille. Swiftly, she finished the last of her calculations, moving her pencil down the page. "*Oui*, it is in order," she finally said. She closed the book and handed it back to Xanthia.

"Lovely!" said Xanthia brightly. "And fast, too."

Camille glanced at the floor. "I kept our accounts at Limousin," she explained. "Economy — and good arithmetic — were necessary."

Just then, a young servant came in carrying a tea tray. They retired to the chairs by the window. For the next half hour, they drank tea and spoke of mundane things, but all the while, Camille's eyes were roving about the room, taking in the charts, the bookcases stuffed with ledgers, and the huge map dotted with bright yellow pins, which covered nearly the whole of one wall. It seemed a new and exciting world to her; a world of commerce and of challenge.

Every few minutes, footsteps would thunder up or down the steps, or the little bell downstairs would jingle merrily as people dashed in and out the door. Even the cries of the boatmen from the river seemed exciting to Camille. Indeed, the entire place seemed to thrum with a special kind of energy, and Camille was suddenly and inordinately jealous of her sister-in-law.

"One would gather you do not darken Neville's door very often," she remarked, as Rothewell helped her back into the carriage. "Indeed, the staff seems to cower at your presence."

Rothewell's expression was inscrutable, his eyes hooded. "I was never a part of it," he said, settling into his seat. "It was my brother's business, not mine. If Zee is away, I go down and bludgeon the staff a bit if I must. Otherwise, I keep out of the way."

"*Oui,* but it is yours, too, is it not?" Camille prodded. "And how very odd that your sister is there."

Rothewell cut his eyes toward the window. "Xanthia is more than capable."

"*Bien sûr*," said Camille. "She seems quite devoted to her work — but devotion and competence are rarely enough to earn a woman respect. And soon, the child will come . . ."

He looked at her impatiently. "What, precisely, are you trying to say, Camille?" he asked, as the carriage jerked, then rocked into motion.

"I think you should talk to your sister," she answered. "I think she wishes to have your help."

His dark, slashing brows lifted. "*My* help?" he echoed, as if he had never before considered it. "Good God!"

Camille regarded him silently across the carriage.

Finally, he spoke again. "Neville Shipping was always something . . . something special, which Xanthia and Luke shared," he said pensively. "Something she has always loved. I never thought of it as a burden to her. It seems unfathomable."

"But she is to have a child now," Camille repeated. "And she is right when she says that no one can run a business as well as an owner. After all, it was you, was it not, who advised me to trust no one else to steward my wealth and steer my future?"

"Did I indeed?" he said quietly. "How very brilliant I am."

Her husband's gaze turned inward, but he seemed disinclined to discuss it further. Wisely, Camille let the subject drop.

For the duration of their journey, Rothewell fell quiet — not his usual grim silence, but more of a pensive lull. Camille wondered what he was thinking. And she tried *not* to think about how much she was enjoying the afternoons spent in his company. Indeed, there was little she would rather do.

She was becoming foolish. She half wished Rothewell would come home raging drunk again, so that she might quarrel with him, and have a good excuse to jerk herself up short. She needed to realize that *that* was the man she had married. He had made himself — and his wishes — plain when he had agreed to marry her. Their short, shared interludes of true intimacy aside, Rothewell's heart was still closed to her. He had given it long ago — given it to a dead woman, for whom he still grieved — and that was the end of it. She must not be a fool. She must be content with what she had.

When they went up the steps at Berkeley Square, it was to find Lord and Lady Sharpe drawing up after them in a large, open carriage. Camille looked down to see that Lady Sharpe wore an elaborate lavender hat and was swathed in a heavy cloak of a deeper shade of purple.

"There are our newlyweds!" she cried up at them. "My dears, Sharpe and I were just going for a drive in the park. Do join us."

But Camille was cold, and far more interested in remaining at home with her husband. After a swift, assessing glance at her, Rothewell declined, and asked them in to tea instead. A footman stepped forward to help Lady Sharpe from the carriage.

Just then, a flash of motion caught Camille's eye. Rothewell's stick went clattering down the steps. Camille turned to watch in horror as his knees seemed to collapse beneath him. Lady Sharpe screamed, startling the horses. The footmen leapt back as the carriage jerked wildly.

"Oh, mon Dieu!" Terrified, Camille knelt.

"Well, bless me!" Lord Sharpe clambered down, heedless of the carriage's movement.

"Kieran!" cried Lady Sharpe. "What is it?"

By now, Trammel had flung open the front door. Sharpe and the butler knelt on either side of Rothewell, and when Camille glimpsed his face in the afternoon light, her terror deepened. Deathly pale was not too strong a term.

"All right, old chap?" asked Sharpe.

Her heart in her throat, Camille could not make out Rothewell's response. Sharpe and the butler somehow got him to his feet and into the house.

"I'm fine," Rothewell managed. "Just . . . light-headed."

"Into the library, sir, if you please," said the butler to Sharpe.

Rothewell tried to shake them off, insisting he could walk. But his pain was obvious. In moments, he was half-sitting, half-stretched out on a red chaise which faced the fireplace, his face still twisted in agony, his hand clasping one side of his ribs.

"Build up the fire, Trammel," Lady Sharpe ordered. "And send for a doctor."

Rothewell reached out, and grasped Sharpe by his wrist. "No . . . doctor," he gritted.

"Rothewell, don't be a fool!" Lady Sharpe bent over the side of the divan. "Where does it hurt? Are you queasy?"

"Yes," Rothewell managed.

The butler returned from summoning a footman for the fire. "The pain will pass, ma'am, I believe," he suggested. "He just needs air and rest."

Lady Sharpe looked indignant. "What do

you mean to say, Trammel? Has this happened before?"

Camille had pulled a chair to the divan, and sat stroking Rothewell's shoulder. His posture, she noted, was relaxing. She tried to remain calm, though a deep sense of despair was spreading over her.

Heedless of the others, she knelt by the chaise. "Where is the pain?" she said softly, taking his hand. "Is it *le cœur?*"

He shook his head. "The heart, no," he rasped. He winced again, and sucked air through his teeth. "Christ, this is humiliating."

"Don't be an *imbecile,*" she said, forcing her voice to be calm. "Just tell me where it hurts."

"I thought" — his breath hitched — "I thought you weren't going to ask questions. That you meant to stay out of this."

Stay out of this? She had threatened as much, yes. But it had been a lie, she now realized. "Is that what you thought?" she said, struggling to steady her voice. "That I would let you quietly kill yourself? *Non.* Now, where does it hurt?"

A look of resignation passed over his face. "The ribs, then. Under them. Everywhere, really."

Camille released his hand and began to

unbutton his waistcoat. She wished desperately she could summon Xanthia, for she might better know how to influence her brother. But Xanthia was with child, and there was always a risk . . .

"What did you have to eat?" she asked.

"Toast," he answered, his head falling back. "Some . . . eggs, I think."

The room had gone perfectly still. With one less layer of clothing to hamper her, Camille set a hand flat on his rib cage and began to feel her way gingerly outward. At a point just below the last rib, he winced again.

"You must have a doctor." Camille's hand was shaking a little. "I insist."

"No doctor, damn it," he swore. "Not yet. Not . . . *yet.* Please, Camille. Don't harangue me."

Camille hesitated, looking around at the others. "*Madame,* the two of you should go. It is possible he might be — how do you say — *contagieux?*"

"Contagious?" Lady Sharpe's expression was anguished. "Oh, no."

"Nonetheless, you must think of the little one," said Camille.

Just then, Rothewell grunted, and drew almost double on a gasp of pain.

"Oh my God!" cried Lady Sharpe. "Something must be done. He needs laudanum."

Camille cupped his face in her hand. "Kieran?"

"Brandy," hissed Rothewell.

Lady Sharpe leaned urgently forward. "Oh, for God's sake, Kieran! You cannot treat every ill with brandy."

Camille looked up at Trammel and dared him with her eyes. He drew back, and did not fetch the brandy.

After a time, Rothewell's pain seemed to relent again. He lay upon the chaise with his legs flat, both his brow and his breathing smoother. Camille looked down at their hands, which had somehow become entwined, and suddenly wanted to cry.

"Buck up, old girl," he whispered, squeezing her fingers. "If I die, at least you'll have Jim-Jim."

"*Mon Dieu,* how can you jest at such a time?" Camille wanted, suddenly, to be alone with him. Still kneeling on the floor in a puddle of silk, she looked up at Lady Sharpe. "Please, *madame,* you should go now," she said, blinking back the tears. "I will see him safely to bed and stay with him through the night. And tomorrow I shall send you word of how he goes on, *oui?*"

Rothewell smiled weakly. "Go on, old girl," he said to his cousin. "Go home. I have a wife to plague me now, remember? Just as you wished."

At last, the countess gave in. After another round of reassurances, Lord Sharpe patted his wife's shoulder, then urged her out. A second later, Camille heard the front door shut behind him.

Still staring at their hands, Camille opened her mouth, but nothing came out. Her husband's blithe words did not comfort her. Pain in one's organs was dangerous. A putrid appendix — or something equally untreatable — and he could be dead by morning. Or he could be up dancing a jig. There really was no knowing. The realization terrified her, even as the memories of her many vigils by her mother's bed haunted her.

Camille bit her lip to keep from crying. He was her husband, and he was suffering. It brought home to her once again the significance of what she had pledged.

Wilt thou love, honor, and keep him in sickness and in health?

Perhaps she had not meant those words when she'd spoken her vows, but she meant them now. She did not have to fail as a wife. Perhaps she did not have to be cold — if she was willing to risk opening that heart she had once wished only to shutter. Camille lifted her head, kissed his hand, then rose.

Rothewell looked up, his gaze holding hers. "Perhaps this is nothing," he rasped. "Perhaps it will pass." But he spoke as a man unconvinced, and she saw an ache in his eyes which went beyond physical pain.

She squeezed his hand, and set her shoulders back determinedly. "Randolph, come here, please," she ordered the hovering footman. "You and Trammel help him up to bed."

"Yes, my lady."

"I can go on my own, damn it," said her husband, moving as if to stand.

"Very well," she said tartly. "Then they shall merely walk beside you holding on to your shoulders."

Rothewell shot her a wry look as the servants did as she ordered, escorting him from the room.

"And Trammel?" said Camille. "We shall want the doctor next, *s'il vous plaît.*"

"No doctor," muttered Rothewell, looking up the stairs as if dreading the climb.

Camille shook her head and looked at Trammel. "Send someone."

Rothewell managed a weak laugh. "Your new mistress is proving persistent, Trammel," he said. "Camille, my dear, you are not a nursemaid."

"No, I am your wife," she calmly returned. "And I think even Trammel will tell you that you would do well to heed me."

"That's as may be," he answered, "but what I want is my bed and my brandy — in that order. I am sure it will pass by morning."

Camille saw the exasperated look which flashed across the butler's face, but Trammel said nothing. Even now, however, some of Rothewell's color was returning. He was no longer grimacing against the pain.

"*Très bien,*" she said, as they reached the top of the steps. "But only until dawn, *monsieur,* will we wait, *oui?* After that, we will do it my way."

"I didn't say that," he growled.

Camille shrugged. "It little matters," she answered. "As you are, you are too weak, I think, to chase me back down the steps and stop me. So it will be done as I wish."

He cursed beneath his breath and shot her a dark look, but Trammel's faint smile was triumphant.

Chapter Eleven

IN WHICH LORD ROTHEWELL
DINES AL FRESCO

To Camille's relief, Rothewell awoke the following morning much recovered. He had passed a bad night, she knew, for even though he had adamantly refused her a place in his bed, Camille had insisted on keeping the connecting door open. Twice he had been up retching, and had paced the floor for a time — during the short weeks of their marriage, she had come to sense his every move and mood, it seemed — but with each instance, he had appeared vaguely mortified by his weakness and demanded she return to bed when the worst was past.

Despite all this, he was sitting up in bed with the dog on his lap when she rose sometime near dawn. Camille perched on the edge of his mattress and watched as Miss Obelienne personally urged upon him a few bites of porridge and some hot tea.

When at last he forced the cook away he lay back, with Chin-Chin tucked beneath his arm. Camille rose to open the door so that Miss Obelienne might carry the tray back out again, then went out into the passageway with her.

"His color is much improved, I think," Camille remarked hopefully.

Miss Obelienne cast a worried look at the door. "*Oui,* for now," she conceded.

Camille laid a hand upon the older woman's arm. "What do you think is the matter with him?" she asked. "Is it just the drinking?"

Miss Obelienne shook her head. "It is the devils eating him." Her voice was grim despite her island lilt. "The past, *oui?* It is like a cancer in the belly."

But it was more than that, Camille sensed, as she watched Miss Obelienne's proud, rigid form descend the stairs. For a moment she stood there in the cool, dark stillness of the passageway, wondering at the cook's strange diagnosis. Guilt and anger, yes, it could eat at a man. But not like this. Not in such violent, irregular attacks.

With a sigh, she returned to Rothewell's bedchamber to begin anew the fight over calling in a doctor. But it was a fight she was destined to lose. By the time she pushed open the door, her husband was up and stropping his razor.

Camille took up a sentinel's position in one of his wide armchairs and watched assessingly as the servants brought his hot water and laid out his clothes for the day. Rothewell's hand was unerringly steady as he drew the blade down in firm, straight strokes, neatly scraping away the soap.

"I am going out later today," he said, his gaze steadily watching her in the mirror. "I won't be back until late."

The argument, Camille realized, was again lost.

He bent over the basin to sluice away the remaining soap, then turned around, toweling off his face. He was naked from the waist up, and he looked incredibly, vigorously male, with his broad chest, and the trail of dark hair which disappeared beneath the drawers, which hung loosely from his lean hips. His eyes were again piercing, his jaw firmly set in its usual manner. It was almost as if the water had washed away not just soap and stubble, but all evidence of the previous night.

Yes, she grimly considered, he was definitely well enough today to chase her back down the stairs. The doctor would not be coming. She tried to feel relieved. To feel hope. Perhaps, as he said, it had been nothing.

"I'm to meet Nash and his brother Hayden-Worth at their club," he went on, tossing down the towel. "And then to play cards. Have you something with which to occupy yourself?"

It was the first time he had bothered to inform her of his plans. Camille had risen and made her way to the door. There, she hesitated, and cut him a sidelong glance. "*Oui,* the new piano will occupy me," she said softly. "I have some practicing, I think, to do?"

He smiled, a soft, faintly wicked smile which definitely lit his eyes. "Ah, a capital notion," he murmured. "Perhaps I shan't be so late after all."

Two days after her husband's sudden illness, Camille went down for luncheon only to find, strangely, that the table had not been set and that no footmen were in attendance. Instead, Miss Obelienne awaited her with a leather satchel in hand.

"What is this?" Camille asked, confused.

Miss Obelienne's eyes were stubbornly narrowed. "Food," she said, tilting her head toward the satchel. "He must get out of this house — in the daylight, I am saying. The night has an evil grip. You will take him to the park today."

Camille frowned. "I — I do not comprehend. To the park as in . . ." She searched her mind for the right word, "— a *picnic?*"

"*Oui,*" said Miss Obelienne. "Out in the air. It is a good day. The Lord has brought us sun."

To her surprise, Rothewell came in behind her, carrying a fold of paper. "Camille, Xanthia has written to ask —" He drew to a halt and looked at them, surprised. "What have you there, Miss Obelienne?"

"Spiced chicken. Cheese. Apple tart. Cassava pone." She glared at him, then hefted the bag onto the table with a heavy *thunk!* "Your luncheon."

Camille turned to him with a specious smile. "Apparently we are going on a picnic."

Miss Obelienne had her arms crossed over her chest. Rothewell's gaze trailed back to the satchel. "A picnic?" he echoed. "In London?"

"*Oui,*" said the cook. She made a dismissive motion with one finger, as if he were Chin-Chin being sent from the room. "Go. The outdoors will give you appetite."

Finally, Rothewell laughed and lifted both hands. "Obelienne has spoken," he conceded. "I'll send for my gig."

Camille let her gaze run down him. "*Ça*

alors!" she murmured. "Perhaps I should engage Obelienne's assistance more often."

Rothewell turned to go, and a look of relief passed fleetingly over the cook's usually impassive face. Only then did Camille realize what Obelienne's bravado had cost her. She had not been at all sure of her employer's cooperation. She had counted, perhaps, on Camille's presence to defuse Rothewell's temper. A remarkable notion.

Half an hour later, they sat beneath a tree near the quiet westerly end of the Serpentine Pond, amidst the bare trees and shrubs. Rothewell's horse was tied nearby. The fashionable rarely came so far, Camille assumed, for this part of the park was empty today and far less manicured.

Camille lifted her face to the sun, and fleetingly closed her eyes. The weather was not warm by any measure, but it was a brilliant, cloudless day rarely seen on either side of the Channel at this time of year, and she found herself in a strange, slightly giddy mood.

Beside her, Rothewell had tossed aside his hat, and was removing the parcels of food carefully wrapped in cheesecloth and setting them out atop his driving cloak, which he'd spread upon the ground. He had not thought to bring a blanket. Certainly she had not.

So far as she could recall, she had never dined out of doors. Her mother's interests had run more to late-night affairs — masques, soirées, gaming salons, and the like. Rarely had the Countess of Halburne risen before midafternoon. Not until those final years, when she had scarce left her bed save to rummage round for a bottle of wine, or the dregs of whatever drink she could wheedle from the servants.

"Chicken?"

"Pardon?" She looked around to see Rothewell leaning toward her on one elbow and holding up a drumstick for her inspection. Impulsively, she leaned over and took a bite.

"Your personal servant now, am I?" he said laconically.

Scowling, Camille chewed the bite into submission, then, "We haven't any plates or forks," she protested.

"Never eaten with your fingers, eh?" Rothewell nibbled at the leg himself.

"Non, I have not." Camille dabbed at the corners of her mouth with her handkerchief. "And you do not seem much of a — a picnicker, either. If that is a proper English word?"

Rothewell laughed, and laid the chicken aside. Her heart sank with it. She had hoped Miss Obelienne knew something that she did not, and that the great outdoors would have miraculously whetted her husband's appetite. On an inward sigh, Camille picked over the food and took a piece of cheese to nibble on, but the taste disagreed with her, as food so often did of late. Indeed, her once-healthy appetite had waned to a mild revulsion. Soon, she would be little better than her husband.

When she looked back, Rothewell was reclined on both elbows, his long, booted legs crossed at the ankles, staring across the water toward the farms and fields of Kensington. A faint breeze came off the Serpentine, gently teasing at his hair, and for an instant, he looked almost boyish. And surprisingly wistful.

"I don't think I have been on a picnic in fifteen or twenty years," he said quietly.

"Have you not?" she answered. "It seems such a quintessentially English thing to do."

"I daresay." His gaze had turned distant. "It didn't seem like much of a lark when one ate out of doors more often than not."

"Did you?" she asked. "Why?"

He glanced up at her. "I lived in the cane fields, Camille," he said. "I was a glorified farmer."

Camille had heard terrible stories about the work of harvesting and processing sugar cane. France had many such interests in the Caribbean. "Was sugar as dreadful a business as they say?"

"Dreadful is such a relative term, my dear." He flashed a sardonic smile. "It was hot, dirty, and dangerous work. For our slaves, though . . . yes, I daresay they found it dreadful indeed."

"*Oui,* I am sure." Camille fell quiet for a time. "Who oversees the slaves, now that you are here?"

"No one," he said. "They are my tenant farmers now."

"*Alors,* you . . . you gave them freedom?" she asked. "That was generous."

He grunted dismissively. "It wasn't generous," he said. "It was *right.* We should have done so when Uncle died, but the estate was so deep in debt, Luke said —" His gaze had turned suddenly inward.

"*Oui?*" Camille encouraged. "What did he say?"

Rothewell shook his head. "He wanted to pay off Uncle's debts," he answered. "And after that . . . we debated it, the three of us. We decided everything together. But the pressure from the other planters — to set so many slaves free at once — it was frowned upon."

"Why?"

"They feared another rebellion," he said. "And slaves who are freed can move about at will. But it little matters now."

"Does it not? Why?"

He shrugged. "The days of slavery need to end," he said quietly. "It is a vile, corrupting institution, and it will eventually be outlawed, if what Anthony Hayden-Worth says is true. It is one of his pet projects in the Commons."

Camille shivered, and tucked her cloak a little closer. "I have always thought slavery dreadful."

He was still staring into the distance. "But when you grow up with it," he said, "you don't think of it at all. It is simply the way of things. Then, as you get older, you begin to see that a slave is just a man like you, with his own hopes and fears and even dreams. And when you know that . . . when the knowledge comes clearer with every passing day . . . well, it takes a hardened soul to look past it."

"A great many people seem to have no trouble looking past it," said Camille a little sarcastically.

"I cannot speak for them," he said quietly.

"I speak only for myself. What I have seen. What I have learnt. Abolition is the only way — and it cannot happen soon enough."

"Perhaps . . . Perhaps you can support Mr. Hayden-Worth's efforts in some way?" she tentatively suggested. "Perhaps if more people believed as you do, abolition would come sooner?"

Rothewell shrugged, and looked away.

Camille recalled the story about their dead brother's wife, the woman Rothewell had loved — and would perhaps always love. No doubt that circumstance, more than any other, had altered his thinking.

"Xanthia told me about your brother's wife," she blurted, staring at her hands, which were clasped in her lap. "That she was of mixed race, and that she was not always welcome in society. I am sure that was hurtful."

She watched his jaw go rigid, a bad sign. "Xanthia spoke out of turn," he gritted. He sounded angrier, even, than she had expected.

"Non," said Camille sharply. "She did not. That woman was a part of your family. Her daughter still is."

"She is dead," he replied, his words curt. "My brother is dead. There is nothing to talk about, and by God, Xanthia knows it.

But apparently I am going to have to remind her of that fact."

Camille's temper slipped. "How can you be angry with Xanthia?" she demanded. "I am your wife, Rothewell, and this has to do with your family. I have a right to know such things, especially if I'm to bear your child."

His sensuous lips turned into a sneer. "Oh, that's high talk, Camille, from a woman who not so many days past, wanted nothing more than my seed," he returned. "A woman who called our marriage a 'transaction.'"

"Rothewell, that is not fair —"

"No, it is a fact," he interjected. Rothewell had turned to face her, his eyes glittering with emotion. "Even now, Camille, you cannot even call me by my name."

"I — I have."

"Aye, once? Twice?" He sneered again. "You said you didn't care where I went, what I did, or who I did it with."

Something inside Camille snapped. "How dare you?" she whispered. "*Mon Dieu*, how *dare* you? You have already made it plain — more than plain — that those things are none of my concern. *Alors,* has that changed? Is this to be a real marriage? You wish to be accountable to me now?"

He turned his head, and glared into the

distance.

"*Non*," she said quietly. "*Non*, I did not think so."

Rothewell cursed beneath his breath, then jerked to his feet and strode away.

"*Zut!*" Camille's hands balled into fists. "You are an ass, Kieran!" she cried after him. "An obstinate ass. *Et voilà!* — I have used your name!"

He went down the slight slope to the water's edge, one hand set at his waist. The other hand dragged through his hair, then fell. His shoulders slumped as if with fatigue. But when she thought that he would turn around, or at least stop, he strode off down the path which edged along the pond.

Should she follow him and plead with him? Apologize? But for what? And why should she? He was wrong — and stubborn in the bargain.

And sick, she reminded herself as he disappeared behind the trees. Guilt began to needle at her. He must have loved Annemarie very deeply. Though it hurt her to think of it, how could she judge him for it? All her girlish infatuations aside, Camille had never loved anyone save her mother and her nurse — well, not until now. And now it was her fate to love a man whose heart was not whole.

Behind her, Rothewell's horse whinnied a little pitifully.

Camille glanced over her shoulder. "He will come back, *Monsieur Cheval*," she said a little sadly. "*Oui,* he must, mustn't he?"

With that, she fell back onto the driving cloak, shut her eyes, and sighed. Rothewell was right — at least in part. In the beginning of this pathetically misbegotten marriage, she had not known what she wanted. She had demanded one thing of him, and secretly begun to long for another — a thing which frightened her, and shook her to her very core. She wanted his love. She wanted a true marriage. And now she had raised the worst possible topic — his lost love. A picnic, indeed!

She was not certain how long she lay there mentally thrashing herself and trying to determine the precise moment when she had fallen in love with her husband. But eventually, she felt a shadow move over her, and opened her eyes.

Rothewell stood above her, but not looking at her, his eyes narrowed against the sun, his mouth grim. "What the devil do you want of me, Camille?" he rasped. "What? Can you tell me that?"

She sat up, and looked at him unflinchingly. "*Oui,* I want you to be happy," she said. "To be whole and happy, instead of sick and angry — angry with the whole world around you. I want you to have a purpose in your life. To feel joy instead of despair. You may believe it or not as you please."

He looked away, his expression strained. "You are going to be disappointed, Camille," he said quietly. "I cannot be the kind of man you need. It isn't in me."

"Wait!" She held up one hand. "Did I ask you to *be* anything? Are my ears and my tongue deceiving me?"

"I know what you want," he said darkly. "But I've disappointed every woman in my life save, perhaps, for my sister."

"Stop, *s'il vous plaît*." Camille still held her hand up, palm out. "You will not play this trick of words on me, *monsieur*. I meant just what I said. You are a vile-tempered, unhappy man, and you worry all who care for you — your sister, Lady Sharpe, *oui*, even your servants." Then, fortuitously, she recalled Xanthia's words. "Your love and your grief for this dead woman is like a boil on your heart, Rothewell. And you will not lance it. You make your whole family suffer the pain."

Some powerful emotion flickered in his eyes, and for an instant, she feared his face might crumple. But Rothewell was made of sterner stuff than that. He set his jaw grimly and looked out across the water.

"I do not hurt for a dead woman, Camille," he said, pushing back his coat as he set one hand on his hip. "In that, you are wrong. Xanthia is wrong."

"*Alors,* what is it, then?" Camille challenged, not certain what folly drove her. "Do you think, Rothewell, that I do not hear you pacing the floors all hours of the night? — when, that is, you choose to come home. You do not eat or sleep, but keep only to your brandy and your solitude. *Mon Dieu,* I have already nursed to the grave one miserable human being bent on drinking herself to death because love was lost to her. I do not relish a second."

"By God, what do you want to know, then?" he snapped. "All of it? Every filthy truth — and the lies that go with it? And be damned sure of your answer, Camille. Be *damned* sure — for once it is said, it cannot be unsaid, and you will have to think of it every time you look at me."

"*Non,* I shan't —"

"*Yes,*" he interjected with icy certainty. "You will. Every time I come to your bed, you will remember this day."

"Will I?" Camille offered up her hand.

"Then I shall risk it. Sit down, *s'il vous plaît?*"

Rothewell still did not look at her, but he sat back down on the cloak and braced his elbows on his knees. After many moments had passed, he exhaled, a sound of surrender and of grief. "Her name was Annemarie," he finally said. "Did Xanthia tell you that, too?"

"*Oui,* she told me that," Camille murmured.

"Annemarie was older than I — and a good deal more polished." His gaze was still fixed in the distance. "She was . . . a fallen woman, I suppose. And I fancied myself in love with her."

Camille resisted the urge to touch him, but the raw emotion in his eyes tugged at her heart.

He dropped his head, and stared at his boots. "Although I was young, I was . . . well, not without experience," he said. "Luke and I — we had lived unsheltered lives, to say the least. But nothing had prepared me for Annemarie."

"*Oui?* In what way?" asked Camille softly.

He shook his head. "She was . . . she was ephemeral and worldly all at once," he said. "She was dark and very French, and her eyes — Christ, they simply smoldered. Men fought one another for the mere favor of helping her across the street. And she was my lover before she married Luke."

"Xanthia suggested as much," Camille quietly acknowledged.

But Rothewell's eyes had gone black and fierce, his fists squeezed tight as if he might pummel someone. The suppressed anger inside him was palpable now.

Suddenly, Camille was anxious. She had said she would risk it, yes — but what if he were right? What if this changed everything? Was not a skilled lover and sometimes-friend better than the nothing she had been living with for so long?

She licked her lips uncertainly. *"Je ne sais pas,"* she whispered to herself. "Perhaps, Kieran, you were right —"

"No." He held up one hand, palm out. "You started this, Camille," he said, his voice hoarse. "You started it. You and Xanthia. So now you can sit there and listen to this . . . this *thing.* This awful thing I wanted to take to the grave. I will tell you — and then I don't want to hear of it ever again. Do you hear me?"

"Mais oui, if you wish it." She curled her fingers into the fabric of her skirt, for to her horror, her hands had begun to shake. "For what it is worth, I have known many women

like your Annemarie."

He swallowed hard, and dropped the hand. "She was not . . . she was *not* my Annemarie," he rasped. "Not ever. I asked her to be my mistress — many times. I gave her money, yes, and a bit of jewelry here and there. But each time I pressed her for an answer, she would hesitate. She wanted me — in her bed, at least. She would even cry, and swear she loved me. But apparently, I was not quite what she was looking for."

"What . . . what did she want, then?"

Rothewell shook his head. "A husband," he said. "Security. I just was too young and too arrogant to see it. So one day my brother asked her to marry him. And she . . . she said *yes.*"

Though Camille had already learned much of this from Xanthia, hearing it from his own lips was entirely different. His pain was still raw, and it told in his tone. He had lost his only love to the brother whom he had adored and respected. And in a way, he had been betrayed by them both.

"Did you know, Kieran, that your brother was in love with her?" Camille whispered.

He shook his head, his glossy dark hair catching the lowering angle of the afternoon sun. "I should have," he acknowledged. "I knew he admired her, and that they were well acquainted. I don't know what Anne-marie told him about us — something less than the truth, I daresay. I should have seen the whole bloody mess coming, but I was so naïve, I did not."

"*Mon Dieu,* you must have been devastated."

"No, outraged," he gritted. "It drove a wedge between us that remained until Luke's death. But he felt I had insulted Annemarie; that she deserved something more honorable than what I had offered. He accused me of toying with her affections. So he married her, and we fought over it. I bloodied his nose, and he broke two of my fingers. Then I moved out of the house."

"And after that?" asked Camille. "What happened?"

Wearily, he lifted both shoulders. "Nothing — on the surface of it," he said. "We made a surly sort of peace between us. Then Luke turned his attention to the shipping business and left me to run the plantations."

"You . . . you never returned home?"

At last, he looked at her. His eyes held a world-weary look edged with something which troubled her. "How could I sleep beneath that roof, Camille?" he whispered. "I couldn't keep my hands off her — and she was my brother's *wife.*"

A sense of dread ran through Camille. There was more to this story, she sensed, than Xanthia knew. "And Annemarie — how did she feel?"

He snorted with disgust. "Annemarie was happy enough," he said. "She had found a way to have her cake and eat it, too."

Camille shook her head. "This cake . . . I-I do not comprehend."

He tore his eyes from hers, and stared at the water. "We were still lovers, Camille."

"Mon dieu!" Camille set her fingers to her mouth.

"She would slip away to see me with any excuse she could find." His voice was dead. "I told myself . . . I told myself it was her doing, not mine. I never sought her out. *Never.* Never even met her eyes over dinner — on those rare occasions I could bear to go home. But God help me, when she would turn up at my door . . . I was weak."

Camille suddenly felt sick.

"Every time I would tell myself — and her — *never* again," he whispered. "It sickened me. I would beg God's forgiveness and swear it was over. And then . . . there she'd be. Standing in the middle of my cottage, with that wide-brimmed hat in her hands, and a desperate look in her eyes. If I told her to get out, she would cry. She

would say . . . she would say that she had
made a mistake. That Luke . . . that he did
not love her as I did. That her life was coming apart, and that if I would just hold
her . . ."

"Mais non," said Camille sadly, "it never
stopped at that, did it?"

He swallowed hard, and shook his head.
"I gave in. Every time. Because she would
tell me she loved me, and for a few minutes,
it would be like before. But it wasn't. She
was Lady Rothewell. And I was just the
younger brother."

Camille set her hand over his. "She . . .
she wanted a title?"

"God, I don't know." His voice was bleak.
Beaten. "She wanted to be something other
than a rich man's mistress. I look back, and
I try to understand. Her honor was stripped
from her when she was very young —
thirteen or fourteen. I forget. He was rich
and lily-white, and she was neither. She had
no say in the matter, and when he was done
with her, he simply cast her off — she and
their child, Martinique. It . . . it did something to her. I cannot explain it."

Camille thought, strangely, of her mother.
And of the deep wounds rejection and
insecurity could leave behind when hope
was lost and love was but a cold memory.

Her mother had turned to brandy. Annemarie, it seemed, had been more clever. Or more desperate.

"Did you brother suspect?" she asked quietly.

Rothewell laughed bitterly. "He should have done," he answered. "But no, we trusted one another completely, the three of us. We had to; otherwise, we would never have survived. Luke was always in Bridgetown slaving away at the office — and soon he began to take Xanthia along. I lived half a mile beyond the plantation house. No, he never suspected."

"How old were you when it started?"

"Old enough to damn well know better."

Camille felt her lips thin. "I wish to know what age, *s'il vous plaît*."

He lifted one shoulder wearily. "Eighteen," he said. "Nineteen, perhaps."

"And you feel you betrayed your brother?" she gently pressed. "Is that it?"

He turned at last to look at her, his eyes as flat and gray as slate. "I don't *feel* it," he answered. "I did it. That's the sort of man I am, Camille. You said it yourself. The very day we met, you called me a devil. Then you offered to pay me a hundred thousand pounds to impregnate you. You knew precisely what I was."

409

"*Oui.* And then I offered to have an *affaire* so that you might divorce me, *n'est-ce pas?*" she responded, her words soft. "Yet is either of us the same person as the ones who met on that night? Are we truly as callous as we sound?"

"Don't look for honor in me, Camille." His voice was rough as gravel. "I lay with my brother's wife — over and over again until I somehow found the will to stop it. But the damage was done. And I can't even begin to tell you the pain I've caused Martinique, out of my own selfish bitterness. Hell, I even cheated at cards to get what I wanted. Yes, I cheated at Valigny's that night. You didn't know that, did you?"

She looked at him blankly for a moment. *"Non,"* she whispered. "And I do not believe it."

He laughed darkly. "Valigny kept drawing the Queen of Spades," he said. "I began to suspect he was palming it — his lucky card, you know. Some gamblers do that. So I found it, and I stole it. I laid it down as if it were mine. I did it and . . . damn it, I don't even know why I did it."

She squeezed his hand. "Perhaps you did it to save me?" she whispered. "Perhaps you knew, as I knew, that you were my only hope?"

His eyes glittered. "Don't try to paint this a pretty color, Camille," he said tightly. "I don't wish the past sugarcoated just to make me — or you — feel better about what happened. I am what I am. Now for God's sake, let that be the end of it."

"But what happened with your brother was a tragedy," Camille murmured.

"Wrong, *oui*. But I know you loved him very much."

Her husband's hands balled into fists, and his jaw went rigid. "Luke — he was *everything* to us," he choked. "Can you understand that? *Can* you? He was both brother and father. He fought to keep us together. Good God, I cannot count the times he kept Uncle from beating me to death. He'd take the lashes himself if he had to. And Xanthia —" Here, Rothewell jerked to a halt, and physically shuddered. "God only knows what Uncle would have done to Xanthia — him, or one of his drunken friends. A young girl, growing up in a house like that — around men of his ilk — it was inhuman, the way they would look at her. Until she was old enough to keep a pistol under her pillow, one of us slept on the floor in her room. Luke at first. Then me."

"*Mon Dieu,*" whispered Camille. "Your uncle was a monster."

She looked at Rothewell, but his eyes were still distant. He said no more.

"What finally happened to him, this uncle?" Camille asked. "A quick and painless death?"

"Aye." Rothewell's mouth twisted bitterly. "How did you guess?"

"Is it not always the way with the wicked?" she asked a little bitterly. "We must hope *le bon Dieu* makes them pay for it in the end, for they surely do not pay for it on this earth."

Rothewell's bitter expression did not abate. "Yes, I have been giving that one a good deal of thought of late."

He was still thinking of Annemarie, she knew. Impulsively, Camille took his fist in her hand and forced it to relax, rubbing the tension from his palm, and then his fingers. What he had done — dear heaven, it really was quite unforgivable. Why, then, did she feel so deeply for him? Why did she sit here rubbing his hand and wondering if his forgiveness was not long overdue? Could a boy — one without a mother's love or a father's guidance — really be a man at nineteen? Or would he define love wrongly, and seek it out desperately?

Perhaps she was just making excuses, but she was no longer sure she cared. She had long ago given up any pretense that they might someday live apart. Frighteningly, perhaps, she was committed to her marriage for the duration — and she would likely be nursing her husband all the way to the grave if he kept up his hard living and self-torment. But there was no other option now. Not for her heart.

When his palm and fingers lay flat and relaxed upon his thigh, she spoke quietly. "How did your uncle die, Kieran?"

"Luke," he said, his voice flat. "Luke pushed him down the stairs."

Camille was not surprised. "Perhaps he deserved it."

Rothewell gave another snort of disgust. "Aye, he deserved it," he answered. "He had quarreled with Xanthia — God, I can't even remember why. He called her an insolent little slut and backhanded her. The blood . . . her lip. It split wide open. And this time, Luke just snapped. He pushed Uncle away and — and somehow, he fell. They were standing at the top of the staircase. Uncle was drunk, of course. He broke his neck."

Camille did not know what to say. A chill wind picked up, ruffling at the edge of her skirts, and tugging her hair from its pins. They were utterly alone amongst the trees, with nothing but the occasional spate of birdsong or the clatter of leafless branches to break the tension.

"Was there trouble for Luke?" she finally asked. "The — the constables?"

Rothewell shook his head. "Just an inquest," he said quietly. "Our uncle's reputation was well-known. It was accounted something of a miracle he lived to see five-and-forty."

Camille narrowed her eyes against the sun. "How old were you when you went to live with him?" she asked musingly. "Do you remember your parents at all?"

He nodded. "Oh, yes," he said. "But as a little child remembers. Impressions. Flashes of memory. Just this . . . hazy sort of happiness. And smells. I remember how my mother smelled — of lavender water. I adored it."

His posture relaxed a little, and his face softened. Camille smiled. "What a lovely memory," she said. "When I was a very little girl, I knew that if *Maman* smelled of fragrance, it meant she was either entertaining or going out. In either case, I knew I would not be seeing her. I came to hate that smell. Utterly hate it. I think it is why I do not wear any scent."

Rothewell looked at her strangely and leaned nearer. "But you must do," he said.

"You smell of . . . I cannot quite say what. Spices and rose petals? Something exotic."

Camille shook her head. "*Non,* you must be mistaken," she murmured. "You have confused me with someone el—"

"No, by God, I haven't," he interjected harshly. And then his gaze softened, even if his tone did not. He took her hand in his, and held it lightly, almost as if he meant to draw it to his lips. "I would know your scent anywhere. Even in the darkest night in the darkest room with a hundred other people." His voice dropped to a husky whisper. "Yes, Camille. I would know it. Always, I would know . . . you."

The sudden catch in his voice was unmistakable. Camille felt at once unsteady, as if the mood — perhaps the very earth itself — had shifted ever so slightly. Her eyes searched his, seeking to understand him, this painfully complicated man she had married. What did he ask of her? Or did she even dare to hope?

He released her hand and looked away, as if regretting he'd spoken at all, and Camille was struck with the strangest impulse to set her lips against his cheek. To tell him that, against all odds and all wisdom, she had fallen in love with him. And that nothing he had done — or could ever do — would alter that. But perhaps she was more a fool than her mother had ever been.

Just then, Camille heard the sound of gravel lightly crunching in the distance. Remembering the very public place in which they sat, she drew away from her husband and began to smooth the folds of her skirt. From one corner of her eye, she could see a fashionably attired gentleman making his way along the path which fringed the Serpentine, a walking stick in hand, and wearing a top hat so silky it seemed to reflect the autumn sun.

Rothewell watched him as he neared, then gave a grunt of dismay.

"Who is that?" she asked

"An acquaintance," he said. "A family friend."

The gentleman had already espied them. Rothewell lifted his hand in greeting, the motion somewhat less than enthusiastic, and the man turned from the path to stroll up the slight slope toward them.

Camille surveyed his approach. "A very handsome gentleman," she murmured. "But a bit of a dandy, *n'est-ce pas?*"

Rothewell merely grunted again. But the man, Camille noticed, looked less like a dandy the closer he came. He was slender and lithe, and he moved like a cat on the hunt. His dark eyes danced with humor, and with something less easily discerned. Cynicism, perhaps?

"Good afternoon!" said the man, lifting his hat. "Have I the pleasure of addressing the new Lady Rothewell?"

"You have indeed." Rothewell had stood. "Camille, this is George Kemble. Kemble, my lovely bride."

"*Bonjour*, Monsieur Kemble," said Camille, offering up her hand.

"*Enchanté, madame!*" he said, bowing low over it. "Of course, your grace and beauty is quite wasted on this barbarian. Nonetheless, my felicitations."

"A pleasure to see you, too, Kem." Rothewell hefted Obelienne's rucksack out of the way. "I suppose you mean to sit down?"

Mr. Kemble frowned at the grass, clearly hesitant. "A dangerous business, sitting upon the ground." His smile returned as swiftly as it had come. "But how can one think of one's wardrobe when met with so lovely a lady? And so heartfelt an invitation as yours, Rothewell?"

Camille's husband finally laughed. "You are rather far from the Strand today, old chap," he said, as Kemble settled gingerly onto the edge of the greatcoat. "What brings you through the park?"

"Why, I've just this instant come from Whitehall." Kemble had begun to pick bits of grass from his trouser hems. "Lord de Vendenheim wanted me — so I made him take me to dine at Rules for the roast grouse. After all, one must eat, mustn't one? And it tastes so much better when dear old Max pays the shot."

"I daresay it would," Rothewell agreed.

Mr. Kemble shrugged. "In any case, now I must sing for my supper," he continued. "I'm off to North Wharf to poke round a bit. There was a little contretemps at the canal basin late last night."

"Someone up to no good, eh?" Rothewell looked suddenly somber. "Have a care, Kemble."

Kemble smiled faintly. "It's not my favorite part of town," he confessed. "But one must occasionally do one's part to placate the Government, mustn't one?"

"I generally don't trouble myself," said Rothewell.

"Yes, well, you don't have to. And speaking of bad parts of town —" Here, Kemble paused to rummage through his pocket. He extracted something wrapped in a scrap of white linen and passed it across the coat to Rothewell. "I think you lost this at Eddie's."

Rothewell folded back the cloth to reveal

a gold pocket watch. He flicked a dark glance up at Kemble, then dropped the watch into his pocket. "I don't suppose you'd care to explain how you came by it?"

Kemble wrinkled his nose. "I think not," he said. "Let's just say I saw you lose it."

"And?"

"And so I retrieved it," he said simply. "Before something untoward could happen."

A warning look passed between the two men. Camille wondered at what was not being said. *"Alors là!"* she said brightly. "Will you join us in some refreshment, Mr. Kemble? We have chicken, apples, and a lovely cheese. And something called a cassava pone." She produced the latter for his inspection.

Kemble cut another dubious glance at Rothewell. "I think I'll take my chances strolling round the wharves," he said, poking one finger into the spongy bread. "I've heard of cassava."

"I used to like it very well indeed," said Rothewell. "But it is admittedly an acquired taste."

Camille smiled at Mr. Kemble. "I confess, *monsieur,* it is a taste I have not yet acquired," she said. "The spices in this are very strong, and a little strange."

"I shall try an apple," said Mr. Kemble, taking one and crunching into it with his flawless white teeth.

Rothewell relaxed onto his elbows again and crossed his boots one over the other. Mr. Kemble's arrival had been inconvenient, perhaps, but it had defused the tension of their earlier discussion.

"I have been thinking of engaging your assistance, Kem," said Rothewell pensively.

Eyes wide, Mr. Kemble finished chewing. "Surely you jest?" he finally said. "*You* are asking for help from another human being? How novel! Do tell me how I may assist."

"I am told my house lacks charm," said Rothewell dryly.

"And warmth," added Mr. Kemble knowingly. "Indeed, a more utilitarian building in London does not exist — unless one counts the Smithfield slaughterhouse."

"*Merci,* Mr. Kemble," said Camille, laughing.

"Utilitarian?" Rothewell winced. "I like to think of it as practical. Simple elegance, and all that rot."

"What a canard!" Mr. Kemble rolled his eyes. "You don't think of it at all — nor did your sister. Oh, I adore her, to be sure. But Lady Nash thinks taste is something one needs only at dinner."

"Pardon," said Camille uncertainly, "but how shall Mr. Kemble help us?"

"He keeps a sort of museum or — or a curiosity shop — in the Strand," said her husband. "The place is filled to bursting with . . . things."

"*Ambience,* dear girl," Kemble interjected. "I sell ambience and old money polish to those who do not have it — or those who simply want more of it."

"*Vraiment?*" Camille laughed lightly. "Pray tell me — how is this ambience delivered? In a bandbox? A portmanteau? Or can it be bottled?"

Mr. Kemble grinned. "Why, I can deliver by the vanload, when necessary," he said. "I am something of a connoisseur, you see, of all things elegant — and one of extraordinary discernment, if I do say so myself."

He was entirely serious. "*Alors,* you have been inside the house at Berkeley Square?"

"Oh, yes," said the dapper gentleman. "I worked with Lady Nash for a time. And the house —" Here, he paused to shudder, "— why, it's rather like a mixture of day-old porridge and river sludge, *n'est-ce pas?* All bland and cold and brownish?"

Camille laughed at the apt if rather odd analogy. "What sorts of things do you suggest?"

Mr. Kemble laid a finger beside his cheek. "Well, let me see," he murmured. "I just acquired a lovely silver epergne which would make for a magnificent centerpiece in that dreary dining room. And a gorgeous pair of Chinese foo dogs made of absolutely flawless jade, mounted on mahogany. Three full sets of medieval armor — and one set is a rare Milanese Missaglia, I am quite certain."

Camille smiled at him. "*Non,* not the armor, I think. But I should love to see all of it."

"I shall set aside the epergne." Mr. Kemble smiled and reached inside his coat. "Why do you not call upon me next week, Lady Rothewell?" He extracted a fine silver case, and withdrew his card. Camille looked at it.

Mr. George Jacob Kemble
Purveyor of Elegant Oddities
and Fine Folderol
Number 8 Strand

"And come alone, if you please," Mr. Kemble added, cutting a glance at her husband.

"Yes, *please,*" said Rothewell. "As in *please spare me.* Just send me the bills. They will be far less painful."

"A capital notion," said Mr. Kemble, springing to his feet. "I'll make tea, and we'll have a lovely little chat."

By the time Mr. Kemble had bowed himself back down to the path, Camille noticed that the wind was growing cooler. It had been a strange day indeed.

"We should go, *oui?*" she murmured, watching as the wind lifted Rothewell's dark hair, making it look somehow softer. "But I daresay we must eat something first?"

Rothewell glanced down at the food. "Aye, Obelienne went to a good deal of trouble," he muttered, picking up the drumstick again. He had little more to say after that, but Camille kept up a light, pleasant chatter, and his black mood seemed to relent. He went on to eat a bit of the cake, a wedge of cheese, and an apple.

Camille accounted it a small success, and repacked the satchel, feeling perhaps a little more hopeful about the world in general. The feeling, regrettably, was to be short-lived.

When the food was in place and Camille safely on the seat beside him, Rothewell put on his greatcoat and drove his gig back through the trees and onto the carriage road which circled toward Park Lane. He glanced at Camille, who sat beside him, her spine perfectly straight, her bearing as regal as that of even the most highborn duchess.

He was sorry Valigny was her father, yes, but for his part, he didn't give a damn about the circumstances of her birth. He should have been proud to drive with her through the park — and he was — but his joy was tainted by the knowledge that he had played her a damned dirty trick in marrying her. And she was beginning to suspect it, too.

Camille had said little of substance since Kem's departure, but Rothewell feared that had more to do with the discussion Kem's arrival had cut short. Good God, he was tired. He felt physically eviscerated, and this time the pain was caused by more than his malevolent innards.

Perhaps it was a just punishment. He was a man in his prime, with a beautiful, deeply desirable bride by his side, a sister who loved him, at least two good friends, and more money than any one man had a right to. And yet the whole of it — all the satisfaction and joy his charmed life should have brought him — was tainted by regret. Regret for the past, and regret for what was to come.

He was ashamed. Always, he had always been ashamed. He wore his grief and guilt like a shroud, cloaking out life's joy, and leaving only the hatred, which had lived inside him so long it had boiled down in the pit of his belly until it was like a black, burning cancer — perhaps quite literally. And now he had shared that shame — at least a part of it — with the last person he had wished ever to learn about it — and to what end? To let it eat at someone else? To make her think less of him than she already did?

Already he held her at a distance. She was right about that. Was he now determined to drive her completely away by telling her the truth of what he was? He had committed adultery with his brother's wife. And then his guilt and his intemperance had sent them both to their deaths.

Annemarie had played him for a fool after her marriage, but he had let her. Perhaps there had been a little part of him that had done it out of spite. He had always loved Luke, but toward the end, he had hated him, too. Hated him for taking the thing he had most wanted — the woman he had burned for, but never really loved. And that was the most unforgivable part of all.

All of these morose thoughts conspired to convince Rothewell that his afternoon could not get much more unsettling. Then he turned the curve to head down to Grosvenor Gate, and saw a familiar red-wheeled phaeton spinning merrily up the hill toward them. The driver wore a driving cape lined in red silk, and a black hat set at an especially rakish — and recognizable — angle.

Damn it to hell.

It was Valigny, all right — and this time he was not alone. Rothewell glanced over at Camille. Her hand was clutching the side of the gig, her mouth a thin, tight line.

"Well met, my Lord Rothewell!" Valigny was grinning ear to ear as he drew alongside them. "And *mon chou!* Never has a bride looked lovelier. I believe you have already met my new friend?"

Rothewell saw Camille stiffen her spine and lift her chin. Good. She was not going to give them the satisfaction of seeing her squirm.

"Bonjour, Papa," she said lightly. *"Oui,* I have had the pleasure of meeting Madame Ambrose."

"Christine," Rothewell acknowledged tightly. "Valigny."

Valigny leaned conspiratorially nearer. "Everyone in town seemed to be staring at Mrs. Ambrose and me today, Rothewell!" he said from the higher phaeton. "I wonder why? Perhaps they will say we have made a curious trade, you and I, eh? My daughter for your mistress?"

Christine tossed her blond curls insouciantly. "Let them talk if they wish," she said, curling her hand through Valigny's arm. "I never shy from gossip — and certainly not now."

Rothewell's horse jerked forward impatiently. He reined him in and leaned toward the other carriage. "Be honest, Christine," he said quietly. "It is your intent to make people talk. Why else would you be with him?"

"*Alors,* my friend, you give no credit to my beauty and charm?" said Valigny, laughing.

But Christine paid Valigny no heed. Her lip curled with disdain as she looked down on them. She was up to something. A sudden chill ran down Rothewell's spine.

"Valigny has told me the most amazing story, Rothewell!" Christine gave a light, tinkling laugh. "My God! One does wonder what society will say when they hear how you met your wife."

The chill turned to a hard, cold lump in his heart. "You would not dare."

Her brittle smile faded to a sneer. "You think not?"

Rothewell leaned over the edge of the phaeton. His voice when he spoke was barely audible. "Madam, I *know* not," he said very quietly. "Do not try me in this regard."

"What balderdash!" Christine tossed her curls again, but Rothewell saw fear flicker in her eyes. "You have no power over me."

Rothewell dropped his voice even further. "One word of this, Christine, and I shall see you ruined, so help me God," he said. "And I'll have no shortage of witnesses — myself included — who can attest to your sorts of debauchery. And then we shall see which lurid tale the *ton* finds more titillating."

"*Mon Dieu,* Rothewell!" Valigny's grin widened. "A gentleman does not kiss and tell."

Christine's eyes blazed. "Oh, if it's gossip you fear, Rothewell, then I suggest your blushing bride leave the park, if not London altogether."

"Perhaps you might flee to the south of France?" Valigny suggested lightly. "I have always found it most agreeable in the winter."

But Rothewell was still eyeing his former mistress. "My wife and I are going nowhere, Christine," he said, taking up his reins. "Be damned to you."

Christine glanced down dismissively. "You might wish to reconsider, for your wife's sake," she returned. "Lord Halburne has returned to Town unexpectedly — for the rest of the year, and into the season, they say. And if I am not very much mistaken, that is he just there — by the Serpentine, do you see? — the gentleman with a newspaper under his arm?"

Camille's head jerked toward the water, her face a mask of horror.

"*Oui, oui,* that is Halburne, to be sure!" Valigny set his fingertips to his chest and pulled a face of specious sympathy. "You see one never forgets, *mon chou,* the face of an old acquaintance!"

Chapter Twelve

THE GATHERING STORM

Camille's skirts swished about her ankles as she paced the floor of her bedchamber. Rothewell had followed her in, and tried twice to touch her shoulder in an attempt to soothe her, but his wife was having none of it. *"Non,"* she finally snapped. "Just . . . Just leave me alone. *Please.* I beg you."

Even the dog had flung himself onto her bed and lay cowering, his silky black ears limp upon the coverlet, his fanlike tail still for once. Rothewell felt frustrated, and very, very angry. He was not, however, leaving.

"I don't think this is the time, Camille, when a husband abandons his wife," he said firmly. "Not if he cares for her."

Camille flashed him a withering, watery look. *"Mon dieu,* how can my father do this?" she cried, turning to cross the room again. "How can he laugh at me? Whatever he is — and even if I am just his bastard child — am I not his own flesh and blood?

Does he not care for me in even the slightest way?"

Rothewell's heart ached for her. By God, Camille had deserved better than this — a faithless father and a distant husband. "I think it's time someone put a period to Valigny," he said almost to himself. "I begin to think I would be doing you the greatest of favors to simply call that bastard out and make you an orphan."

It was not, apparently, the best way to comfort his wife. Camille turned on him, her face twisted with grief. "*Oui,* a brilliant notion!" she cried. "That will solve all my problems, *n'est-ce pas?* I shall be left a widow! And Valigny will waltz away laughing, as he always does."

Rothewell did stop her then, catching her firmly by both shoulders. "Camille, he won't walk away," he vowed. "Not from me."

"*Très bien,*" she said, dashing away a tear with the back of her hand. "The alternative, then? My husband will shoot my father dead and be banished forever. That will damp down the gossip, *assurément.*"

He bit back a curse. "Camille, I just want to — to *fix* this for you."

"Oh, Kieran, don't you see?" She set the heel of her hand to her forehead as if it ached. "You cannot fix who my father is.

431

You cannot make him love me."

Rothewell did then what he should have done at the outset — he forced her to stop, and drew her into his arms. He was learning, it seemed, for Camille came willingly, all but collapsing against his chest. "I am so sorry, my dear," he murmured, as she set her cheek to his lapel with a sob. "I am as angry with myself, I daresay, as with Valigny."

"Pourquoi?" she said through tears. "What did you do to cause this travesty?"

Rothewell struggled to find the words. "I should have stopped that damned card game," he said. "I should have put an end to Valigny's mockery then and there. But I didn't, because I was half-drunk and — well, truth be told, half-maddened by you — so I left the truth of it hanging over your head like a sword."

"Oui, you could have walked out," she answered. "And left me with him. Would I be any better off?"

Rothewell bit back a curse. "I could have *stopped* it," he said vehemently. "All of it. A gentleman would have done so. Afterward, when I considered the risks, I warned Valigny to keep his mouth shut but —"

"Did you?" she interjected. "When?"

"The day after I left you at Pamela's," he

said. "And I don't think, honestly, he gives a damn about spreading rumors — but Christine — oh, she's spiteful and unpredictable."

"Non." He felt Camille shudder in his embrace. *"Non,* this was all predictable, Kieran. All of it. Especially Lord Halburne. The moment I set foot on the ferry at Le Havre. The moment I wrote my letter to Valigny to ask his help. *Oui,* even then the die was thrown."

"Camille, that simply is not so."

"Oui, predictable!" she insisted. "I should never have done it — but I did, because I am little better than the blood in my veins. Like Valigny, I was greedy. I wanted my inheritance. I thought . . . I thought I could become — oh, independent, I suppose, if I had to. To protect myself — and my child, if *le bon Dieu* were gracious enough to give me one."

"Oh, Camille!"

"Do not say that!" she cried. "It sounds mad, *oui,* but I had no choice. I knew I could not live as my mother had done. But I should have known my coming to London would stir up the past. And now Lord Halburne is here — and suddenly I cannot face that past. To think that he — and the rest of London — will learn of what Valigny did to me . . . *Mon Dieu,* Kieran, is it not enough that *I* must know my father laughs at me? Must all the world know it, too?"

He pulled her toward the bed. "Sit down, Camille," he said, urging her onto the mattress. He joined her there and began to smooth away her tears. "I am so sorry, my dear. You are a lovely and gracious woman. If Valigny does not see how lucky he is — and if you will not let me throttle him — then at least let me speak to Lord Sharpe."

"Lord Sharpe?" she said, snuffling. "Why?"

"If my threats haven't frightened Christine into silence, Sharpe's will, for he pays her allowance, and a great deal more, too," he answered. "Whatever pleasure he is taking from her now, Valigny cannot mean to marry Christine or maintain her in any way — and Christine is cunning enough to know it."

Camille gave a lame shrug. "Valigny scarcely has two sous to rub together," she admitted. "But to involve Lord Sharpe again? *Mon Dieu,* even that is a mortifying notion."

"*Christine* is the one who should be mortified." Rothewell squeezed her hands. "Not you, my dear. You are the only victim in this whole debacle."

She held his gaze for a moment as if searching for the truth in his face. And then her lower lip trembled tellingly, and she launched herself against him, sobbing in deep, gulping heaves.

"Come, now," he murmured, pulling her onto his knee as if she were a child. "What's all this?"

She refused to look at him. "I am ashamed!" she cried. "Ashamed of my mother. Ashamed of Valigny. How could I let this happen? Why did I imagine someone as scandalous as I could come to London and magically avoid a scandal?"

"Shush, my dear, shush." Soothingly, Rothewell kissed the arch of her eyebrow, then her cheek. "You are not scandalous."

Rothewell wasn't an intuitive man by any stretch, but even he could see that her despair had little to do with Halburne and far more to do with the pain of her father's very public betrayal. Her mother's vain foolishness. The sad circumstances of her birth.

With loving parents, Camille could have brazened out the whispers and society's sidelong glances. Instead, this afternoon, Valigny had used her plight for his own amusement — and not for the first time. Rothewell was beginning to think that perhaps there were worse torments a child could face than a malevolent uncle's whip.

"I shan't let anything blight your future, Camille," he said firmly. "I swear it."

That brought her head up. Her damp, faintly accusing gaze caught his. "But what if you aren't here?" she whispered hoarsely. "Do not lie to me. Oh, Kieran, do not make me a promise you cannot keep."

God knew he was no hero, but he didn't know what else to be. So he let his hands cradle her face as he kissed her again, this time on the lips, long and lingeringly. "I shan't," he vowed, knowing even as he said it that it was likely a lie. "I will do it, Camille. I will take care of you. Of *this*. All of it. I swear it. I'll even take you away if you wish. To — to Cheshire, if you like. To my estate."

"It is far away?" she asked as his lips brushed over her cheek.

"Two hundred miles," he said. "And if that isn't far enough, we have Barbados."

She had closed her eyes almost dreamily. *"Je ne sais pas,"* she whispered. "I — I do not know. I am not a coward, Kieran. I am *not*. And I think perhaps I wouldn't like myself very much if I became one."

"No, my dear." Rothewell pulled her fully into his lap and reclined against the head-

436

board. "No, you are no coward, I have discovered, much to my peril."

She made a little sound, something between a laugh and a sob. He kissed her again, tilting his head low to do so. It was a kiss, he hoped, of reassurance.

He felt strangely proud of her. Camille had kept her chin up in the face of Christine's venom and her father's cruel laughter. She had a grit few people possessed. She was a survivor.

From the first, Camille had given the impression of a woman in control of her destiny, but now that Rothewell knew her — really *knew* her — even he could see that it was abandonment which had always driven her. She had been determined never to entrust her fate to a man — not insofar as she could avoid it.

Alas, it was too late. She was Lady Rothewell now — and selfishly, perhaps, he was glad. And he would do anything in his power to protect her.

"Look on the bright side, my dear," he murmured, lifting her chin with one finger. "I know it isn't much, but you do have me. And Jim-Jim, or whatever the devil he's called."

She did laugh then, her dark eyes crinkling at the corners. *"Chin-Chin,"* she said, casting an affectionate glance at the spaniel. "And I thought you were returning him to Lord Tweedale? Instead, he is sleeping in your bed and getting fat."

Rothewell looked away. "I cannot seem to catch Tweedale at home," he said vaguely. "But if he's to stay here, he'll need a proper name. I'll be damned if I'll call a dog Chin-Chin."

She stilled in his arms for an instant, her face calmer now, her eyes shifting swiftly from humor to something altogether different as they searched his face. "Oh, Kieran," she whispered. "It is not true, what you said today. It is *not.*"

He looked down at her, confused. "What did I say?"

"I will not think of it — of *her* — every time I look at you," she whispered. "Every time you come to my bed, I will remember this day, *oui.* But not, I think, for the reason you believe."

He looked at her gravely. "Camille, my dear, you are —"

"*Non,*" she said. "Do not say it, *s'il vous plaît.* Do not tell me what I think."

"No, I gave that up weeks ago," he murmured.

Just then, the mantel clock struck the hour.

"*Zut!* Look at the time." Camille stood, and dashed a hand beneath her eyes. "We should dress for dinner."

Kieran eyed her from the bed. "Let's not," he softly suggested. "If you meant what you said — if you still feel . . . something in your heart for me, Camille, then undress instead. Undress, and let me make you forget all this."

Camille turned to look at him. "I care for you, Kieran," she whispered. "My feelings — *oui,* trust me when I say this — my feelings for you are unchanged."

He was watching her steadily, his gaze softer than she had ever seen it. "Then lock your door, Camille," he ordered. "And come back to bed. That is a husbandly command, by the way."

It was one command she was more than willing to follow. After this tumultuous day, Camille was emotionally spent, and she wanted only Kieran, and his arms about her — not a roomful of servants, with course after course of food she would not taste and could barely eat.

She went to the door and snapped the key in the lock. She turned and leaned back against the cool, hard wood, her hands flat against it as if she might keep the world and all its ugliness from bursting through.

Kieran still reclined upon her bed, one booted foot set upon the floor, the other crossed over his knee. His cravat was disheveled from her tears, and he looked darkly, disarmingly handsome, with his stern face and sensuous mouth.

She shivered when Kieran's gaze slid languidly down her length. "What witchery, Camille, have you worked on me?" he murmured. "Even now, I cannot fathom it."

Camille left the door and started toward the bed. She dared not ask him what he meant, dared not press him for the answers he had always been so unwilling to give. He cared for her — more than he wished to admit. And in this moment, it was enough.

At the corner of the bed, she stopped and began to pull the pins from her hair.

"Wait." Kieran unfolded himself from the bed. "I wish to do it."

He walked behind her, and set his searing lips to the turn of her neck. Camille closed her eyes and let the familiar, aching warmth go twisting through her. She wanted him — *needed* this — and she was tired of denying it. "Make me forget," she whispered. "Oh, Kieran, make me forget."

"You are a fool, you know, Camille," he murmured as if to himself. "A fool to want me — for anything other than this."

Camille did not answer him. The truth was, nothing he had said in Hyde Park had jerked her back from the emotional precipice she seemed destined to tumble over. And if she was a fool, so be it.

One by one, he drew the pins from her hair, threading his fingers through the loosened locks with unerring gentleness as he pulled them down. When he was finished, Kieran's lips brushed the shell of her ear. "I'd best cancel dinner," he whispered, "before Trammel comes looking for us."

"Très bien," she agreed.

He turned and snapped his fingers at the dog. "Jim! Out, old boy."

Dutifully, the little spaniel leapt off the bed. Camille watched Kieran's lithe, muscular form pace across the room to the connecting door, the dog trotting happily at his heels.

By the time he returned to lock the door behind him, Camille wore only her shift and her stockings. Fleetingly, he hesitated, his expression softening as he watched her.

"What?" she whispered. "What is wrong?"

His smile returned, wistful and vague. "Nothing," he answered. His warm, long-fingered hands came up to cup her face. "It is just that . . . you are so beautiful. Too beautiful."

Camille rose onto her toes, and slid her arms about his neck. "Kieran, why do you say —"

He silenced her with his lips. The kiss was long and deep, his mouth demanding. She turned her face willingly to his and let him possess her. When they parted, she looked at him through the dying light, and watched as his face shifted yet again, into something which looked hesitant, and a little despairing.

She held his gaze, willing him to speak. It was as if he wanted her, yet watched from a distance, afraid to come too close. He was a man eaten with regret for his past and unwilling, perhaps, to hope for a future. But with her eyes, she begged him to let her in.

In response, his thick, black lashes fell shut. Acting on feminine instinct, Camille lifted an unsteady hand to his face. Sliding her fingertips across the turn of his cheek, she caressed him, then brushed the pad of her thumb across the corner of his mouth.

With his eyes still closed, his nostrils flared at her touch. And then, as if searching for home, he turned his face into her hand and pressed his lips into her palm with a sigh.

"Kieran," she whispered as his breath came more roughly against her skin. *"Mon chéri."*

He was drowning, he thought. Drowning in Camille's touch; a simple, gentle caress which was neither seductive nor demanding. And yet those small, warm fingers skimming over the hardness of his face made him ache for more — not just a carnal longing, but a deeper desire he could not explain. This moment was a joy, a tenderness; emotions undercut by a bone-deep sorrow in the knowledge he had wasted his life. Sorrow that fate in all her cruelty had chosen now to gift him with this woman who instilled in him a yearning he could neither subdue with his own acrimony, nor obliterate with alcohol.

Camille drew away, and some sense of reality returned. He watched as she set her foot to the bed, drew up the hem of her shift, and began to roll down her stockings revealing, inch by inch, the perfect, silky length of her legs. And as he watched her, Kieran's mind returned to their afternoon in the park. He had finally told her — knowing full well that he owed her the truth. And that the truth would be the end of it. Yet here she was, slipping off her stockings. Untying the ribbon of her shift.

He reached out, mesmerized, and drew the soft white linen off her shoulder. Her neck, the hollow of her throat, that tiny pulse point which he foolishly imagined beat only for him; all of it was perfection. Dear God, what had he pledged to her? He had tried to measure his words, and yet he had made promises he likely could not keep. She probably knew it, too — and another betrayal was the last thing on earth she needed.

He set his lips to the turn of her throat again, and let his cheek rest upon her shoulder. Once upon a time, he had foolishly believed Camille cold. But she was not cold, she was *strong* — and there was a world of difference between the two. Without him, Camille would survive. Without her, Kieran feared, he might not. He loved her. Completely, fully, he loved her. It was not an emotion he welcomed, and yet it came to him with a searing certainty.

Kieran was silent for so long, Camille began to feel worried. She whispered his name, and he lifted his head, opening his eyes to reveal the desire which burnt there. "Good God, Camille, I need you," he rasped. "Beside me. Beneath me. Just . . . *with* me."

Relief surged through her at his words. "Kieran, *mon cœur,* I am here," she whispered, her lashes dropping shut. "I am with you. Always."

"I want you, Camille," he rasped.

"Oui."

Slowly, Kieran undressed, shrugging off his coat, and unfastening his waistcoat with a languid, masculine certainty. Camille raised her hands to unfurl the snowy white cravat about his neck. He lifted his chin, quietly watching her.

He surprised her when he spoke. "I desire you, I think, more than I have ever desired anything in my life," he said abruptly. "Should I have told you that? I daresay not."

Camille smiled, her heart almost bursting. "Why should you not?"

He looked away. Her eyes took in the slightly gaunt bones of his cheeks, and the faint stubble of beard which shadowed his face. He looked neither old nor young, but merely beautiful. And alone.

"Perhaps some things are selfish to say?" he suggested, jerking his shirttails free.

Camille pushed the shift from her shoulders. His eyes followed it to the floor. "Perhaps the time for talking is done," she answered.

It was almost dark inside the room now. She drew down the bedcovers, then watched as Kieran shucked off the last of his clothes. By the faint, wintry light she let her gaze drift over the sheer bulk of his body. Despite whatever weight he had lost, Kieran was a large man in every sense of the word. There was nothing of grace or beauty in his lean, hard-muscled form, for it was a body forged by long hours of hard work and scarred by deprivation and abuse. Yet he *was* graceful. To her, he *was* beautiful. And when he turned to toss aside the last of his clothing, and the dying light caught the long, layered scars across his back, Camille found herself blinking back tears.

"Come to bed, *mon amour*," she whispered.

To her surprise, he caught her up in his arms, one arm beneath her knees, and laid her on the bed as if she weighed nothing. He crawled over her, his eyes dark with need, his erection heavy and jutting. One heavy lock of hair fell forward, shadowing his high forehead. Impulsively, she lifted her face to kiss him. Their lips met once, twice, then his mouth took hers in earnest. Camille's hands settled on his hips, drawing them to hers.

"I want you, Kieran," she whispered when the kiss ended. "I am impatient."

His hand seemed to shake as he set it to her inner thigh. "I mightn't be gentle," he answered. "You are sure?"

Her arms came up to embrace him. "*Oui, very sure.*"

He slid his hands beneath her hips and dragged her down the bed. One knee pressed her thighs wider as his hand went to his erection. Camille drew up her knees and guided him to her. When he entered, it was swift and a little forceful. At her sharp exhalation, he cursed beneath his breath.

"*Non,* do not stop," she choked. "Please just —"

With a soft, guttural sound, Kieran pushed himself deeper, bracing one arm above her shoulder. Slowly, so slowly, he rocked himself into her, his eyes closed, his nostrils flared wide. "Sweet Jesus, Camille," he whispered. "You are — oh, Lord. So tight. So . . . like home to me."

She felt her heart lift, rising unburdened to him. As her body relaxed to take his, she lifted one leg and twined it over his heavier, stronger one. Kieran kissed her possessively, with his lips and his tongue, plumbing her depths as she rose to him. When she returned the kiss, darting her tongue into his mouth, he groaned and deepened the kiss. The sweetly familiar desire drew at her, making her sigh beneath him.

"You are mine, Camille," he rasped when their lips parted. "Tell me you are."

"Kieran, *mon trésor*," she whispered. "Always."

Over and over he thrust, his powerful thighs taut, his eyes closed. The heat of his body began to surround her, tantalizing and seductive, as the tension built. Beneath the weight of his thrusts, the bed began to creak in a faint, steady rhythm. Camille felt caught up in him, a part of him.

The longing deep inside her swelled until she began to sigh with each stroke. She was spiraling, higher and higher. His body drew hers, possessed hers. He took her long and hard as the afternoon gave way to evening, and a soft, cool gloom settled over the room. The hearth was empty, the lamps cold. And yet, a fine sheen of sweat glistened on his forehead and trailed down his throat to pool in the hard-boned vee below his throat.

Suddenly, his eyes opened, his silvery gaze mesmerizing. "I can't give you up, Camille," he choked. "I *won't*."

A little shaken by the fervency his voice, she faltered.

Kieran responded by dropping his head to kiss her, swift and hard. "Don't draw away from me, Camille," he murmured against her lips. "Please. Not now. Not when it is too late."

He was not speaking, she understood, of this simple act of lovemaking. The words went deeper, to the heart of what they were together. Man and woman. Lovers joined by something more than a physical act. And what it cost him to make such a request, Camille could not imagine. She let her hands slide down to the taut muscles of his buttocks, urging him to her.

Kieran tried to clear his head. To *think.* But a sort of madness drove him now, a dark need to possess her. There was an edge somewhere in the darkness, and he had crossed it. Given himself to her irretrievably. He deepened his thrusts, and she cried out, her voice thready in the dusky light.

"Camille, Camille," he chanted, stilling her to his thrusts. Skin against silken skin. The scent of desire swirling about them in a sensual heat. It was ecstasy, and he was lost. Lost to her. She was panting now, soft, rhythmic sobs of need. He lifted himself higher, holding that sweet, perfect angle as he drove himself into her. And then she cried out again, her warm, silken sheath drawing at him as her hips rose to his.

"Kieran," she gasped. "Kieran, oh . . ."

He tried to gentle his thrusts, to draw out the pleasure, but her breathless cries of urgency spurred him on. Camille clung to him, trembling, her nails raking down his buttocks as her head went back into the softness of the pillow. And then her release seized her, shook her, and left her sobbing beneath him. Kieran felt his groin spasm uncontrollably, and on a harsh, guttural cry, he spilled himself inside her as a perfect, brilliant light exploded inside his head.

The room was nearly dark when Camille stirred to awareness. Kieran lay beside her, his legs entangled with hers, their bodies slick with perspiration. She closed her eyes and drew in the comforting scent of him.

It was over. There was nothing left of her heart to hold apart from him, this man she had once thought harsh and unlovable. A man she had hoped to hold at arm's length, emotionally if not physically. And even as his body warmed hers, and his masculine scent comforted her, the uncertainty which lay ahead was a bleak and frightening thing.

Oh, what a fool she had been to underestimate him. Camille drew a deep, shuddering breath.

Kieran leaned nearer and set the back of his hand lightly to her cheek. "Camille?" he murmured, nuzzling her neck.

When she did not respond, he lifted his head to look down at her, a quizzical smile curling one corner of his mouth. "What's wrong, *hmm?*"

She closed her eyes and exhaled a little roughly. "*Mon Dieu,* Kieran, I am sometimes afraid of this," she whispered. "I do not wish to lose my heart to you. I cannot."

For an instant, he went perfectly still. "No," he said quietly. "No. It would be best for you if you did not, I daresay."

He dropped his hand, and the loss of his touch was like a physical ache.

"I know — I *know* — that I said it was not possible," she continued, her voice thready and nothing like her own. "But this line I drew in my mind — something is changing, Kieran. Once it was so sharp. So clear to me . . ."

His faint smile faltered. "You are too wise, Camille, to fall in love with me," he assured her. "Today, after all that we have shared, you feel sorry for me, perhaps. But I assure you that I am unworthy of either sentiment — particularly your love."

But it was too late for her, Camille realized. She could neither look away nor leave him. Not in any sense of the word. His silvery gaze held hers warily, seeing, she was sure, into the pit of her soul. "Kiss me," she whispered. "Kiss me, Kieran. And let me decide your worth."

Something like regret sketched across his

face. Then his hand came up, hesitated, and slid round her face. His eyes dropped shut, and when his lips touched hers, Camille flew to him, her arms going round his neck. This time his kiss was infinite and aching in its sweetness. Not a kiss of heated lust or of tempting invitation, but a gentle, languid thing, which was almost reverent. A kiss which was not his, and yet was the very essence of him.

Kieran's hands cupped her face gently, his thumbs stroking slowly across her cheekbones as he kissed her mouth, her brow, and the delicate bones beneath her eyes. Finally, he kissed the length of her neck, his mouth warm and soft against her skin, then set his forehead upon her shoulder

"My beautiful girl," he murmured. "My beautiful Camille. What in God's name have I done?"

"Nothing," she said fervently. "*Mon Dieu,* you have done nothing."

He gave a muffled, humorless laugh. "I thought you so wonderfully coldhearted," he murmured, one hand making soft, soothing circles between her shoulder blades. "But I miscalculated, did I not? Beneath that hard façade of yours beats a heart as tender as a ripe peach. And I am sorry for it."

"Just kiss me again," she whispered. "*Vraiment*, Kieran, we think too much, you and I."

He obliged her, kissing her languidly and thoroughly, then rolled a little away. Camille turned onto her back, still watching him. His gaze drifted down to the slight swell of her belly. His hand settled over it, heavy and warm.

"What do you think, my dear?" he whispered. "Is there . . . any chance?"

Camille hesitated. "It is too soon, *chéri*."

He must have caught the uncertainty in her tone. His gaze jerked up, catching hers. "How much too soon?"

Camille caught her lip between her teeth. "I . . . I do not know," she finally said. "I have no experience in such things."

His hands caught hers, squeezing them urgently. "But there *is* a chance?" he said. "You have a reason to hope?"

Slowly, she exhaled. "*Oui,* a reason to hope," she agreed. "But a very tenuous one."

He settled back onto the bed, and slid an arm beneath his head. "Nine months," he whispered. "It seems an eternity."

But to any normal man, it was not an eternity. It was a very short while indeed — and in terms of raising one's child, it was a mere twinkling of an eye. But to Kieran, perhaps it really would be an eternity.

Vowing not to think of it — refusing to let a moment of uncertainty cloud her pure and certain joy — Camille drew up the covers, tucked herself against her husband, and fell into a restless sleep.

Camille passed a night fraught with snatches of half-formed dreams, then awoke to find herself alone when Emily came in to draw the curtains and pour her hot water. The door to Kieran's room was closed, and though she had not felt him leave her bed, Camille knew he had risen and left the house sometime in the early hours before dawn. In the short weeks since their marriage, she had developed an innate sense of his presence.

After putting on her best walking dress, a deep burgundy redingote of wool ottoman, which she hoped flattered her coloring, Camille went down to breakfast. Once there, however, mild nausea overcame her, and she left after a slice of dry toast and half a cup of tea. She glanced at the longcase clock as she ascended the steps. Half past eight. Far too early for her purpose this morning.

She returned to her room to hear Chin-Chin scratching at the connecting door. She opened it to see the butler at Kieran's washstand, a deeply troubled look upon his face.

"Good morning, Trammel," said Camille, scooping up the wiggling dog and settling him across her shoulder. "His lordship left early, I see."

"Yes, my lady." Swiftly, Trammel snatched a towel from the floor, and picked up the basin. Camille watched him suspiciously as Chin-Chin dashed her cheek with a kiss.

"Have you any idea where he went?"

"I couldn't say, ma'am," said the butler. "He called for his phaeton well before dawn."

"His phaeton?" Camille echoed. "*Ça alors.* Was he in some sort of rush?"

"I daresay," said the butler. "His lordship keeps his own counsel, ma'am."

"*Oui,* I noticed," said Camille dryly.

Trammel hesitated, then relented. "He did have a pair under the pole, ma'am," he remarked. "And he had me put up his kit — just in case, he said."

"He might be away the night, then." Camille frowned.

Trammel smiled wanly. "Well, if you will excuse me, ma'am, I shall —"

"Wait, *s'il vous plaît.*" Camille stepped into the room, and looked pointedly at the towel.

"How ill was he this morning, Trammel? And please do not pretend. I am, after all, his wife."

Something like sympathy sketched across Trammel's dark face. "Just a touch of nausea, ma'am," he said. "We must hope that it is nothing."

Camille set her shoulder to the door frame and regarded him pensively. "But I think we are both beyond hoping it is *nothing,*" she softly challenged. "It is — how do you say it? — *un maladie du foie?*"

"His liver?' A little unsteadily, Trammel set the basin down, and this time Camille saw the bright red bloodstain on the towel. "I simply cannot say, ma'am. His lordship does not confide in me. Indeed, he confides in no one — not even Lady Nash."

"But he knows what it is, *oui?*" Camille pressed.

Trammel lifted one shoulder. "I believe he suspects, ma'am," he answered. "But his . . . his habits are unchanged, and one would think —"

"You mean his drinking?" Camille interjected. "Not to mention the fact that he rarely sleeps? Scarcely eats?"

The butler's gaze fell. "Yes, those things," he agreed. "I find it strange he wouldn't do — but then, it really isn't my place, is it?

And his lordship is . . . well, difficult, at best."

Camille surveyed him levelly. "Ah, *difficult!*" she echoed softly. "Perhaps, Trammel, it is time that came to an end?"

Trammel cast her one last glance — one which seemed to say *good luck!* — then picked up the basin and hastened from the room.

Forcing away her grief and fear, Camille spent the morning going over the household accounts, and meeting with Miss Obelienne to sort out the linen press, but she went through the process like an automaton. Her crates had finally arrived from Limousin, sent at Camille's request by the elderly housekeeper, and together with Emily, Camille busied herself with unpacking them.

The landscapes she hung in the withdrawing room, assisted by Trammel and one of the footmen. The needlepoint pillows she arranged on Kieran's bed to give his room some much-needed color. But the rest of the crates could not hold her interest, and by midafternoon, she had sequestered herself in the upstairs parlor to sit by the fire with Chin-Chin in her lap.

What on earth had prompted Kieran to leave at such a frightful hour this morning? He had not gone merely to one of his low clubs or gaming hells, she was sure. Not in his phaeton — a vehicle made for speed — drawn by two horses. And he had asked Trammel to pack his things — after yet another spate of illness.

She remembered the urgency of Kieran's questions last night and absently set a hand over her belly, mimicking the gesture she had so often seen from Lady Nash. Fleetingly, she closed her eyes. *It was too soon.* It simply was.

She had hated to disappoint him, given the emotionally wrought day they had shared, and the yearning in his eyes. But however desperately either of them might wish otherwise, a week late — or even a fortnight — meant nothing.

Except that she had never, ever been so much as a day late. Moreover, she just *knew.* God help her if she was wrong, but she was simply certain. She was with child — in a world where she knew almost no one. A world where her husband was gravely ill, if not dying.

It had seemed such a simple thing in the abstract to raise a child with no father, and almost no family. It was the way in which she had been raised, and Kieran, too.

Well. Perhaps she had just answered her own question. Perhaps that was why it seemed such a horrific fate.

Camille opened her eyes, and stared at the world beyond her window — the fine brick town houses and glossy, crested coaches which went flying past, their liveried footmen clinging to the rear. *That* was the world in which her child would live; the world of aristocratic England. Not some far-flung colonial outpost like the West Indies, or the anonymity of rural France.

With or without two parents, her child would need to be a part of a society in which neither she nor Kieran was entirely comfortable. Which made her errand this morning all the more critical — and Kieran's absence, perhaps, all the more convenient.

Camille rose and walked to the window, considering that moment in Hyde Park when she'd first glimpsed Lord Halburne. What was he like, this man her mother had once wed? He had worn a sweeping gray cloak, she recalled, but no hat, having removed it in order to greet two young ladies by the Serpentine Pond. His hair had been snowy white, and at first glance, he'd appeared remarkably tall and thin, but then he had leaned forward to address a little black poodle which one of the ladies held on a leash.

Camille wished she could have heard Halburne's words — or at least his voice. Had he been sincere? Kind? Surely an *unkind* man would not have wasted his time cooing at a mere dog? It wasn't much comfort to seize upon, but it was all Camille had. So when she heard the clock strike four, Camille gathered her courage and went back downstairs. As she pulled on her gloves and cloak, she informed Trammel she was going for a long walk. She declined the escort of a footman. This was a deeply personal errand, and one which did not need an audience.

By noon, rain had swept in from the Channel, drowning all which lay in its path as it made its way toward London. Confined to the house, the Duke of Warneham was in his butler's office by the great hall at Selsdon Court when a racket arose in the carriage drive beyond.

"What the devil?" he said, looking up from the papers they had been reviewing.

Coggins rose. "I shall have a look, Your Grace," he said, going to the window. He turned almost at once. "It is a phaeton, sir, coming in fast. Looks like he's taken out the upper gatepost."

"The devil!" said Warneham again, striding out and round the corner into the great hall.

Here, the roar of the storm was louder. Two footmen had already thrown open the door and gone down the steps before him, bearing great black umbrellas with which to greet the guest and protect whatever luggage there might be from the now-torrential rain.

Warneham glowered down at the familiar, solid black carriage drawing up at the steps, and at the pair of lathered black horses still prancing in the downpour.

"You!" he shouted irascibly. "You and my damned gateposts! It's constant carnage, I tell you!"

The duke was already choosing the words with which he might further lash his friend when Lord Rothewell awkwardly gripped the edge of the phaeton's calash and attempted to descend — attempted being the operative word, for the baron did not so much leap from the high-perched conveyance as fall forward, almost tumbling onto the graveled drive.

"Good God!" The duke was out and down the steps in a trice.

The footmen had tossed down their umbrellas and were hitching Lord Rothewell up by both arms by the time the duke reached him. "Good God," he said again, shouting over the rain. "What has happened?"

Despite the calash, Rothewell's clothes were drenched by the rain, his hat sodden, his heavy black hair plastered. His expression when he looked at his old friend was bleak. "Get me inside," he rasped. "I need to speak with you."

"What were you thinking to ride south into the face of a storm?" the duke demanded when he had the baron ensconced in his private study and was more certain Rothewell was not apt to die. The baron had at first appeared to be in some pain, but was steadier — and a little dryer — now.

"I didn't know a storm was brewing." Rothewell was wrapped in a dry robe by a roaring fire, his expression pensive. "I have some papers in my coat — something I must discuss with you."

"And it could not wait?" Warneham had gone to the sideboard and was pouring two tots of brandy. "And never mind the papers, Rothewell. You look ill. Too dashed ill to ride hell-for-leather from London into a drenching rainstorm."

The baron looked up and held his gaze as Warneham pressed the brandy into his hand. For an instant, their fingers wrapped round one another's, and a long, expectant moment passed.

"Yes, I am ill," Rothewell finally agreed. "And no. I very much fear, my friend, that this is something which cannot wait."

Outside Berkeley Square, the air was cold and heavy with the tang of smoke and fresh horse dung. Camille could feel a strong rain blowing up from the south, tossing the last of the dead leaves along the near-silent streets. An umbrella hooked over her wrist, she set off at a brisk clip, ducking her head against the wind and pulling her long, sweeping cloak close about her.

In Grosvenor Square, Halburne's imposing town house seemed to loom up from the incipient autumn mist, daunting as a citadel. And in looking at it, Camille's heart gave a strange little lurch. This was the house in which her mother had briefly lived. Here, she had begun her life as the Countess of Halburne. A respectable life of wealth and privilege. Could it have been as dreary and loveless as *Maman* had made it out?

Her mother's tragedy aside, the house appeared to be quite the nicest in Mayfair, so it was unlikely Halburne had moved elsewhere in the years since her mother's leaving. Camille paused on the steps to extract her card, which unfortunately still bore her maiden name, then rang the bell and stiffened her spine. Perhaps Halburne would think better of her for having paid this call and discourage whatever gossip and questions came his way. Or perhaps not. But she would have the satisfaction of having attempted to make peace, and of having taken a little wind out of the sails of society's gossips.

The servant who answered the door was old and frail to an almost startling degree, and attired in ill-fitting butler's garb. He opened his mouth to speak then, to her horror, staggered backward with a strange, guttural sound, barely clinging to the doorknob.

"Monsieur?" said Camille uncertainly. "Might I help —"

To her shock, the butler's eyes rolled back in his head. As if in slow motion, he collapsed in a heap on the rug. The last to go was his hand, which slithered limply off the brass doorknob to the sound of Camille's short, sharp scream. Her umbrella clattered to the marble floor.

Camille had no recollection of stepping inside the house, but by the time a footman came rushing down the stairs, she already knelt in the foyer, her cloak puddled about her as she loosened the butler's starched stock.

"*Mon Dieu,* he collapsed!" she said as the servant knelt. "I am so sorry. When I rang the bell, he answered . . . then he just fell. Is he ill?"

"No, just old, poor devil." The footman smacked him lightly on the cheek. "Fothering? Fothering?"

"Oh, *mon Dieu!*" Camille whispered again. She had killed Halburne's butler! Could this ill-conceived visit get any worse?

"I think he's all right, miss," said the footman uncertainly. "But he ought not be answering doors at all. Yank the bellpull, if you please. I'll need help getting him up."

Camille did as he asked. "He's frightfully pale," she murmured, as the butler began to groan and flutter his eyes. "*Monsieur,* can you hear us?" She knelt again by the footman, praying. "I think we must send for a doctor."

Just then, a tall form came striding down the hall. "Fothering? Good God! What the devil happened here?"

Camille looked up into the deep brown eyes of Lord Halburne. He had jerked to a halt halfway across the hall and was looking at her strangely. For the first time she noticed his left sleeve hung empty and was pinned to his coat.

Swiftly, she rose, heat flooding her face. "I am so very sorry," she managed. "When he opened the door, your butler collapsed. I do hope it is not his heart."

"Who the devil are you?" Lord Halburne barked.

Something inside Camille withered at his tone. Hastily, she presented her card. A second footman had come to help, and the two of them were lifting the butler under his arms as he moaned.

"I am Lady Rothewell," she said, making a quick curtsy. "My card, I fear, is not current."

She passed it to him, and he glanced at it. His right hand, she noticed, shook as if palsied. "I see," he said, his mouth twisting. "Well. My God."

He walked to his left and pushed open the door to a large, well-lit drawing room. He was not a pale man by any means, but his color seemed to have drained away. "Kindly take a seat. I will join you once I've seen to Fothering."

Camille curtsied again. "*Merci,* my lord." Clearly he was worried for his servant, as well he should be. Just as clearly, he knew who she was — and he was not pleased to see her.

Camille's every nerve was on edge as she awaited Halburne's return. Through the open door, she could hear Fothering grumbling at the footmen who were helping him up the last of the steps. He had recovered enough to become querulous, thank God.

In an attempt to ward off her anxiety, Camille let her gaze roam about the room. It was an elegant, high-ceilinged chamber hung with pale blue watered silk and adorned with a great deal of opulent molding and woodwork. The furniture, surprisingly, was French and heavily gilded, whilst the painted ceiling — a view of the heavens and the apostles — was the work of a near master.

A matched set of massive full-length portraits flanked the fireplace; to the left a beautiful woman in a high Elizabethan collar carrying a terrier pup in the crook of one arm. In the other hand, a pearl rosary lay across her open palm, the small gold crucifix dangling from her fingers. The right portrait was of a distinguished-looking gentleman with a pointed black beard wearing the stiff, brocade doublet and paned hose of an earlier century. A golden globe and a brass sextant sat beside him on a carved desk. The Halburne dynasty was a long one, it would appear. And a wealthy one, too, given the opulence of the art and décor.

As her gaze traveled from the paintings to a lovely rosewood pianoforte, Camille heard a noise behind her and whirled about to face the door. Lord Halburne stood upon the threshold, watching her warily. She had the strangest feeling he had been doing so for more than a moment.

"Your butler," she uttered. "How is he, my lord?"

"He will doubtless recover," said Halburne, coming fully into the room. "At the moment, he is merely bruised and embarrassed. Will you have a seat, Lady Rothewell?"

"*Alors,* this has happened before?" asked Camille, taking the chair he indicated.

Halburne sat down opposite, still holding her card in his hand. "Once, yes," said the earl coolly. "Fothering has weak blood. He was pensioned, but insists upon working when the regular butler is off."

Camille felt a little relieved. "How admirable," she replied. "I hope, *monsieur,* I did not give him a fright."

Halburne's next words were blunt. "What do you want of me, Lady Rothewell?"

Camille could not hold his gaze. "You know who I am, then?"

468

"Oh, I rather think I do," he said tightly. "But perhaps you should explain."

Camille dredged up her resolve. "I am Dorothy's daughter," she said, keeping her voice emotionless. "I arrived in London some weeks past. I would have called upon you as a courtesy to tell you so, but I understood you were in the country."

"So I was." Halburne narrowed his eyes. "Might I ask why you've come to London after all these years?"

Camille hesitated. She had expected indignation — perhaps even outright dismissal — but not this combative suspicion. "I came to be married," she said. "My father brought —"

"Your father?" he said sharply.

Camille felt her cheeks grow warm. She felt like the worst sort of fool. "The Comte de Valigny, *oui*." On impulse, she jerked to her feet. "I beg your pardon. This was a mistake, *monsieur*. I came merely to apologize in advance for the gossip which my presence — and my father's — will inevitably generate. If I could spare you from it, I would."

"I am afraid I don't perfectly understand, Lady Rothewell."

Camille had already started toward the door, but she stopped and turned around.

Halburne's hand was clutching his chair arm as if he meant to spring from his seat, but he did not.

"My mother was a vain and foolish woman, *monsieur,* but I loved her," she finally said. "And yet one cannot be insensible to the . . . the inconvenience, I suppose, which her behavior caused you. I regret it. That is all I wished to say."

At that, Lord Halburne did jerk from his chair. "Good God!" he said affectedly, pacing toward the front windows. "The inconvenience? The *inconvenience?*"

Camille watched the stiff set of his posture. "Whatever one would properly call it, my lord, I do not wish to make it worse," she said quietly. "*Bonjour,* Lord Halburne. I shall find my way out."

"Wait." His voice was gruff; he still would not look at her. "What . . . What did she tell you of me?"

Camille shifted her weight uncomfortably. "Little, my lord," she said. "Indeed, she rarely spoke of her life in England."

"Little?" he rasped. "Not how we met? What I looked like? How long I courted her?"

Camille swallowed hard. *"Non, monsieur."*

At last he turned from the window. "Did she tell you why we parted?"

Camille hesitated, then hung her head. *"Oui,"* she whispered. "Because she wished to go with Valigny to France."

Halburne set his fingers to his temple. "But he never loved her. *Never.* It was . . . just a lark to him." The man was shaking now. "All of life was but a lark to him. For God's sake, could *none of you see that?"*

"*Maman* could not, *monsieur,"* said Camille quietly.

Halburne came away from the window then and paced twice across the drawing room. Camille was uncertain what she should do. Stay? Go quietly? Tell him to go to hell? But that would not do. And in truth, she understood much of his anger and confusion.

Suddenly, Halburne stopped pacing. "She was just too young," he muttered. "Just seventeen, and I nearer thirty, and far too stern. I know that now. And I was not a handsome man, God knows. But after all those months — when she finally said *yes* — I . . . I thought she meant it."

Camille did not know what to say. She wished very desperately she had never come here to witness this man's pain. "I am so sorry, *monsieur.*"

Halburne's jaw was set at a grim angle now. "I forgave her, at first," he gritted,

471

turning to face her. "Did you know that? Did she tell you?"

"*Non, monsieur.*" Camille dropped her gaze. "She did not."

His hand was clenched into a fist. "Valigny left me no choice but to demand satisfaction," he gritted. "But I brought Dorothy back here. To start again. To wait out the duel and the gossip. I was willing. I loved her that much. But even then, her only thought was for Valigny. She begged me to spare him."

Camille tried to smile sympathetically. "She never realized he would fire first."

"Fire first?" Halburne looked at her incredulously. "The notion is ludicrous! I was known to be a crack shot. No, I deloped. I did what Dorothy asked. I fired into the air."

"I . . . I beg your pardon?"

"*I deloped,*" Halburne slowly repeated. "Then the bastard shot me."

"*Mon Dieu!*" Camille sank into a nearby chair, horrified.

It was the worst breach of gentlemanly etiquette imaginable. To shoot an unarmed man? Particularly one who had just forgiven so egregious an insult?

"Your . . . your arm?" she managed to whisper.

Halburne gave a terse nod. "The shot severed an artery," he said. "They said it was hopeless. That I was as good as dead. Dorothy fled with Valigny to France."

Camille swallowed hard. "What madness!" she whispered.

The earl misunderstood. "What choice did I have?" he asked. "Had I killed him as he deserved, he would have died a romantic death — a poet's death — and she would never have forgiven me. I could not win. I know that now."

He was quite right. Camille wished the earth would open and swallow her whole. She opened her mouth to say something — anything — but words failed her.

At last, Halburne approached her. "But after all these years, Lady Rothewell, there is still one thing I cannot fathom."

"What is that, *monsieur?*"

"Why did your mother never marry him?" His voice was hoarse now. "Wasn't that what she wanted? I divorced her. By God, I set her free. And yet she did nothing."

Camille swallowed hard. "Valigny, too, was divorced," she whispered. "He lied to *Maman,* saying he'd learnt the church would not permit him to wed again. *Maman* discovered his perfidy years later. It was . . . the final blow."

Yes, the final blow indeed. To her mother's love for Valigny. To her very life, really. But if Camille had expected triumph to flare in Halburne's eyes, she was mistaken. The heated emotion turned to pity.

"And so she knew," he rasped. "In the end, she knew. Our lives — yours and mine — perhaps even hers — all were ruined. And for what? Nothing but a lark."

Camille looked away. "The truth, I think, sent her to an early grave."

Halburne collapsed slowly into a chair. "So she is dead, then?" he said hollowly. "I knew, of course, from your words that she was."

"Oui, monsieur," said Camille quietly. "She is dead."

Lord Halburne did not respond.

"Monsieur?"

But Halburne was a beaten man. He would not so much as look at her.

Camille left him sitting limply in a chair, his shoulders slumped forward, his eyes unseeing. This time when she told him good-bye, he said nothing.

Halburne's entrance hall was blessedly empty. No one having bothered to take them, Camille still carried her cloak and umbrella. So she simply let herself out, wondering what manner of harm she had just done — to herself, and worse, to Lord Halburne.

CHAPTER THIRTEEN
IN WHICH LADY ROTHEWELL STANDS FIRM

Camille arrived home to find the house as empty as she had left it. Alone, she moved restlessly from room to room, picking up her books and her letters — anything to occupy her mind — and finding solace in nothing until some hours later, Chin-Chin came up from the kitchens to comfort her.

She sat with the dog in her lap until well past dark, eschewing dinner, then finally going to bed sometime past midnight. It was scarcely the first night she had passed in this house without her husband — without even knowing where he had gone, or whose bed he might be warming. So why tonight did it feel such a tragedy?

Because of last night. Because of the day they had spent together. And because she wished desperately to talk to him about Halburne. She had needed a shoulder — and now she fully understood that only his would do. But perhaps Kieran was sending

476

her a message? He had never intended to get so close. Could he be drawing back from her, perhaps, in the only way he knew how?

She rolled over again in the big, too-empty bed, and drew Chin-Chin against her side. The dog snorted sympathetically and licked her cheek.

"Oh, Chin-Chin," she whispered. "What a fool I was to imagine I could do this — marry a man I was altogether too attracted to — then keep my distance."

No, there was no distance — not on her part. And sometimes, she believed, not on his. To console herself, she got up and pushed open the connecting door to Kieran's room so that she might hear him if he returned. Back in bed, Camille sighed and stared into the low fire, which flickered in the hearth. But she kept seeing Lord Halburne's stark, grief-stricken face in the flames and had to roll over and confront the grim emptiness of her room.

Once again, as she had been throughout most of her marriage — perhaps most of her life — Camille was alone, save for the dog. But Chin-Chin was lightly snoring now. Camille tucked him tight against her and tried to go to sleep.

It was almost dinnertime the following day

when Rothewell made his way back from Surrey. He had been a fool to hope to make the journey down in one day, even without the rain. In Berkeley Square, he leapt down with only a little more grace than he had done at Selsdon Court, and looked only marginally better, he suspected. Fighting to stand straight, he passed the carriage off to a waiting footman and went gingerly up the steps to see that Trammel awaited him.

"My lord." The butler all but winced as his gaze swept over him. "You look —"

"Never mind that," Rothewell interjected, pushing past him. "Where is my wife?"

Trammel followed him up the stairs. "Lady Sharpe came for tea," he explained. "She insisted Lady Rothewell return with her to Hanover Street for cards and dinner."

Camille, gone? Rothewell stopped, his heart sinking with disappointment. He had rushed back to London with pain burning a hole from his belly to his backbone, and a vise round his heart, longing for Camille. He had simply assumed she . . . but how arrogant of him.

His shoulders fell. Good God, he felt at death's door. He wanted . . . her. Simply *her* — selfish though such a desire might have been. He strolled along the empty passageway of his home, listening to the hollow echo of his bootheels on the fine wood floors. The sound of an empty house. The sound of what his life had once been.

Was it too late, he wondered, for him and Camille? Too late for them to find their way into each other's hearts? And was it even fair to her that he should contemplate trying? His days were numbered, and there was little, it seemed, to be done about it.

Just then, a spasm of pain wracked him. Rothewell floundered, the corridor swimming dizzily before him. "Christ!" he choked, his hand clawing at the balustrade.

"My lord." Trammel caught him by the arm. "Let's get you into bed."

Rothewell forced himself upright and shook him off. "Just fetch me my brandy," he rasped. "I don't want a damned nursemaid, Trammel. I can put myself to bed."

But the gnawing beast had been his constant companion the past day or more, and Rothewell knew it was gaining in strength. There was no escaping it this time, he feared. Even Gareth had seen the fiend at work. Rothewell had passed a nearly sleepless night at Selsdon, and had found himself unable to eat much more than dry toast this morning.

Trammel, however, did not fetch his

brandy, and for all his high talk, Rothewell wasn't sure he could stomach it anyway. Instead, the butler busied himself by going unobtrusively about his job; drawing down the bedcovers, removing Rothewell's boots, then laying out a fresh nightshirt. Perhaps Trammel knew the signs, for within the hour, Rothewell was heaving up bloody bile, nearly doubled by the agony. When at last the spasms relented, he found himself in bed, the shafting pain dulled to a sickening ache.

The dog lay upon the coverlet, his chin upon his paws, staring forlornly up at him.

"Well, what do you make of it, Jim?" Rothewell rasped, when Trammel went downstairs again. "Am I to meet Old Scratch before the night's out? Or do they mean to torture me a while yet?"

The tiny spaniel made a strange sound, something between a howl and a whine, and inched farther up the bedcovers. Rothewell closed his eyes and laid his hand over the dog's silky head. He shared the spaniel's sentiments. He had spent the better part of his life hell-bent on killing himself — and now that life had suddenly become worth living, he was fairly confident he had succeeded.

■ ■ ■ ■

In Hanover Street, Camille had just taken three tricks in a row and was passing the deal to Lord Sharpe when his butler entered the drawing room. He bent low over the card table, holding a silver salver in her direction. "A note for you, my lady," he said. "From Mr. Trammel."

"Oh, dear," said Lady Sharpe. "What can it be?"

Camille's eyes darted over it. "Rothewell is ill," she said, jerking to her feet. "*Mon Dieu,* I must go."

Within two minutes, she was bundled back into her cloak and out the door, having gently but firmly refused Lady Sharpe's offers to accompany her. Her heart was in her throat. It must be very bad indeed for Trammel to have sent for her.

She arrived home to find one of the footmen hovering at the front door.

"Where is Trammel?" she asked, stripping off her gloves.

"Upstairs, ma'am." The footman lifted her cloak from her shoulders. "He says to tell you that his lordship is resting comfortably now."

"Merci." Camille hastened up the stairs and

turned down the passageway. Trammel met her by Kieran's door, his brow deeply furrowed. "How is he?" she demanded. "What happened?"

Trammel gave a stiff half bow. "He went down to Selsdon Court, my lady," he said quietly, "and was taken ill on the drive, I collect. But this time, the pain was slow to abate. I believe he suffered terribly last night."

Camille's eyes darted toward the door. "*Alors,* he is retching blood?" she asked. "Tell me the truth, Trammel."

The butler nodded. "Not a great deal — it never is — but the spell has lasted longer than before." Then he leaned into her. "I did not tell him I sent for you, ma'am."

Camille set her hand on the butler's forearm. "And he does not need to know, *n'est-ce pas?*"

She went in to find Kieran's lamp turned down and a warm fire blazing in the grate. The covers were drawn halfway up his chest, and one hand rested upon Chin-Chin's back. Seeing Camille, the dog lifted his head and wagged. Kieran's eyes fluttered open.

"Aye, he sent for you didn't he?" Kieran muttered, surveying her approach. "Damned interfering old hen. I'm well

482

enough now."

Camille settled onto the edge of his bed and took his free hand in hers. He was colorless and a little drawn, but otherwise seemed himself. "If you have enough energy to complain of the servants, *mon chéri,* perhaps you have enough energy to tell me where you have been? And how you came to be ill?" she gently suggested. "And kindly do not tell me it is none of my business. I think I have decided that it is going to become my business."

He cut a dark, irritated gaze at her, but a smile, she thought, toyed at one corner of his mouth. "And how long have we been married?" he complained. "A month?"

Camille pursed her lips. "Thereabouts," she remarked. "My questions, *s'il vous plaît?*"

After a moment, the dark gaze relented. He closed his eyes, and squeezed her hand affectionately. "I went down to Selsdon."

"*Oui,* but where is that?"

"Warneham's estate," he answered. "Down in Surrey."

"I see," she said quietly. "In the future, would you be so kind as to leave word for me?"

A ragged sigh escaped his chest. "I thought — foolishly, as it happened — that I could

483

get back in one day if I pressed on."

"But you did not," she said calmly. "And I have been very worried."

"Have you, my dear?" A faint smile curved his mouth. "No one has ever worried about me before."

"Xanthia does," she softly challenged. "When you will allow it."

But the fact was, Camille inwardly acknowledged, he spoke the truth. For much of his life, Kieran had had almost no one in his life to care whether he lived or died.

Suddenly he stirred, withdrawing his hand from hers, and pushing up in the bed. "Speaking of my sister, there are some papers inside my coat," he said, nodding toward a side chair. "Be so good as to fetch them, will you?"

Camille hesitated. *"Non,"* she said. "No papers. Not until we discuss your illness."

He sucked in air through his teeth. "Just . . . *please* do as I ask, Camille," he said. "And then — well, we shall see."

Reluctantly, Camille rose, and the dog leapt down to follow her, his tiny claws tapping on the wood floor, an incongruously merry sound. Kieran's coat hung over the chair, and inside the pocket, she found a fat fold of papers. She took them back to the bed, wondering if she should have refused him. But she had questions — and for once, perhaps, he seemed disposed to actually answer them. After that would come the argument about a doctor — and it was going to be a short one, she vowed.

She handed the fold of papers to him, stroked a hand over his face, then perched herself on the bed.

"I had to discuss this with Gareth first," he said, passing the first several pages to her. "This is a conveyance for my share of Neville Shipping. The second is for ownership of this house. Xanthia needs to sign the last, but she will. Gareth shall be your trustee."

Camille looked at him blankly. "I — I do not understand."

"They are yours now," he said quietly. "Take them."

"Pourquoi?" she asked, confused. "I do not understand, Kieran. I am your wife."

His lips thinned, and fleetingly, his eyes closed. "Camille, I want those things in your name," he said fervently. "Everything else I own is entailed to a son — and if I have no son, to some distant relation whose name I don't even know."

She nodded. *"Oui,* I understand this is the English law."

He reached out again for her hand. "God

485

forbid the worst happens, I want these things clearly separate from the barony," he said. "I want there to be no question but that this is your home, and that my share of Neville's assets now belongs to you. They are not part of the entail, and they were not acquired with entailed assets."

"*Mais non,* Kieran, I do not want this," she said.

"Camille, listen," he whispered. "If I should die childless —"

"*Non,*" she said quietly, handing back the papers. "You married me to have a child. Do you think me so stupid I don't know that was your reason?"

Guilt sketched across his face. "Things change, Camille," he said quietly. "It mightn't work out as we'd hoped."

To her humiliation, tears sprung to Camille's eyes. "We are going to have a child," she said, placing her hand over her abdomen. "I feel it. I *know* it."

"Camille." He looked askance at her. "You said yourself that you cannot be sure."

"We are going to have a child," she insisted. "Eventually, we *will.*"

"Camille, what if I die first?" he whispered.

This Camille had refused to consider. But now, her hand still on her belly, she pondered it. Kieran was trying to *protect* her. Why then did it feel as if he were driving a stake through her heart?

"A decent father would have insisted on a marriage settlement to protect you from such a possibility," Kieran continued. "Instead, all the ready cash you will have is the fifty thousand pounds your grandfather's solicitors are holding in trust."

"*Mais oui.* Fifty thousand pounds is a lot of money."

"It isn't enough, Camille," he said. "Not for the life you deserve. Trust Xanthia to run the business, or go and help her if you like. You could do it, I know. Gareth has stepped down, but he can give you advice. And I want you to —"

"*Très bien,*" she interjected, snatching the papers back. "I have taken them. Now, *s'il vous plaît,* you will answer my questions?"

His eyes darkened. "I am sick, Camille," he said quietly. "I haven't been well in months now. There is nothing more to say in the matter."

Camille laid aside the fold of papers. She forced her voice to be calm but unyielding. "*Mais oui,* there is much to say," she insisted, leaning over the bed to cup his face in her hand. "What is the nature of this illness, *mon cœur?* Why have we not called a doctor?"

His mouth twisted grimly. "Perhaps God means to strike me down for my iniquities," he said acerbically. "In any case, my dear, there's nothing to be done about it."

"Nothing to be done?" she echoed, drawing back. "You do not mean even to try?"

He fell back against the pillows. "Christ Jesus, Camille!" he rasped. "Are you listening to me?"

Camille felt her temper slipping, and desperation setting in. "*Mon Dieu,* Kieran, this self-punishment — this *martyrdom* — it is insanity," she cried. "Why must you be so hard and unfeeling, save for those moments we are in bed? How can you be one man there, and another one here? What is it, Kieran, that you cannot say to me?"

His gaze shuttered, and he shook his head.

Camille curled her fingers into his nightshirt. "Are you already lost to me, Kieran?" she whispered. "Is that what you are so certain of?"

"Camille, I . . ."

Wearily, she let her head fall forward to touch his. "A man such as you," she whispered, "giving in to what? To hopelessness? *Pour l'amour de Dieu,* Kieran! You are a better, stronger man than that. You are not honest, not even with yourself."

"Camille," he finally said, his voice flat. "We all make our choices in life, then we live with them. As to honesty — are you honest with yourself?"

"I see the truth of what life is," she answered, straightening up. "But I do not let it defeat me."

"What about your grandfather's letter?" he gently countered.

"*Oui?* What of it?" she asked.

"I read it carefully," he answered. "That's why you were left with nothing, Camille. And for the life of me, I cannot understand why you are not angrier about it."

"Angrier at whom?" she asked. "My grandfather? Bah. I do not waste my time."

"No," said her husband. "At your mother, for hiding it. My God, it wasn't just a dowry or an inheritance, Camille. Did you read it? The man offered to take you. To raise you. To get you away from the father you hated and a life of impecunity. He wanted to give you life's every luxury."

Camille cut her gaze away. "My mother did not wish to lose me," she said quietly. "I was all she had. That is how I must look at it now."

"Very well," he said. "Let us concede, then, that she was merely selfish instead of thoroughly spiteful. Why did she not give you the letter on her deathbed? Why not then? Instead, it took you what? — six weeks? Six months? — to find it?"

Camille dropped her head. "A little more."

"And all the while, the clock was ticking," he said. "You had mere weeks left in which to find a husband, Camille, when you met me. So now you are saddled with me because I was the best you could do. And now I'm the only one who's angry about it? Why is that, Camille?"

Camille clasped her hands in her lap. She did not wish to answer that question; did not wish to revisit the pain of those last, awful years — nor did she wish to consider that there might well be more such years ahead of her if she did not stand firm.

"I know, Kieran, that my mother was a selfish woman," she said quietly. "I lived it. I *know*. Many times, *oui,* she wounded me, and a part of me is still angry. But *Maman* did not know about the letter on her deathbed. Or I should say, she could not remember it."

"I beg your pardon?"

"My mother," said Camille. "She became a — a — what is the word? A drunkard? I spent the last three years of her life watching her slowly kill herself because her beauty

490

was gone, and Valigny had forsaken her." She paused to drag in a ragged breath. "On a good day, Kieran, *Maman* scarcely knew her own name, let alone her father's. At the last, *mon Dieu!* — she didn't even know mine."

He was stunned into a moment's silence. "I am sorry, Camille," he said, reaching out for her hand. "I ought not have said anything."

Camille shrugged. "No, you ought not have," she agreed, her husky voice bitter. "You must pardon me, Kieran, when I do not know if we are sharing our lives with one another or not. It is so very hard to tell."

"I just don't wish to worry you, my dear, or to hurt you."

"Et alors," she rasped, pulling away. "I have hurt before. I will hurt again. Perhaps, Kieran, I am already hurting?"

"Camille, listen —"

"Non!" she said sharply. "You listen. I hurt when you are cold to me. I hurt when you stay out all night, and I do not know where you are. I hurt when I watch you poisoning yourself with too much drink and never —"

"Camille, I told you when we married —"

"I know what you told me!" She cut him off with a chop of her hand. "But it is over, that marriage! Do you hear me? Whatever we said, whatever we agreed — *it is over.* Can you not see it, Kieran, in my eyes? I — I need you now. Our child will need you. I am not begging you. I am *telling* you."

The pain and the weariness were pressing in on Kieran, weighing him down. "Perhaps, Camille, if you —"

She shook her head. "Perhaps I do not wish to waste more of my life sitting by the bed of another invalid who has brought his troubles on himself?" she whispered, her eyes welling with tears. "Perhaps that, Kieran, is what I think unfair."

She was angry, and by God, he hated to admit she had a point. At least Camille had never said she loved him. That, he could not have borne. "Camille," he said quietly, "this is who I am. It is who you married. I made that plain."

"*Menteur!*" she rasped, springing off the bed. "Liar!" It is not who you are. *Oui, oui,* I know what you said — and if you were that man I met at first, perhaps I would not care. But you do not enjoy this life you have made for yourself, Kieran. You come home as restless and as unhappy as you were when you left. You scarcely eat. You scarcely sleep. I tell you it is the life of a coward."

"A *coward* — ?"

"One who will not fight," she answered,

leaning over him. "Not his devils. Not his illness. You promised to give me a child — a child I need you to help me love and bring up, Kieran — and now you are all but willing yourself to die."

The word *coward* was ringing in his ears. "Oh, I see." His voice was flat. "I see what this is about."

Camille crossed her arms over her chest and turned away from the bed. "Whatever this is *about*," she said quietly, "you promised me. And you cannot keep your promise if you are gone, *n'est-ce pas?*"

"I didn't promise you a damned thing," he answered. "I saved you from marrying a sick, perverted bastard because you were too bullheaded to listen to reason. *That* is what I did for you. And as you say, perhaps you are already carrying that child. Why do you think I demanded this travesty of a marriage?"

"A travesty?" she whispered in her husky voice. She turned around and walked slowly back to the bed. "*Mon Dieu,* is that what you think this is?"

His lips thinned with frustration. "No," he returned, dragging his hands through his hair. "I am sorry. I misspoke."

But it was too late. He could see the tears beginning to trickle from her eyes. God damn it, he should have known it would come to this. He should never have let another woman into this house. Into his life. The pain in his gut he could bear. Camille, crying, was harder.

"*Sacré bleu,* Kieran," she whispered, "do you think I am going to let you just lie there and die?"

"We aren't apt to have much choice, my dear," he returned. "God makes those decisions."

"*Non!*" she replied sharply. "No, I will *not* believe that. God gave us brains so that we might use reason."

She was fishing through her pocket now, looking, most likely for a handkerchief. Hell and damnation. "In the top drawer of the chest," he said, gentling his tone. "Help yourself."

"*Merci,*" she sniffled, turning away.

Rothewell's hands were balled into fists, his frustration turning to fury. Fury at fate. Fury at himself. But somehow, through all the rage and frustration, he knew it was not Camille's fault. And he knew in his heart that everything she had said was right.

"I am sorry, Camille," he said, as she returned from the chest. He held out his arms. "Please, may we just forget all this? Just for tonight? Tomorrow you can scold me anew. Come here, my dear."

She blew her nose then returned to sit beside him. He enfolded her in his arms, and she came against him, pressing her cheek to his nightshirt. "Oh, Kieran!" Her small, warm hands went round his neck.

Rothewell closed his eyes and inhaled deeply. Camille smelled of roses, and of that exotic spicy scent he could never quite identify. It was simply *her*. And he loved her. He had come to accept that now.

Whether he was worthy or not, he felt for her a deep, profound, bittersweet love which was tinged with regret. A love he could never have imagined, and would never shake off, no matter how far he roamed or long he stayed away. One which would, ultimately, transcend the grave.

And if he loved her that much, what harm would it do to simply acquiesce to her wishes? There was nothing to keep from her now. He could no longer shelter her, or obscure the truth. He had meant to keep a distance between them — to spare her, to spare himself — but he was weak, and it was no longer possible. His every thought was of her. Of how it would feel to lose her. Worrying about how she would go on, financially, and yes, emotionally. Moreover, he was not ashamed to admit to himself that he was frightened of what lay ahead. That he needed her.

"Go on, then," he said, murmuring into her hair. "Tomorrow morning, call the doctor if it will make you feel better."

"Tomorrow?" Her voice caught on the last syllable.

He stroked a hand down her hair. "Camille, will one night make a difference?" he reassured her. "I feel well enough now. Truly. Just . . . stay with me tonight. Sleep here. Please."

She lifted her cheek, her smile halfhearted. *"Très bien,"* she said softly, dabbing at her tears. "But I do not know a doctor to call. Will Trammel know of someone?"

Rothewell stared into the fire which had caught to a roaring blaze now. This was another coil he'd snared himself in. Finally, he spoke. "There is a doctor in Harley Street," he said quietly. "Dr. Redding. I cannot recall the number — somewhere near the street's end. I shall tell Trammel to send for him first thing."

She drew back, her eyes searching his face. "You know him," she whispered. "You have seen this doctor before."

Reluctantly, he nodded. "A few days before we met."

Understanding dawned in her face. *"Je*

vois," Camille murmured. "And . . . what did he say?"

Rothewell gave a wry, sideways smile. "That I drink too much and smoke too much," he answered. "That I have lived too hard and waited too long. That I likely have a cancer in my stomach — or a cancer that has spread from my liver. And given the blood loss, he thought it was . . . far gone."

He watched her face crumple; watched her fight for control as her lower lip trembled. *"Oui?"* she whispered. "What is . . . what is the treatment?"

He cupped her face in his hands. "Camille," he said, his voice gently reproachful. "You and I both know there is no treatment. A doctor can do nothing but treat the pain when it becomes intolerable."

She shook her head. *"Non,"* she whispered. "This cannot be. It must be something else. Or . . . or it might just go away, if you are careful. Doctors are often wrong."

Rothewell squeezed his eyes shut. He wanted, suddenly and desperately, to believe her. He wished to God he'd changed his ways the moment he'd left Redding's office. But he had not bothered. This was the fate he had long expected. Awaited, really.

It was as if Camille read his mind. "You . . . you just accepted it, *n'est-ce pas?"*

she said weakly. "You thought it was God's will. What you deserved."

At last, he tore his gaze from hers. "It crossed my mind, Camille," he acknowledged. "I never expected to live this long, truth to tell. And when he told me . . . I thought, well, this is it. I've done it to myself. And now I'll finally see Luke again, somewhere out there. I shall have my chance at last."

Camille frowned and turned his face back to hers. "*Oui?* Your chance for what?"

Lamely, he lifted one shoulder. "I — I hardly know," he whispered. "To beg his forgiveness, I suppose."

"Perhaps, *mon cœur,* he should beg yours?" she suggested. "He took the woman you loved."

Rothewell set his head to one side and studied her. "He felt I had wronged her."

"*Oui,* perhaps," she acknowledged. "But his solution was to *marry* her. He did not even give you the chance to make things right."

He shook his head. "What do you mean, *make things right?*"

She shrugged. "He could have told you to marry her, or he would do so," she suggested. "Would that not have been the gentlemanly thing to do?"

He dropped his gaze. "I wonder if I would have done," he said softly. "Even then, I think I knew the difference between a dangerous obsession and true love. If I did not know it then, I surely — well . . . I just know it."

Camille dipped her head to better see his face. "So you grieve for . . . for the *affaire* which came after," she remarked. "It was wrong, *oui,* very wrong. Yet he married her knowing she cared for you."

Rothewell laughed harshly. "Yes, that story about my having slept with my brother's wife would haunt anyone, wouldn't it?" he muttered. "But that wasn't enough for me. To put a properly tragic twist on the tale, they both came to a sad end. An end for which I was responsible."

She held motionless for an instant, waiting for him to continue. When he did not, she shook her head. *"Non,"* she said quietly. "You did not kill anyone."

His gaze caught hers, but it was flat. Hard. "No, they were burned to death in a slave revolt," he said. "But I caused it. I caused it as surely as if I had lit the fire myself."

She searched his face as if looking for the truth. "And why do you think this?" she finally asked. "*Oui,* it sounds terrible. But you cannot have been the cause."

He couldn't bear it. He looked away again. "I was to attend a dinner the night they died," he murmured. "It was Easter Sunday, and the parish planters were meeting to discuss rumors of slave unrest. But I was drunk — too drunk to be fit company for anyone. I had learnt, you see, that the nastier I was and the drunker I was, the less I would see of Annemarie."

"Oui?" Camille was watching him, her gaze steady. "Go on."

Rothewell hesitated. Having given words to it, the truth was suddenly easier to see. The darkness in him, the temper and the irascibility — it had served him as both sword and shield. It had kept people away. Indeed, it had almost kept Camille away, and might still do so. His rage had been a lethal weapon indeed — perhaps literally.

He drew a deep breath, and went on. "When Luke came round and saw I was deep in my cups, he was enraged," he said. "He said . . . he said that one of us had to go, so he would, since I was incapable. He ordered Annemarie to dress and go with him. But in the middle of dinner, someone rushed in and said the slaves in St. Philip's were in revolt."

Camille made a soft sound of anguish, one hand going to her mouth.

"Houses and fields were set afire," Rothewell whispered. "Luke set out for home, but on the way back, someone set our cane fields afire. Both sides of the road. The winding lane back to the house was so bloody narrow. No place to turn. No way to go backward. They were trapped. Just . . . hopelessly trapped."

"Mon Dieu." Camille's eyes swam with pity.

Rothewell swallowed hard. Since the inquest, he had spoken aloud of the tragedy but once — to Martinique, in some pathetic, ill-thought-out attempt to explain himself to her. And speaking of it now left him feeling the same as he had felt then. Dead. Cold. As if hope was lost all over again.

"They came to fetch me near midnight," he finally managed to continue. "Luke — he was still alive. But Annemarie . . . it was too late. The horses . . . dear God. Someone had to shoot them. But Luke . . . we couldn't shoot him, could we?" His voice cracked, and he realized in some shock that tears had sprung to his eyes. "At first, when you're burned that badly, you — you can't feel it. But soon enough he was begging us. Begging *me.* He . . . he didn't last long, thank God."

Camille stroked her hands down his arms, then caught her fingers in his. "It was a terrible tragedy," she said. "And you know in your mind, Kieran, that you did not cause this. But in your heart — *oui*, in your heart, you still hurt. I understand that."

Rothewell gave a bitter bark of laughter and let his head fall back against the headboard. "Ironic, isn't it?" he said softly. "Luke was everyone's white knight. He saved people. That was what he was good at. I thanked him by bedding his wife and drinking myself into a stupor. Annemarie, she admired Luke — as everyone did. But she was drawn to me. Drawn like a moth to flame. And in the end, she was burned to death in it."

"Kieran," said Camille softly. "That is not what happened."

Slowly, he shook his head. "No?" he said quietly. "Then why does it feel that way? Why wasn't I in that carriage? I should have been. Perhaps they wished to kill me? God knows I had enemies. Perhaps they did not even know it was Luke?"

"Or perhaps it was just an angry mob running mad," she whispered, touching him lightly on the cheek. "Perhaps there was no rhyme or reason to it. And you will not make it right by allowing yourself to die."

It was the best answer Camille had. She shifted closer, curled her legs beneath her skirts, and reclined fully against him. "Kieran, *mon cœur*," she said, settling her head onto his shoulder. "You have carried your pain too long. And I cannot make you stop. But perhaps I can try with all my heart to make you look beyond it? There can be a future for you — for *us*. I have to believe that."

He set his hand between Camille's slender shoulders and began to make small, soothing circles. She did not seem disgusted, or even particularly shocked by what he'd said. And she was right — it had been a mob run mad. Still, it should have been he trapped inside that burning carriage. *It should have been.* And he had spent more than a decade trying to right that old wrong.

But now, perhaps, there were others to think about? Or perhaps it was too late. But he had never been a coward, and he would not start now. A journey to Surrey in the pouring rain whilst bent double with pain was easy. What Camille was asking was harder. She was not simply asking him to try to get well, she was asking him to hope. For the future. For them. For *himself*.

Rothewell tilted his head to kiss his wife's temple. "Send for your doctor in the morning, Camille," he said again. "Send for him then, if that is still your wish. And if Redding says there is anything to be done, I . . . I will do it."

Chapter Fourteen

IN WHICH
DR. HISLOP STEPS IN

Shortly after dawn the next morning, Camille sent Trammel off in Rothewell's gig to personally fetch Dr. Redding from his office in Harley Street. Kieran was pacing the floor again in his dressing gown, the pain having returned in the night. But when Trammel reappeared at the bedchamber door well over an hour later, he was alone.

Camille set down the porridge she'd been more or less forcing upon her husband and went out into the passageway to speak with the butler.

"I'm afraid the doctor was away, ma'am," he said uncertainly. "He's been with a patient in Marylebone the whole night."

Camille's heart sank. *"Zut!"* she muttered. "I think, Trammel, we must find someone else whilst his lordship is amenable."

"I did bring someone, ma'am," said Trammel, looking doubtful. "A fellow down the street. Dr. Hislop is his name — an army man, he says, formerly attached to the physician-general in India. A bit rough around the edges, but I thought . . . well, I thought he'd be better than no one?"

"*Oui, certainement,* Trammel," said Camille, relieved. "Show him up at once."

Dr. Hislop took his time in climbing the stairs, huffing and puffing, but at last he arrived, a bedraggled, voluminous satchel in hand. Camille at once understood Trammel's apprehension. The physician was a stout, stooped man of indeterminate years who looked as if he had slept in his coat. His white hair was disorderly, with a cowlick the size of Camille's hand up the back, and his trouser hems appeared to have been nibbled upon by rats.

Upon introduction, the doctor cocked his head and looked at Camille with a squint. "Well, now, where's our patient?" he said cheerfully. "Best get to 'em before the undertaker, I always say."

Disconcerted, Camille showed him in with some reluctance. Chin-Chin leapt from the bed and waddled over to give the man a thorough sniffing. Ignoring the dog, Dr. Hislop set down his tattered satchel, shook Rothewell's hand, then bade him remove his dressing gown and sit on the edge of the bed.

"Trouble in the gut, eh?" he said, throwing back the buckles of his bag, one of which was broken. "Nothing more annoying, I always say. Pain's a sharp one, is it?"

"Yes, at times," said Kieran, wincing.

Humming to himself, Hislop began to extract a number of legitimate-looking and reasonably clean medical tools from within. Once or twice, he glanced at Camille as if expecting her to excuse herself. Instead, she crossed her arms over her chest and stood her ground, Chin-Chin at her feet. The spaniel was making a low, wary rumble in his chest.

Kieran surveyed them good-naturedly. "I collect my wife and the dog mean to stay, Hislop," he said. "The butler, too, I do not doubt."

Trammel sniffed and backed out, drawing shut the door.

The doctor drew a long wooden tube from his bag. In response, Chin-Chin leapt up on the bed beside Kieran and gave the physician a territorial growl, baring his sharp white teeth. He had clearly appointed himself Kieran's protector.

The doctor looked at him and chuckled. "A mighty small dog, your lordship, for such a large job as me," he said. "Has he a name?"

"Jim," said Kieran.

"Chin-Chin," said Camille at once.

The doctor looked between them and smiled. "Ah, newlyweds!"

Kieran's black brows went up. "Why do you say so?"

"If you'd been married any time a'tall, my lord," said the doctor, extracting a set of lancets, "you would *know* his name is Chin-Chin. The wife, you will soon learn, is always right. Now, kindly remove your nightshirt and lie down, if you please."

His point made, Chin-Chin retreated to the middle of the bed, observing the doctor with a dubious eye. Camille shared the sentiment, but she was desperate.

Rothewell was already regretting his promise to Camille, and he was not at all sure of Dr. Hislop. But he *had* promised, so, with one last withering look at the doctor, he stripped off the shirt, loosened the tie of his drawers, and lay down.

Hislop spent the next quarter hour quizzing him on all manner of intimate and highly personal things — things which men simply did not discuss — whilst probing and poking him from his neck to his nether regions. It was damned humiliating, particularly in front of Camille. And beneath his ribs, it hurt like the devil.

"Ouch, damn you!" Finally, Rothewell tried to rise up and push away the doctor. Chin-Chin leapt up, and began to snarl, his feathery black ears atremble.

"Chin-Chin, *chut!*" Camille scolded, plucking him from the bed.

The cool hand bore Rothewell back down onto the bed, and the doctor resumed his interrogation. "Does it hurt when I do this? No? And what about this?"

Another searing pain shot from Rothewell's belly to his backbone. This time he did sit up. "The examination is finished," he said roughly.

With a muted smile, Hislop turned round and motioned between Camille and the dog. "Well? Which one of you is going to bite him?"

Camille stepped forward. "I shall," she said, glaring.

Cursing beneath his breath, Rothewell lay back down.

Hislop took up the wooden tube, pressed it to Rothewell's chest, then set his ear to the other end. "Ah, a good, strong heart!" he announced, listening. He straightened up and put the tube away. "You may put your shirt and robe back on, my lord."

In an instant, Rothewell was up and dragging his shirt over his head.

Camille set the dog down and came forward. For the first time, her motions looked tentative. "What do you think it is, Dr. Hislop?" she asked. "Is it . . . is it a cancer as Dr. Redding believes? Could it be fatal?"

"Oh, cancer is always fatal," he said almost cheerfully. "No cure for that! But is it cancer? Hard to say. Certainly the symptoms are there."

Camille's shoulders fell. Rothewell resisted the urge to go to her; to tell her it would all be well. It mightn't be, and he knew it. Hislop knew it, too, for despite his outward nonchalance, Rothewell could feel the tension. He motioned them all to chairs by the hearth. Dr. Hislop sat down with a sigh, both knees cracking ominously.

"As you already know, my husband is losing blood," said Camille when they were settled. "I understand, *bien sûr,* that this is grave. But please tell us what else it might be."

"Good Lord!" said the doctor. "It *might be* a hundred things. It might be that your butler is slipping broken glass into his morning coffee, or that he swallowed a fish fork and forgot to tell me about it, or that —"

"Point taken," Rothewell interjected. He managed a grim smile. "Well, I daresay we are finished here. I thank you for your honesty, doctor."

But the doctor remained silent in his chair. "Or it might be, my lord," he finally said, "that you are a man on the verge of killing yourself with drink."

"With drink?" Rothewell lifted his brows, and scrubbed a hand round his unshaved jaw. "I somehow doubt it. I have been trying to kill myself with drink for years to no avail."

Dr. Hislop simply shrugged. "Men who drink to excess, my lord, tend not to mind their health until it is too late," he said. "A bad habit, that. How long has it been since you went a full day from your brandy?"

Rothewell considered it. "A few weeks past," he answered honestly. "I just . . . well, I just needed to clear my head for a day or two."

The truth was, a fortnight before Xanthia's wedding, he had stopped drinking altogether. He had wanted to be sure he was judging her future husband with the utmost care, and he had wished to be stone-cold sober to do it. And he had stopped again two days before Xanthia's fateful dinner party — again, because he'd wanted his wits about him.

The doctor set his hands over his ample

belly and drummed his fingers for a moment. "And when you stop, do you suffer any side effects, my lord? Shaking? Hallucination?"

Rothewell gaped at him. "Good God, man! The rum fits?"

"The delirium tremens," the doctor corrected. "Frightful things! Do you?"

"Certainly not." Rothewell was affronted. To his way of thinking, delirium was for sots and for weaklings — men who had no business drinking to begin with.

The doctor was nodding jovially. "And how long before that?"

Rothewell managed a wry smile. "Occasionally, doctor, a man of my ilk must surrender one vice in order to better indulge in another — or I did do, before my marriage," he belatedly added. "It was not unusual for me to go a day or two without a drink if I found something willing enough and pretty enough to distract me."

"Ha-ha!" The doctor slapped his thighs, and winked at Camille. "And other than your carnal appetites, my lord, can anything else dissuade you?"

"Not often," said Rothewell. "I do recall that on my crossing from Barbados last year, several of us aboard ship took ill. For nearly a fortnight, I'd no wish to drink, or even eat or breathe, frankly. The cook died of it, whatever it was."

"On a ship? God only knows!" The doctor scratched his head. "In any case, it would appear you are not dependent on drink."

"Brandy is a fine servant, sir," said Rothewell. "But it must never be a man's master."

"A remarkable philosophy," said Hislop dryly. "Nonetheless, my lord, you *do* drink too much — particularly spirits. And it must come to halt, at least for a time."

"Will that fix it?" asked Rothewell hopefully. Brandy seemed suddenly a small sacrifice.

"Hard to say," answered Hislop. "But in any case, my lord, a man of your age can no longer afford to drink as if he means to kill himself — particularly one with so lovely a young bride, and perhaps a wee one on the way? So far as a diagnosis, however, I know only what I can guess from a cursory examination."

"*Accursed* examination, you mean," Rothewell complained. "Very well then, hazard a guess."

The physician shrugged. "Certainly you have a case of acute gastritis," he said. "Beyond that, it could be an ulceration of the duodenum. That is the point at which your stomach connects to your bowels."

Rothewell winced. "Is that fatal?"

"Oh, Lord yes! Quite often." Hislop had apparently decided Rothewell was not a man with whom one minced words. "Particularly if it eats through to your entrails. However, since you are not putrid, feverish, or dead, I fancy that isn't the case. Nonetheless, it is possible something has begun to eat holes in your gut."

The beast. He had always sensed it. Rothewell considered his odds.

"What causes this — this ulcering, *monsieur?*" asked Camille.

"Drink, worry, and tobacco are prime suspects, my lady — and it is not a problem easily healed."

"*Alors,* there's no hope it is ordinary dyspepsia, then?" Camille pressed.

The doctor smiled grimly. "No, no," he said. "Not a chance in the world."

"Very well." Rothewell gave a terse nod. "If not ulceration, what else?"

Hislop waggled his head from side to side equivocally. "Well, as Dr. Redding suggested, a cancer of the liver — or perhaps a cancer of the stomach which has spread to the liver — both are still quite likely."

"A cancer," Rothewell echoed.

Well. There it was again. Brutal honesty. He felt that strange, almost numb-inducing chill settling over him once more, wrapping round his heart, weighing down his limbs, and leaving a faint roar in his ears. Good God. He was in the prime — or what ought to have been the prime — of his life. And for the first time ever, he was in love. He had everything, he now realized, to live for. A wife and a home. A sister and a family. Hell, even a silly little fluff of a dog to which he'd become strangely attached. Rothewell wanted to live. To love his wife. To care for the child he hoped she carried. Such seemingly simple things.

For a time, he had actually wished to die, though he had never consciously admitted it until today. Perhaps that was why he sat here with that steel-cold certainty spreading like lead over his chest, but without panic or denial. That would come later, he did not doubt, if the worst were to happen. Men were always afraid to meet their Maker. God knew he was.

Ah, but this would not do! A man must die as he had lived. He had already faced his own worst nightmare in the cane field that fateful April night. The other side of the grave could hold no worse than that. Somehow, he cleared his throat. When he spoke, his voice was perfectly steady. "Thank you for your candor, doctor. Is there anything else it might be?"

Dr. Hislop threw up his hands. "Oh, what the devil!" he said. "I think you've got a bleeding ulceration. I'd stake my best pair of carriage horses on it, for I've been at this for forty-odd years. You drink too much. You smoke too much. You get no sleep — and God only knows what you've been eating — or what's eating *you.* Something you need to get a choke hold on, I can tell you that much."

Camille exhaled audibly.

"Do you think that's it?" asked Rothewell hopefully.

Hislop's grizzled eyebrows snapped together. "Well, that's not good news!" he barked. "It might not be cancer, but it will bloody well kill you, and a good deal quicker, too. We must heal the stomach, and it shan't be easy."

"*Mon Dieu,* just tell us what to do." Camille slid forward in her chair, her slender hands braced on the arms. "Tell us, and I shall see it is done."

Hislop eyed her up and down. "Aye, you will, won't you?" he said. The doctor rummaged through his coat and extracted a wrinkled bit of paper and a stub of a pencil. On his knee, he began to jot out a list. Rothewell tried to relax in his chair. He watched Hislop's face carefully. The doctor was telling the truth, he believed. Moreover, the man seemed to have a sort of horse sense about him.

Hislop lifted his list, and cleared his throat. "Well, then," he announced. "Here is what you may eat, my lord, and mind what I say, for you mustn't vary from it in the slightest! Boiled roots — potatoes, parsnips, and the like. Soft rice, beef tea —"

"Beef tea?" said Rothewell. "*Beef tea?* What the hell good is *that* going to do me?"

Hislop shot him a nasty look. "Bite him," he said, motioning at Camille.

Rothewell held up a surrendering hand. "I shall acquire a taste for it," he said. "Go on."

"Stewed chicken, poached eggs, mushy peas, snap beans — well-cooked, mind — and perhaps a slice of bread — no butter."

"Good God!" said Rothewell.

"Oh, and very weak soda water," added the doctor cheerfully, squinting as he jotted it on the list. "It will neutralize the gastric secretions, and perhaps ease the pain. No other liquid of any kind — not even watered wine. That, my lord, is your diet for the next six weeks."

"Six weeks!"

Hislop waved the list as if to torment him. "Yes, and the first week is to be total bed rest," he continued. "*Total* bed rest. The next week you must rest comfortably at home, with no vigorous activity of any kind — and I think you know what I mean. Then, and only then, may you begin to take a little exercise. And at the end of all this, my lord, you shall be either alive or dead."

"Or starving," said Rothewell glumly. "Or perishing of boredom."

Unsympathetic, Hislop ignored him. "Provided you are still alive and breathing at the end of six weeks," he went on, "and provided the bleeding and pain have stopped, we may safely assume it is not a cancer."

Camille made a sound of relief and shut her eyes.

"On the other hand," the doctor continued, "if you keep on as you are — drinking, smoking, and fretting over whatever the devil it is you are fretting about — and one of those ulcerations eats through to your innards, then you may well wish you had a cancer."

"He will do as you say," said Camille, snatching the list. "I shall see to it."

Rothewell was smiling grimly. "So the two of you mean to starve me to death instead, eh?" he said teasingly. "Without even the comfort of my brandy? Good God, Doctor, this is a sorry way for a man to go."

The doctor had the audacity to lean forward and pat Rothewell's knee. "Keep on as you are, my lord," he said again, "and you'll soon be praying for the Angel of Death. There won't be a bloody thing I can do about it, either, so do me a great kindness and don't send for me. I really do dislike watching strapping young men writhe in agony, particularly when a bit of temperance could have avoided it."

He had painted a vivid picture in Rothewell's mind. "Yes," said Rothewell, much subdued. "It does seem a waste."

"Well, that's that!" Hislop rose, his knees cracking back into place. "I'd bleed him with my lancets, my lady, just to get his attention, but he can't spare it right now."

"Très bien," she said, shooting Rothewell a warning look. "We shall let him off that hook — *this* time."

Hislop took up his bag. "Well, that will be ten pounds sixpence, my lord, for the call," he said. "Might I ask that you settle your account now?"

"Ten pounds six?" Rothewell echoed, horrified. "Why, highwaymen don't make that!"

"Yes, but I find an exorbitant fee tends to

dramatically increase the value of my advice," said the doctor. "And I like the terminally ill to pay straightaway. After all, one never knows."

Rothewell blinked uncertainly. "But . . . But I thought you said . . . if I ate stewed chicken . . . ?"

"Ha-ha!" said the doctor, elbowing Camille. "Just making a point, my lord! Six weeks — and no cheating!"

Camille escorted the doctor down the stairs and sent Trammel off to the cash box. At the front door, she paused to thank Hislop.

The doctor puffed out his cheeks. "Pray do not thank me yet, my lady," he warned. "This will not be easy. I know his lordship's type."

"*Oui*, perhaps," she quietly acknowledged. "But you do not quite know mine."

Dr. Hislop smiled as a footman threw open the door. As they said their final goodbyes, a fine barouche pulled to the pavement, and Mr. Kemble climbed gingerly out, carrying a canvas bundle before him.

Camille was taken aback. "Good morning, Mr. Kemble," she managed to say. "We were not expecting you."

Kemble nodded at the passing doctor, who lifted his hat. "Yes, but I was expecting you," he said brightly. Then, leaning into her, "*Quelle horreur!* What was that?"

"I fear it is a long story," she said wryly.

Kemble shrugged it off at once. "Well, may I come in just a moment? I have something I wish you to see."

"For a moment, *oui*," she said. "But I am afraid my husband is rather ill."

Kemble looked instantly grave. "All the more reason, then!" he said, swishing past her. He set the canvas bundle on the floor.

"*Alors,* what have you brought?" asked Camille, confused.

Kemble bent over and lifted the canvas bag with a soft *whoosh!* An ornate arrangement of glistening glass bowls and silver branches sat upon the hall carpet, rising to Camille's hip. She drew in her breath sharply.

"Indeed, the epergne!" he proclaimed. "Is it not magnificent? Jean-Claude left it out by mistake, and Lady Sallwart nearly got hold of it, so when you didn't turn up, I thought I'd best bring it by — but never mind that! Where is Rothewell? What has he done to himself now?"

"*Now?*" asked Camille pointedly.

Kemble smiled tightly. "Oh, he has a death wish, that one," he said quietly. "I trust, my lady, that you can disabuse him of the notion?"

"*Oui, certainement,*" she said grimly. "You may depend upon it."

Kemble started up the steps as if he knew where he was going. "Frankly, the life that man has led quite chills one's blood," he said, tossing his hand theatrically. "I shan't terrify you with the details — but never say I did not warn him!"

"*Vraiment?* Did you warn him?"

"Oh, Lord yes!" said Kemble. "Scarcely six months ago, in this very house. We quarreled horribly over it, you know, but Rothewell is most unamenable to persuasion."

"Is he indeed?" said Camille dryly. "I had not noticed."

Kemble turned at the top of the stairs but nearly strode past Rothewell's door.

"This way," said Camille, lightly touching his shoulder. "We have changed rooms."

Kemble turned and followed her in.

"*Mon cœur,* I have brought you a visitor," she said.

Kieran lifted his head from the pillows. "Good God," he said. "You!"

"*Oui, c'est moi!*" said Kemble cheerfully. "Try to contain your enthusiasm."

"Do draw up a chair, *Monsieur* Kemble," said Camille, going to the opposite side of the bed and beginning to fluff Rothewell's pillows. "I am most eager to hear your story."

Rothewell shot her a dark glance. "What story?"

"The story of how *Monsieur* Kemble warned you about your health," she said lightly. "Six months ago, *n'est-ce pas?*"

"A little more," said Kemble, settling into the chair he'd pulled to the bed. "It was May Day, actually. I remember it well."

"Do you?" said Rothewell irascibly. "I certainly do not."

Kemble turned to look at Camille. "I was warning him, you see, that the Satyr's Club was a nasty, pernicious place, and that he ought not frequent —"

Camille dropped the pillow. "The *Satyr's Club?*" she interjected. "What a vile name."

"Yes, the place is rife with disease — I shan't be specific, mind — *and* opium," said Kemble knowingly. "Moreover, the poor devil was practically *living* in that hellish hole." Then Kemble dropped his voice to a more somber tone. "And I warned him, too, that he was in grave danger of losing his looks from all the drinking and smoking," he said gravely. "Can there be a greater tragedy, I ask you?"

"Oh, good God!" said Rothewell again. "What nonsense! You said no such thing."

A tight smile curled Kemble's lips. "But I did, my dear Rothewell, and you know it," he said, cutting a chiding gaze toward him. "I told you quite plainly that you had all the charm and beauty of a violent death. That your skin tone was gone, your eyes were shot bloodred, and that it appeared a drunken stonemason had carved those lines into your face with a hammer and chisel. My *exact* words, I believe."

"*Très drôle,*" said Camille. "It now appears my husband has made a habit of ignoring good advice."

Rothewell stared at the ceiling. "I do not recall any of it."

"Probably because you were half-sprung and in an ill humor at the time," said Kemble blithely. "But never fear. I recall the rest of it, too."

"Yes, right up until the moment I tossed you out on your arse, I hope?" Rothewell suggested.

"Thereabouts, yes." Kemble laid a pensive finger to his cheek. "Now let me see! I warned you that your skin was losing its resiliency, and that if you hadn't a bit of your island bronze left, you'd have no color at all. And then I wondered — presciently, it now would appear — what would become of you in another six months."

Rothewell looked at him sarcastically. "And I said?"

Kemble crossed his legs, and set his hands atop his knees. "Why you said you might as well hang yourself!" he declared. "*Once a chap's looks are gone,* you said, *what else has he to live for? Good tailoring and a tight corset can only go so far.*"

"Oh, good God!" Rothewell rolled his eyes heavenward. "I didn't really mean that."

Camille circled around the bed and sat gingerly at Kieran's feet. "I fear, *Monsieur* Kemble, that the trouble is far worse than merely losing his looks," she said, settling a soothing hand over Kieran's ankle. "That, really, is bearable. But Dr. Hislop fears that my husband might have ulcerations — is that the word?"

Glumly, Kieran nodded.

"*Oui,* ulcerations in his stomach," she went on. "It is very dangerous, he says, and my husband must rest for many weeks."

"And eat a very bland diet," said Kemble, nodding. "That is of the utmost importance. And you don't want to eat *anything* they serve at the Satyr's Club, old chap, if you catch my meaning."

Just then, one of the footmen came in bearing a huge covered platter. "I beg your pardon, my lord," he said, jerking to a halt.

525

"Miss Obelienne said since you didn't come down, I was to bring up a late breakfast?"

"Zut!" said Camille, as if to herself. "I must discuss with her the new diet." Then, to the footman, "His lordship cannot eat that, Randolph. You must take it back down again."

The servant swallowed hard. "Must I, ma'am?" he said. "Miss Obelienne won't like it."

Kieran motioned to the empty side of the bed. "Just set it here, Randolph," he said. "What Obelienne doesn't know won't hurt her."

The footman did as he was bid, shot a parting look at Camille, then hastened from the room.

Chin-Chin leapt at once onto the mattress, tail madly wagging. Clearly, the spaniel had expectations — well-founded, too, it soon appeared.

Mr. Kemble asked another question about Dr. Hislop's evaluation. Camille reiterated much of what the physician had said, and the details of the new diet, all the while watching from one corner of her eye as Kieran lifted the lid from the platter and began to feed Chin-Chin from it.

"And so drink and diet might be eating his stomach away?" Kemble mused when she finished.

"*Oui,*" she answered. "But it is more than that, I think."

Just then, Kieran dipped his finger in a pat of butter, and offered it to Chin-Chin to lick. Finally, mildly exasperated, Camille turned round on the bed. "*Ça alors!* How long have you been doing that?"

Kieran lifted a guilty gaze. "Doing what?"

Camille pointed at the dog. "*Mon Dieu,* he is going to explode," she said. "He has got fat, Kieran. And that is not fit food for a dog."

"But Jim likes it," said her husband defensively. "Well, all but the spiced herring and the cassava pone."

"Jim — ?" said Kemble, standing to lean across the bed. "Jim's no sort of name for a dog, Rothewell. And what the devil have they done to those kippers? The smell is peeling off my nose hair."

"Those?" Kieran poked at the herring with a fork. "Some sort of West Indian seasonings. Obelienne has a strong hand at the spice box."

Kemble's face contorted. "Spiced breakfast kippers?" he said. "Now *that* is a sin against nature."

Kieran shrugged. "I rather like them," he said. "And they do take the edge off a

527

hangover pretty nicely."

"*Oui,* that may be," said Camille primly, "but you may no longer eat them." She moved to put the cover back on the platter.

"Wait!" said Kemble, poking his finger into the cassava pone again. "The dog won't touch this, will he?"

Kieran shook his head. "Did I not just say so?"

Mr. Kemble looked at Camille. "Dogs are intelligent creatures," he said, holding her gaze intently. "And cassava is deadly, if one does not know how to use it. Wrongly prepared, I daresay it would eat the lining out of anyone's gut."

"Mais non, monsieur." Camille shook her head. "Obelienne is most careful with it. Indeed, she would not even let me touch it."

His lips thin, his expression mistrustful, Kemble sat back down again. "How long have you employed her?" he asked Rothewell. "Has she any reason to wish you ill — aside from your frightful disposition, I mean?"

"Oh, balderdash!" said Rothewell. "The woman is the salt of the earth."

Mr. Kemble, Camille decided, had a dark view of human nature. She shooed the dog away, covered the platter, and moved it to her husband's dressing table by the door.

"All the same," said Kemble, suddenly standing up again, "I think I should visit Miss Obelienne. Might I do so, Lady Rothewell?"

Camille looked at her husband. "*Oui*, I suppose," she replied. "I must go down to see her about Dr. Hislop's diet. Kieran, will you excuse us?"

They found Miss Obelienne at her worktable darning table linens. Upon being introduced to Mr. Kemble, she regarded him suspiciously. "*Oui,* Mr. Kemble is well known to me," she said. "How do you do, sir?"

Swiftly, Camille explained Dr. Hislop's requirements. Again, the cook looked displeased. "But no one can live, *madame,* on such a diet!" she protested. "It is flavorless, and without spirit."

"But that is the very problem, Miss Obelienne," Camille firmly explained. "Rothewell has had a little too much — er, *spirit* in his life — his doing, not yours. And it is only for six weeks. I am afraid Dr. Hislop insists."

Obelienne tucked the list into her pocket with a sour look.

Camille smiled, and thanked her. "Now *Monsieur* Kemble would like to ask you some questions about your cassava root, since he has never seen it," she said, not entirely sure she spoke the truth. "Will you kindly explain to him what you explained to me? And show him your spice cabinet, perhaps?"

"*Bien sûr, monsieur,*" she said, rising regally.

Mr. Kemble beamed. "Oh, thank you, Mrs. Trammel!" he said, clutching his hands theatrically. "I am something of an amateur herbalist, you know, and a bit of a cook myself, from time to time."

Miss Obelienne looked over her shoulder, her expression dubious. "Follow me, *monsieur,*" she said, extracting the key ring from her pocket.

"It is so exciting to see cassava from the islands," he said. "A rarity, as I am sure you know. Tell me, how do you come by it?"

"Miss Xanthia has it brought out to me, already made into a sort of flour, or packed in barrels of damp earth." She unlocked the wide mahogany doors and threw them open to reveal the apothecary drawers.

As she had done before, she pulled open the large bottom drawer. This time, there were but two roots, and they looked a little withered. Miss Obelienne extracted one, and presented it to him. "Cassava is a good staple," she said firmly. "But one must never eat it raw. Preparation is key."

Mr. Kemble examined the still-dirty root. "How does one do that, Mrs. Trammel?"

She shrugged. "It depends, *monsieur,* on how you wish to eat it," she said. "But always, the poison must be drawn off. Often it is boiled or fermented, or the starch is extracted."

Kemble handed it back to her. "How does one know if it is safe?"

"If it is bitter, one mustn't eat it," said the cook a little haughtily. "But only a fool would do so. The taste is quite unpleasant." She stood impassively, still suspicious, awaiting his next question.

"Well, that's clear enough, is it not?" Kemble remarked. "I believe I shall leave cassava to the experts. Thank you, Mrs. Trammel, for educating me."

"Miss Obelienne, why do you not show Mr. Kemble your herbs and spices?" Camille cajoled, trying to appease the cook. "Your collection is perfectly fascinating."

Again, Kemble brightened. "Oh, yes!" he said rapturously. "Do let me see. I am sure, with Lady Nash's ships going all around the world, you have a splendid array. Ooh, I smell saffron — and oh my! Is that tamarind?"

Warming a little to her task, the cook dutifully pulled open the little doors and drawers, going through the exotic names just as she had with Camille, and allowing Mr. Kemble to smell and examine those he wished.

"Most come from Miss Xanthia's ships," Obelienne explained, "but a few can be had in the markets." She drew open the drawer which held the shriveled white root Camille had seen before. "This one, for example," she said, dumping it from the cloth bag into Kemble's palm. "It is very rare. Even Miss Xanthia cannot bring this."

Suddenly, Mr. Kemble seemed to quiver like a bird dog on point. Gingerly, he picked it up. "What is this, Mrs. Trammel?" he asked sharply. "It is ginseng, is it not?"

Obelienne shook her head. "*Non, monsieur,* it is called *rénshēn.*"

"Where do you get it?" The fawning fop was gone, and Kemble's voice was suddenly strident.

Obelienne drew back. "Covent Garden Market," she said a little defensively. "A Chinaman named Ling sells it there. I trade him green peppercorns from Bangalore."

Lightly, Camille touched him on the wrist. "What is it, *Monsieur* Kemble?"

Kemble turned to look at her, his brown eyes alight. "I do much of my shopping in Covent Garden," he said. "I know Mr. Ling vaguely. This root is Chinese ginseng."

"*Oui?*" Camille blushed. "Obelienne says it increases a man's — well, his . . ."

"His stamina," Kemble supplied diplomatically. "Some call it 'manroot,' and it costs a bloody fortune." He turned to the cook again. "Have you been giving raw *rénshēn* to Lord Rothewell, Mrs. Trammel?"

Obelienne drew herself up an inch. "*Oui,* of course," she said. "Mr. Ling says it will keep him strong and potent. My husband says Rothewell must have a son. Now he has a wife. And I have the *rénshēn.* After all, someone must keep him healthy, *non?*"

Kemble's knuckles had gone a little white where he clutched the root. "How do you give it to him, Mrs. Trammel?" he asked sharply. "And how often? Be precise, if you please."

The cook looked suddenly frightened. "I . . . I put a little in the cassava," she said. "Like gingerroot, *oui?* A little in this thing or that thing. Anything spicy which hides the taste. Otherwise, he is very difficult."

"*Oui, oui,* we know that he is," Camille reassured her. "How often, Obelienne? How long?"

She blinked her eyes rapidly. "But every day, *madame.* Since the early winter." Her voice was thready. "On the boat, *mon Dieu,* the master, he was so sick. My husband, he feared the master would die. Why do you ask me this? Is this a bad thing, *monsieur?* Mr. Ling tells me it has powers to make Lord Rothewell strong. Has he lied to me?"

Mr. Kemble's eyes met Camille's. "Raw ginseng is harmless to most people," he said quietly, "but too much of it can make one bleed more freely, it is thought."

Obelienne gave a sharp cry, her hand going to her mouth. Her keys hit the stone floor with a discordant jangle. *"Mon Dieu!"* she rasped. "The bleeding? I . . . I have caused this?"

"No," said Kemble firmly. "No, you did not cause it." He set his hand on her arm and urged the cook back to her chair by the table. "You did not cause anything, Mrs. Trammel," he said again, when she was seated. "Ginseng, in small amounts, it can actually settle dyspepsia. But too much can have an ill effect."

Obelienne's eyes were pooling with tears. "I — I have poisoned him?" she whispered. "I have *poisoned* the master?"

Kemble sat down beside her. "Absolutely not," he said. "Lord Rothewell poisoned himself with his dissolute habits, and we all know it. But once he had begun to bleed . . . well, then a great deal of raw *rénshēn* was perhaps not *quite* the thing. I think, my dear, that from now on, you should probably keep your green peppercorns and let Mr. Ling be."

"What do you make of it, *Monsieur* Kemble?" Camille asked, as they went back up the stairs. "Obelienne seems sincere, *n'est-ce pas?*"

They had settled Miss Obelienne with a pot of tea and Camille's repeated reassurances, then called for Trammel to come down to sit with her and hear a somewhat gentler version of what might have happened with the *rénshēn* root. Camille had never seen the cook distraught, and she got the distinct impression that perhaps Trammel had not, either. In the end, Obelienne pledged faithfully to adhere to Hislop's diet and never to use Ling's magic root again.

"I do not believe it was intentional," Kemble agreed. "If Obelienne wished to kill him, she'd use cassava, or good old arsenic from the chemist's."

Camille had never considered that it might have been deliberate. While it was true Obelienne had come to Barbados with Annemarie, she seemed devoted to Kieran. Certainly Trammel was. No, it had been overzealousness, perhaps, on Obelienne's part, but not maliciousness.

"How, precisely, does this root work?" she asked.

On the landing, Kemble hesitated. "As I said, it is hard to know," he answered. "I have but a passing acquaintance with the stuff. Certainly it causes a stimulation in the body, something like strong coffee. One should generally not consume them together."

Something in Camille's brain seemed to snap into place. "His insomnia and restlessness," she whispered. "Kieran often stays awake all night, and he's constantly on edge. Xanthia said — why she said he'd been like that for months!"

Kemble's lips thinned. "I daresay it is related," he agreed. "Ordinarily, one makes an infusion or a tincture of the stuff, but Obelienne has been grating the root like ginger. We've no way of knowing how Ling told her to use it. The poor devil's English is abysmal, and given the lilt in her voice, her native tongue must be French *Kwéyòl?*"

"*Oui,* she said as much," Camille answered.

Kemble resumed his climb up the stairs. "Well, it isn't the *cause* of his troubles, though it almost certainly has worsened them," he said pensively. "Whatever it was doing to him, Rothewell certainly mustn't have any more of the stuff. And I think we've put the fear of God in poor Obelienne."

Rothewell sat alone on his bed, thinking of his brush with death and stroking the dog's silky head. It had been, by God, a near run thing. And it was not over. But Hislop thought that this disease — this *beast* — might be within Rothewell's control. Hislop had given him hope.

The truth was, although he gave every impression of a man who was fully in control of his destiny — and of nearly everything around him — Rothewell knew in his heart it was just a façade. He had let his entire life run to ruin ages ago, he had never dreamed it might be possible to get it back again.

But it was possible. And if it was remotely possible, he would do it. Yes, he would eat Hislop's damned diet and lie abed for what would doubtless feel like weeks on end with his beautiful, seductive wife just beyond his reach — in the most important way, at least. Yes, he would do anything and everything which was required of him to survive this illness and ensure its eternal banishment from his life. He would pray to God that

Hislop was right. *Because he had a life to live.* He always had, but for some reason, it had taken Camille to make him see it.

He closed his eyes, and remembered his own foolishness. He had lost a lot of blood — more than he wished anyone to know. He had driven his body to near exhaustion, and for reasons even now he did not fully grasp. But now his life had perhaps been returned to him, and he was not fool enough to waste a God-given second chance.

As if sensing his mood, Jim shifted nearer, and laid his head upon Rothewell's thigh. He cast his brown eyes up at Rothewell and gave a faint, enquiring snort.

"Yes, I wonder, too, Jim," he said, his hand never leaving the dog. "She's been gone a while now, hasn't she?"

Suddenly, the spaniel pricked up his ears. Then Rothewell heard her footsteps coming up the stairs, light and quick. Unmistakable to him now. Like her delightful scent, the sound of her movements and even the soughing of her breath as she slept — all of it was unique, comforting, and instantly familiar to him.

When she entered the room, her gaze alit on him, and she smiled, her brown eyes softening. Kemble came into the room behind her, looking his usual arrogant self.

As if unaware of Kemble's presence, Camille flew across the room and bent over
him to lightly kiss his lips.

"Mon cœur," she said in her soft, throaty
voice, "I missed you. And you will never
believe the story Mr. Kemble has to tell . . ."

CHAPTER FIFTEEN
A RETURN TO TATTERSALL'S

Rothewell was in the conservatory enjoying the life of a semi-invalid, stretched languidly out on a chaise in the midmorning sun, when his wife came in looking especially radiant. In the fortnight since Dr. Hislop's visit, she had nursed him faithfully and nagged him unmercifully. Rothewell had savored every minute of it.

Today, Camille wore a yellow silk day dress which contrasted beautifully with her dark, opulent hair, and a smile so new and so brilliant he was only now becoming accustomed to it. *"Bonjour,"* she said cheerfully, dropping the *Times* onto his lap. "Trammel has brought your paper."

"Have you finished your chores?" he asked in a faintly injured tone. "If you are going to force me into seclusion, the least you can do is bear me company whilst I suffer."

Camille grinned and held up the book which she'd hidden behind her skirts. *"Oui,*

540

mon chéri," she said. "Trammel has brought me one of Mrs. Radcliffe's novels from Hatchard's — *Gaston de Blondeville.* I am going to be a lady of leisure this afternoon."

Rothewell watched her settle onto a comfortable settee opposite him and tuck one leg girlishly beneath her — a most unladylike pose. But in all other ways, Rothewell reflected, Camille was every inch a lady: well-bred, intelligent, and lovely. Rothewell still marveled that he'd won her hand, and wondered if he would ever stop feeling guilty about the way in which he'd done it.

When she looked at him now, it was with hope and with joy. It was as if she loved him; her face lighting up, her smile and her eyes going instantly soft. Was it possible she did love him? And was it remotely possible he could do that love any justice? Perhaps. Perhaps he could, at the very least, show her how he felt about her when he was cut loose by this damned interfering physician they had set upon him.

Irritated, Rothewell snapped his paper open, then wisely quashed the feeling. The truth was, Hislop's advice, Kemble's interference, and Camille's nursing had likely saved his life, he inwardly admitted. He was feeling better than he had in years. He did not care for his diet of poached eggs, beef tea, and boiled chicken. His beloved cheroots had been surrendered forever, and his brandy, too, quite probably. He was rising at dawn and going to bed at dark like some rustic farmer. But at least he could eat a little now and sleep like the dead. His eyes were no longer bloodshot, and Miss Obelienne had finally got over her terror at having very nearly killed him.

But what would it have mattered, really? The truth was, he had been well on his way to killing himself — and Obelienne had seen the signs of it. She had merely tried to help in her own way. Perhaps if he had been less prideful, and a little more amenable to the advice of others . . . but he had not been.

No, he had been his usual angry, arrogant self, wallowing in his own grief and intent on doing himself harm without troubling himself to see what he was doing to those around him. Those who cared deeply for him. Xanthia, Pamela, the Trammels, Gareth, and most of all, Camille, he hoped.

And then there was Luke, of course. Luke had never been vindictive. He had been protective. Of him. Of Xanthia. And of Annemarie and her daughter. Luke would never have wished him ill, and mourning Luke's death inside a bottle of brandy would never bring him back. Rothewell's mind had always known that, of course, but only now was his heart beginning to accept it.

Rothewell was stirred from his reverie by the sound of a servant approaching. One of the footmen entered the conservatory and presented a silver salver to Camille. She looked up from her novel, startled.

"A caller, ma'am," said the footman. "The Earl of Halburne."

"Ça alors." A little unsteadily, Camille picked up the card. "Lord Halburne?"

Rothewell sat more erect. He had heard quite enough about Halburne's ugly interrogation of his wife. But she had come to peace with the man's bitterness and put it behind her.

"You do not have to see him ever again, my dear," he said. "Would you like me to send him packing?"

For an instant, she hesitated, her hand shaking ever so slightly. *"Non,"* she finally said. "I shall see him. What more can he say to make me feel worse about *Maman* than I already do?"

"Very well," said Rothewell to the servant. "We will receive him here together."

Camille nodded. *"Merci."*

Rothewell watched as Camille straightened her leg and smoothed the pleats of her skirt. She was anxious, and it made him angry that it should be so. She did not deserve to be stung by the lash of Halburne's diatribe. She was no more responsible for her mother's actions than she was for that bastard Valigny's.

But then, Camille felt guilty for Valigny's sins as well. And Rothewell was beginning to understand what she, perhaps, already knew. As a parent, her mother had been selfish, yes, but Valigny was reprehensible — and knowing that the blood of such a scoundrel coursed through her veins was perhaps the greatest burden Camille bore.

Rothewell was surprised when the Earl of Halburne entered the brightly lit conservatory. Beneath his expensive, well-tailored clothing, Halburne seemed somehow more frail than Rothewell had expected, though in fact he could not have yet reached sixty. And though he carried himself like a man to the manner born, there was an aura of unmistakable weariness about him; one which Rothewell would have sworn was not normally in his nature.

Rothewell stood as his wife made the introductions. "Do have a seat, Halburne," he said coolly. "But for my wife's sake, I do hope this can be brief."

Halburne looked back and forth between

them, as if judging his welcome and finding it wanting. "I rather fear it mightn't be," he said quietly. "Thank you, Lady Rothewell, for granting an old man a little of your time."

"*Bien sûr,* my lord." Camille smiled weakly. "I hope your butler has recovered from his fall?"

Halburne blinked almost owlishly. "In truth, Lady Rothewell, that is in part what brings me."

Camille looked alarmed. "*Mon Dieu,* he still suffers?"

"See here, Halburne," said Rothewell gruffly, "this is a sad business, but my wife did nothing but drop the knocker on your door, with every intention of —"

"No, no." Halburne held up a commanding hand, looking suddenly like the aristocrat he was. "That is hardly what I meant, Rothewell — and this business is far sadder than you know."

Camille looked worried. "Pray continue, *monsieur,*" she urged.

Halburne looked fleetingly at a loss for words. "Fothering, as I told you, is an old man," he said awkwardly. "Indeed, he was in the employ of my father, and — very briefly — my grandfather before him. And when he saw you, Lady Rothewell, standing on our doorstep that day, he knew, I suppose, what no other person on earth knew, save one — the Comte de Valigny."

"What?" Rothewell demanded. "And what can your butler possibly have to do with my wife?"

An uneasy expression flitted over his face. "Because your wife, Lord Rothewell," said Halburne quietly, "is my daughter."

A moment of dead silence held sway, then, "*Mon Dieu,* you must be mad," said Camille breathlessly. "How can he have imagined such a thing? How can you have believed it?"

Halburne shook his head. "In truth, he imagined very little, Lady Rothewell," said the earl. "He knew precisely what he had seen, once he regained himself. Indeed, I suspected it, too, from the moment I saw the name on your card and the look of your face. But I had to be sure. Dear God, after so many years . . . I had to be sure." His voice had fallen to a whisper. "I can't think how this happened. After almost a fortnight's time, I am still — well, heartsick, I daresay, is the word."

Camille looked stricken. "*Mais non,* this cannot be."

Rothewell was worried. All the color had drained from Camille's face. He set his hands on his knees and leaned forward. "This does sound like a pack of nonsense, Halburne," he said brusquely. "You mean to suggest that Camille is your daughter, and you did not know? Her mother had to know. What are you saying? That she lied?"

Rothewell realized there was a ring of truth in his own words. Camille's mother had to have been a tad unhinged to abandon a gentleman like Halburne to chase a ne'er-do-well of Valigny's ilk. Could it be she had *wished* to believe Camille was Valigny's?

Halburne had opened his hand expressively, but his gaze was fixed on Camille, drinking her in. "It is possible, perhaps, that Dorothy did *not* know," he said almost apologetically. "Or that she simply convinced herself otherwise."

Camille was slowly shaking her head, her eyes glistening with unshed tears. *"Non, c'est impossible,"* she said quietly. "It cannot be. You wish to persuade me that *you* are my father? Not the man I have believed all my life? How can you even suggest such a thing after all these years?"

"My dear girl, please forgive me." Pain sketched across Halburne's face. "I do not mean to distress you. I did, however, get the impression that you were not . . . well, overly attached, perhaps, to the comte? I know it is far too late to right old wrongs. Do you wish me to the devil now? You have only to say the word, and I shall leave you."

Rothewell was still studying his wife. "No," he said, rising to join her on the settee. "It is best, I daresay, the truth comes out. My dear?"

"Oui." Camille cast a sidelong look at him, and he glimpsed hope in her eyes. "It is best — if it can be true."

"Rest assured, my dear, that it is." With his only hand, the Earl of Halburne reached inside his coat beneath his carefully pinned sleeve and withdrew a silk pouch. "It was your dark red dress that so distressed Fothering," he said, awkwardly shaking a gold frame from the little bag. "He thought, you see, that he was looking at a ghost." He offered the frame to Rothewell.

Gingerly, Rothewell took the miniature portrait and tilted it from the sun's glare. He barely suppressed a gasp. The woman in the frame could very well have been Camille. Her dark hair was piled high, and the squared, ruched neckline of her wine-colored gown was reminiscent of fashions some six or seven decades past. But the eyes . . . the dark, honeyed complexion . . . good God.

With a warning in his eyes, he tilted the

frame toward Camille. She drew in her breath sharply. *"Mon dieu!"* she said. "Who is she?"

"My mother," said Halburne quietly. "Her name was Isabella, and she always favored red. Beautiful, is she not?"

"Breathtaking," Rothewell said.

"As a very young man, Fothering was her personal footman. He was deeply attached to her."

"Isabella," Camille whispered, still staring at the miniature. *"Alors,* she . . . she was French?"

Halburne shook his head. "Andalusian," he said. "From a great trading family in Cádiz, but her father was a diplomat. It was an arranged marriage, and brief. She died when I was six."

Rothewell lifted both eyebrows. "The likeness is amazing."

Halburne gave a dry laugh. "Lord Rothewell, that is nothing," he remarked. "Gainsborough painted my mother shortly before my birth. The portrait hung in the library of my country house until I sent for it last week. I should like you both to see it. The portrait is utterly haunting when one compares it to Lady Rothewell. The same hair, with the deep widow's peak, the same high cheekbones and slender nose. Identical eyes.

549

It is no wonder poor Fothering keeled over."

Camille still looked disbelieving. "But my mother . . . she always called Valigny my father," she said quietly. "I was born in Paris almost ten months after my mother left England."

"How do you know?" murmured Rothewell. "Have you anyone else's word?"

Slowly, she shook her head. "There was a Bible," she said. "Some papers."

All easily forged, thought Rothewell. This was making a frightening amount of sense.

Halburne's expression softened. "Sometimes children enter this world on their own timetables, not ours," he said. "Ten months is not unheard of."

"But what if she simply lied?" asked Camille. "Why would she do that? Why would she do that to *me?*"

Lord Halburne looked faintly embarrassed. "Far be it for me to defend your mother, Lady Rothewell," he said. "We were together but briefly. I can tell you this: she never saw my mother's portraits. She would have had no way of knowing what my mother looked like."

"I have often been told I look nothing like my mother," she confessed, "but very like Valigny. I do have olive skin and dark eyes, but you must forgive me, my lord, for having doubts. A similarity in appearance can be misleading."

"Your doubts speak well of you, my dear," said Halburne gently. "When you came to call upon me, I expected . . . well, I expected something altogether different."

Camille's gaze darkened. "*Oui,* you expected me to make demands."

He nodded, his expression morose. "I was angry, and I was confused," he admitted. "I could not understand quite what I was seeing. What you wanted of me. And no, I was not certain — but Fothering was, for he knew my mother well. He watched you depart, you know, from an upstairs window. But I . . . I required more."

"What do you mean by *more?*" Rothewell demanded, taking Camille's hand.

Halburne's lean form shifted uncomfortably in his chair. "I sent Mr. White, my man of affairs, to France that very evening," he said. "I wished to know more of the Comte de Valigny and his past."

"And what did he find?" Rothewell's voice was bitter. "Another pack of lies?"

Halburne lifted his grizzled eyebrows. "No, the truth," he replied. "Valigny's maternal family was from an obscure village in the Pyrenees, and this is where White's inquiry took him. Valigny was married there at a young age to the daughter of a wealthy colliery owner."

Rothewell snorted. "Fancy that."

Halburne smiled faintly. "I think her family came to understand Valigny quickly," he said. "And by the way, my dear, there was not a divorce, but an annulment."

Camille gasped. "An annulment?" she asked. "*Ça alors!* On what grounds was this given?"

"What grounds indeed," Rothewell muttered. In France, a divorce was one thing, but an annulment was not easily obtained.

"The union was childless amongst other things." Again, Halburne's smile was faint. "At the age of seventeen, Valigny had apparently suffered with mumps — and in some men, this is thought to have a very bad result. But he failed to share this fact with his bride's wealthy family. The Catholic Church keeps meticulous records of such proceedings."

"Good God, he . . . he was unable to father a child?" asked Rothewell incredulously.

The earl shrugged. "It seems likely," he answered. "The colliery owner's daughter immediately married a cousin, and died in childbed soon after, so she was not barren. Valigny, of course, was handsomely rewarded to go away and forget he had ever known the poor girl — which likely was his hope at the outset."

"Why would he lie?" Camille whispered. "Why lie to *Maman?* Or to me?"

Rothewell squeezed her hand, and fought down his anger. "To give the devil his due, I daresay he was fond of her in his way," he murmured. "In the beginning, he doubtless believed your grandfather would forgive her, and they could marry. He hoped to obtain money from him, perhaps — or, barring that, he hoped *you* might obtain money. And in time, his patience was rewarded, though not on the scale he had hoped."

This time, Halburne's smile was sour. "Men do not like to admit they cannot father children, my dear," he said. "Not even to themselves, for it is a point of masculine pride. But in all these years, despite his many exploits, I find it odd Valigny has never fathered a child with any of his paramours."

"*Oui,* and there have been many," said Camille. "Toward the end, he threw them in *Maman's* face."

Despite his soothing words to Camille, Kieran was fighting that all-too-familiar urge to punch someone. Temperance, apparently, didn't quell his temper. "That traitorous dog knew the truth at the outset, and simply did not tell you," he finally said. "It explains too much." Like why Valigny treated his supposed flesh and blood like an unwanted burden — or a joke to be cast up for the entertainment of others.

"I am so sorry, my dear," Halburne said again. "Had I known of your existence, I would have taken you, as the law allows, and seen you properly brought up."

Camille seemed to waver on the edge of tears, yet Rothewell sensed she was not yet convinced. "And my mother?"

Halburne looked away. "God help me, but I could not forgive her," he whispered. "Not after she left me there, believing I was bleeding to death. Not after she shamed us all by fleeing with that man to France. No, I could never have taken her back. But I would never have divorced the mother of my child."

Suddenly, a notion struck Rothewell. "So you married again?" he asked. "You have other children. Camille . . . Camille might have brothers and sisters?"

Sadly, the earl shook his head. "I meant to do," he said. "But after Dorothy, I . . . I just never found anyone. I have a nephew, however, who is my heir, and many other nieces and nephews. I believe that they would welcome you, Lady Rothewell, as one of their own. The choice, of course, must be yours."

Rothewell forced his fist to unclench. "It can never make up for what Valigny has taken from her," he said. "He has taken from her a happy, wholesome childhood. A life of ease and plenty instead of a life as a poor relation. If all you say is true, then Valigny should be made to rue the day his greed was discovered."

Halburne's voice, when he spoke, was calm. "Let us forget, my dear, about Valigny's perfidy," he suggested. "Your husband wishes to defend you, and that is admirable. But I would submit that living well is the best revenge."

Rothewell disagreed, but he wasn't sufficiently impolitic to say so.

"What do you mean, living well?" Camille was looking, perhaps ironically, at Halburne's empty coat sleeve — just one more thing Valigny had so callously taken.

"When you are ready, my dear, when you are truly convinced that all I say is true, come and be a part of my family," the earl suggested, his voice suddenly tremulous. "You and your husband and his family, too. Let me get to know you, and embrace you. *I have a child.* After all these years! And yet

I do not know so much as your favorite color, your favorite poem. Can you imagine, even for an instant, what a hell that is to me?"

Strangely, Rothewell *could* imagine. Perhaps it was because of the hope he held in his own heart — hope that he and Camille would soon have a child, and eventually, many. Or perhaps it was the fact that he had never really known a father's love and had long ago accepted that he never would. Whatever it was, it tore at him, and on his wife's behalf — perhaps Halburne's, too — it enraged him.

But Camille and the man who Rothewell desperately hoped *was* her father were still talking. Halburne had slid forward on his chair and had taken Camille's hand in his.

"Though what we have lost can never be regained," he said humbly, "I long to hear about you. How you grew up. How you were educated. And when the two of you have your own" — here, Halburne faltered and squeezed his eyes shut — "have your own children, if you have any forgiveness in your heart, if you can believe what I say is true, please let me be a grandfather. Will you do that? Can you? It would make the last years of my life so very much happier than these past three decades have been."

Camille's eyes were tearing up again, this time with hope. Abruptly, Rothewell stood.

Camille flicked an uncertain glance up at him and wiped her eyes with the back of her hand. "Where do you go, Kieran?"

He smiled down at her. "Out for a walk, my love," he murmured, brushing his knuckles affectionately over her cheek. "I believe the two of you should have some time alone. Halburne, I invite you to dinner, if you can stay. In the meantime, the two of you should — oh, I don't know. Go for a drive, perhaps?"

Halburne smiled. "No sight would better please me — or the town gossips — than to see my daughter in my carriage being squired round Hyde Park."

Camille looked up at Rothewell and laughed a little nervously. She was thinking, he knew, of how vastly different this would be than the last occasion she had seen Lord Halburne in Hyde Park. Then her face fell. "*Mais non,* Kieran," she demurred. "You really are not well enough for a walk, I think."

Rothewell did not let his smile flag. "Remember that Hislop said I might take light exercise, my dear," he said gently. "Besides, I was doing far worse things just a fortnight past, and in far worse shape. A leisurely walk in the autumn air is just the thing, I believe."

"*Oui,* perhaps," she reluctantly acknowledged, still holding her father's hand. "But you must promise it will be light exercise."

"Very light," he agreed. "Indeed, my dear, I shall barely move at all."

"And where do you go?" she further pressed. "Until you are fully recovered, I must insist upon knowing."

"Yes, and when I am recovered, you will still insist upon it," he teased. "It's sale day at Tattersall's. With your permission, Halburne, I think I shall stroll down to tell Lord Nash and some of the fellows of your shocking suspicions. One might as well get the gossip rolling, don't you think?"

Rothewell left the two of them in the conservatory, leaning near one another as Lord Halburne explained to Camille the intricacies of his ancient and very noble family tree. Upstairs, he put on his boots and a heavier coat, then took up his walking stick. His heart was filled with relief and sadness — and underlying all of it, the simmering anger at what Valigny had done.

As he went out into the street, ignoring Trammel's sidelong look of disapproval, Rothewell felt strangely free. He believed, even if Camille could not quite, that Halburne was correct in his conclusion, and it was as if a burden had been lifted from him. The weight of Camille's inherent sorrow. The torment of having to tolerate a man whom he had come to despise. Valigny was nothing — almost nothing — to him now.

As to Camille, she needed to forget Valigny altogether. Until she was able to do that, the most nightmarish part of her past would never be quite over. She needed to begin her life anew, with a father who would love her and treasure her for the extraordinary young woman she was. And she deserved to float through life and through society with her head held proud, without worrying who might cross her path and dim her joy. But most importantly, she needed to be *certain*.

It was the least he could do under the circumstances, Rothewell decided as he left Mayfair to stride across Park Lane. He was not so caught up in his desire for Camille he could not see the ugly truth. Camille married him because she had no choice. And because in part — despite her outward confidence — she felt unloved and unlovable. Her mother had been emotionally selfish, her father outright malicious.

Along the edge of Hyde Park, Rothewell stopped, staring almost blindly at the swans gliding across the Serpentine. He remembered the day he had brought her here. How he had bared his soul, and waited for her censure. For her disgust at what he had done to his brother. But there had been only understanding, and more kindness than he could ever deserve.

Now Camille had a father; a father who would have loved her all her life had he been given the chance. And the beloved daughter of Lord Halburne — scandal or no — would never have stooped so low as to wed the likes of Rothewell.

Even now Camille might be placing her hand in Halburne's, and climbing up into his fine carriage. She would begin to move in that rarefied world he had once hoped to give her, but as Halburne's daughter, that world was hers by rights. Would she now regret having married him? It scarcely mattered. It was done. Now it fell to him to ameliorate her regrets. Rothewell turned back to the pavement. His heart was heavier, yes. But his cause was still just.

At Tattersall's, the Jockey Club's large subscription room was empty of all but the most hardened of gamesters. Today's serious buyers had already drifted outside to await the auction's afternoon commencement. As he was most every auction day, Lord Nash sat at his corner table, holding court with his fellow turfites. Today, their heads were bent together as they quarreled about some entry that had been placed in the betting books. Several gentlemen nodded at Rothewell as he made his way into the crush, a few even greeted him by name. His eyes scanning the crowd, Rothewell absently returned their nods.

When he was halfway across the room, Nash caught sight of Rothewell and called out his name. Rothewell lifted a hand in acknowledgment, but pressed on. By the archway which gave onto the courtyard, he espied his quarry. The Comte de Valigny had propped one shoulder against the door frame, spinning some sort of tale which held in thrall a crowd of young bucks who hadn't better sense.

Valigny, perhaps sensing the weight of Rothewell's gaze, glanced up and broke into his nauseating grin. "My lord Rothewell!" The comte lifted his hands in welcome. "Look, gentlemen, my *beau-fils* approaches."

"Valigny." Rothewell's voice was cool.

Noting Rothewell's approach, the young men parted like the sea, several of them choosing that moment to drift away with uneasy, sidelong looks. Perhaps the tension was palpable.

"*Alors, mon ami,* you have taken leave of your lovely bride?" asked Valigny on a laugh. "I hope you have not come to return her! After all, a hard bargain is a bargain nonetheless, *oui?*"

One of the youngsters snickered with laughter. A dark glance from Rothewell cut it short — very short. Then, however, as he turned back to threaten Valigny, Rothewell's fist chose that instant to draw back and collide with Valigny's face.

The blow might have been unpremeditated, but it was damned satisfying. As if in slow motion, the comte's eyes widened, his head snapped back, and he staggered backward into the cobbled courtyard, arms flailing. Rothewell stalked out after him.

Deep in the shadows of the corridor, a dead silence fell over the subscription room and beyond. Rothewell snatched the comte by his gaudy neckcloth and yanked him up short. "How long," he slowly gritted, "have you known Camille was Halburne's daughter?"

Panic lit Valigny's face, but he recovered. "*Oui,* show the world what an uncouth pig you are, Rothewell." His voice was disdainful. "I am afraid I must demand a gentleman's satisfaction."

"Best get your satisfaction now, you bastard." Rothewell gave him another hard yank. "Only a fool would trust you on the dueling field — and I'd far more enjoy killing you with my bare hands."

The comte looked up — far up — and fear sketched across his face. *"Aidez-moi!"* cried Valigny, his eyes darting round the yard. "This man is unhinged! He attacks like some felon."

But Valigny's reputation preceded him. The gentlemen milling about in the yard simply turned round to their conversations. Valigny laughed nervously.

"Answer my damned question!" Rothewell got his other hand round Valigny's throat, lifted him onto his toes, and squeezed. "How long," he slowly repeated, "have you known that Camille was Halburne's daughter?"

The comte's mouth twisted bitterly. He jerked back, bringing his fist up to blindside Rothewell. The blow connected, but badly.

Rothewell let him down, then set his fingertips to Valigny's chest. "I asked you a question, you son of a bitch," he growled. "And I will have an answer."

Valigny sneered. *"Mon Dieu,* you colonial rustic!" he said. "How stupid do you think me?"

Something inside Rothewell snapped, and

a red-hot rage shot through him. He threw another punch, an uppercut which caught the comte solidly beneath the chin, snapping his head back again. Thirty years of pent-up fury exploded, and Valigny looked like the perfect target.

Valigny hitched up against the cupola in the center of the yard, looking desperately about the enclosure. Seeing no alternative, he came after Rothewell. Rothewell swung a glancing blow to the left ear. To his delight, Valigny threw a rounder, connecting solidly with Rothewell's jaw. Just what he needed. An excuse to beat the living hell out of the bastard.

It was a free-for-all then, with Rothewell pummeling Valigny into the dirt whilst at least a score of gentlemen quietly checked off their auction lists, as if nothing out of the ordinary was occurring. The comte landed a few punches, then caught Rothewell around the waist and kneed him ineffectually in the knackers. Once, Rothewell got him down in the filth of the yard and planted a knee in his chest, but Valigny threw him off-balance.

They both rolled and scrabbled to their feet, Valigny gasping for breath now. Rothewell moved to throw him down again, and in a quick, desperate maneuver, Valigny caught him behind the knee with his foot. Down onto the cobbles they went, fists and knees flying, but the comte was at least three stone lighter, and obviously hadn't scrapped his way through life. Soon, Valigny was down for good, retching onto the cobbles. It took all Rothewell's self-control not to throttle him.

"Hold still," he rasped, "or I will kill you." Rothewell set a knee to his breastbone and drew back.

Valigny's hands waved back and forth frantically. *"Arrête! Arrête!"* he cried. "Not the face again! *Mon Dieu,* not the face!"

Rothewell hit him in the face. Blood spurted from his nose, running down his jaw to stain his collar. Righteous satisfaction flooded Rothewell. "That," he gritted, "was for me. The rest of it was for Camille."

He twisted Valigny's face and shoved it cheek first into the vomit and blood. Then he bent low, nearly setting his lips to the comte's ear. "Now answer my question," he rasped. "How long have you known Camille was Halburne's daughter?"

Again, the nervous laugh. Valigny looked up, his eyes shying sideways like a frightened horse. *"Et alors!"* he finally said. "I claimed her, *oui.* Of what use was Halburne's daughter to me?"

"Lady Halburne told you the child was yours?"

Valigny managed to shrug one shoulder. "*Oui,* she suggested it." He laughed lamely. "And what had I to lose in denying it, eh? Lady Halburne's warm bed anytime I wished it? Even a little of her father's money, perhaps, if I bided my time?"

"So, on the off chance you might get your forty pieces of silver, you ruined that girl's life and denied her a father who would have loved her and wanted her?" Rothewell sneered into his face. "You are not worthy, Valigny, to lick the dirt from Camille's shoes — and the truth is, you couldn't father a child if someone paid you."

The comte managed to look insulted. *"Mais bien sûr!"* he declared. "Why not? But I have never been fool enough. *Non,* my lord Rothewell, the little shrew is not mine — and thank *le bon Dieu* for that mercy."

Rothewell hauled Valigny onto his feet, and dragged him back through the archway. Nash stood in the shadows with a pair of his cronies, one shoulder propped against the wall, his thumbs hooked in the bearer of his trousers as they passed.

"Rough justice, old chap," said one of the gentlemen, glancing down at Valigny. "But long past due."

Rothewell grunted, hauled Valigny through to the other side, and tossed him into the lane beyond. The comte staggered, attempting to keep his feet. "You have until noon tomorrow, Valigny, to quit England," said Rothewell coldly. "If ever I lay eyes upon you again, the beating you got this afternoon will pale by comparison to what you'll get then."

"You cannot order me away," Valigny hissed. "Those gentlemen have seen what you did to me. You are younger, Rothewell, and hulking in the bargain. They know you for what you are — a big, brutish thug."

Rothewell eyed him nastily. "What those gentlemen *know* is that you once unfairly shot Halburne in a duel, damn near killing him," he returned. "And soon they will know you have kept him from his only child. But they don't know anything about the beating you got today. If you do not believe me, Valigny, fetch a magistrate down here and see if you can find a witness."

For an instant, Valigny managed to draw himself up like a bantam rooster. Then, suddenly, his shoulders fell. With one last dark glance at Rothewell, he spit at his feet, then turned and went slinking up the narrow lane toward Hyde Park Corner.

Rothewell turned around to see that Nash

had followed him out. His brother-in-law stood quietly surveying Valigny's departure, his arms crossed languidly over his chest. Humor, and a certain amount of sympathy, lurked in his eyes.

"And let that be a lesson to us all," he said. *"Sic transit gloria mundi."*

Rothewell cocked one eyebrow. "And for the less literate amongst us?"

Nash smiled. "Thus passes the glory of the world," he said, just as Valigny turned the corner and vanished. "He will be forgotten soon enough."

Rothewell began to laugh.

Nash came away from the door frame. "That was not a bad piece of work for an invalid," he said calmly. "But what the hell are you doing down here, Rothewell?"

"Taking light exercise," said Rothewell, dragging a coat sleeve over his forehead.

"Indeed." Nash's gaze swept over him.

"That's my story," he said darkly. "And it's the story you're going to tell my wife, old chap."

Nash just smiled, turned, and clapped a fraternal arm about Rothewell's shoulders. "Valigny is right, you know," he said as they went back inside together. "You *are* a bit of a thug."

CHAPTER SIXTEEN
JOYEUX ANNIVERSAIRE

"What happened?" Camille whispered in bed that night. She was looking, of course, at the faint bruise which was beginning to appear at the corner of his left eye.

Rothewell drew her nearer and laid his head beside hers on the pillow. "A lamp-post," he said, holding her gaze. "The ones in St. James's are quite vicious, my dear."

Camille lifted her head enquiringly. "*Mon Dieu,* how did this happen?" she asked, instantly anxious. "And what were you doing in St. James's? I thought you said you strolled along Hyde Park?"

He looked at her, and stroked the backs of his fingers across her elegant cheekbone. "First I went to Hyde Park," he said. "And then to St. James's. I had an errand I wished to take care of."

"And you think that is light exercise?" she asked, mildly perturbed. "It is a good thing, I daresay, that I was still driving in the park with . . . with Lord Halburne when you returned."

Rothewell cupped her face in his hand. "I hope, my dear, that you will someday be able to call him *Papa*," he said quietly. "I confess I feel for Halburne in that regard. I can only imagine how he longs to hear the words."

Camille wriggled onto her back and stared up at the ceiling. She sighed deeply, her bare breasts rising and falling with the effort. "This is all so very hard to accept," she whispered. "And we shall never know for sure, *n'es-ce pas?* I feel . . . I feel a fraud, Kieran. I have never believed I belonged here, in this world. And now . . . can it be that I *do?*"

Kieran rolled onto one shoulder. By the light of the dying fire, he searched her face, then kissed her lightly on the lips. "I saw him, Camille," he said quietly. "Valigny, I mean."

She lifted her head. *"Où?"* she murmured. "At Tattersall's?"

Rothewell nodded. "We had a frank exchange of views," he explained. "And Valigny realized the game was over. So he admitted it — oh, not that he was infertile, and one couldn't expect that. But yes, he said . . . he said he knew all along that you were not his child. He confirmed it, Camille. What Halburne told us today is entirely true."

Camille's head fell back into the softness of the pillow. *"Mon Dieu!"* she whispered. "He . . . He *admits* this?"

Rothewell tucked a curl of hair behind her ear. "With a little convincing, yes," he said softly. "So it is over, Camille. Whatever you had with Valigny — whatever hell he has put you through — it *is* over. Whatever you make with Halburne is to be your choice. Not his, and not mine. But your life with Valigny, that much is done."

Her soft gaze holding his, Camille exhaled again, a long sigh of relief. *"Grâce à Dieu!"* she whispered. "Oh, Kieran! I just don't want his blood in my veins. I am just like my grandfather, *n'est-ce pas?* And I do not care. I am just so relieved. I do not know if I wish to thank Valigny or throttle him."

Rothewell did not have the nerve to tell her the throttling had already been done. "You shall have the opportunity to do neither, my dear," he said. "Valigny returns to France tomorrow."

"Bah!" She might have been a quarter Spanish, but her language was still laced with French disdain. "Valigny can never remain long in one place. He is always on the run from his creditors. He will be back."

"No, not this time."

Camille turned to look at him, her fine black eyebrows drawing together.

"Not this time, Camille." Kieran tried to look innocent, but it was a stretch. "I have persuaded him that the air on the Continent will be far better for his health."

Her eyes narrowed in irritation. "*Mon Dieu,* Kieran, you are not yet well!" she scolded. "What did you do?"

He lifted one bare shoulder. "Nothing remarkable," he answered. "Ask Nash. He was there."

"*Oui,* I shall," she declared. Then she closed her eyes as if savoring the moment. "But you *are* sure, are you not? And *oui,* it is a great burden lifted. As to what you have done, I shall discover the truth in time, I am sure — and report you to Dr. Hislop, most likely — but for now, I will just float here on this strange feeling of relief and . . . and of hope."

Unable to resist, Rothewell threaded his fingers through the fine hair at her temple and kissed her again, this time more thoroughly. They had made languorous love but half an hour past, and already he wanted her again.

"It is my life's ambition," he said when

her lips looked thoroughly ravished, "to make you happy, Camille. I have my life back because of you — and because of you, it is a life worth living. I love you, Camille. Do you know that? Can you see it in my heart?"

She snared her bottom lip between her teeth and shook her head. "I . . . I did not know," she whispered. "But you are a good man, Kieran. I know you will always be a good husband —"

"A *true* and *faithful* husband," he interjected.

She nodded, her black curls scrubbing on the pillow, her eyes dampening. "I know that," she answered. "I thought I married one sort of man, Kieran, but it was not long before I realized you were a complete and utter *imposteur.*"

Her arms came round his neck. Her body to his body. Their lips became one, as they were one. It was absolute and eternal, and the reassurance the knowledge brought would comfort him, Rothewell was certain, into the waning years of his life.

But his life was not waning. It was just beginning. He was increasingly certain of it. Gently, he pulled away, planting lighter, smaller kisses across her mouth, her cheek, and even her nose. "I have something for you," he rasped. "Wait."

Rothewell rolled over to fumble at his night table. When he rolled back to her, he pressed a carved rosewood box into her hand.

She looked up, blinking. "*Ça alors!* What is it?"

He smiled down at her. "My errand in St. James's," he said. "Happy Birthday, my love. A day early, yes. But then I have never been known for my patience, have I?"

Camille laughed, a remarkably happy sound. "*Mon Dieu,* I have not had a birthday gift in years and years!"

Rothewell tipped up her chin with his finger. "And that, my dear, is a tragedy," he said quietly. "I love you, Camille. You have changed my life — no, *given me back* my life. And for as long as we are together, we will celebrate your birthday — and with a gift, too. Every year."

"Why?" she asked softly. "It sounds like a lovely gesture, *oui,* but not necessary."

Rothewell hesitated, searching for the right words. "I will celebrate it because it was your birthday which brought us together," he finally said. "*This* birthday, Camille. Otherwise — admit it — you would never have spared me so much as a disdainful glance — and trust me, your glances can be supremely disdainful."

Fleetingly, she looked ashamed. "I was wrong about you," she began.

"No, you weren't," he interjected.

Camille set her fingertips to his lips, gently pressing them shut. "I was wrong about you," she said, looking into his eyes. "And what is worse, *you* were wrong about you. You have been wrong about yourself, *mon amour,* for so very, very long. And I love you, Kieran."

"Do you?" he asked quietly.

Her eye were soft, almost dreamy now. "I have loved you, I think, from the moment I saw you standing in Lady Sharpe's back parlor," she confessed. "You . . . you were tapping that crop against your boot, so very impatient, and looking — *ooh la la!* So very large and wicked."

"Oh, come now, Camille!" He gave a self-deprecating laugh.

"*Non,* it is true," she insisted. "You . . . you made my breath catch, Kieran. For a moment, I could not breathe. *Oui,* even then I knew. I knew that there would be trouble for me. With you. And I feared that I was destined to . . . to fall in love with you. You see, my heart knew, from the very first moment I saw you, what my mind did not — that you were a good and honorable man.

That I could trust you."

"Camille." He lifted both hands to cradle her lovely face. "Camille, my love."

He started to kiss her again — this time with more serious intentions — and then he remembered the box. "I thought women were supposed to be inquisitive creatures," he teased, pulling back. "Do you mean to open that box tonight? Or must it wait until tomorrow is officially here?"

"No," she said, grinning. "No, *mon cœur*, it cannot wait."

She looked down and opened her hand to reveal the little box. Gingerly, she lifted the lid, then gasped. A short strand of diamonds lay upon white velvet, a ruby teardrop pendant dangling from the center. "*Mon Dieu,* such gems!" she whispered.

"To match your wedding ring," he whispered. "Because I love you madly. Because I am so proud that you are my wife — even if I do not deserve you. And because I think, my love, that like your grandmother, dark red is destined to be your color."

He lifted the necklace from the box. "Here, goose, turn round."

Camille did so, her long, slender neck lovely in the firelight. The diamonds twinkled as he lifted it, making her gasp again. Carefully, Rothewell set it around her throat and snapped shut the clasp.

It was a perfect fit.

EPILOGUE

THE TELL-TALE KIPPER

Lady Rothewell sat at her desk, so deeply absorbed in a voyage reconciliation report, she did not hear the faint squeal of the door hinges, or feel the rush of cool air which washed up the stairs to stir the draperies behind her.

"Where is my little princess?" sang a soft voice from the threshold.

At that, her head jerked up to see a thin, familiar face peeking round the door. "Papa!" she cried, tossing aside her pencil. "What a lovely surprise!"

"Good morning, my dear." Lord Halburne came in as his daughter dashed from behind her desk.

Swiftly, she embraced him. "I certainly did not expect to see you today," she said, setting him a little away so that she might study his lined face. "What on earth brings you to Wapping?"

His expression turned wistful. "Ah, my

princess, of course," he replied, laying his cloak across a chair. "I was just struck by the wish to see her this morning. Remember, my dear, I am an old man, and must be indulged."

Camille laughed and kissed him lightly on the cheek. "Nothing would please me more than to indulge you," she said. "Isabella is next door in the nursery. Will you have a cup of coffee first?"

"That would be most welcome." Halburne's gaze was drifting about the room now. "Do you know, my dear girl, I still cannot fathom this." His tone was musing, but not disapproving. "The fact that you come here — all the way to this place — just to . . . to do what, precisely?"

"Papa!" she chided, drawing him to a chair. "It is but two days a week, and I come because I wish to, not because —"

"Oh, no, my dear." Halburne patted her hand affectionately, then sat down. "I do not criticize. I mightn't understand what you do, but I do understand this is what you want."

"*Merci.*" She smiled at him affectionately.

Halburne's gaze went to the map which covered the adjacent wall. "What I would have envisioned for you, Camille — an easy life as a lady of leisure — well, I see now that it never would have done at all."

Camille laughed. "I am a lady of leisure — five days a week."

"That's nonsense, and you know it," he calmly answered. "The other five days of the week you are poring over those papers and ledgers your grandfather's solicitors keep sending. I have seen the stacks, dear child, in the study in Berkeley Square."

"Kieran is helping with all that," she replied. "After all, what is the difference, really, between a cotton mill and a sugar mill? Together, we are learning how to go on."

Her father's gaze returned to her face, his eyes softening. "You have a good husband, my dear," he said quietly. "If I had had the honor of choosing a husband for you, I could not have chosen better. I account myself fortunate that you have done so well for yourself — and all by yourself, I might add."

Camille patted his hand again and blinked back a tear. Her father — her newfound, much-loved father who had come to her by such an amazing twist of fate — was but one of the many new blessings in her life. And since Isabella's birth, she inwardly considered, the woman who rarely cried had become something of a silly watering pot.

After the coffee came, they passed a few moments in idle conversation, catching up on the fortnight which they had spent apart, and discussing Halburne's visit to his country estate. The earl had remained almost the whole of the year in Town, even venturing out into society again, once or twice with his daughter on his arm. Society's whispers about Valigny had faded by mid-season, and with them, much of Halburne's reclusion and melancholy.

Halburne had just broached the subject of a hobbyhorse he wished to buy for Isabella when Mr. Bakely came in with the morning's post, distributing it evenly over the three desks which the office now contained.

"Well!" said Camille's father, rising. "Bakely has things for you to do, I collect. Let me leave you to it. Perhaps Isabella's nurse will permit me to read to her again today?"

"She would not dare stop you." Camille rose and kissed his cheek again. At only three months of age, Isabella paid no attention to books, but she had learned the rhythm of her doting grandfather's voice. "May we expect you for Wednesday dinner as usual?"

When Halburne was happily ensconced in the nursery, Camille returned to her desk and to her reconciliations, but her efforts were short-lived. In moments, Kieran came elbowing his way through the door, a wicker basket in the crook of his arms.

"Oranges," he announced, setting the basket down on his desk. "The *Queen Anne* just came in. I plucked these right off the top of the best barrel."

"Kieran, *mon amour.*" Camille rose, set her palms against her husband's lapels, and kissed him lightly on the lips. "How did you find things at the docks?"

"All on schedule, just as Xanthia said." Kieran tilted his head at the dark gray cloak which lay draped across one of the chairs. "Halburne has dropped by?"

Camille smiled. "He's just back from the country and could not wait to see Isabella."

"His little princess," said Kieran, studying his wife's face.

She laughed. "Yes, he treats her like a princess, too."

Kieran kissed her again, swift but hard. "I think someone should treat *you* like a princess," he said suggestively. "Tonight, perhaps?"

Camille leaned nearer. "Oh, *you* may certainly do so, *mon amour,*" she murmured against his ear. "But I am no princess."

To her shock, his hand came up to cup

her cheek. "Oh, but I think you might be," he murmured, his voice oddly gentle. "Indeed, I think you have known it all along in your heart."

She drew back and laughed. "Whatever are you talking about?"

"Do you remember, Camille, that story you once told me? About being a kidnapped princess?"

She nodded. "A child's fantasy. Lonely children have a great many, I fear."

He set his hands lightly on her shoulders. "But if you think about it, Camille, this one turned out to be true," said Kieran. "You really *had* been kidnapped by the evil Comte de Valigny. You really were stolen from your father. Perhaps . . . Perhaps something deep in your heart knew that all along? Perhaps you always knew that something was missing?"

Camille had never before thought of it in that way. It sounded tragic indeed. "Ah, but there is one difference between the fantasy and the reality," she said, her face brightening. "In reality, it was not my kingly father who rescued me from the evil comte, but instead a dark and dashing prince — the Black Prince, I shall call him."

"And you, my dear, are my Black Queen," he answered, his gaze holding hers. "That, at least, is how I once thought of you. So dark. So aloof and so utterly regal in your disdain of me. Indeed, you made me feel like a lowly commoner by comparison."

"Kieran, *mon cœur,* you will never be that," she murmured, her eyes searching his face. "Every morning when I awake to find you beside me, I feel rich beyond measure. It occurred to me yet again today when Papa arrived unexpectedly. How very blessed I am to have the three of you in my life when, little more than a year ago, I had nothing. No, less than nothing."

Her husband shook his head. "No, my dear," he answered. "It is the three of us who are fortunate, for we have you, the center of our little universe. The thing around which we all revolve. The thing which gives us light and warmth."

She looked away, a little embarrassed by the fervor in his voice. After more than a year of marriage, Kieran was still a serious man of few words, but from time to time . . . yes, he could say enough to set her to blushing.

"How very silly you are today, my dear," she said, returning to her desk. "Now, do not let the time get away from you. Mr. Hayden-Worth is still expecting you for luncheon, *n'es-ce pas?*"

Kieran's expression shifted to one which was far more serious. "Yes, we are to dine with the Anti-Slavery Society at one." Swiftly, he glanced at the clock. "Mr. Buxton plans to bolster his push for abolition, and we want to see how we can help."

"I still don't understand," said Camille stridently. "Why won't Parliament simply *act?* Can anyone doubt the rightness of Buxton's cause?"

Kieran shook his head, his eyes grim. "Whitehall is dragging its heels by continuing to negotiate with the colonial governments," he said, beginning to sort mechanically through his post. "Hayden-Worth says it is time we built the fire a little hotter, and I am beginning to agree."

Camille lifted her eyebrows. "Indeed," she murmured. "What sort of fire does Anthony have in mind, I wonder?"

"Buxton says we must take our case to the British public." As if the post could not hold his attention, Kieran tossed it down and went to the window which looked out over the Pool of London. "Once the people understand what slavery is, Camille," he said, staring out into the cold brilliance of the morning, "once our citizens see that simply stopping the slave trade was not enough, and that the horrors will go on until we have total abolition — then Parliament will have to act. The pressure will simply be too great."

Camille joined him at the window and stood beside him, shoulder to shoulder. It was how they lived now. The very foundation of their marriage. Shoulder to shoulder.

She was so very proud of him, and of his many efforts — here, helping Xanthia at Neville's. At home with the estate and all the other business interests which required his constant attention. But she was especially proud of his new association with Anthony Hayden-Worth, a politician who was still young enough and energetic enough to think all the world's ills could be fixed if one simply worked hard enough. Perhaps he was right.

"With Anthony in the Commons, and you and Nash in the Lords . . ." she said musingly. "Well, the three of you will make a formidable force, I think, allied with Mr. Buxton."

He turned to face her, his smile faint. "And speaking of that alliance, I suppose I'd best head back to Westminster." He paused to embrace her again. "I shall just go and kiss Isabella, then see you both at home, shall I?"

"Kieran, wait," she said, following him as

he strode toward the door. "What am I to do with all these oranges?"

He regarded her a little sheepishly. "You know, I've a desperate wish for one of Obelienne's orange sponge cakes," he confessed. "After all, I am not precisely *fat* yet. And I thought — well, I thought if we mashed one of the oranges up with a little sugar, perhaps Isabella might think it a great treat?"

"Oh, Kieran, she is still far too young!" Camille laughed. "Besides, Isabella is not a pet, you know, to be fed wicked tidbits from your pockets. And speaking of wicked tidbits, did you by chance slip Chin-Chin one of those overspiced kippers this morning?"

Kieran's expression went blank.

Camille shot him a warning look. "Oh, don't come the innocent with me, my dear," she said darkly. "They are perfectly indigestible, as Mr. Kemble says. Trammel found the resulting evidence next to the sideboard — and it stained the carpet, I might add."

Kieran drew her back into his arms and kissed her again, this time more thoroughly. "Don't scold," he said when at last their lips parted. "I warned you, my dear, when you agreed to marry me."

"What?" she demanded. "What, precisely, did you warn me of?"

"That I was a very wicked man," he said. "And hopelessly unrepentant."

"Well," said Camille, her eyes twinkling, "that, at very least, will make Chin-Chin happy. After all, he actually *approves* of your bad habits."

ABOUT THE AUTHOR

During her frequent travels throughout England, **Liz Carlyle** always packs her pearls, her dancing slippers, and her whalebone corset, confident in the belief that eventually she will receive an invitation to a ball or a rout. Alas, none has been forthcoming. While waiting however, she has managed to learn where all the damp, dark alleys and low public houses can be found.

Liz hopes she has brought just a little of the nineteenth century alive for the reader in her popular novels, which include the first and second novels of her latest trilogy, *Never Lie to a Lady* and *Never Deceive a Duke;* the trilogy of *One Little Sin, Two Little Lies,* and *Three Little Secrets;* as well as *The Devil You Know, A Deal With the Devil,* and *The Devil to Pay.* Please visit her at www.lizcarlyle.com, especially if you're giving a ball.